Evergreen Ivy

Ada Taylor

Copyright © 2023 Ada Taylor
All rights reserved.
ISBN:

To all the girlies that are reading this in public right now

CONTENTS

Chapter One	8
Chapter Two	18
Chapter Three	47
Chapter Four	66
Chapter Five	99
Chapter Six	121
Chapter Seven	144
Chapter Eight	169
Chapter Nine	194
Chapter Ten	230
Chapter Eleven	256
Chapter Twelve	270
Chapter Thirteen	285
Chapter Fourteen	293
Chapter Fifteen	315
Chapter Sixteen	329
Chapter Seventeen	340
Epilogue	358

CHAPTER ONE

Dane

I was going to have a fucking heart attack.

If I had one more cup of coffee my heart was going to rip out of my chest. I knew she was lying. I knew just to spite me she had made up the rule but I had no room to argue. So, as I sat and watched people go in and out of the restaurant across the street I finished off my cup.

I had been sitting here for a few hours hoping to see anyone important stop by. At our last meeting with the Russians we knew they were hiding something. They hadn't been completely honest about their plans for the future, or who they were working with. Apollo was upset they had lied to us. It meant they had found someone else to work with, and we needed to know exactly who that was.

I went unnoticed for almost an hour at the table by the window before she came by with another coffee. Now that she knew I wanted to stay she hadn't left me alone. I made the mistake of looking over my shoulder and made eye contact with her. I couldn't help it. Her hair curled and bounced high above her. Her heart shaped glasses could be spotted a mile away. She had the attention of everyone in here, and yet she acted unbothered by the stares, including my own. Smiling when she saw me she quickly grabbed another cup that she had ready.

"I saw your cup was a little low. I thought you could use another." She smiled.

Oh my god, she's trying to kill me.

I hesitated to take the cup from her, and she knew why.

"Unless you're tired of drinking coffee, and you're planning on leaving?" She teased.

I couldn't leave yet. I knew the Russians were meeting someone today. I couldn't afford to leave. I grabbed the cup from her with shaky hands. I had barely sat the cup down on the table before spilling the hot coffee on the cheap vinyl tablecloth.

The barista tucked her serving plate under her arm and let out a quiet laugh as she walked away. She grabbed a few empty plates from other customers, and then made her way back behind the counter. With the dirty dishes in hand, she walked back into the kitchen.

I returned to watching out the window. Not a single car had pulled up in two hours. I knew there was someone inside, but they hadn't moved in a while. After a few minutes I heard a familiar laugh from behind me. Turning in my seat I found her walking back out to the bar. She handed a few clean washcloths to her coworkers, and then started cleaning the counters. I took a break watching the Russians to watch her instead. I watched a single strand of her hair continuously fall out from behind her ear no matter how often she tucked it away. I watched her apron ride higher on her hips as she stretched to reach the corners of the counter. All of it was distracting. I picked this tiny bakery to keep watch on the Russians and instead I was distracted by a barista who was trying to give me a caffeine overdose.

I felt the table shake and looked around to see what was causing it to move. I looked down and saw my own leg shaking. I had to get out of here. I would try to come back tomorrow, but first I needed to go run a few miles, maybe a dozen.

I grabbed my jacket and walked over to the front counter. The mystery barista walked over to the cash register.

"Would you like a cup to go?" She asked, grabbing the twenty from me.

"I- You- I'm-"

"I'm kidding." She smiled.

"Oh."

I grabbed my change back from her and gave a polite nod.

"Come back soon." She grinned, already distracted with another customer.

Leaving the bakery I hoped the next time I visited she wasn't working. It was impossible getting any work done while she was here. Tomorrow I'd pray for anyone else to be working.

I turned left down an alley and found my car parked in the lot behind the bakery. I knew Apollo would be upset to know nothing had happened with the Russians, but it could have been worse. No news is better than bad news. I drove to his office and hoped he would agree.

He did not agree. If anything my update made him angrier than any bad news I could have given him. He hated not knowing, wondering what was happening behind closed doors. I'd known Apollo for close to ten years, and never in those years had he learned the true meaning of patience.

The gods must have noticed that about him too because they found him a fiancé that tested his patience every day. There hasn't been a boring day since Eliana and Apollo's engagement dinner. I could count on one hand the nights that I hadn't been bothered since she had moved into his place.

"Dane." Apollo shouted from across the room.

"Yes?"

"Where the fuck did you go? Your eyes did that glossy stare again. It's creepy man. It's like you disappear."

"Sorry."

"I asked you if you had any plans for tomorrow." Apollo said.

"No, I have Romeo checking in on the warehouses for me."

"Good, I need you to go back to that bakery and keep waiting for the Russians to make a move."

"Do I really need to go tomorrow? I doubt they try anything this soon after our last meeting. We might be wasting time waiting for something to happen."

"Are you suggesting we wait for something to happen? Just sit and miss an attack or trade because we thought it was a *waste of time* to do surveillance?" Apollo asked, tossing a few papers on his desk.

"No, of course not. I'll go as soon as they open."

"If you would rather not go back I can send someone else. I know Junior wouldn't mind watching the place-"

"No!" I shouted.

Apollo snapped his eyes to mine. Surprised to hear my outburst, Apollo leaned onto his desk.

"First you're hesitant to go, and now I couldn't pull you from the bakery if I tried. Dare I ask, what has you acting like this?"

"It's nothing. Blame it on all the coffee I drank today. I'm a little bit jittery."

"You don't drink coffee." Apollo said.

"Trust me, I know. But there was no getting out of drinking it today. Maybe tomorrow I'll try a dessert. Can I leave now? I can literally feel my blood circulating through my body. It's starting to itch."

"Go, I'll call you tomorrow."

Apollo waved his hand to the door and watched me leave. Right before I left he called my name one more time.

"I'm only paying you to work, Dane. I don't plan on reimbursing you for all the treats you eat while you're there." He laughed.

"Fuck off." I mumbled, leaving his office.

I took the stairs back to the lobby of Apollo's office. I needed to start sweating the caffeine out of my body. I ran down the stairs from the eighteenth floor and drove home.

I promised Apollo I would get to the bakery when they opened tomorrow which meant I had less than twelve hours before I had to be back. I had time to work out, eat dinner, catch up on paperwork. There was no chance of getting any sleep tonight. Not now that my brain knew I'd be going back to the bakery tomorrow. I'd be up all night and it wouldn't be the coffee's fault.

I stood across the street from the Russians and watched the clouds decide if it was going to snow. It had been cloudy all day, but they couldn't make up their minds. I considered staying outside but I hadn't brought a warm enough jacket. I had no choice but to return to the bakery.

Letting out one more deep sigh to prepare myself, I dragged the broken door of the bakery open and found my way back to my table. I made a note of the door and reminded myself to tell someone it needed to get fixed.

"You're back!"

Shit.

"What can I get you today?"

Shaking my suit jacket off of my shoulders I turned. She closed last night, why the hell was she here so early? I wonder how hard it would be to get a copy of the schedule. I knew they kept it in the kitchen.

I looked back at the waitress; she stood there waiting for me to give her my order. Her heart glasses were gone, and her hair was tied down. I hardly recognized her. Today she matched the dark weather outside.

"I think I'll try your desserts today. Please."

"No coffee?"

"No, please, no."

"Do you have any particular dessert in mind?" She asked.

"I'll eat anything. I'm sure it's all fine."

"Honey it's better than fine, why don't I get you a few different pastries and you can see for yourself."

Honey. Did she just call me honey?

"That would be great, thank you." I replied, waiting for her to leave.

She took the menu I wasn't going to use from the table and went over to the display case. I took note of everything happening across the street while I waited for her to return.

There were a few cars from yesterday still parked in their same spot. I texted Apollo a few plates to have Alex run. Most of the lights were off just like yesterday too.

A clank of a plate interrupted my scanning of the restaurant.

"See anything exciting today?" She asked, handing me a fork.

"Excuse me?"

"Has anything changed since you were here yesterday? It hasn't been too busy over at Darbazi's but that look on your face tells me something different. It looks like you noticed something important."

"I don't think that's any of your business." I replied.

"I'm pretty sure it is my business what you do at one of my tables. I'm responsible for all guests that sit here. And I'll have you know it's been a little boring here lately. Sue me for watching you and hoping something exciting would happen."

"You've been watching me?" I asked.

"It's silly to ask questions you already know the answer to. How could I not? A guy like you walks in here and I'm just supposed to ignore him?"

"Okay, if you think you know so much then tell me, what happened over there after I left? Anything stand out to you?"

"I'm sorry, that information is personal and quite frankly none of your business. Enjoy the cake. Let me know if there's anything else I can get you." She smiled, walking away.

I blamed my irritability on the coffee yesterday, but now I was certain it was definitely her that had me so bothered. If she had any idea who I was or who I worked for she wouldn't be so brave to talk to me like that. She had no idea I wasn't just some guy stalking the restaurant across the street.

I looked around the bakery hoping to find a manager. I needed the waitress's name. She could be helpful to our Russian search. She knew more than she was telling me.

Unfortunately I found no one else in here except for me. No one else was at the counter, no one was sitting near the back with their computers like yesterday. It was just me and her. A few pots of coffee were warming up behind the counter, and soft music was playing in the kitchen. That was the only noise made in the entire shop.

My new plan was to wait for a few hours until her shift was over and then get my information from her replacement. I grabbed my fork and took a small bite of the cake. She was right. It was amazing. If I had known how incredible her desserts were I wouldn't have killed myself yesterday with coffee.

I was a few cakes in when she came back to my table.

"You're scaring away my other customers."

"I don't think that's true." I said.

"It is true. They walk in here and the first thing they see is you sitting here with a frown on your face. You look like you're being forced to sit here and eat my food."

"I am being forced to sit here and eat your food." I said.

"Well they don't need to know that. Give a smile when the next person walks in. I don't make money when they take orders to go. I need people at tables."

"I'm not doing that."

"Yes, you are. Or I'm making you go to the table in the back by the storage closet. You don't get to sit at the window table if you're going to continue looking mean."

While I doubted she'd be able to move me herself to a different table I didn't want to risk it. She'd nearly killed me yesterday. Who knows, maybe if I kept being an ass she'd poison my cakes.

"I'll try looking less miserable, but I can't promise anything."

"Thank you. Now, can I get you anything else? A coffee maybe?"

I held back the glare and forced a smile, "No."

"No, what?" She asked, enjoying every moment of this.

"No thank you."

Satisfied she left me alone for another hour. Every once in a while she pointed at the door to remind me I was not doing a good job at being welcoming, but her sighs of disapproval became less and less as the day went on.

Hours had passed and I had learned even less about the Russians than I did the day before. All I'd done was help improve the bakery's atmosphere. I was getting restless waiting for something to happen when I got a text from Apollo.

The Russians would have to wait because he had another job for me. If I didn't know any better I'd say I felt a little disappointed that I had to leave.

I had a few things to grab from my place before leaving for Apollo's job, so I left some cash under my bill and grabbed my jacket. I thought I had made it out unseen, but I was stopped only a few steps from the front of the bakery.

"Excuse me!" She shouted.

"Yes?" I asked, turning around.

"I know how much that watch you're wearing is worth."

"And?"

"And I never thought a man with a watch like that would leave such lousy tips. You're bad at this whole bribery thing."

"And what do I stand to gain from trying to bribe you?"

"You know I know who's been going in and out of that restaurant over there. I've seen a lot of things, important things, and lousy tips are incredibly unmotivating. If you want my information you're going to have to earn it."

"How do I know I can trust your information? You haven't proven yourself to be a credible source. I can't even leave without getting a shake down in front of your bakery. Why should I trust you?" I asked.

"You probably shouldn't trust me." She laughed.

"And why not?"

"Well for starters yesterday I made a bet with a coworker."

"And what bet was that?"

"I wanted to see how many cups of coffee you would drink before I had to call the paramedics." She smiled.

I should have been mad, but I wasn't. Instead I enjoyed the smile she struggled to hide.

"How much is an appropriate tip for your valuable information?" I asked.

"How much do you have in your wallet?"

I dug around in my coat for my wallet. I found nearly a grand in hundreds.

"A grand."

She laughed as she walked closer to me. She stopped laughing when she realized I wasn't kidding. She looked up at me, and then back down at my wallet.

"You shouldn't carry that much money on you at one time. I'd hate for you to get robbed on the streets."

"You don't consider this a robbery?" I asked.

"Think of this as more of a donation."

"Fine, here." Pulling out all the money I had, I folded it up in her hand. I hoped no one could see how much money I'd given her. I'd hate for someone to try and take it from her.

"Stop, take it back. I was kidding." She tried to shove the money back to me, but I slid my hands in my pocket.

"Same time tomorrow?" I asked, walking away.

"Sir, I can't take this!" She shouted after me.

"Go back inside, it looks like it's going to snow."

She eventually gave up running after me and went back inside. Before I went home tonight I made sure to stop at the bank. I would hate to build a reputation for being a bad tipper.

CHAPTER TWO

Kate

I hadn't slept a minute last night. I couldn't possibly accept a grand in cash. That was absolutely ridiculous. He's a mad man. It didn't matter how captivating or handsome he was, he was insane.

I was hiding in the kitchen because I was terrified I would see him again today. I knew he had to be someone important. He was dangerous, no doubt about it. I couldn't see him again; I didn't have the guts.

"Kate!" Becca shouted, as she ran into the kitchen. "He's back."

"Who?" I asked, even though I knew her answer.

"The grim reaper, he's back."

"Becca, I told you not to call him that. That's mean." I sighed, taking out the tray of muffins to the counter, Becca followed close behind.

"It's not mean if it's true. Look at him! He's dressed in all black again, he looks like he's dressed for a funeral. Plus look at the size of him! He barely fits through the door." She explained.

I hate to admit it, but she's right. He was intimidating. He had to know how other people perceived him. It was easy to see his strict personality through his style. His suit was perfectly tailored to his broad shoulders and hugged his arm muscles. His short hair was cleanly styled and his dark eyes never gave away any emotion. He was hard to read and devastatingly handsome.

"Go take care of the display case. I'll go talk to him." I said.

Becca shook her head and left. She relaxed, relieved she didn't have to serve him.

I grabbed his money from my apron and walked up to his table.

"Take it back."

"No." He said, not even looking at me. He gave all of his attention to Darbazi's.

"I can't accept this. It's too much."

"You were right. I was using you and the bakery."

"I don't care, take it back."

"If you don't want the money, give it to the owner or something, I'm sure they're smart enough not to turn down a generous tip." He said.

"I am the owner, and I'm smart enough to know there's no way this money is clean. I'd rather not get involved in whatever you're a part of."

"And what lifestyle would that be?" He asked, shoulders tensing.

"You're sitting in a run-down bakery so you can stalk a shady restaurant across the street. The suit you're wearing costs more than all of my mortgage payments combined for the entire year. I don't trust you." I said.

"Good, because I don't trust you." He said, crossing his arms.

I refused to back down. I continued to hold his money out towards his chest.

"Look, it's clean. It's fine that you don't trust me, but I'd never do anything to put your business at risk. It's probably smart of you not to trust me but know that accepting a tip from me won't put you in harm's way. This is my way of saying thanks. If you aren't comfortable keeping the money then put it in the tip jar and share it with anyone who might need it. Next time I leave a big tip I'll be sure to leave enough for everyone here to share."

I was surprised by his words, turns out the grim reaper is a big softie. So I was right, he was involved with the Russian family across the street. I had told him yesterday I'd seen things, and I wasn't lying. I'd seen them bringing in guests after business hours, and sometimes they never walked back out. Call me crazy, but it calmed my anxiety a little having him here. I felt safe having him visit, and that was the only reason I was going to agree to take his money. We both needed each other.

"Well then, thank you."

He smiled and looked down at the table. He was hiding his face, but I saw his cheeks blush.

"What would you like today?" I asked.

"Surprise me. You were right, everything here is delicious. I trust you."

"Okay, I'll be right back."

I walked away, heading to the kitchen. I did as he asked. I separated his tip and split it amongst all of my staff. After making sure the money was safe in my office I went to grab an almond croissant for the Grim Reaper. While I grabbed a plate I promised myself I would ask him what his name was so I could stop calling him that. I felt even worse calling him that now that I knew how generous he was. I knew he was going to love our croissants. It was the only thing on the menu that sold out daily. It didn't matter how many we made; they were always gone by lunch.

I rounded the corner and brought him his croissant. I also brought him a small coffee. I was done trying to kill him, but coffee with a croissant was a must.

I set down his plate and coffee while he watched across the street. Something must have possessed me because before I knew it I was sitting down next to him. He was just as shocked as I was to be sitting next to me. I tried to act like I planned on sitting here, but it wasn't very smooth.

"So." I said, looking up at him.

"So."

"I was hoping now that we're friends you'd tell me your name." I said.

"We're friends now?"

"I think technically we're partners in crime, but I'm more comfortable labeling it as friends."

"My name's Dane, but you should know you aren't breaking any laws by helping me. If you're worried about getting in trouble for helping me then you have too little faith in me."

"What happens if someone finds out I helped you spy on Darbazi's? I don't want something to happen to me because I helped you."

Without breaking eye contact with me, or looking the least bit afraid he said, "I'd never let anything happen to you."

The way he said it was so definitive, so promising. He truly meant what he said. I had nothing to be afraid of. Unable to stare into his eyes any longer I broke my gaze. I cleared my throat and began to stand up. Before I could walk away he grabbed my arm. I turned around and tried to ignore the electricity running through his fingers.

"I um- I should probably get back to work. It's been busy, busy. Nice to meet you Dane."

"Wait, you never told me your name."

"Kate."

Dane whispered it back to himself while he looked down at his fingers laced around my arm. I pulled away and took a step back.

Before I embarrassed myself any further we were interrupted by Becca, "Kate, the drawer is stuck again."

Dane dropped his hand so that I could walk over to Becca and we both pretended the last minute of our lives hadn't happened. I knew better than to get involved with someone like him, no matter how dreamy. It was going to be near impossible pretending I had zero feelings for the mystery customer near the window, but it was the smart, sensible thing to do.

For hours I pretended like Dane didn't exist. I was afraid to look over at him because I knew he was already looking at me. Around two the bakery got really busy. There was a light rain that caused everyone who was out on the street to look for a dry place to wait out the storm. I was a waiter short and running around like a mad woman. There wasn't an empty table in the entire shop. When I finally found the courage to look over at Dane I was disappointed to find his table empty. He had snuck out before saying goodbye. It was probably for the best, but that didn't make it hurt any less. I grabbed a tray and walked over to clean his table. Under his plate I found another large tip and a note. He had written his goodbye on a piece of his torn napkin.

Tomorrow, Kate.

Two words, that was all he wrote. I took the tip back to the office and hid his note in one of my desk drawers. It felt wrong throwing it away. I went back out to the floor and distracted myself with customers to try and ignore the possibility I'd get to see him tomorrow.

Dane showed up the next day, and the day after that. Most days he showed up as soon as we opened. Sometimes early in the morning the only two people here were me and him. No words were shared, but the moments felt intimate. Every day he ordered a croissant and a coffee and every day I brought it to him at the table by the window. Some days when we were slow I'd catch him staring, other times when we had a room full of customers he disappeared into his own little world. Sometimes he would leave to the back patio to take a phone call, and other days he would leave early. I know he wished he could stay later than our closing hours, but he hadn't found the courage to ask me to stay.

It was Sunday and Dane was nowhere to be found. I thought maybe he was just running late but by noon I knew he wasn't coming. I had no real reason to be upset, but something deep down hurt. I was hoping to see him again. I knew he was dangerous, and my coffee shop was as far as our relationship could go, but I still enjoyed his visits.

It was almost six and I had started to clean up the front of the shop. My last customer had left a few minutes ago and the odds of getting another before we closed was slim.

I flipped the chairs onto the tables and then took a pile of dishes to the back room. Setting down the tray of dishes I heard the bell chime from the front of the store. I looked at my watch and saw it was a minute past six.

I loved my job, I really did, nothing made me happier. But today I wanted to close up, and head upstairs to sleep off the worry I felt.

I dropped the dishes in the sink and walked back out to the front of the store.

"I'm sorry, but we're closed, if you'd like to come back-"

"Kate."

"Dane? It's past six, what are you doing here?"

"I got caught up with something at work. I thought I had enough time to make it here before you closed but I guess I was wrong. I'm sorry, I'll come back tomorrow."

"Dane, wait! Would you like a cup of coffee?" I asked.

I can't believe I just asked that. Of course he doesn't want coffee. He probably wants to leave and go home.

"I'd love a cup." He smiled.

Dane walked over to his table while I grabbed him his coffee and sugar. He took his jacket off like always, laying it on the chair next to him. I walked over to his table and watched him slowly roll his sleeves up to his elbows. It was the first time I'd ever see him without long sleeves. I looked up and down, at every drop of ink on his arms. He was completely covered in tattoos. They varied in size, but all of them were black ink. A few bruises on his hand pulled me from the tattoos on his arm. His knuckles were red and looked like they'd been recently used. I pretended not to notice as I looked back up when I heard my name being called.

"Kate…"

"Huh?" I asked, snapping out of my daydream.

"I asked how your day was?"

"Oh, fine, great, busy, the usual." I said, trying to play it cool.

"Good." He said, taking a sip of coffee. "Anything exciting happen while I was gone?"

I sat down next to him and looked out the window, "Nothing, not a single person in or out. It was quite boring. You didn't miss anything."

"Nothing may have happened at Darbazi's, but I'm sure I missed something exciting today. Did you try to kill or bribe any customers?"

"I'm hurt, I would never."

Dane let out a small laugh, and then continued to watch across the street.

"Where were you?" I blurted out before my brain could process what I'd just said.

Dane looked over at me. He went from relaxed to tense in a second. The smile he had was now gone.

"I got caught up at work. It wasn't anything important."

"It was important enough for you to not show up today, it must have been pretty important."

"I don't want to talk about it."

"Don't want to, or can't?" I asked.

"Kate..." He warned.

I could have pushed him further, but if I did he would leave, and I really wanted him to stay.

"Is there anything about your day that you can tell me?"

"I don't think so."

"Come on, there isn't a single thing you can share, not a single good thing happened?"

Dane paused and looked right at me again. He looked like he wanted to say something but was holding back. I knew what he wanted to say. I knew right now was his something good, but he was too afraid to admit it.

He didn't have the nerve to say it, so I said it.

"I missed you today, Dane."

"Really?"

"Yeah, I've sort of gotten used to you showing up."

"Please, you were probably so busy you didn't even notice I was missing." He said.

"That's not true, we were busier than we'd ever been today, and I still noticed."

Dane tried to deflect, "How busy were you?"

"I had someone call out which meant I had to cover, and like we weren't already short staffed every table was full from open to close. I didn't even have time to grab lunch. I had to sneak back to the kitchen and steal muffins and one of our ovens stopped working. We had to call in someone to come fix it."

While I talked and told Dane about everything that happened he sat and listened. He gave no attention to Darbazi's. I had his undivided attention. Before I knew it, we'd been talking and sitting for over an hour. He hadn't even touched his food or coffee.

"Anyway, I'll give you a few minutes to eat and have a minute to yourself. It sounds like you had a rough day. I have some cleaning left to do in the kitchen. Just holler if you need me."

Dane nodded and grabbed a fork. I had met a lot of people, especially at the bakery, but there was no one quite like Dane. He hardly ever talked, but I always knew what he was thinking. He did a terrible job hiding the true emotions on his face. Tonight I could tell how tired he was.

I worked in the kitchen until I heard a phone ringing out front. I looked out and saw Dane on the phone. He looked upset. He spoke what I can only imagine was Italian, at a speed I'd never seen Dane speak before. When he heard me behind him he turned around.

He was quick to hang up the phone. I'm not sure why, considering I don't speak Italian, but he still ended the call.

"I have to go." He spoke, tossing his jacket back on.

"Okay. Will I see you tomorrow?"

"I don't know."

It was now my turn to simply nod. I was afraid he'd hear the disappointment in my voice. Before he left, a man came up to the front of the bakery. I had never seen him before, but he was dressed similar to Dane. The man knocked on the door and handed Dane a brown paper bag. After that he stood and waited near a car down the street.

"Here." He said, holding the bag out to me.

Confused, I took a short step forward.

"You said you didn't have time for lunch. I had one of my guys pick up some dinner for you."

"You didn't have to do that."

"I know." He said, cutting me off. "Goodnight, Kate."

As soon as Dane left I looked down at the bag in hand. What Dane lacked in words he made up for in kind gestures. Maybe Becca was right, there's more to him than I've seen.

"Becca I can't find my glasses." I shouted from my office.

"Why do you need your glasses? Aren't you wearing your contacts today?"

"I was wearing them, but I forgot I was wearing them and rubbed my eyes while unloading the dishwasher because of the steam. I thought I had a pair of glasses in my office, but they aren't in the place I usually keep them." I explained.

I walked out to the front with Becca and continued looking.

"I thought I saw the blue pair near the cash register."

"I moved those upstairs because I couldn't find the pair I keep in my apartment."

"I can't help you if you don't keep the right pair in the correct spot. We have a system for a reason Kate."

"We have a system for a reason Kate." I mimicked as I walked by Becca.

"I heard that, and I'm done helping you look for another pair." Becca shouted from behind me.

I went out to the tables to try and find a spare pair. I knew I had a few lying around. While I was looking near the small library the doorbell rang. I looked up and found Dane. Unbelievable, even blurry he was hot.

"Good morning."

"Good morning Kate." He said, walking to his table.

I thought maybe the more he came the more he would open up, but he's been here every day for two weeks, and I still haven't cracked him. He is still as mysterious as the first day he showed up. I know he enjoyed our conversations and late-night talks, but sometimes it felt like I was the only one doing the talking. He was a great listener, but some days he still felt like a stranger.

"Becca, can you check in the kitchen?" I yelled out to her.

"No! I'm busy!"

"Did you lose something?" Dane asked.

"I can't find my glasses." I said, pulling out my notepad.

"The red pair?"

"No, I haven't seen those in a long time. I'm trying to find literally any pair I can, and Becca is trying to prove a point and is refusing to help me. I swear she acts like I do it on purpose. It's not my fault. She sees how busy I am-"

"Kate." Dane tried to interrupt.

"I don't complain when she needs help every time she breaks the register drawer, and I definitely don't keep a tally of how many times she's jammed it. All I'm saying is she could keep an eye out for them while she works. I don't think that's too much-"

"Kate." He spoke louder.

"What?" I asked.

Dane let out a laugh and pointed to my apron pocket. I looked down and found a pair of glasses tucked down in the bottom of my apron.

"Oh, fuck me." I sighed, grabbing out my old pink glasses I'd lost nearly a month ago.

Dane looked up at me and shook his head.

"Don't tell Becca, she'll kill me." I begged.

"Your secret's safe with me." He laughed.

As if she'd heard her name one too many times Becca came out to say hello to Dane.

"Where did you find that pair?" She asked.

"Around." I answered.

Dane hid his laugh and pretended not to be paying attention to our conversation.

"What would you like today?" I asked Dane.

"Nothing, unfortunately I can't stay long. I just stopped by to see if anything happened, and make sure things were okay here."

"Nothing exciting happened since yesterday, but I did make a new scone recipe! Meet me at the counter, I'll grab you a few to take home."

Dane tried to protest, but I walked away before he could say anything. He followed me to the counter while I disappeared to the kitchen.

"Here you go! Let me know what you think of the recipe. I can always make more." I said, handing him his bag of scones.

"Kate this is too much, please you shouldn't have. How much do I owe you?"

"Oh no, they're free today."

"No, I can't."

"Dane, for the love of Mary take the bag of scones." I snapped.

He quickly took the scones that were sitting in front of him on the counter and walked to the door. I felt terrible for raising my voice at him, but I was desperate. How could a man so mysterious be so terrible at reading between the lines?

Dane

What the fuck was I supposed to do with a bag of scones? I'd never seen Kate act like that. While I walked back to the car I tried to think of anything I might have done to make her angry. I thought we'd gotten closer over the past few weeks. She'd never raised her voice like that, even after a long day. Something was wrong and I was dying to figure out what.

Opening the car door I tossed the bag to Junior.

"What's in the bag?"

"Scones."

"Scones?" He asked.

"They're yours if you want them." I said, pulling out into traffic.

"Did you get any news about the Russians?" He asked.

"No."

Junior had more questions, but he waited until we got back at the warehouse to ask them. He wasn't going to risk pissing me off even more than I already was while he was trapped in a car with me. Junior made it back to the warehouse unharmed. He followed behind me into my office. I tried ditching him at the elevators, but the little shit was fast.

"How much longer do you plan on spending time at the bakery? Apollo said he'd send someone else to watch over Darbazi's." He asked, sitting down at the coffee table.

"I'm not sending someone else."

"Why not? It sounds boring. You have to be tired of sitting and watching the Russians by now."

"Just shut up and eat a fucking scone already."

"Alright, alright." Junior said, opening up the bag.

Maybe now I'd get a few minutes of quiet.

"Holy shit." Junior laughed.

"What?"

"These aren't scones." He said.

"What are they?" I asked.

"Look."

Junior held up something covered in plastic wrap. I grabbed it from him and ripped it open. Holy shit was right. Kate had snuck me a thumb drive under the scones. She wasn't mad, she was just desperate for me to take the bag. What an absolute genius.

"What do you think's on it?"

"I don't know. Get out of my office."

"Oh come on, I want to see what's on the thumb drive. This is so exciting. You know what this means right? You've got an inside man at the bakery. That's insane."

"Junior, you have ten seconds to leave before I put a bullet in your knee." I warned.

Junior left without another word.

Finally alone I plugged the USB into my computer. A file downloaded; it was the bakery's security footage for the entire month. Since the first day I started watching Darbazi's. I sped up the footage so that I could watch what happened across the street at night. While it was playing I called Apollo.

"Dane?"

"She gave me everything."

"Who gave you everything?"

"The owner of the bakery, she gave me her security footage. I'm watching it right now."

"How much did it cost?" He asked.

"It didn't cost anything. She just gave it to me."

"For free?"

"Yes, for free."

"No threats?"

"No threats." I answered.

"Well shit, okay, call me if you find anything on it. I have dinner with Eliana's family tonight, but if something comes up, call."

"Do you need me to fake an emergency?" I asked.

"No, I promised Mom I'd try to make it through the whole dinner."

"I'll keep my night free just in case."

"That's probably for the best." Apollo agreed, hanging up.

I had hours of footage to watch, so I sent Junior and a few other guys on some runs for me. If I sped up the footage there was a small chance I could make it to the bakery before they opened.

I had been watching footage all night. Absolutely nothing exciting had happened. Turns out Darbazi's was just as boring at night as it was in the daytime. If someone did show up to the restaurant they drove down the alley towards the back of the shop. I could only see customers or workers going in or out. I knew someone was there at night because of the lights, but other than that I had nothing.

I was just about to give up when I saw a few men leaving from the front of the store. The video had been taken a week ago. I watched Jozef and a man that looked familiar get into the same car. I paused the video and called Apollo.

"I was sleeping. You better have found something good."

"I'm sending you a picture. I need you to tell me who this guy is. I know I've seen him before." I said.

I sent a photo of the man to Apollo and waited for him to open it.

"Fuck."

"Who is it?" I asked.

"It's Laurent."

Shit. I knew I recognized him. Every family that I've ever worked with, including the Costa's live by a code. Even the cruelest of Don's had respect for human life. Laurent was evil. The only thing he cared about was money. The last I heard about Laurent he was working in Europe. He was untouchable, he was Europe's best arms dealer. Him working with the Russians meant they were looking to increase their supply, and the only reason they'd need weapons was if they planned to use them.

"When was this?" Apollo asked.

"Last week."

"I need to know how much time he's been spending there. No one's safe if the Russians are dealing with Laurent so publicly at their restaurant. I don't want you going back to the bakery until we know more." Apollo said.

The bakery. Kate.

Kate had been living across from the Russians and Laurent for who knows how long. She wasn't safe there, I had to get her out of there. I looked at my watch and saw how early it was. The bakery wouldn't be open for another hour.

"Dane." Apollo shouted through the phone.

"What?"

"You zoned out again. I told you I need you here as soon as possible. I think I know how to take care of the Russians."

"I'm leaving right now." I said, hanging up the phone.

Leaving the garage I had a choice to make. Apollo knew how long it took to get to his house from the warehouse. If I went to check on Kate he would know but I had to make sure she was safe. I had to warn her about Laurent. If something happened to her because of me I'd never forgive myself. Fuck it. I had to go to the bakery.

I parked in the parking lot behind the shop and ran up to the front door. I saw a few lights on in the back. I knew she was in there. She always got here early to do paperwork and get the kitchen ready. Not caring who heard me I started banging on the front door as loud as I could. I needed to see her, to see that she was okay. She didn't hear me the first few times I pounded, so I hit harder. I shook the door with every knock, the windows rattled.

I was a minute away from breaking the door down when a very tired and confused Kate walked out from behind the counter.

She tossed her apron onto the counter and walked over to unlock the door.

"Dane, what are you doing here? Is everything okay?" She asked.

"We need to talk. Can we go to your office?" I looked out the window to make sure no one from across the street had heard me or seen me here.

"Sure, do you need any coffee, you look like you haven't slept in a while."

"No, please let's just go to your office."

"It's to the left of the kitchen." She said, leading me back through the bakery.

Kate leaned against her desk and crossed her arms. She had to be startled by my surprise visit. I'd never come this early, and I had never been so loud.

"Dane, what is going on?"

"Do you recognize this man?" I asked, pulling up the photo of Laurent.

"No, where would I have seen him?"

"You've never seen him leave the restaurant, maybe late at night, probably leaving with Jozef?"

"No, I try not to make it a habit of watching my neighbors through my curtains after work. It's not a hobby of mine. Is he someone you know?"

"I know of him."

"And?"

"And if you ever see him around here or at Darbazi's I need you to call me immediately."

"Why?"

"He's dangerous Kate. I don't care what time it is; you call me as soon as you see him."

"If he's as dangerous as you say he is then why would I risk myself to help you? What if he finds out I helped you?" She asked.

"I promise, he doesn't even know you exist. You would be saving so many lives by calling Kate. I would never ask you to do this if I didn't think it was important."

"I don't know-"

"Kate, do you trust me?" I interrupted.

After a moment of silence Kate shook her head yes. Before I could tell her anything else my phone started to ring. I knew it was Apollo asking me where I was.

"I have to go now Kate, but first I need you to give me your phone."

Kate scrambled around her office digging under piles of paperwork to try and find her phone. I saw her hands shake and felt like shit knowing I was the one who did that to her.

"Here." She shouted, tossing me her phone.

I added my number to her contacts and then handed it back to her.

"I'm not going to be able to stop by for a while, so if you need me you'll have to call me."

Kate looked down at her phone while walking me back to the front door. I stopped and turned around to face her.

"Kate." I paused waiting for her to look up. "I'm sorry. For everything, I really am sorry."

Kate gave a sad smile and nodded her head. I didn't deserve it, but I was already forgiven.

I walked out of the bakery and turned to make sure Kate locked the door behind me. She waited near the window, watching me walk away. It killed me having to leave her, but I needed to get to Apollo's. We had a slight advantage now that we knew the Russians were working with Laurent but there was no time to waste. We still had no idea what the Russians were planning.

Everyone was waiting for me when I entered Apollo's office.

"You're late." Apollo announced.

"Traffic was bad."

He looked up from across the table. He knew where I was but said nothing. He'd wait until after the meeting to talk to me about Kate. I found my seat next to him and ignored the stares from the rest of his men.

"We know the Russians are working with Laurent. We're screwed if they're building up their supply. It means they plan to use it. I want them taken care of by the end of the week." Apollo explained.

"I have a plan." I said.

Apollo turned to me.

"I think the Russians should take out Laurent."

"The Russians won't kill the man they're using for weapon imports. They need him, more than we want to get rid of him." Apollo argued.

"Not if we convince the Russians he's playing them. We all know they're quick to pull the trigger. They always shoot first and ask questions later. It wouldn't take much to get them to turn on him. Trust me, we want the Russians to be the one to take him out. It would bring us too much heat right now if we did it. And we can't sit and wait to find out what the Russians are planning."

Apollo looked upset, but he knew my plan could work.

"Once we get Laurent out of the picture we have more weight with the Russians. They'll think they can trust us. We might even stop getting push back from them." I continued.

"We have no way of knowing when or how the Russians have been meeting up with Laurent. We can't pay them a visit without them knowing we've been watching them." Apollo said.

"I have someone watching Darbazi's. We can wait until we know Laurent is there and then we join their meeting. If we can make it past the front doors it will be easy convincing the Russians we showed up because Laurent told us to. We play Laurent like he's playing the Russians."

Apollo's jaw tightened at the mention of Darbazi's, "Who do you have watching the restaurant?"

I stared back at Apollo refusing to give in. He wanted me to admit to everyone I had Kate watching from the bakery. I couldn't risk anyone finding out about her.

"Someone I trust. They know to call me when they see Laurent."

"It could work." Junior blurted out. "Worst case scenario we kill Laurent and the Russians and blame it all on someone else. It would cause problems, but it would be easier than dealing with the problems we'd get taking out Laurent alone."

"So your plan is to sit around and wait for a call that Laurent is meeting with the Russians and then we go in and take over their meeting. Then we hope the Russians kill Laurent before they kill us?"

"Yes." I replied.

"How do we even know Laurent will meet with the Russians at Darbazi's or that they'll even meet again?" Apollo asked.

"I saw him on the security footage a week ago. He didn't leave with anything. He wouldn't finish a job without leaving with some type of payment. If in a week we don't see anything then we can change the plan, but this could work."

"You have four days. If we don't hear anything in four days we go after Laurent." Apollo said.

"I'll go get ready, make sure we're prepared in case the Russian's don't take the bait." I said, starting to stand up.

"No, you stay. Everybody out."

All of Apollo's men quickly left his office. Junior took his time, but quickly closed the door behind him when he saw the look on Apollo's face.

I turned to face Apollo, waiting to see what he had to say. His shoulders dropped as he leaned back into his chair.

"Apollo-"

"I told you not to get involved with her. I told you this is how it'd end."

"You have no idea what you're talking about. There's nothing going on between the two of us."

"Does she even know what you've dragged her into? Does she realize what would happen if Laurent found out it's her that's been helping us watch the Russians? Did you ever think about what this would do to her?" He yelled.

"Apollo, how many times do I have to tell you? There's nothing going on between me and Kate. She knows what she's doing to help me is dangerous, and she also knows exactly how dangerous I am. She's smart, I know she's already figured it out." I argued.

"What's your plan Dane? When she calls, and you know she will, what will you do to protect her? I can't have my best man leaving to go protect the girl next door. I told you from the very beginning that she was a distraction and you ignored me." He said.

"She's not a distraction."

"Bullshit. You spend every minute of every day eating scones and drinking coffee with her. You haven't spent a day at the warehouse in weeks, and everyone's starting to notice. I need to know now if she's going to be a problem."

"You have nothing to worry about, I promise. After she helps us with Laurent I promise she won't be a problem anymore. I'm only doing the job you asked me to do, which was to watch Darbazi's."

Apollo stood up from the table. He was right. I was distracted, I'd put her before work. After we took care of Laurent I had to stop whatever this was between Kate and me.

"You're staying here until we hear from your friend. I can't risk you going to visit her and blowing up the whole plan." He told me.

He knew if I could I'd wait down the street from the bakery just to make sure she was safe. He knew if I could she was the first place I'd run to.

"I'll be in the basement if you need me." I said, walking out of his office.

It was day three and I hadn't heard from Kate yet. We were running out of time. Apollo had made other arrangements to take out the Russians. There was a huge risk running his plan, but because of my connection to Kate he doubted me. He was waiting for everything to go wrong.

I had spent the last three days avoiding Apollo. I didn't need him trying to tell me I was getting too attached to Kate. I was in the basement when my phone rang.

"Hello?"

"Dane, he's here!" Kate shouted.

"Who is he with?" I asked.

"Jozef, Jozef's uncle, and a few other guys I've never seen before. Dane, what do I do?"

"Do nothing. Turn off all your lights, make sure all of your doors are closed and then go upstairs. Do not move until I call you or come find you. Do you understand?"

"Dane I can't-"

"Kate, do you understand?" I interrupted.

"I got it. I'm going upstairs right now."

"Good, go to your room and lock the door. I'm hanging up now but keep your phone close. Only pick up the phone if it's me calling."

"How long do I have to wait?" She asked.

"Until it's safe."

"Oh God." She whispered.

"I'll find you as soon as I can, just stay put." I said, hanging up.

I ran out of the basement and went looking for Apollo.

"Apollo!" I shouted through the house.

Apollo came to the staircase and looked down at me.

"It's time, Laurent's there. We have to go, now!"

"Call Junior and Alex, have them meet us a few blocks down from Darbazi's. This is your plan; you're going into Darbazi's with me. I don't want anyone else in there until we know it's safe."

"I'll go get the car." I said.

I drove with Apollo to Darbazi's. I parked across from the bakery and saw all of the lights off. Good girl, she did exactly as I asked.

"You better pray this works." Apollo whispered, walking to the front of Darbazi's.

"Let me do all the talking and it will."

Apollo rolled his eyes while picking the front lock. As we walked back to the kitchen we heard Laurent and Ivan talking about payment. Apollo waited for me to give the okay. I nodded and opened the door wide for him.

He stepped into the kitchen with me right behind him. In a second guns were aimed right at us.

"What the fuck are you two doing here?" Ivan asked.

"We were invited." I said.

"And who invited you?"

"Laurent. He thought we should be here."

Ivan looked over at Laurent.

"Bullshit." Laurent laughed.

"Then why are we here?" Apollo asked.

I continued to walk closer to Ivan, "This has been his plan all along. Every meeting, every shipment drop, we knew about it the whole time. We know what you've been doing since the very beginning. He called us last week after your last meeting. He wasn't happy leaving empty handed."

One of Ivan's men whispered something to him while he looked back at Jozef.

"Did you bring Laurent here last week? After I told you not to?" He asked.

"He wanted to see the layout of the restaurant before today's meeting. I thought he'd back out if I said no. I thought you knew." He explained.

"You use my men behind my back, invite the Costa's to a meeting, what else are you hiding Laurent?"

"This is ridiculous. I have no idea what any of them are doing here. I came to do a job."

Laurent tried to pack up, but Ivan stopped him. Ivan's men drew their guns at him. Apollo walked over to stand behind Ivan.

I watched as Ivan's distrust in us turned to anger towards Laurent.

"You don't want to do this." Laurent warned. "I can and will make you millions. Whatever scam the Costas are playing isn't worth killing me over."

"He could have made you millions if what he was selling wasn't already promised to another buyer." Apollo lied.

"What are you talking about?" Ivan asked, turning to Apollo.

"He's sold off the guns you were going to buy for double the price. They're on a boat in the Atlantic already. Why do you think he's changed tonight's meeting so many times? He's stalling. He needed us to take you out before you got suspicious."

"Liar." Laurent spat.

The only good thing about Laurent is that he worked alone. We could count on no one waiting around the corner to come save him. This wasn't the first time Laurent had been ambushed, but it would be the last.

Laurent could feel the pressure of being trapped in a corner. He wasn't making it out alive tonight. If the Russians let him leave Apollo wouldn't. We'd been looking to take him out for years.

Laurent turned to see he was surrounded; Ivan's men still had their guns aimed at him. I waited for Apollo to give me the okay to shoot, but he shook his head. It looked like I wasn't going to have to kill Laurent tonight. Knowing there wasn't a way he could talk himself out of this one Laurent took a few steps back. He tried to pull his gun out from under his coat, but he never stood a chance. The Russians fired before he could pull his gun out. A few more shots than necessary were fired into Laurent.

Apollo pointed to the back of the kitchen. All that was left to do was to give Apollo a few minutes to renegotiate with the Russians. We considered not taking them back as clients, but business was business. I was followed out of the restaurant by Ivan's men.

I leaned against the Darbazi's delivery van and waited with Jozef while Apollo and Ivan talked.

"You got lucky tonight." I said to him, "You shouldn't have been sneaking around with Laurent."

"Fuck off." He mumbled.

What I didn't tell him is that he was lucky because Apollo and I considered using him as our distraction. It would have been just as easy to turn Ivan on Jozef.

Even though I knew I couldn't see the bakery from the alley I still caught myself looking over there every few minutes. I wouldn't relax until I was sure Kate was safe. Half an hour later

Apollo walked out with Ivan. Jozef went in to clean up the kitchen and I walked back to the car with Apollo.

"He agreed to our increase in payments." Apollo said, opening his car door.

"What about Laurent?" I asked.

"Russians want credit for what happened tonight. Ivan wants to use him to send a message."

"Are we done here?" I asked.

"We're done." He answered, looking over his shoulder at the bakery.

I ignored Apollo's glare and left him alone at the car. I wasn't in the mood to argue. I needed to see Kate.

It wasn't hard picking her front lock. The door handle hardly turned on a good day, and sometimes when it rained it never fully shut. As soon as I got through the front of the bakery I ran to the back and looked for the stairs that led up to the second floor.

"Kate!" I shouted in front of an even older door than the one I'd just broken.

I heard nothing, it was dead silent.

"Kate!" I yelled again.

Finally a light turned on and I heard footsteps.

Kate opened the door with tears in her eyes. A pair of glasses held her curls above her head. She looked exhausted, like she hadn't slept since the last time I was here.

"Is it over?" She asked.

I walked forward into her apartment, closing the door behind me.

"It's over."

"Good." She sighed, her shoulders relaxing.

"Kate, I promise you're safe here. There's no chance of this coming back to you."

"We'll see."

"Kate…"

"No, you don't get to make me feel better right now. If you keep talking you're going to apologize and say the right thing and I'll feel bad and forgive you. So please leave."

"I know you're upset, but please-"

"I'm not upset Dane. I'm absolutely, positively pissed! I know what you did tonight. That man I saw today is just like the others that go into Darbazi's. He's never going to walk back out. I can't keep pretending like I don't know what you are. It was selfish of me to pretend you were spending all that time in my shop because you enjoyed being there. Now that you've taken care of that man you don't need to lie anymore."

I took a step towards her stretching out my arm.

"Don't, Dane. I think you should leave."

"I can't just leave, please."

"Okay fine, you can stay if you tell me what you did at Darbazi's tonight. Tell me everything or leave." She said.

I didn't want to leave, I desperately wanted to stay close to the shop tonight just in case, but I couldn't tell her what she needed to hear.

Kate knew I couldn't say anything, so she grabbed for the door and waited for me to walk back out. I stopped in the hallway.

"Kate…"

She waited one more time for me to say anything, but I couldn't, not even for someone like Kate.

Before I found the courage to say anything she spoke, "Do you have any idea what the past week has been like for me? I sat at that stupid fucking window all night and watched Darbazi's for you. I hated every minute I spent downstairs working. I was too afraid to even turn my back to the street. I wasted an entire week being terrified of a man I've never met and now you don't even have the balls to tell me if he's alive or dead. I'll never know if what I did was the right thing or if you played me and I ruined a man's life."

"I didn't use you Kate."

"Then why do I feel used, Dane?"

It killed me to admit it but she was right, I used her.

Without another thought she left me to find my way out of her apartment. I waited for another minute hoping she'd change her mind and turn around one more time but she never did. I waited until I heard her front door lock and then I left Ivy's for the last time.

CHAPTER THREE

Kate

Dane hasn't shown up since that night in my apartment. I wasn't surprised, I knew now that he wasn't watching Darbazi's he didn't need me anymore. There was a time I really thought he did enjoy being here at the bakery, but I think I told myself that lie so I could avoid having to say goodbye to him.

I was working on icing for our cookies when I heard Becca's yell from the front. I found her sweeping up coffee grinds from the floor.

"What happened this time?" I asked.

"I grabbed the filter thinking it hadn't been used yet and I burned my hand."

"You're the reason my risk and liability insurance rates are so high, you know that?"

"Yeah, yeah." She mumbled.

"Do you need to take a break?"

"I'm fine. It's almost lunch time. I don't want to miss Dane stopping by."

"Dane won't be stopping by anymore." I told her.

"Why not?" She asked.

"Because." I answered, avoiding her concerned frown.

"Go put some ice on your hand."

Becca hesitated for a second before leaving to go get ice. A part of me wished he would surprise me and stop by, but I knew he wouldn't. It was better if we never saw each other again. I made the mistake of talking to him in the first place.

My brain knew we were better off not seeing each other anymore, but my heart was screaming at me. It was telling me I was making a mistake. If Dane walked in right now I wasn't sure what I would do. I mean I would panic for a second or two, but besides that I had no idea what would happen. I like to think I'd stand my ground and throw a donut at him or something but I knew if he came in right now I'd invite him to sit down for a cup of coffee.

The best thing I could do was to forget about Dane and focus on work. It had been a long week and it wasn't even over yet. Fridays were long days for me. There were the customers who stocked up on desserts for a weekend trip, the happy couples who came in after date night, and the lonely guests who had nowhere else to go. I'd been making cookies and coffee for over twelve hours. Becca usually offered to open on Saturday's, but she was visiting her grandma and I couldn't ask her to cover for me tomorrow. I haven't slept much since the Darbazi's incident, so tonight I'll be going to bed early.

I went almost the whole day not thinking about Dane. We were so busy I didn't have time to stop and wallow. It wasn't until we closed and I sent Becca home that I had time to doubt asking him to leave. I was getting ready to take out the trash in the kitchen when I heard the bell ring. I don't think I forgot to lock up. No, I definitely did lock the front door, so who had gotten in? I looked through the kitchen door window and found a nervous Dane holding a basket that was almost as big as him.

"Dane?"

"Kate!" He shouted from behind the basket.

I walked out of the kitchen and helped Dane with the basket. We barely managed to set it on a table before he lost control of it.

"You really need to get that door fixed." He smiled.

"Why are you here Dane?"

Dane dropped the smile from his face and tried again.

"I came to apologize and to start over. I need you to know Kate, that I wasn't using you."

I rolled my eyes, taking a step away from him.

"Even if you don't forgive me I needed to say the words, so here it goes, I'm sorry."

I leaned forward waiting for him to continue.

"I should have never asked you to do what you did. I took advantage of our relationship, and I promise not to put you in danger like that again. Spending time with you was the best part of my day. Job or no job I don't regret meeting you."

I was really trying to play it cool, but I could tell Dane didn't apologize often. It looked like it physically made him uncomfortable. I couldn't stand his stare any longer, so I pointed to the basket sitting on the table as a distraction.

"What's this?"

"A friend gifted me a wine and cheese basket. It's part two of my apology to you."

"Your apology contains a regift?" I asked.

"You're the only one I could think of that I wanted to share this with. There's enough food for thirty people. I couldn't let it all go to waste." He said.

For a minute Dane's charming smile, and kind gestures were causing me to forget why I was mad at him.

"I didn't want the other night to be the last memory I have of this place. I came because we both deserve a better ending, a better goodbye."

"A better goodbye?" I asked.

"I just want to spend one more night here, with you. My sister says closure is good for the soul, it's healing." He convinced.

"Well, I could use some healing, and a glass of wine wouldn't hurt either." I agreed.

God, I shouldn't have caved, but I also wanted one more night.

"I'll go grab some glasses and a few plates. Figure out how to get into all that wrapping paper." I told him.

While I grabbed a few things from the kitchen I heard Dane do his best to get the basket free from all the plastic wrap. When I came back, an out of breath Dane was throwing the plastic wrap onto my clean floors.

"You're cleaning that up before you leave." I said.

"Of course." He smiled.

"Here." I said, handing him two wine glasses and my wine opener.

Before Dane could even grab the wine from the basket I grabbed his arm and pulled it back.

"Holy shit, Dane!"

"What's wrong?" He asked.

"Do you have any idea how much that bottle is worth? We can't drink that! Don't open it, don't waste a bottle like that on me." I answered.

Dane ignored my complaints and popped the cork, "Too late."

He poured me a glass and then poured one for himself. As he handed me my glass I tried to do the math in my head to figure out how much he had just poured out. Dane searched through the basket and found a few jams and breads.

"Who gave this to you?" I asked.

"It's a long story."

"Oh right, I forgot I'm not allowed to ask any questions." I spoke.

"Kate." He sighed.

I grabbed a knife and spread some peach jam onto a cracker.

While pretending like this peach jam required my full attention to spread, I watched Dane from the corner of my eye. I saw his face turn from frustration to defeat.

"A friend sent it as a peace offering." He confessed.

"And why did this friend feel like they needed to send you a peace offering?"

"Because I've been nothing but cold to her since we've met."

"Well fix whatever problems you have with her because she's got good taste."

"I'll do my best." He smiled, grabbing his wine.

We sat in comfortable silence for a few minutes. I picked at the table cloth to avoid Dane's intense stares.

"I missed this." Dane spoke, breaking the silence.

"I missed it too. Ever since you've left I've had no one to talk to about the shop." I told him.

"How's Becca?" He asked.

"Oh you know Becca is Becca. Everything is terrible, and the world is ending. Last week she went on a date and had to call me to come rescue her."

"It couldn't have been that bad."

"It wasn't the first date she has fled from, but I can't blame her for wanting to leave this one. Her date brought a puppet that looked like him. He made the waiter find an extra chair for it. She didn't even make it to the appetizers."

"Poor Becca." He laughed, taking another sip of wine.

"She's decided to swear off men. I give it a week."

Dane let out a quiet laugh, but soon we were back to sitting in silence.

This time it was me who watched Dane. I watched his Adam's apple bob as he took long sips of his wine. His jaw tightened every time he looked at my broken door. He turned back to me, surprised I was staring at him.

"You look like you have questions."

"Just one." I replied. "I want to know how close I was to breaking you."

"To breaking me?"

"Every day you sat here with me and listened to me talk. I thought maybe one day you'd break and finally be the one to share. There was that one night you came in late that I thought I might learn something about you, but you left to take a phone call before I got anywhere."

"That night was a close one, but it wasn't the night I almost gave in." He admitted.

"So there was a night that I almost met the real Dane?"

"The snowstorm." He smiled.

"The hot cocoa night?" I asked.

"I was tired, hadn't slept in a few days and you brought me a mug with fucking marshmallows in it. It was almost enough to make me snap." He laughed.

"So all it would have taken were more marshmallows?"

"I didn't give a damn about the marshmallows Kate; it was why you gave them to me. You knew something was wrong that night, so you tried to make me smile, tried to make me feel better. It didn't matter how busy you were or how tired, you were always doing kind things for me even though I didn't deserve it."

Dane looked down at his wine, he watched the few drops left in his glass bounce around. He refilled his glass and tapped his ring against the glass. It hurt knowing Dane didn't think he deserved my kindness.

"God I can't even look at you." I sighed, throwing a piece of bread back onto the table.

"Why not?"

"Because we'd be absolutely incredible together Dane. Don't even try to deny it, I know you feel it too. Maybe in another life I'll get to meet the real Dane and the timing will be right."

"You have met the real Dane, Kate."

"No, I don't think I have." I smiled, biting my cheek to hold back the tears.

Dane nodded his head; he knew I was right. For some reason there was a part of his life he'd never be able to share with me. Dane knew I'd never survive the secrets, and I could never ask him to share them.

I finished off my glass and then remembered I had saved a gift for Dane over by the window.

"I have something for you." I told him, walking over to the pile of newspapers.

Dane turned in his seat, watching my every step back to the table.

"You're my only customer who actually likes the crosswords. I saved the pages from the newspaper every day in case you came back. It felt wrong throwing them out."

As Dane grabbed the newspapers from me our hands met. I'm sure we'd accidentally touched hands before today, but right now in this moment it felt like the first time. The warmth that spread to my hand caused my entire body to turn ice cold.

"Do you have any idea how many newspapers are thrown away every day? People don't even have the respect to recycle them anymore." He complained.

"Don't even get me started on the price of the paper going up." I teased.

"I've complained about it that much huh?" He asked.

"Only every morning."

Dane looked at his watch and slid the newspapers into his coat pocket.

"You have to leave." I spoke.

"I do."

"You were right. I think we both needed one more night, a final goodbye."

Dane stood, trying to clean up his glass and plates.

"Please, you brought this incredible basket. The least I can do is clean up. Besides, it will give me something to do after you leave."

Dane walked with me to the front door. Stalling, he grabbed just below my jaw with his hands, stroking his thumb over my cheek.

"Goodbye Kate." He whispered.

"Goodbye." I said, barely holding it together.

He took one more look around the bakery before walking back onto the busy street.

I locked the broken front door and watched him leave. I waited until he turned into just another stranger on the sidewalk before I started to clean up.

Cleaning up the basket I found a note. I thought about throwing away the card knowing it was written for Dane, but temptation got the better of me.

I pulled the card from its envelope.

If I find out you threw this away I'll kill you

- *Eliana*

I didn't have the heart to throw the note away. I grabbed the note and took it to my office drawer where I kept all the other notes Dane had left me. Dane had never mentioned an Eliana to me, but it sounded like she was an important person in his life. It was another memory I got to keep of Dane.

I went back out to finish cleaning up. I was nearly finished when a knock on the door almost gave me a heart attack. I dropped the plates onto the table, hopefully not chipping them.

Looking behind me I saw Dane standing outside. I ran to unlock the door. Before I could ask him why he'd come back he pushed his way back into the shop.

"My name is Dane Russo. When I was nineteen I met Apollo Costa and I've been working for him ever since. I have four sisters, they never let me forget I'm the youngest. They all still live in Jersey. I have twelve nieces and nephews, and I don't visit them as often as I should. Two weeks ago at Darbazi's I killed an arms dealer named Laurent. If anyone asked me why I killed him I would tell them it was because he was a threat to the Costa family, but the truth is that knowing he was only a few feet away from you and your bakery made me physically sick. If I could go back to that night I'd change nothing about what happened to Laurent. The world is a better place now that he's gone."

I went to say something, anything, but Dane stopped me.

"Let me finish. I don't regret stumbling into your bakery that day. It's selfish of me to be standing here, and if I was a better man I'd walk away but I can't. No more secrets Kate, and now that you know everything about me I think you should know that I'd really like to kiss you."

All of the air in my lungs had been knocked out of me.

"There are some pieces of my life I can never share with you Kate, but I'm willing to bend a little if it means giving us a chance. I've done terrible things in my life, and it would be unfair of me to share them with you, but I can't stay away from you."

I didn't need a mirror to know I looked like an absolute idiot right now. The longer I stared at Dane with surprise the longer he doubted he made the right choice by confessing his life to me.

"Kate."

"Yes?" I asked, looking back up at Dane.

"I said I'd like to kiss you now."

Oh.

Dane looked at me, waiting for me to say yes. Even now he hesitated. I'd only been dreaming about this exact moment for weeks, and still he paused.

"Dane."

"Yes?"

"Just fucking kiss me already."

That was all the confirmation he needed. Dane quickly slid his hands through my hair, pulling me closer to him than I'd ever been. Forgetting his strength he nearly pulled me off the floor. Keeping his lips connected to mine he leaned down further and held me tighter. He didn't wait a minute before he slid his tongue in, searching for mine. His deep sighs were causing me to ache. I could feel the grumble of his frustration with every kiss.

Dane and I fought back and forth for control. I'd never kissed someone like Dane, someone who knew exactly what they wanted. He knew exactly where to hold me, where to kiss me. I finally gave in and let Dane take over. My body was practically screaming at me, begging me to let Dane take it further.

Realizing I was waiting for his move he grabbed my hips and lifted me off of the floor. I wrapped my legs around him as he carried me to the closest table. His hands still wrapped tightly around my ass he sat me down. I locked my legs around his waist refusing to let him go. His kisses grew fiercer, he struggled to hide how turned on he was.

He let out a deep sigh, causing me to moan. Pulling away he softly pulled at my bottom lip.

"There's no chance I'm letting you go now that I've gotten to taste you Kate."

Using his hands still stuck in my curls to his advantage he pulled my head to the side, leaving sloppy kisses down my neck. He bit and licked until he found the fabric of my dress. He pulled it off of my shoulder, continuing to explore. I leaned my head back, arching into him to give him more room to kiss whatever he wanted. Pulling back up he kissed me, this time softer than before. I could tell he was holding back.

He was hesitating, the confidence he had just shown was disappearing.

Something in him changed, and now it seemed as though he was trying to remember this moment with every kiss. He dipped his tongue just below the curve of my top lip, waiting for permission again.

Before I had the chance to invite Dane up to my apartment his phone rang. He grabbed his phone from his pocket, not even bothering to look at who was calling. With his one free hand he ran it all over my body.

"What?" He asked into the phone, kissing my temple.

While he listened to the person on the phone he kissed up and down my jaw.

"No." He spoke, muffled by the kisses of my neck.

Another minute of silence went by before he pulled away.

"I'll be there in fifteen."

Hanging up he kissed me just as deeply as before, once again making me forget where I was.

"I have to go." He said.

"I know." I laughed.

"I'd stay if I could, but it's a work thing."

"A dangerous work thing?" I asked.

"No more than usual. I'll be sure to stop by tomorrow as soon as I can. Do you have the day off?"

"I work tomorrow. I'm covering for Becca."

"I'll be here at six to pick you up for dinner. I know you need to be here to open, but I can steal you away for a few minutes." He said. "As much as I love your croissants and coffee it's about time I took you on a proper date."

"I'll be waiting." I smiled.

Dane helped me jump off the table and pick up the sugar packets and creamers we knocked over.

I walked with Dane to the front door one more time.

"I'll see you tomorrow." He spoke, putting on his jacket.

"Be safe tonight, I'll be absolutely pissed if you cancel dinner tomorrow."

"I'll be on my best behavior tonight, promise."

He turned around and gave me one more kiss on the cheek before walking out the door. I watched him stumble back to his car. Every few seconds he turned around to see if I was still watching through the window. On the third turn he couldn't see where he was walking and ran into an older gentleman on the sidewalk. I watched an embarrassed Dane apologize and turn around to silently blame me for his reckless walking. Closing the blinds on my windows and locking the door I began cleaning up my bakery for the third time.

Everything that could have gone wrong today did go wrong. I slept through my alarm, I didn't have time to prep the muffins this morning, then I crushed my hand in the fridge door and it didn't matter that this was the busiest day of my life it somehow still wasn't time to close.

If I knew Amanda was going to call in I would have asked for Becca to come in after her trip with her grandma or found literally anyone else to come in today.

I was running around like a mad woman trying to keep myself busy. And worse than anything else I dropped purple food coloring on my favorite green pants. Now it looked like I had dark grease stains all over my cute pants. I hadn't stopped to look at a clock since two, but I knew it had to be past five with how dark it was outside.

Like I hadn't suffered enough, I turned to the sound of the bells and found Dane standing there, smile beaming bigger than I'd ever seen before.

Shit. I knew I was forgetting something. I ran over to apologize, but Dane beat me to it.

"You look like you've had a day." He said.

"I let Becca have the day off and then Amanda called out, and on top of that the universe hates me and this is the worst day of my life." I replied.

Okay, so maybe that was a little dramatic, but I had to get my point across.

"I'm sorry Dane. Even if I close up right now there's no way I can get out of here before nine. I have too much to do. I should have called earlier so you didn't waste your time coming all the way down here."

"Kate, look at me." He said, grabbing my arm.

I took a deep breath and relaxed my shoulders, looking up at him.

"I don't care about dinner, and I didn't waste my time coming down here to see you." He spoke softly.

Pulling me to the side he walked right around me and started to walk behind the counter.

"How can I help?" He said, grabbing a few mugs and dropping them into the sink.

"I'm sorry?" I asked, my brain short circuiting seeing Dane behind the counter.

"If I help you close you'll get out of here sooner, so what do you need me to do?"

I continued to stare at Dane, unable to speak. He needed to stop doing charming shit like this or I swear to God I was going to fall in love with him.

"Um, well I need someone to help me clean out the display case and box up any treats we didn't sell today." I explained.

"Seems easy enough." He smiled.

I walked behind Dane towards the cash register to get ready and check out the last couple of customers who hadn't left yet. When I turned around to see if he'd started working yet I saw him taking off his jacket. An act so simple, but when done by Dane it was holy. I would have sat and watched him all night, but something on his back brought me back to reality.

"Oh, Dane, nope, no, why don't you take your jacket off in my office, so you don't set it down somewhere and forget about it." I half shouted at him, pulling his jacket back onto his shoulders.

Dane looked back at me confused for my outburst. I slowly ran my hand down his back and stopped when I got to the gun he had hiding in his belt.

I nodded my head waiting for him to get why I had freaked out. He finally put two and two together and rushed into the kitchen.

"I'll be right back." He spoke, embarrassed to have forgotten what he had hiding under his jacket.

I laughed my way back to the drawer and helped the last of my guests with their last-minute purchases.

Dane came back out when my last customer was walking out. I followed behind them to lock the door. When I turned around I found Dane standing there wearing my pink fucking apron.

Lord, give me strength.

"Better?" He asked, giving a spin.

"Mhmm." I mumbled, physically unable to say anything without bursting into thin air.

Dane, proud of himself, went to work cleaning up the display case. He quickly boxed up the leftovers for the shelter and spent the rest of the time cleaning out the cookie shelves. When he'd finished he turned around to find me.

Technically two people closing was faster than one, but I had gotten zero work done because every two minutes I stopped to watch Dane. I'd probably gotten less done than if I was alone.

"Is there anything I need to do in the back?" He asked, tossing his rag onto the counter.

"Yeah I have some inventory that came in today. It usually takes two people to bring in from the back and put away."

"Just show me where you want it and consider it done." He spoke.

Dane finished every chore faster than the one before. I was running out of things to give him.

"Can you go make sure I didn't leave the back door by the alley open?" I asked.

When he locked the door he walked back to the front of the store in an almost sprint. It's like he knew I was trying to keep him busy. He snuck up behind me while I was grabbing for a mixer. He laid his hand on my hips and tried pulling me closer to him.

I jumped at our sudden closeness and grabbed the bowl, tightening it into my arms.

"I've got it!" I shouted.

Dane lifted his arms in defeat, taking a step back.

"Sorry."

"It's not- I should be the one apologizing. But please, you have to stop doing that, I just can't…" I rambled.

"You can't what Kate?" He asked, waiting for anything to explain my behavior.

"You're just being so, you know? And it's killing me, and I can't even look at you. I just want to-"

I twisted my hands in frustration, wishing Dane would take a step back so that I could focus.

"Use your words Kate, complete sentences please."

"You have to stop being so charming." I confessed.

"I don't understand."

"You're being too sweet, too gentlemanly. I can't take it anymore."

"I'm sorry, I was just trying to help. I can go if you're uncomfortable."

"Damn it, Dane. I want you, like bad. Like all the health codes we'd be breaking are starting to not bother me so much. You're getting in my head, clouding my judgment. I can't even look at you in that fucking apron without imaging what you'd look like taking it off."

My outburst was a surprise to Dane. He processed my words and let a smile slip.

"I can't believe I just said that out loud. Oh my God that's so embarrassing. I shouldn't have said anything, I'm so sorry. You're here helping me close and all I can think about is our last kiss and what it would be like to get to kiss you again." I said.

This was so embarrassing. I needed to shut up before I said anything else.

"I haven't been able to stop thinking about it either." He said.

I froze.

"And as much as I'd love to kiss you again, we have a small problem."

"And what is that?" I asked.

"Well, I'd hate to be the reason the health department shuts down Ivy's, and my mom would kill me if she found out I had ever invited myself up to a girl's apartment without being properly asked."

I smiled, the tension relaxing from my shoulders.

"Would you like to come upstairs for a minute Dane? It's the least I can do after everything you've done to help me tonight."

"I don't know Kate; I'd hate to intrude. Are you sure?"

"I insist." I laughed.

As soon as I gave him permission he grabbed me by the waist and lifted me up. I struggled to get out of his hold because of how hard I was laughing. I did my best to kick and wiggle out of his arms, but I wasn't escaping anytime soon. Dane carried me up the stairs into my apartment. Closing the door behind him.

He finally let me down to give me a chance to unlock my door. As soon as it was open I grabbed his hand and brought him into the living room. I let out a laugh when I scanned over Dane.

"You're still wearing the apron."

"I think pink is my color."

I grabbed the front pocket of the apron and pulled him closer to me. I looked up at Dane and waited for confirmation that this was what he wanted. He didn't make me wait a second longer. He grabbed me and pulled me into him.

Dane dipped down and licked my lips. He pulled away after a short, sweet kiss.

I waited for him to lean back down and reach behind my neck. Like he could read my mind he did exactly that. We couldn't have been closer to each other if we tried. Dane took control of the kiss and teased my lips with his tongue. I took one more kiss of his soft lips before giving him a chance to kiss me deeper.

The two of us were lost in each other for who knows how long. Dane had me forgetting where we were. Dane kissed me just like that first night after his confession. He kissed me like what we were doing was forbidden. Like we'd get in trouble if we got caught. Every kiss he savored like it would be out last.

Surprising me, Dane pulled away and took a step back.

"What's wrong?" I asked.

"Nothing, I just think we need to stop." He answered, running his thumb across my lip.

Did I do something wrong?

"I can see your brain going into overdrive trying to figure out why I stopped Kate, but I promise it's not what you think."

"If it's not what I'm thinking then why did you pull away?"

"Because if I hadn't I'd be fucking you right now, right on that couch." He confessed.

My cheeks blushed; his confession surprised me.

"And that's a reason to stop because?" I asked.

"Because I'd like to take you on a date first. You're worth more than just a quick fuck in your living room. I'd be an ass if I didn't take someone like you out on a proper date first."

"We could always go to dinner after." I smiled.

Dane dropped his head back, letting out a laugh, "Nice try babe."

I let go of Dane's arms and rolled my eyes. I left him in the living room to go grab my hair clip from the kitchen counter.

"I'm free Thursday." I told him.

"What?"

"For dinner, I'm free Thursday. I have no allergies, I love all cuisines, and I'll be ready at seven. I'm sure I don't have to worry about you being late." I said.

Dane smiled and walked over to give me one more kiss before walking me back towards the door.

"I'll see you Thursday." He whispered in my ear.

"Thursday." I repeated, finally moving to let him leave.

CHAPTER FOUR

Kate

"Are you sure you don't need any help? I'm not doing anything." I tried to offer to Becca again. I'd been offering to help all afternoon, but every time I walked back down into the shop she kicked me right back out.

"Kate, I love you, but if you don't leave and finish getting ready for dinner I'm going to lock you upstairs like your evil step mother. I promise Amanda and I can handle the shop. Go, he'll be here soon."

"I'll go back up in a few minutes. I just forgot to check some things in the office. I forgot Steve was coming tonight to drop off some stuff. I'd hate not to be here when he comes to deliver. I should call him." I said.

"Nice try, I already talked to Steve. He's bringing his nephew with him to help with unloading, and I've already paid. The invoice is sitting on your desk which is where it will be tomorrow, when you get to work. Leave." She said.

"Becca I can't! He's going to be here any minute. I'm going crazy waiting for him upstairs, please I need something to do."

"Fine, go work on the schedule or something in your office, but stay out of the kitchen. I will be so annoyed if you get a stain on your new dress. I didn't spend all day yesterday helping you find an outfit just for you to spill jam on it ten minutes before your date."

"You'll let me know when he gets here?" I asked.

"Yes, now go!" She shouted after me.

I locked myself in my office and pretended to work for a few minutes. I hadn't been able to focus on work, or anything other than Dane for the past week. All I could think about was our date. Tonight was the first night our relationship, situation, whatever you want to call it, was leaving the bakery. Up until now I was safe in my own little world. I've never had to consider what Dane and I were outside of here, but tonight that was all coming crashing down. What if real life Dane is a completely different person than bakery Dane? What if the only reason we worked was because we had only spent time here, at my shop?

A knock on the door pulled me back to reality. Jacob opened my door with a scared smile on his face.

"Dane's here. You might want to get out there. Becca is giving him the talk."

"The talk?"

"The birds and the bees, protection of the physical and emotional kind, *the talk*." He explained.

"Oh my God." I cried, running through the kitchen.

In the front of the shop a terrified looking Dane was being educated by Becca in front of all of my very embarrassed customers.

"I'm sure I don't have to warn you what would happen to you if you hurt her or upset her in any way but let me be very clear. If you ever hurt her I will find you, and I will personally rip your-"

"Becca!" I shouted. "I think he gets the picture."

Dane looked up from Becca and gave me a warm smile. His eyes showed appreciation for stopping Becca when I did. He whispered a small thank you as Becca took a step back from Dane and walked towards me.

"Becca, please don't scare him away before our date has even started." I said.

"If Dane's thinking about running after our conversation then he doesn't deserve you. Are you scared Dane? Ready to run?" She asked.

I looked at Dane and raised my eyebrow, waiting to hear his answer.

"Well?" I asked.

"Don't worry Becca, you haven't scared me away yet." He said.

"You sure?"

"Positive." He confirmed.

I smiled at Dane and took his hand, "Goodbye Becca!"

"Home by ten please." She shouted after us.

Dane laughed the entire way from Ivy's to the restaurant. He told me all about his conversation with Becca. I would have completely understood if he did run away. If my customers heard what Dane heard I'd have to give out a free apology treat with every order this week.

Dane parked around the corner from the restaurant. When we were walking I realized we were so distracted by Becca on the way to dinner I hadn't asked where we were eating tonight.

He'd brought me to a busy Italian restaurant. When we walked in he didn't wait for a host to seat us. He led me to a back table hidden by a corner in the restaurant.

"Really? Italian?" I asked.

"You seemed to really like Italian last night. Thought you'd want some more." He smirked, pushing in my chair for me.

Touché.

Dane's smile disappeared when our waiter came up to us with menus. While I looked through their dishes Dane ordered wine for the table. He came back a few minutes later with our glasses and to take our orders. He left quickly leaving Dane and I alone. The rush of the restaurant was muffled by the wall we sat by. It felt like we were the only two in the entire restaurant. I took everything in, appreciating the art on the walls and the rush of the kitchen. When I looked back at Dane he was staring.

"You look beautiful tonight Kate."

I bit my lip, hoping I wasn't already blushing. Dane was quite the gentleman, always ready to charm.

"Thank you." I smiled. "I didn't get the chance to say so when you picked me up, but you clean up nice."

Now it was Dane who was a little embarrassed. He took a sip of his wine, fixing his knife and spoon so that they sat straight.

"How was work today?" He asked.

"No complaints. We were busy, but that's a good thing. Becca spent the day experimenting with new desserts. She's looking for a few desserts to display for spring when the weather gets warmer. She thinks it will pull in customers."

"What classifies a dessert as a spring dessert?" He asked.

"I'm not really sure, and I don't think Becca knows either. Right now she's just wasting my money on new paints and fruit that she ends up not using. It's costing me more than what we'd probably make on new desserts, but she's happy. I'd hate to tell her to stop. She's excited about them and who knows, maybe she'll surprise me and create something incredible."

"Who taste tests all of your experiments?" Dane asked.

"Usually me, but if this is you volunteering I'd be happy to share her unique creations with you."

Dane shook his head no. He was still traumatized from his first few days at Ivy's. He ate more treats than anyone ever should. I would have to wait a while before expecting him to be a taste tester.

"So how was your day?" I asked.

I wasn't expecting him to give me an honest answer, but it was worth a shot.

"I helped Apollo get ready for a trip to Chicago."

"What's in Chicago?"

"A potential business partner." He answered.

"I gotta say, your whole mysterious mob vibe used to drive me crazy, but it's really growing on me. Leaves a lot of room for imagination." I said.

Dane looked around the room at my sudden confession. Before he could remind me we weren't supposed to talk about his work in public the waiter came over to order.

While we waited for our food I asked Dane a few more questions about his life.

"Are you and Apollo friends or just coworkers? Like do you actually hang out?" I asked.

"I don't think we've ever talked about it before but I guess we're friends. I imagine it's like how you and Becca are friends and work together."

"Yeah, but I met Becca in college and I doubt you met Apollo in college."

"That's technically true, but I met Apollo when I was in college, so that kind of counts." He explained.

"How did you two meet?"

"That's a story for another day and another place." He said looking around.

After dropping off our food our waiter disappeared, leaving the two of us alone. We ate for a few minutes in silence. After a few bites of his chicken Dane set down his fork.

"You know, you pretty much know everything about me and I don't know anything about you." He said.

"Well what do you want to know?" I asked.

"Anything you want to share. College, opening the bakery, family. I want to know everything about you."

"I went to the University of Michigan on scholarship. I liked their business and administration program."

"So you always knew you wanted to open up Ivy's."

"Oh no! I'd never even considered it. I always thought I'd work in something like marketing or human resources but then I met Becca. We both lived in the same apartment complex our sophomore year. I don't really remember how it happened but we opened an underground cookie company. We sold on weekends out on the street. We would wait for everyone to start walking back from the bars and sell our cookies for a crazy price."

"That's impressive." Dane said.

"Impressive and illegal. We got shut down by campus police for selling without the correct licenses."

"So you quit?"

"No, we didn't quit. We just had to be sneakier." I smiled.

Dane gave a proud smile.

"We kept selling, we just had to be smarter about where and how we sold our cookies. After graduation I took my savings and used it to buy Ivy's."

"What about Becca? Didn't she join you?"

"No, she moved back home to Buffalo for a few months after graduation. She helped her mom with their family accounting firm. We tried to stay in touch, but it got harder and harder with how busy I was at Ivy's. Then one day I woke up and Becca was standing at my front door with a suitcase and an

Evergreen Ivy

envelope full of cash. She became a sort of partner and never left."

"How long ago was that?" He asked.

"We've been running with a full kitchen and full menu for about four years. The first year was barely a functional bakery. We had the basics and coffee to sell. Every profit was turned into making the downstairs of the building a functional bakery."

"You're living your dream. That's incredible." Dane said, full of sincerity.

"I guess I am." I smiled.

"Not everyone makes their dreams a reality. There are millions of people out there going to a job they hate, hoping one day they'll find the courage to do what you did."

"You're too kind, Dane. Really it's not that big of a deal. Plus owning your own business isn't all great. I haven't taken a vacation in years and the reviews people leave me online keep me up at night." I joked.

"Still, it's very brave."

I needed to change the conversation and get the spotlight off of me. Dane was saying too many nice things all at once. It was causing my head to spin.

"What's your dream?" I asked.

"I don't think I really ever had one."

"Oh come on, what was your dream before you met Apollo? Everybody has a dream, even if it's a small one." I told him.

Dane sat and thought for a few minutes. When he looked back at me I knew he'd thought of a dream but he didn't say anything. He just went back to eating.

"I know what that look means Dane. It means you know what your dream was but you don't want to tell me."

Dane bit his lip in worry, but finally caved.

"It sounds really selfish but I wanted to be rich."

"Your dream was to be rich?" I asked.

"I wanted to give back to my parents. I didn't want them to have to work anymore. That's the only reason I went to college. I saw how tired they were working day and night for the five of us to have a better life than they did. That's why when I met Apollo I didn't refuse his offer to work for him."

"That doesn't sound selfish at all, Dane."

"I guess not." Dane shrugged.

I get the feeling Dane didn't believe me.

"I'm serious Dane. That's not a dream to be embarrassed about. It comes from a place of love for your family. It's admirable."

I quickly learned that Dane didn't know how to accept compliments, but he was taking this one harder than others I'd given him. He hid his face from me, dropping his head low.

"Are your parents retired?" I asked.

"They retired a few years ago, but not because of me. Even with the money I send every month they would have worked until they died. We convinced them to retire to spend more time with the grandkids." He said.

"What about your parents?" Dane asked.

Crap, I knew this would come up. I panicked, unsure how to bring it up to him without ruining dinner.

Thankfully the waiter interrupted to ask us about dessert and the question about my parents was forgotten about. It saved me having to have the awkward 'both of my parents are dead' conversation. I'd bought myself more time.

Dinner and dessert were quick, but Dane and I stuck around at the restaurant talking about anything and everything for hours. I asked Dane if we should be worried we were taking up a table the restaurant needed to flip, but he said they wouldn't mind. If I had to guess I would guess this was one of Apollo's restaurants. Customers began to leave one after another and we knew it was time for us to leave too. As much as I enjoyed dinner with Dane I was hoping to enjoy the rest of our evening. I hadn't been able to stop thinking about our make out session in my apartment.

Dane grabbed my hand as we walked back to the car together.

"Becca wasn't serious about your curfew right? She won't hunt me down when you come home late will she?"

"There are no guarantees when it comes to Becca. We just have to hope she hasn't figured out where you live."

"Oh, so we're going to my house?" He asked.

"Did I mistake you saying you couldn't fuck me until you'd taken me out to dinner?" I asked.

Dane looked around to see if we were alone on the street.

"I might have said that." He said.

"I don't know if you've noticed, but dinner's over." I smiled.

"Yeah, it is." He said, grabbing my hips and leaning me into the car.

He ran his hand from my hips up my back, wrapping around my neck. His other hand searched lower, messing with the hem of my dress. Then he pushed me further into the car. He let go of my neck and ran his finger across my lips.

"Are you going to kiss me?" I whispered.

He shook his head no. He stepped away from me and dropped his hands to his sides.

"Dane…"

"Get in the car Kate."

"Why should I?" I asked.

"Because I don't like sharing and as much as I want to fuck you right here on the car I won't do it in front of the whole city to see. Now, get in the car."

He didn't have to ask again. I was in the car, seatbelt on before he'd made it over to his side. The entire drive to his house he kept a tight grip on my thigh. He'd squeeze every so often to remind me where I was, and where we were going.

When Dane pulled into the driveway of a house I'd only ever seen in movies I thought for sure I was dreaming. As we drove up to the house I had to pinch myself to make sure I actually was awake.

"Dane, this is insane." I said, as he held out his hand to help me out of the car.

"What's wrong with it?"

"This is your house?" I asked.

"I'll give you the tour later." He said, grabbing my hand and walking me through to his living room.

"Take your dress off." He ordered.

"Why?"

"Because ever since that night in your apartment I haven't been able to stop thinking about what it would be like to lean you against a couch and eat you out. I want to taste you, and every second you stand there not taking your dress off is killing me."

This wasn't the same Dane I met at the bakery, but it didn't matter. I very much liked this version of him.

I grabbed my dress by its hem and slid it off. I was left standing in Dane's living room half naked. His eyes raked over my body; his breathing slowed down. He looked back up at me and smiled.

"Take off your bra."

Again, without question I took off my bra. Dane seemed to enjoy how quickly I followed his orders. With any other partner I'd feel uneasy to do as I was told, but with Dane there was a level of excitement involved. I was curious to see what he'd ask for next. It made my legs clench, and my clit throb watching him. He looked pleased.

"Good, now turn around. Hands on the back of the couch."

I held onto the couch and waited for Dane to move closer. He grabbed the back of my thighs and pulled me towards him. I had to catch my feet and spread them wide to keep from falling.

He traced his fingers along my thigh and around my ass. He played with the fabric of my panties. He pulled them down and helped me step out of them. I tried to shift my weight to not feel so exposed, but he stopped me. He grabbed me back so that my ass hung out.

"Your safe word is cupcake."

He didn't waste another second before he began playing with me. He slid his fingers in and out of my folds, exploring my clit. I gasped at the coldness of his fingers, the sudden contact between us. I bit my lip trying to restrain myself. We'd barely just started and already I was unraveling.

"We're the only ones here Kate. Don't hold anything back. I want to hear you. I want to hear how I make you feel."

Dane got on his knees and pushed my back down, arching out my ass. It gave him a better angle to rub my clit while he licked the rest of me. The more he explored the more my legs began to shake. I had to put all of my weight onto the couch to keep from my knees giving out. Dane didn't hide how it made him feel watching me fall apart. Every moan I let slip gave him more energy, more need to keep eating me out.

I had almost completely lost all control of my legs and was about to come when Dane stopped. His lack of touch made me cold. Shivers ran down my spine as I waited to see what he was going to do next.

"Why did you stop?" I asked.

"I want to see your face when I make you come for the first time. Go sit on the couch."

I once again did exactly as he asked. I sat down on his couch with my ass as far up on the edge as possible. I was leaned back with my head resting back when he walked in front of me. Now it was my time to enjoy the show. Dane began taking off his shirt and tie. He tossed his tie next to me and let his shirt drop on the floor. He popped the button on his pants and let them hang low on his hips.

This was my first time seeing Dane shirtless. That alone almost sent me over the edge. I wanted to kiss and lick him from his collarbones all the way down to the ridges on his hips. I wanted to explore every tattoo on him. I looked but couldn't find a single untouched piece of skin. He was covered in dark ink, just like I'd been picturing.

"Keep staring at me like that and I might fuck you before I get the chance to finish what I've started here."

"Maybe I want you to fuck me already. Maybe I'm bored." I teased.

I was very much not bored, but I wanted to see his reaction. I wanted to frustrate him like he frustrates me for merely existing.

"Put your hands behind the pillow."

I did as he asked then watched him lower to the floor again. He grabbed my knees and spread my legs apart. Dane's long fingers slid in and out, setting a slow pace that matched the kisses he left all over my thighs and folds. When he made his way back to my clit he picked up the speed a little to match his tongue.

"Fuck Dane." I gasped.

I felt his lips form into a smile before continuing to suck me. I tried to reach down and press against his shoulders but his hand was ready to stop me. He felt me move, he knew what I wanted and he wasn't going to give it to me. His hand held down my hips, keeping me still. My mumbling let him know I was close. He continued to circle with his fingers but leaned up for a sloppy kiss. His tongue licked my lips and trailed down my jaw.

"I want to hear you scream, Kate. Stop holding back."

I got out of my head and gave everything I had left to give to Dane. He kept his pace the same but eased up his hold on my hips. It gave me enough freedom to circle and twist with his movements. I had enough space to grind against his fingers and lips. I finally let go, shouting out his name, before calming my hips.

Dane kept his fingers in me and felt me tighten around him. He kept a tight grip on my thigh as I rode out my high.

"Jesus." I sighed.

"That was so fucking hot." He said, pulling out and leaning up to kiss me again.

His hands were on either side of me. He lowered until his chest was pressed against mine. Shifting his weight to one side he brought his left hand up and pushed my hair out of my face. He wiped my lips dry, cleaning up his kisses that left a mess from before.

"That all you got?" I asked.

It was a risk considering my entire body was still tingling, but I wanted to see how far I could push Dane. He didn't give me the reaction I was expecting. He smiled and grabbed my hand.

He led me to his bedroom before leaving me there alone. He came back with his tie that he had left on the couch.

"Do you remember the first time I came into Ivy's?" He asked.

"Yes."

"You were wearing those tight jeans and that tight little blue shirt. Every time you moved or stretched over the counter I watched your apron ride up higher and higher on you. I watched how tight those strings clung to your hips."

I watched Dane walk around to the part of the room I had moved to. He reached for my hips.

"I couldn't stop picturing what it would look like tying you up tight. I wanted to watch the curves of your body struggle every time I tied you up to my bed. I dreamed of getting to grab your hips and press into your stomach while I fucked you. I wanted to feel you, touch you wherever I wanted while I was inside you. I wanted to fuck you so hard my neighbors could hear you screaming."

I walked over to Dane and took the tie from his hand. I ran it over my wrist and knuckles while he watched me.

"Is this what you want? You want to tie me up and fuck me?" I asked.

Dane nodded his head yes. I handed his tie back to him.

"Then tie me up and fuck me."

Dane didn't waste a single second. He grabbed my hips and threw me onto the bed. He kneeled next to me and grabbed my arms. He pulled them over my head and tied my wrists to the headboard. He left just enough room for me to wiggle my fingers.

Dane leaned off the bed and pulled his zipper down, dropping his pants. Watching him walk over to me almost naked answered a question I'd been wondering about since the first day I met Dane. Dane was completely covered in tattoos. His legs were covered in more ink than his chest and back. Dane walked over to his bed stand and pulled open the first drawer.

"I'm on birth control and I get tested regularly." I blurted out.

Dane looked over at me with a smile on his face.

"What are you trying to say Kate?"

"I'm saying I want you to stop wasting your time digging around in your nightstand for a condom and I want you to come fuck me. That is unless you're irresponsible and don't get tested regularly. But considering you've been dreaming of fucking me since the first time you met me I find that hard to believe. I bet your first week at the bakery you went to get tested."

"You're a cocky little thing aren't you?" He laughed.

"Am I wrong? Did you not go get tested the minute you saw me in those tight little jeans, as you described?"

Dane closed the drawer and bit his lip.

He took off his boxers and sat back on the bed. I watched Dane's dick hit his thigh as he leaned over to me. He was bigger than I was expecting but it didn't matter. I wanted him to ruin me, I wanted him to fuck me until I couldn't breathe.

He leaned between my thighs and left a few kisses in-between my folds. He played with how wet I was before reaching and coating his dick with his now wet fingers.

He sat on his knees and stroked his dick a few more times through my folds before slowly pushing in. I took a deep breath in when he first entered. He paused at my reaction. I went to reach out and grab him but remembered I couldn't. Dane watched my struggle and waited for me to give him the okay to push in deeper.

"Don't stop, keep going."

"Are you sure?" He asked.

"Yes."

"What's your safe word?"

"Cupcake."

Dane slowly thrusted his entire cock into me. I felt him tense when he filled me. It took a few deep breaths to adjust to him, but when I was ready I gave him a nod. He slid out almost completely and then quickly snapped back into me. My heart dropped, it nearly exploded. No one had ever made me feel this way. I desperately wanted to reach out and grab Dane's arms as he fucked me but I couldn't. I watched him raise my hips higher onto his lap to fuck me deeper.

"Fuck." He cursed.

Dane was going slow. He thought he was going to hurt me but I desperately needed him to go harder, faster.

"Stop holding back."

"Are you sure?" He asked.

I nodded yes and watched as Dane came undone.

"I wanted to go slow tonight, really enjoy watching you writhe beneath me but now that I'm inside you I can't slow down Kate."

"I don't want slow. I want you to fuck me as hard as you can." I told him.

Dane smiled and pressed my legs into my stomach. At the new position I panicked. I knew with my knees pressed up to my chest Dane would see my stomach curled in, no longer flat. I tried to shift my hips so that Dane couldn't see me, but he caught on to what I was doing right away.

He grabbed my waist and pulled me back onto the bed so that all of me was exposed.

"Try and hide your body like that from me again Kate and see what happens."

"I just didn't think-"

Dane grabbed my cheeks and shut me up. He pressed his fingers into my jaw hollowing out my lips. He dropped down to give me a sloppy kiss.

"I can't make you feel good when you hide from me like that Kate. A body like yours is meant to be worshiped. How could you ever think this isn't exactly what I want?"

I had no response to his question. Instead I looked in his eyes for any doubt or lies. Dane didn't wait for me to decide he was telling the truth.

He spread my legs out to the bed and leaned down onto my stomach with his left hand right above my pussy. He picked up his pace and pressed against my stomach causing a deep throb to form in the pit of my stomach. Dane smiled when he saw what he'd done to me. It was a sensation I'd never felt before. My vision was literally blurring.

"Fuck!" I screamed.

Dane let out a satisfied laugh and continued to thrust into me. He showed no mercy. Relieving the pressure from my stomach he traced his hand back down to my clit. He rubbed it with the same pace as his cock.

I watched him spit onto his hand before continuing to rub my clit.

"Dane." I cried.

"That's it baby. Let go."

I locked eyes with Dane and gave him full control. I couldn't even move if I tried. I watched Dane play with me while he thrusted. I wiggled underneath him to let him know I wasn't going to last for much longer.

He took that as his cue to keep doing exactly what he was doing. Dane's right hand held my hip firm on the bed while the other continued to circle around the throb of my clit. When I couldn't hold back any longer I let out a cry and let my orgasm take over my body.

I shook as the orgasm pulsed through my body like it never has before. Dane continued to fuck me as he watched me lose it. He sighed as I tightened around his cock. I could feel him slow down. He let go of my hips and pressed my knees back into my chest.

I rode down my high and rocked with Dane. He picked up his pace and started to get sloppy. He started to pull out further and further with every stroke.

He thrusted one more time then released his cum deep inside of me.

"Fuck Kate."

Dane fell onto me and calmed down his heart rate. I was itching to run my hands through his hair, but I was still tied up.

"Umm, Dane?"

He lifted off my chest and looked up at me.

I wiggled my fingers above me and laughed, "Help."

Dane rolled over and sat up to the front of the bed. He untied my hands and brought them to his lips. He left soft kisses along my irritated wrists.

"We need to get something better to tie you up in. I can't have you showing up to work like this."

"I don't mind it."

Dane smiled then pulled me up to his side. He gave me a slow kiss and dropped my hands to his chest.

We sat there in silence trying to soak up the moment together for a few minutes. Finally I looked up at him.

"I was right."

"Right about what?" He asked.

"We're absolutely incredible together."

After our first date Dane stopped by Ivy's as often as he could. He would stop by for a coffee in the morning or he'd come help me close at night. He spent almost every night at Ivy's. On the mornings I woke up early to open he was always there to help. Things were great between us.

It wasn't until a few weeks later I noticed something was off. He became more distant. He would show up to my place late at night and be gone in the morning. He would stop by for a coffee but leave after a quick kiss on the cheek. I pretended not to notice his change in behavior, but it was getting harder to not worry I was the problem.

Finally, a few nights ago I figured out it was definitely something happening with Apollo, or work. The only reason I figured out something was wrong was because of a phone call I overheard when he thought I was in the shower. He only spoke in English when he thought I couldn't hear him. Feeling bad for eavesdropping I left him to his phone call and went back to the bathroom until I heard him end his call.

I was afraid if I brought up the phone call he'd get upset so I pretended it never happened. He was weird when it came to talking about his work. He didn't want me anywhere near it. He refused to talk about any of it, the good or the bad.

I hated the distance that grew between us, but there was nothing I could say to fix what was going on in his personal life, so I left it alone. Until he was ready to talk I'd support him any way I could. For now that meant I was there for him at night after a long day. If I was lucky he'd stay for a few hours after I fell asleep, but he was never there when I woke up. Every morning there was no proof he had spent any time at my place.

Dane knew I'd started to notice his weird behaviors. It was getting harder for him to pretend he wasn't building up walls around me. In an attempt to make our weekend feel more normal he invited me to dinner. It wasn't anything like the dinner we shared only a few weeks ago, but it was still nice to be spending time with him.

I sat across from Dane and watched as he slowly picked at his steak.

"Dane."

"Yes?"

"I asked you if the food was good? If they didn't cook it right you should send it back." I said.

"I'm fine. I'm just not as hungry as I thought I was going to be." He explained.

"Well if you're not hungry then we should leave. No point in wasting time sitting here, pretending to enjoy our food."

Dane looked up at me, guilt in his eyes. He was trying his best, but he was failing at pretending to care at all about this dinner.

The longer I sat here the more I hated myself. Why did I think whatever this was between us was going to work?

"I'm sorry, Kate. I'm just in a weird place right now." He apologized.

"Why don't we call it a night?" I suggested.

Dane agreed and wasted no time running to find our waiter and grab our check. While I waited for him I watched the other guests in the restaurant. Just when I started to walk to the front to find Dane a man caught my eye.

I could have sworn I'd seen him at Ivy's. It was hard forgetting a man like that. He was somehow scarier than Dane. He carried himself like Dane, like his sole job was to intimidate anyone he met.

Before I could stare any longer Dane's arm wrapped around my waist.

"Are you ready to go?" He asked.

"Sure." I answered, unable to look away from the man in the booth.

Leaving the restaurant Dane held my hand as we walked back to my apartment. He looked down at his feet, once again lost in thought. Our shoulders brushed as we walked and our fingers linked together, but I had never felt farther away from him.

He only looked up to make sure he didn't accidentally run into someone or cross the street too soon. It was like the Dane I had met a month ago was gone.

A few blocks later we were standing in front of Ivy's. I knew it meant that it was time for me to let go of his hand, but in a way it felt like the last time I'd get to hold it, so I held it tighter.

Dane looked up at me and watched, waiting to see my reaction to being home. I didn't want to walk in without him, but I also knew I couldn't invite him in. He'd say yes even though he had somewhere better to be.

Right before I found the strength to let go, Dane spoke, "I'm sorry."

"What for?"

"For how I've been acting, for how I've been treating you. It makes me sick to see you look at me with this- this pity and regret in your eyes. I deserve every bit of hatred you feel towards me right now, so please know I am sorry."

"I don't want an apology Dane, I want to know why you've been acting like this, acting so cold."

"I can't tell you that Kate. We made a deal; it would put you in too much danger. Believe me it's killing me not telling you, but I just can't."

"Well I can't keep living like this. You're shutting me out Dane. How much longer are we supposed to pretend like nothing is wrong between us? I'm really trying to be patient and trust you're doing what's best, but I can't do *this* for much longer."

"I know, baby. I'm so sorry." He whispered, pulling me close to him. "It will be over soon. I promise."

I didn't get the chance to ask how much longer before Dane pulled me into a kiss. The longer he held me the more I relaxed. My fears faded, and all I could think about was Dane.

Against my better judgment I pulled away and grabbed his jacket to pull him back with me into the bakery. My brain was trying to tell me Dane needed space away from me, away from Ivy's but I just couldn't give it to him. I wanted him here with me. I wasn't ready to say goodbye.

Dane took a step forward, closing the door behind him. While he locked the door I found the light switch to the main room. Walking back to Dane I looked out the front window. There at the corner, right across from us, was the man from the restaurant.

Dane tried to pull me back towards him, but I put a hand on his chest. I walked over to the window and looked for the man again. This time when I looked he was gone. I turned around to try and tell Dane what I saw, but he'd already started closing my blinds. Once he'd finished he pulled me away from the window.

"That man was at the restaurant." I said.

"I know." Dane replied.

"Is he following us?" I asked.

"We should get upstairs, Kate. Let's go." Dane said, ignoring my question.

"I'm not going anywhere until you tell me if you knew that man was following us."

Dane sighed, running his hands through his hair.

"It's complicated Kate."

"No it's not fucking complicated Dane. Either that man was following us or not. What's so complicated about that?"

"Yes, he was following us. Now please, can we go upstairs?"

"Why was he following us Dane?" I asked.

"Kate, please."

"Why was he following us?" I asked one more time, my voice cold.

"He's not following us; his job is to follow me." He said.

"I saw that man a week ago right here in Ivy's. How long has he been following you?" I asked.

"A while."

"Why is he following you?"

"I can't tell you."

"Oh my God." I laughed. "I can't fucking believe this."

"Kate, you know I would explain if I could. Me telling you who that man is only puts you in danger. It's better if you don't know."

"That's bullshit Dane and you know it. After everything we've been through, you still can't tell me why a man has been following us for weeks?"

"He's not following you Kate, he's following me."

"How is that any better? I've spent all of my free time with you. If he's following you, that means he knows who I am. Don't stand there and lie and tell me that man doesn't know as much about me as he does you. He was in my fucking shop Dane! I've been serving that man tea for a week."

"If I thought him knowing about you was a risk I wouldn't have even come back here Kate. I promise you aren't in any danger."

"You can't be serious right now. I know you're a private person and I respect that, but not telling me about this is a new low for you. I've tried really hard to give you space Dane, but this is too much. Do you have any idea how violated I feel right now? You knew this entire time we were being followed and you didn't think that was an important piece of information to share with me."

I couldn't even look at Dane right now. I felt sick. I wanted to throw up my dinner. How could he not see how much this affected me? He'd brought this man into my life, against my own knowledge or will.

I looked back out at the window and tried to find the man again. Unable to find him, I turned to Dane.

"You need to leave."

"I can't." He said.

"You can and you will. Goodbye."

"You knew from our first date there would be things I couldn't tell you. This is one of them." Dane said.

"There's a difference between keeping your work life private when you need to and not telling me we're being followed by a stranger."

"He's not a stranger Kate. There's a reason he's following me."

"That only makes it worse!" I shouted.

Dane tried to take another step into the bakery, but I stopped him.

"If I hadn't been paying attention, or if I never confronted you about your weird behavior these past few weeks, would you have ever told me?" I asked.

Dane didn't answer.

"I didn't say anything a week ago when you shut me out. I didn't say anything when you stopped picking up my calls. I trusted you enough to know you needed space, but this? This is too much for me Dane. I don't trust you. I can't trust you."

"Kate…"

"Goodbye Dane." I said, walking around him and opening the front door for him.

I felt like such an idiot. How many times had I kicked Dane out before? How many times did I promise it would be the last time I let him in? It only hurt me to keep making excuses for him. Whatever we were had to end. I think Dane knew that too. He knew he'd lost my trust and lost me. He didn't argue on his way out. It was our last goodbye.

When my first alarm went off at four I was already awake. I grabbed my phone and left for the kitchen. If I couldn't sleep I could prep the morning pastries. While I cleaned the kitchen my argument with Dane ran around in my head. He had to know how awful I'd felt finding out he kept such an important piece of information from me. It was getting harder and harder to give him the benefit of the doubt.

A few hours passed and it was time to open. It was rare to get any customers before the rush of people trying to get to work. Only rarely did anyone get here at exactly six. While keeping busy and cleaning the counters I heard the front door open. In walked a woman I'd never seen before. I knew she wasn't a regular, but she seemed familiar with the layout of the bakery.

It was clear she wasn't here for a coffee or a breakfast scone. No, she was here to see me. She looked at me in awe, in pure disbelief.

"Oh my God, Alex owes me fifty bucks." She laughed.

"I'm sorry, do I know you?"

"No, probably not. Dane and I aren't super close, but I know him well enough to know he wouldn't tell anyone about me."

"I think you might have me confused for someone else." I lied.

"This must be so confusing for you, I'm so sorry. I wanted to give you a heads up I was coming over, but I wasn't even sure you'd be here today. I knew Dane had been spending a lot of time here, but I wasn't sure why. Now that I'm here it's pretty obvious. You must be the reason he's been so distracted."

"I don't know a Dane. Maybe you're looking for one of my employees. Would you like to leave a message?" I asked.

Until I knew who she was I couldn't risk her knowing I knew about Dane. Only a few hours ago I found out he was being followed. I couldn't trust anybody that came into my store looking for him. Dane and I didn't work out, but I couldn't put him in more danger.

"You're smart. I can see why he likes you."

I continued to clean the counters. I thought if I ignored this stranger she would just leave but it didn't work. When I looked up again she was still here.

"Where are my manners? You must be so confused. I'm Eliana Mariano-"

"Eliana?" I asked, lifting my glare up to her.

Eliana dropped her hand that she had held out for me to shake. Now she looked just as shocked and confused as I probably looked.

"So he did tell you about me. I'm flattered."

"He doesn't know I know about you, technically." I admitted.

Eliana tilted her head, waiting for me to explain.

"I found your letter on the gift basket. He told me you were a friend."

"That little shit. He told me it never got delivered."

I laughed, that sounds like something Dane would do.

"Well, he's a liar. I still have the note. I wasn't sure if he'd ever want it, but I couldn't throw it away." I smiled.

"I can't believe I'm finally meeting you." Eliana smiled, "I've known for a while Dane must have had a good reason to spend all his time here, but now that I'm seeing you I'm shocked. I knew if I needed answers I would have to come here myself. I can't even get Dane to tell me his favorite ice cream flavor. There isn't a chance in hell he'd ever tell me about the beautiful girl he met at a bakery."

I laughed at Eliana's confession. I'm not even sure I know his favorite ice cream flavor.

"It's nice to meet you." I said, reaching out my hand for her to shake, "I'm Kate, and it if makes you feel any better I don't know much about Dane either. He's quite the mystery."

"You may think you don't know a lot about Dane, but I'm going to guess you know more than most people. He's become slightly less miserable since he started making regular visits to come see you." She said.

My smile dropped, it hurt to hear that. All the nights Dane spent here came flooding back.

Eliana could see the pain I was in. If we weren't total strangers I'm sure she'd be looking to comfort me. I knew she didn't come here because she was concerned about me, she came here because she needed something from me.

"It was really nice meeting you, but I have some work to finish before the breakfast rush. You're more than welcome to have a seat and stay awhile if you want." I said, starting to walk away.

"Wait, please." Eliana almost shouted.

"What?" I asked.

That came out a bit more aggressive than I intended, but I'd had a long night. I didn't have the energy to appease Eliana today.

"I know something happened between you and Dane last night. He's a mess, I'm really worried about him."

I rolled my eyes and walked away from her. Dane wasn't the only one hurting.

"Whatever he did to you I need you to forgive him, please. We're strangers, you owe me nothing, but please believe me when I tell you that Dane needs you more than ever now. It would be a mistake to leave him."

"You're right, we're strangers. You don't know anything about me."

"I know exactly how you feel right now. I know that even though you're mad at him the only person you want here with you right now is Dane. I know you'd do anything to erase the fight you had with him last night. I know you're lying even though you say you're moving on." She said.

"Dane and I are too different. Last night was proof I will never fit in Dane's life. There are too many secrets between us. Nothing is more important to me than honesty and it's the one thing Dane can't give me." I explained.

"You're wrong about him." She said. "Let me guess, a few weeks ago he shut you out. He's been distant, cold. When you spend time with him it's like he's not really there. You thought maybe if you gave him space he'd open up to you, but instead he pushed you away even more."

The hairs on my arms raised, my stomach flipped.

"Last night, something happened, didn't it?" She asked. "You finally snapped. Demanded the truth, but he couldn't give it to you."

"Stop, please."

"How much do you know about Dane and what he does?" She asked.

"Not a lot."

"Do you know about Apollo, my fiancé?"

"Yes." I answered.

"So you know Dane is the fixer, the one the Costa family calls when they fuck up?"

"Yes."

"Well they fucked up. Two weeks ago Apollo left me. He ran away to hunt down his own cousin. The only person in the entire world that knows where he is right now is Dane. For weeks I've been watched and questioned by men far scarier than Apollo and Dane. They think I know something. They're convinced I know where Apollo is, and they'll stop at nothing to get any information out of me. The past two weeks have been hell for me, so I can't even begin to imagine what they've been like for Dane."

Eliana paused, trying to calm herself down.

"There are men that want to ruin me and my family. They want to burn the Costa family to the ground and the only reason they haven't succeeded yet is because of Dane. The only reason he didn't tell you about Apollo is because he's trying to protect you. That's what he does, he protects the ones he cares about. He is single handedly running Apollo's company by himself. On top of keeping Apollo alive and safe he's been taking care of me. I'm not a selfish person, and I rarely ask for favors, but I'm asking for one now. You are the only thing keeping Dane sane right now. If he loses you then I lose everything. I lose Apollo, I lose my firm, I lose my family, I lose all of it. So please, I know you're hurting but don't leave him."

"It's too late, I'm sorry." I whispered.

"I know it hurts. I know what it feels like to be second. To always wonder what other secrets he's keeping from you, but I promise it gets easier. One day it just clicks. One day all the pain won't hurt as much, and you'll be glad you stayed. Dane's world is chaos right now. He's drowning, and even if you can't see it you're the only thing keeping him afloat. He chose you to run to when he needed a break. How many nights have you woken up and found him lying next to you?"

"He's here every night."

"Tonight when you're lying in bed without him I want you to imagine a tired Dane wandering around because he can't sleep without you. Because that's what he did last night. For hours, he walked the halls of my empty house and distracted himself with work to try and forget about you."

"Stop." I begged.

"He was still walking around when I woke up today to come and find you. He lied and told me he'd gotten a few hours of sleep, but I know he only said that to make me feel better."

Eliana was interrupted by the bell ringing at the door. In walked the first commuter coming in for coffee.

Eliana walked over to the front door, "If you change your mind Dane can never know I was here. He's finally beginning to trust me. I want him to tell me about you when he's ready."

I nodded my head in agreement.

"I can't convince you to give him another chance, but I can promise you'll never forgive yourself if something happens to him before you get the chance to hold him one more time. Trust me. You'll be stuck replaying the last time you ever saw him over and over in your mind for the rest of your life."

I wanted to say something, but there was nothing I could say to make her situation any easier, so instead I watched her leave. She held the door open for one of my regulars before giving me one more smile and walking away.

I worried about Dane all morning. I thought back to last night and how hard it was for him to walk away. I thought I was the reason he'd grown distant. I hadn't considered I was his relief from reality for a few hours. Eliana was right. Dane was a protector; he would always put others first. Last night he could have told me everything. He could have told me about Apollo, and whoever had ordered men to follow him, but instead he stayed loyal to his oldest friend. I accused him of growing tired of me when the truth was that his world was falling apart.

The only thing that kept me from having a mental breakdown was the bakery. I kept busy until we closed. It wasn't until the door was locked and I was back in my apartment that I snapped. I found myself on the floor of my kitchen as the tears I had been holding back all day began to fall.

I pictured Dane running around, getting ready for another night of no sleep. Soon his body would shut down, soon he'd make a mistake, and it would be fatal.

Trying to take deep breaths I searched for my phone. I searched through my recent calls and found Dane's name. My phone was ringing before I had even processed what I was doing.

He didn't answer until I was almost sent to voicemail.

"Kate?"

"Please come back." I whispered.

"What?"

"Come back." I cried.

Before I could ask again the call dropped.

I sat in my kitchen and listened to the buzz of the dead phone line. Maybe it was too late. I'd pushed him away too many times. He was busy dealing with Apollo's family, he didn't need to worry about me too.

I gave myself a few minutes to sit and wallow in self-pity before picking myself up off the floor. I grabbed my phone and walked back to the living room to clean up a little. I grabbed my jacket that had been laying on the back of my couch for a week and went to put it up. While grabbing a hanger for it I heard a crash downstairs. Soon after I heard footsteps running up my stairs. There was a chance someone was breaking into my apartment to hurt me and all I had to defend myself with was a coat hanger.

Before I could process what was happening my apartment door swung open. Dane ran in, nearly crashing into my coffee table. He caught his balance and began looking around for me. He found me hiding in my coat closet, ready to use the hanger.

"Kate." He sighed.

"You came back."

Dane closed the space between us and crushed me against his chest. He wrapped his arms around me so tight I thought I was going to pop.

He took one more deep breath, and then leaned into me, "We really need to get your front door fixed."

"It worked perfectly fine before you started breaking and entering because you're too impatient to ring the doorbell." I said.

"Missed you too, Kate."

"Will you stay here tonight?" I asked.

"Of course."

Dane took my hand and led me to the bathroom. He helped me take off my clothes and started the shower for me. I stepped in and watched Dane leave. A few minutes later he came back with a warm towel. He sat against the sink and looked over at me in the shower.

"Why did you call me?" He asked.

"Because I missed you."

"No, that's not the only reason. That wouldn't have been enough to get you to call me."

"I was worried about you."

"You were worried about me?" He scoffed.

"I've known for weeks now that something's wrong Dane. When I asked you to leave I did it because I was angry. I was so mad Dane."

"I know." He said.

"And then I imagined what would happen if you left here angry. I had this feeling like something bad was going to happen, so I called you."

Dane stood up, "So what happens now Kate? Am I only here until that bad feeling you have goes away? Will you send me away every time you get angry? Because I can't live like that Kate."

"I'm done asking you to leave Dane." I told him.

"You really mean that?"

"Yes."

Dane waited for my answer then took off his suit. He threw his jacket and shirt over by the door and kicked off his pants. In only his boxers he opened the shower door and stepped in.

"Come here." He whispered.

I closed the distance between us and rested my head on Dane's chest. We held each other in the shower until the water ran cold. Eventually Dane turned off the water and pulled me out with him. He dried off my body and wrapped my hair up. He took my towel and dried himself off enough to walk back to bed with me.

He sat me down in bed then left to my closet. He tossed me an old shirt and then grabbed a pair of shorts of his that he'd left here a few weeks ago.

Dane was quiet tonight, even more than his usual self. Maybe it was because of how tired he was. If Eliana was right then this would be his first night of sleep in days.

It made me sick thinking about him staying up late, pushing through the exhaustion with more work.

"Please don't leave me tonight." I told him.

"I won't." He said pulling the covers over the both of us and turning on his side to wrap me in his arms.

As I fell asleep I prayed that when I woke up Dane would still be here, holding me like this.

CHAPTER FIVE

Dane

The next month was a blur. After weeks of covering for Apollo he was back, and he didn't need me anymore. Things went back to normal, and everybody pretended like nothing happened. No one mentioned his traitor cousin or the fact that Apollo was missing for two months.

Kate and I were slowly building trust. She never forced me to talk about work, but I knew eventually it was something I would have to open up to her about. I didn't know how to explain to her I wasn't keeping her in the dark on purpose. The only way to keep her safe was to not involve her. I'd never forgive myself if something happened to her because of me or the Costas.

After everything we'd been through Kate and I needed a chance to start over, to take a break. She'd been working overtime at Ivy's and I had been working with Apollo to catch up on everything he'd missed.

Apollo gave me the night off, so I grabbed a few things from my house and started driving to Kate's. When I got to the bakery I found her front door locked. Trying to prove a point I rang the old door bell. It sang out a few notes and then fizzled into a sad screech.

Kate came down the stairs laughing harder than I'd seen in a while. It was nice seeing her happy after all the stress I had caused her. She caught her breath and waved at me to come in.

"Can we please fix that?"

"You can't fix something that isn't broke." She said.

"You should see the new systems they have. They use passcodes that actually work and you can even pick a song to play as your doorbell."

"Shut up, no way!" She teased.

"I have a guy that could set it up tomorrow, please let me call him."

"While I love the idea of me getting to answer the door to a song you hate every time someone rings it I think I have to pass. I can't accept something like that from you. I'm saving up for a new system I promise."

I rolled my eyes and took Kate's hand. I walked back upstairs with her and found her living room set up for a movie night. She had all of her blankets pulled out and a few bowls of snacks on the table.

"What's this?" I asked.

"I didn't know if I'd see you tonight so I was planning on having a movie night and then going to bed early." She said.

"What movie are we watching?"

"I haven't picked one yet. I was interrupted."

I sat down on the couch and pulled a few pillows behind me. I made sure there was enough room for Kate next to me before I lifted the blankets and invited her to sit with me.

She quickly sat down and leaned in closer to me. I paid no attention to what movie she picked to watch. Instead I paid attention to how she crossed her legs over mine, how she felt safe enough with me to rest her arms on my chest. Every time she touched me a hot flame spread through me.

It took my full concentration to remember to breathe. I looked down and watched as she gave her whole attention to the tv. I'd never met someone so comfortable being around me. My height intimidated everyone I met, not to mention how much space I took up in a room. My size was enough to scare anyone away, but Kate never seemed to be bothered by me. From day one she wasn't ever afraid to share her personal space with me. Even now while we watched a movie together she used me as her own personal pillow.

Before her I tried to take up as little space as possible everywhere I went. But Kate didn't mind how much space I took up, in fact I think she enjoyed it. I was her own personal buffer to the outside world, and nights like this reminded me how much I liked her close to me.

I didn't pay much attention to the movie. I was too busy watching Kate. Half way through she fell asleep. When I woke her up she denied falling asleep. She said she was resting her eyes for a minute during the boring part of the movie.

When it ended neither of us moved. We watched the screen turn black after the credits ended. I'm not sure where what I said next came from. It just sort of came out.

"We should go on a trip."

Kate sat up on her elbow to look at me.

"A trip?" She asked.

"Yeah, just the two of us. I could take a few days off and I'm sure you could fix the schedule to cover you while we're gone. Nothing crazy, let's just get out of the city for a few days." I explained.

"I don't know. The shop is in its busy season right now. And you know I'm short staffed." She said.

"The two of us need a break from work. If you're worried about taking too much time off we could drive somewhere for the weekend. Or we could fly out Friday and be back by Monday. You'd hardly miss anything." I tried to convince.

"Let me think about it." She said. "My brain is too fried to make plans like that right now. I have to be up in a few hours. I'll look at the schedule tomorrow, promise."

"Deal." I whispered, kissing her temple.

I was driving to Apollo's when Kate called.

"I can make it work!" She shouted as soon as I answered.

"Explain."

"Next weekend, I'm all yours. Becca's grandma is taking the bus to the casinos so she agreed to cover. I told her to only put out the basic pastries and go easy on the coffee bar, and she should be good without me until at least Tuesday."

"Where should we go?" I asked.

"I'll go anywhere. Car, train, plane, I'll take anything. I haven't taken off in forever. Hell, we could go a mile down the block and hide out in a hotel and I'd be happy."

"Don't tempt me. If I got you alone in a hotel room for three days we'd never leave."

Kate laughed through the phone, "Then maybe not the hotel idea. Looks like you'll have to find a different place for us to go."

"I'll come over after work and we can look at flights. Sound good?" I asked.

"I'll keep a pot of coffee warm for you." She laughed.

"If your coffee pot breaks between now and when I see you I had nothing to do with it."

I hung up to Kate laughing her ass off. She thinks I'm kidding but I bet I could call and pay whoever's working to accidentally knock it off the counter.

As soon as I walked into Apollo's office I wished I was at the bakery. Every time I walked in there they were happy to see me. Right now Apollo did not look happy to see me.

"Junior said you needed to talk to me. Said you couldn't talk over the phone. What's going on?" I asked.

"We need to talk about Gio." He said.

I sat down across from Apollo and waited for him to continue.

"When Leonardo told me I had permission to take care of him I didn't think he'd be so hard to find. I thought after Leonardo killed his dad he wouldn't have enough resources to keep hidden for this long."

"He has to come out of hiding eventually, Apollo. You'll be able to find him." I assured.

"I don't think I will. I can't do it again Dane. I almost lost Eliana the first time I went after him. I don't know what to do. I want Gio dead for what he did to me, but I can't leave her."

"So you're giving up? You're going to let him walk away." I asked.

"I can't do that either. I want to hurt him as much as he's hurt Eliana and me."

I watched Apollo fall back into his chair. I'd never seen Apollo look so defeated. Before Eliana, Apollo wanted revenge more than anything in the world. I knew this had to be killing him. I also knew Eliana would never forgive him if he left again.

Staring at Apollo I finally figured out why he called me in here. I sighed, clasping my hands together and dropping them into my lap.

"You can't leave to go find Gio, but I can." I said.

"I talked to Junior. He says you've done a good job training him. I asked him to be in charge of shipments until you get back."

"When do I leave?"

"The planes waiting. There was a sighting of him in Italy. I want you there on the ground looking for him. I have a few men sending you everything we have on him. Eliana made me promise no matter what happens you'll be back for the wedding."

"Well, thank goodness for that. I was worried I'd miss it." I said, standing up and leaving the room.

Apollo tried to call after me, but I ignored him. I didn't have time to hear his excuses for sending me. As much as I hated leaving I had to go find Gio for him. There wasn't another option.

I walked back to the guest room I used when I stayed at Apollo's house and tried to call Kate. I'd been sent to voicemail twice. There was no time for me to make it into the city to say goodbye to her before I left for the plane. If I didn't get a hold of her I'd be leaving her a voicemail like an asshole. She finally agreed to take some time off and go on a trip with me and now I was leaving her.

I continued to call her while I packed. I heard a quiet knock on my door and then saw Eliana let herself in.

"Can't talk right now El, I'm a little busy."

"I know, but I wanted to come and say sorry. I asked Apollo not to send you, but you're the only one he trusts to find Gio."

I listened to my phone ring and ring while Eliana talked. Why the fuck wasn't Kate picking up her phone?

I ignored Eliana's thanks and apologies as I dialed Kate one more time. While grabbing a few things from the bathroom I heard Eliana following me around. The phone went to voicemail one more time and I lost it.

"Damn it!" I threw my phone onto the bed and sat down.

"What's wrong?" Eliana asked, standing in front of me.

"I'm trying to get ahold of someone, but it's sending me to voicemail. And now I'm leaving and she won't know why. She's going to be sitting there alone, wondering why I didn't show up. Fuck, I just got her back. I promised her things would be different, I promised her a vacation and now I'm leaving her. She's going to hate me. Once I get on that plane she'll have no way to reach me. She'll be calling and calling and she won't know if I'm alive or dead. And then in a few days she'll give up on hearing from me. I just got her back; I can't lose her again."

"Dane!" I looked up, snapping out of my rambling.

"I'll go to the bakery; I'll tell Kate what happened. Just breathe, you're freaking out." Eliana said.

"How do you-"

"It wasn't hard to figure out. When Apollo was missing I wasn't sleeping much. I could hear you leaving late at night and trying to sneak back into the house without waking anyone up. Also, there's no person alive that needs as much coffee as you've been drinking."

"You knew? This whole time?" I asked.

"Maybe." She smiled.

My cheeks flushed red. Of course she knew.

"Look, nobody but me knows. Not even Apollo, I mean I'm sure he knows, but we are both pretending we don't know what's got you so distracted. I promise not to say a word about her to anyone. I'll go check in on her and keep an eye on her while you're gone. You need to focus on finding Gio and making it back for the wedding. I don't want to get married to Apollo if you're not there to celebrate with us. You're family Dane, you were there for me when Apollo left, let me be here for you now."

Before I could thank Eliana, Apollo shouted from down the hall, "Let's go! Plane's ready."

"Go, I'll keep her safe until you get back." She smiled.

I squeezed her arm as I ran past her and out of the room. I made it to the stairs before I turned back around.

"Eliana!" I shouted.

She came out to meet me in the hallway.

"I need your help with something." I said.

Kate

Eight missed calls.

I left my phone in my office all day and didn't have a minute to check it. I tried calling Dane back, but he wasn't picking up. I tried a few more times before finally admitting to myself that his phone was turned off. He wasn't going to see my calls, no matter how many times I called.

While opening up our messages and starting to type out a text for him to see when his phone was turned back on, I heard Amanda come into the office.

"I'm going to head out, unless there's anything else you need help with?" She asked, putting on her coat and flipping her hair out from under the collar.

"No, I'm good. Go home before it gets dark. You still good to come in and help Tuesday?" I asked.

"Yeah, Becca said she'd pick me up on her way over."

"Thanks." I smiled.

"I left a few crates out in the kitchen to be picked up for milk, and I already counted the register. Oh, and that friend of yours is still here. I asked her if she needed anything else before I clocked out, but she said she was good. I told her you'd be back out on the floor in a few minutes."

"What friend?" I asked. I wasn't expecting anyone.

"Not sure who she is. I haven't seen her around before, but she definitely knows who you are. Seemed anxious to talk to you. Want me to ask her to leave?"

"No, I'll go talk to her."

I followed Amanda out to the front. I looked around at all the tables and found a familiar face sitting alone in the back. She sat there picking at a donut.

Amanda was right, she looked stressed.

I sat down across from her and looked around to make sure no one was close enough to hear our conversation. When I was sure we had some privacy I asked her about Dane.

"Where did he go?" I asked.

"How do you know he's gone?" She asked.

"Because if Dane was still in New York he'd be here right now. He wouldn't be sending someone to pass along a message for him."

"He's in Italy... probably." She said.

"For how long?"

Eliana shook her head, "I don't know."

The first time I met Eliana she was confident and direct. I found myself looking away because her constant eye contact was intimidating. Right now she was timid, afraid to look up at me.

"There's something you're not telling me." I said.

"It's my fault he went."

"How?" I asked.

"Dane went because Apollo can't. I almost left the first time Apollo chased after Gio. If Apollo left again it would be the end for us."

"I just don't understand."

"What don't you get?" She asked.

"Any of it. I don't get how you live like this. I don't get how you're fine living with the unknown. Aren't you tired? Look how easy it was for Dane to leave today. I don't know how much longer I'll be able to handle all this."

"It's not usually like this Kate. You met Dane at a dark time in our family's life. This isn't about work. This is about revenge. Dane went to find the man who almost killed Apollo and got close to killing the rest of us."

"Doesn't it scare you? This world you live in, if I lived in it I'd forever be looking over my shoulder for the next attack. I'd never get any sleep. It sounds exhausting."

"I hate to break it to you, but you're already in this world." She said.

"How?"

"I wouldn't be sitting here if you weren't important to Dane. Do you think Apollo would be pretending not to know about you if he thought you and Dane were just a fling? He'd have ended the relationship before it ever began. Dane doesn't plan on letting you go anytime soon Kate."

"I'm not- we haven't even talked about that yet, so-"

Eliana smiled, "Oh poor thing, you have no idea. Hell would freeze over before Dane ever let you go. You might not see it yet, but you're stuck in this world just as much as I am."

It felt like yesterday that Dane walked in here for the first time. Were we really already at that stage in the relationship? Eliana could see my doubt, it was all over my face.

"Let me ask you something. When you saw me sitting here and you knew something was wrong, what were you thinking about?"

"I was thinking something happened to Dane. That he was gone and I didn't get a chance to say goodbye."

"And how did that make you feel?"

"Like I was going to throw up and pass out all at the same time." I admitted.

Eliana smiled, "And how do you feel when you're with Dane?"

"Safe."

"Welcome to the family Kate." She laughed.

"So now what? Is there an initiation? Do I have to pass a bunch of tests and swim with sharks before we make things official?" I asked.

"No, there's something much worse. I'm getting married in a few weeks, and I would love it if you could be there. Consider that your soft launch into the family. You can meet Apollo, get to know the men who work with Dane. And if at the end of the night you've survived meeting my family and all of Apollo's relatives and you still want to be with Dane then I promise nothing could split the two of you apart."

"Two weeks, isn't that a little last minute to be adding an extra guest? I mean, we're practically strangers." I asked.

"God no, my mom will have no idea if I add another person to a table. Plus the majority of the people coming to my wedding secretly hate me, so it will be nice having one genuine friend there to support me. And I know Dane would be very excited to see you."

At the mention of Dane's name I sat up a little straighter.

"Dane will be there?"

"Dane is Apollo's best man; I'm not getting married without him. Work can wait until after the celebration. I'll send over an invitation. I don't need an answer right now, just think about it please. It might help you to meet the other important people in Dane's life. He'll deny it until he dies, but I know he really does care about all of us."

"I can't promise I'll be there, but I'll think about it."

Even though Eliana's life was full of chaos she was still trying to make me feel more comfortable about my worries about Dane. It meant a lot to me for her to show up and try to ease my anxiety.

"Oh, I almost forgot!" She said, pulling out her purse. "Dane asked me to give this to you."

Eliana handed me a small silver flip phone, "He wanted me to tell you to call or text him using this until he gets back. He left his phone at our house, so that no one could track it. He asked me to tell you to please call him any time you were missing him."

I smiled, taking the phone from Eliana. I clicked through to the contacts. There was only one number saved. I ran my fingers over the small keypad. How soon was too soon to call him? I already missed him.

"I have to get back to work, but I really do hope to see you soon Kate. Please consider coming to the wedding."

"Thank you, Eliana. You didn't have to come here, but you did. It means a lot." I said.

"Of course." Eliana wrapped her leftover donut into her napkin and grabbed her purse.

I continued to sit at her table even after she'd left. I spun the phone around in my hand a few times. A crash of dishes pulled me back to the real world. I wanted to call Dane, but I had work to do. I put the phone in my apron and ran back to the kitchen.

It was almost eleven before I made it back up to my apartment. After cleaning up a little I found the flip phone in my pocket. I thought about calling Dane all day. I wanted to hear his voice more than anything, but I was afraid that Eliana was right. That I was in this world now whether I liked it or not. If I called Dane I was in his life to stay.

Letting go of my doubts I hit the call button.

The phone hadn't even rung twice before he answered.

"Kate."

God, I missed hearing his voice. All of the doubts in my mind settled, all that mattered was that he was alive and safe.

"Hey." I replied, like this was just a normal phone call.

"You have no idea how good it feels to hear your voice right now." He said.

"Eliana told me what happened, why you left." I said.

"Are you upset?" Dane asked.

"No, I'm not upset."

"Promise?"

"I promise."

"I didn't want to go." He said, hurt in his voice.

"I know."

I listened to the sound of his breaths. Each one longer than the last.

"I miss you." I finally spoke.

Dane cleared his throat. Even now he still wasn't a man of many words. I wish I could see his face right now. I'm sure his forehead was all scrunched up trying to say he missed me too.

"Are you getting ready to go to bed?" He asked.

"No, I'm not tired yet. Why?"

"I thought maybe you'd stay on the line and tell me about your day. Unless you have something else to do?" He asked.

"No, I'm not doing anything!" I answered a little too quickly. "You really want to know how it went at the bakery today?"

"Listening to you tell me about Ivy's is my favorite part of the day." He said.

"Well then you're in luck because today kept me busy." I smiled.

"Really?"

"Mhmm, Jacob broke half of our bowls, the good bowls I just bought. That old couple I was worried about finally came back, they said they hadn't been walking as much because of the snow. I packed them up a few extra pastries to freeze in case they didn't come back for a while. Becca didn't work today, but she came in to tell me she met the love of her life at the grocery store. Said they both like the same type of oranges..."

As I told Dane about my day I listened to his quiet laughs and sighs. I didn't know how to ask him about Gio or how long he'd be gone, but tonight that didn't matter. Even for just a few minutes we both gave each other a break from our reality and that was enough.

"Kate you have ten seconds to get your ass over here before I drag you in!" Becca shouted at me.

It was Friday night and Becca and I were out with a few of our old college friends. I was hiding from a drunk Becca, but she found me. Unlike Becca I couldn't drink as much as I used to in college. It took a serious amount of pregame tums and Tylenol to prevent a hangover the next morning. I had successfully hidden from Becca during shots, but now I was being called to the dance floor. She grabbed my hand and pulled me along with her to the center of the dance floor.

I let loose and danced with Becca for a few songs. I forgot about the bakery, Dane searching for Gio and my invitation to Eliana's wedding. All the unknowns were forgotten about tonight. Right now all that mattered was that I was taking a much needed night off.

In desperate need of water I left Becca and went back to the table. Rena was waiting for me with a tray of shots.

"I know you didn't drink the last round of shots you sneaky bitch." She said.

"I don't know what you're talking about." I lied.

"Drink." She ordered.

"Fuck it." I sighed, tossing back a few tequilas.

Proud of herself Rena took me back to the dance floor. I danced until I couldn't feel my feet. If I didn't go outside soon I would overheat. I waved to Rena I was taking a break and went out to the front of the bar. While cooling down I searched for the flip phone in my purse.

I took a deep breath of the winter air and waited for Dane to pick up.

"Kate, it's past midnight there. Why are you still up?" He asked.

"Because I miss you." I answered.

"You should be sleeping."

"Well, I'm definitely not sleeping." I laughed.

"Where are you? Why does it sound like you're outside?"

"Because I am. Becca took me out for drinks."

"Kate, please tell me you're not outside alone right now. Please tell me your friends are right next to you waiting for a cab or something."

I didn't answer.

"Kate."

Shit. That was Dane's angry Kate.

"The reception is really spotty; I think I'll have to call you back." I said.

"Hang up and see what happens Kate." He warned.

"What would you do if I did hang up? You're in Italy. Would you fly back to spank me?" I asked.

Jesus, what the fuck was in that tequila?

"Have you been drinking?" He asked.

"No."

"You're a terrible liar Kate. Tell me how much you've had to drink."

"I wasn't counting."

"You're fucking killing me here. I need you to go back inside."

"It was too hot on the dance floor. I can't go back inside until I've cooled down."

I heard Dane curse under his breath.

"Are you even wearing a jacket?" He asked.

I didn't answer him.

"It's below freezing outside."

"I'm not cold."

"Inside, Kate. Now."

"If I go back inside I'll have to hang up the phone." I said.

Dane sighed, "It scares the shit out of me knowing you're outside alone right now. Please go back inside baby. I'll call you the minute you're home."

"Promise?" I asked.

"Promise."

"If you don't call me I might just fly to Italy and kick your ass." I threatened.

"I believe that, now go."

I hung up the phone and walked back inside. Becca was back at the table looking over the crowd of strangers. When she saw me she raised another glass and gave a cheer. I smiled and walked back to the table.

I took out my phone and sent Dane a photo of the two of us at the table.

** Back at the table, miss you **

A few minutes later I got a text from Dane.

** When I get back I'm fucking you in that dress **

I had to hide how red my cheeks probably were. I thought I was being subtle, but Becca saw how flustered I was. She gave me a knowing smile.

"What?" I asked her.

"Nothing, but you look quite smitten with whoever you're texting right now. I wonder what dirty things Dane is texting you to have you blushing like that." She laughed.

I hit her shoulder causing her to nearly fall over into the next seat. Rena looked over at the two of us and saw a very drunk Becca. She pointed over to the bar and gave me a thumbs up. I watched her pay our tab and then round up the rest of the girls. It was my job to get Becca out to the taxi. I linked arms with her and pushed through the busy crowd towards the entrance.

I was helping Rena and Becca into our cab when my phone buzzed. I pulled out my phone and saw a text from Dane.

** Look to your left. Black Mercedes.**

I looked around and saw the man that came to pick up Dane from the bakery a few weeks ago. He was waving at me. I shouldn't be surprised Dane arranged a ride home for me.

I kissed Rena and Becca goodbye, made sure their driver knew where to drop them off and then walked over to the car.

"Kate?" He asked.

"Did Dane send you?"

"I'm here to make sure you get home safe."

"Of course you are." I laughed, opening up the car door.

Dane's driver waited until my door was closed before he walked over and got in himself.

"So, you work with Dane."

"I work for Dane." He clarified.

"What's your name?" I asked.

"Junior, Ma'am."

I laughed quietly to myself. Junior couldn't be older than twenty, but he was trying his hardest to act tough. I only see Dane outside of work. I hadn't considered how he acted when he was working. From the way Junior acted around me I'm guessing Dane was a terrifying boss.

"Is Junior your real name or a nickname?"

"It's complicated." He answered.

"How so?"

"I was named after my father, Alessio. After he died everyone started calling me Junior."

"Oh Junior, I'm sorry I didn't know."

"It's easier for everyone to call me Junior so they don't have to be reminded of my father."

"Well which do you prefer? Junior or Alessio?" I asked.

"Junior's fine." He sighed

"It doesn't sound fine. If you don't like Junior then why don't you go by Alessio?" I asked.

"I haven't earned it."

"Earned it?"

"I haven't done anything to earn being called Alessio. My father sacrificed his own life to save my family. It would be weird to ask others to call me Alessio." He said.

"Well, maybe one day you'll earn it. Maybe you'll do something incredibly heroic, something that would make your father proud."

Junior let out a short laugh, "Yeah maybe." He smiled.

I did my best to make small talk for the rest of the drive but with how much I'd had to drink that night it wasn't easy. After an awkward drive back to Ivy's Junior got me home safely and helped me get into the shop. He made sure I locked my front door and then drove off.

I began to kick off my heels and unzip my dress when my phone rang.

"Hello?"

"Did you make it home?"

"Don't pretend like Junior didn't call you the second I walked up my stairs. What are you doing to that poor boy at work? He was terrified to be driving me home. Have you heard of workplace morale?" I asked.

"Drunk Kate is mean." He said.

"Drunk Kate is honest." I replied.

Dane sighed. I couldn't see him, but I'm sure he rolled his eyes.

"What are you thinking about?" I asked.

"I'm thinking about how much stress you caused me tonight. I nearly flew home just to make sure you were safe."

"I wish you would fly home." I told him.

"And why is that?"

"Because you're really hot when you're angry."

"Kate..." He warned.

"I'm serious. The other night I came so hard thinking about what you'd do to me if I pissed you off."

Dane's breathing slowed down.

"How many times have you touched yourself since I've been gone Kate?"

I didn't answer him. I knew the answer would only upset him.

"Kate?" He asked.

"Yes?"

"You wish you were playing with yourself right now, don't you?"

Again, I didn't answer him. He knew my answer.

"Go take that dress off and lay down on the bed, baby."

I set my phone down on my pillow and unzipped my dress. I grabbed the phone again and crawled under the covers.

"You lying down?" He asked.

"Yes."

"Good, now run your hands over your stomach, just like how I would." He ordered.

I put Dane on speaker and did as he asked. One hand gripped the covers, the other ran down my stomach.

"Don't touch yourself until I tell you to." He said.

I continued to circle my fingers over my chest and stomach.

"Run your finger over your pussy and tell me how wet you are Kate."

I ran a finger through my folds and dipped into me just a little. I let out a short breath.

"Fuck I love hearing you moan baby." He whispered into the phone.

"What do you think about when you touch yourself like this?" He asked.

"I can't tell you."

"You know the rule Kate. I can't make you feel good if you aren't honest with me."

"I picture you working." I confessed.

"I don't understand."

"I imagine you come home from work and fuck me with the bruised knuckles you used to hurt someone with. I imagine I get to calm you down after a stressful day of work."

"And how do you do that?" He groaned.

"I suck your cock and then I ride you."

"You like my cock don't you?"

Listening to Dane's low voice was driving me crazy. I circled my clit and pretended it was him playing with me. My thighs were tight, I was starting to ache.

"Answer me Kate."

"I like your cock."

"I hear you shuffling around in the covers, tell me what you're doing."

"I'm playing with myself."

"Fuck I wish I was there. I want to taste you."

I let out a whimper.

"You want that too? You want my tongue on your pussy, eating you out?"

"Yes."

"Keep touching yourself. I want to hear you come."

I closed my eyes and pretended it was Dane here with me.

"What do you want Kate?" He asked.

"I want to hear your voice. Keep talking." I told him.

"I was serious about taking you out to dinner in that dress then fucking you in it. When I saw you in that picture I wanted to rip that dress off of you. Why haven't you worn that dress for me before? Why is tonight my first time seeing you in it?"

I slid a finger inside me, "It's an old college dress. I only wear it out to clubs."

"What else have you been hiding from me?" He asked.

"That's for me to know and you to find out. I have this pink mini skirt that makes my ass look so good it'd give you a heart attack."

"Jesus." He cursed. "You're killing me Kate."

"If I take even one step in it, it rides up my thighs. It's definitely a no panties skirt."

"Just wait until I get home Kate, you're going to regret teasing me like this."

I was enjoying driving Dane crazy, but I was close. I wasn't going to last for much longer.

I put more pressure on my clit and relaxed my muscles. I grabbed the phone and cried out for Dane.

"I'm coming." I moaned.

I listened to Dane curse through the phone. It was like he was here with me. I let go as my body shook and my stomach flipped. I touched myself until I was too sensitive for it and then laid there listening to Dane's breathing.

"I miss you." I told him.

"I miss you too, baby."

"Come home soon please."

"I'll come back to you as soon as it's safe. Go to sleep Kate. I'll call you in the morning."

"Goodnight Dane." I whispered before hanging up the phone and falling asleep.

CHAPTER SIX

Kate

    Dane called when he could, but it got harder to call with how busy we both were. The last time I talked to him I told him about my visit from Eliana. I thought maybe he wouldn't want me to come to the wedding, but he said it would be good for me to go. He almost sounded excited at the idea of me being there. I know he said it was fine, but I was still nervous.

    There were only so many times I could change my outfit before I had to give up. If I didn't leave now I was going to be late. I grabbed my coat and a small purse, almost forgetting Dane's phone. He hadn't called me since his flight back to New York took off, but he had to be back in the States by now. While I turned off my lights and made sure the windows were locked I called him.

    I was half expecting him to not answer. I'm sure he was busy.

    "Hello?"

"Hey." I said.

"Why are you calling? You're still coming to the wedding right?"

"I'm just making sure you're okay with me coming tonight. I know how hard you've worked to keep me separate from your work life. I'd totally understand if you didn't want me there." I said, walking down the stairs.

"Kate, listen to me. I'm not having second doubts, I want you there, and I'm excited to introduce you to everybody. It's going to be absolute madness when people find out I'm bringing a date, but it's worth it if I get to spend the night with you. Do you not want to go?" He asked.

I messed with the lock on my door and held the phone to my ear with my shoulder.

"No, of course not! I'm just nervous. I think I'll feel better once I see you in person."

"Good otherwise this would have been really awkward."

"What would have been really awkward?" I asked.

"Showing up at your bakery in an attempt to be romantic and mysterious."

I turned around and saw Dane standing there, phone in hand. He looked incredible. He'd somehow gotten hotter since I'd last seen him.

"Are you done staring or should I give you another minute to check me out?"

"Holy shit. Why are you here?" I asked.

"I came to pick you up."

"You're Apollo's best man. Don't you have more important things to be doing than picking me up?

"I didn't want our first time seeing each other in weeks to be at Apollo's wedding."

"And why not?"

"Because then I wouldn't be able to do this."

Dane wrapped his arms around me and leaned me into a kiss. I would have fallen if not for Dane's strong embrace. He stood me up straight and pulled me into another kiss. We were snapped back to reality by a honking car.

"How long are you back for?" I asked.

Dane looked down at his feet.

"Just tell me."

"I leave early tomorrow." He said.

"Then we better get going. If I've only got twelve hours with you I need to make them count."

Dane smiled and held out his arm. I locked arms with him and let him walk me to the car. He held my head while helping me into the car. I was blocked from getting the seatbelt because of Dane. He continued to lean into the car, resting his elbow on the car door.

"We're going to be late."

"One kiss." He said.

I looked around and saw we were alone on the street. I grabbed Dane's tie and pulled him closer to me. He slipped his hand behind my ear and tilted my chin up. I tried to give Dane a quick kiss, but he had other ideas. He bit my lip and begged for me to let his tongue slide in. For only a minute I gave in. The hour I spent on makeup was a complete waste.

"Dane, the wedding." I tried to say between kisses.

"One more minute."

"If we keep this up we aren't going to make it to the wedding."

"Fine by me." He said, kissing me again.

"Dane!" I laughed, slapping his chest.

"I will not be the reason you don't make it to Apollo's wedding.!"

"Apollo won't mind."

"It's not Apollo I'm worried about. Eliana would never forgive me if I stole you from her wedding."

Dane looked nervous, "You're right. Oh my God, we're going to be late."

Dane let go of me and ran around the car. We pulled into traffic and drove to the wedding.

"How was Italy?"

"Not good. I'm closer to finding Gio, but he's still too many steps ahead of us."

"You'll find him."

Dane looked over at me and kissed the back of my hand. We drove the rest of the way in silence. I watched as the Dane's relaxed energy disappeared. He was turning back into Apollo's best man, not the man that I just made out with in front of Ivy's. By the time we parked I was sitting next to a Dane I hardly recognized.

I waited for him to open my door and help me out of the car. He rested his hand on my back and walked me through the halls of the church. As soon as he opened the door whispers echoed against the stained glass of the church. Dane walked me over to a group of people, only one of which I recognized as Junior. He ignored the stares and gasps of the guests around us. I tried to turn my head, but I was pulled closer to him. He made it impossible to look anywhere but up at him.

"Junior." Dane said, drawing the attention of everyone standing around us.

"Sir."

Dane nodded his head over to the empty corner of the room. He left me alone to go talk with Junior. He came back a few minutes later and grabbed my hand.

"I have to go help Apollo find the rings. How he already lost them is beyond me, but he's freaking out. I've asked Junior to help you find your seat. He's also going to take you to the reception. If you need anything between now and then tell Junior. He'll be able to get a hold of me. Do you understand?"

I nodded my head yes. Dane dropped my hands back down to my sides.

"Don't talk to anyone that makes you uncomfortable. If anything happens tell Junior and I'll take care of it. You're here as my guest tonight Kate, if anyone gives you shit I want to know about it."

He pushed my hair behind my ears and kissed my forehead.

"I'm glad you're here." He whispered so only I could hear.

"Me too. Now go, Apollo needs you. I'll be fine."

Dane walked away with a few men following behind him. I watched until I lost sight of him and then went to stand by Junior.

"Is there anything I can get you while we wait?" He asked.

I took a deep breath trying to ground myself, "Vodka." I answered.

Junior started to pull out his phone and send a text, but I raised an arm to stop him.

"That was a joke Junior."

"Oh, of course." He said, putting his phone away. "If you change your mind just let me know. There's no shame in needing a little something to calm the nerves."

"And you'd know that because you're of legal drinking age?" I asked.

"Well… no, not exactly."

I laughed and took a step in front of him, "Come on, let's go find our seats."

There were no appropriate words to describe Dane. My stomach was in knots the entire night. He was just so… hot.

I'd never seen this side of him before. He was dangerous, intimidating and looked fucking delicious. I couldn't stop picturing what it would be like seeing this version of Dane in bed. Don't get me wrong, I loved the sweet and caring Dane that I met in the bakery, but oh the things I wanted this Dane to do to me. He was the scariest man in the room and yet when he looked for me across the room I melted. I don't remember most of the night, or any of the names of the people I met. I was too distracted by Dane to remember anything.

Almost an hour had passed since Eliana and Apollo had left and the party was coming to an end. Dane left me for a few minutes to say goodbye to a few people and to talk to Apollo's men.

When he came back he grabbed my hand and started walking me to the car. I squeezed his hand as he walked. I was as excited as he was to finally be alone.

When we were alone in the car he turned to face me.

"Are you okay? You've been real quiet tonight."

My brain was short circuiting. How was this hot scary mafia man the same man that baked muffins with me in the morning? Was there a polite way to ask a man to fuck your brains out?

"I'm fine, tonight was just a lot to process. I'm still trying to wrap my head around it."

"Alright, let's go then. We can relax back at the house."

Dane started the car and I leaned back into my seat. I got comfortable for the drive back to his place. We had almost hit the highway when Dane got a call. He debated picking it up in front of me, but I gave a quick nod letting him know it was okay.

Dane answered the phone and in less than a minute was spitting out a string of curses. He was not happy with whoever was on the phone. It wasn't like Dane to lose his composure like this. He hung up the phone and turned the car around.

"What happened?" I asked.

"Change of plans. We aren't going home yet."

"Where are we going?"

Instead of answering my question Dane ignored me. We drove in silence for the entire ride. Half an hour later we pulled into an empty warehouse. It looked like it was under renovation.

"Where are we?" I asked.

"One of Apollo's storage facilities. He keeps some product here."

"It looks half blown up." I said.

"It looks like that because Giovanni tried to blow us up. We stopped using it when Giovanni attacked us. I haven't been back here since that night."

"Then why are we here?"

"Apollo asked me to pick something up."

Dane got out of the car and motioned for me to follow him. He went left down a dark hallway. He messed with an electrical box which sent rows of lights to turn on. In front of me were rows and rows of crates. Some larger than others, all of them stacked on shelves as high as the ceiling.

"What does he need you to pick up?"

"It's complicated. I need you to wait here for me. Alex is on his way with a few others. They're bringing a van. Once they get here we can go, but for right now I need you to stay here. No wandering."

I nodded my head yes and continued to explore the aisles. Dane said no wandering, but I'm sure exploring was okay. I looked around the ground floor and confirmed I was alone. Dane was long gone. I really shouldn't have taken a look into any of the crates, but I was bored. And if you think about it it's Dane's fault for leaving me here alone.

I pulled off a crate that was half open. Inside underneath recycled packing paper was old car parts. Some that were so rusted I almost wouldn't have recognized them. I opened another crate and found more car parts. These looked like new exhaust pipes. What the fuck could Dane possibly be picking up in a warehouse full of car parts? What was so important for Apollo to call him on his wedding night?

I went further down the aisles hoping to find a crate that didn't match the others but they were all from the same manufacturer. I made it to the other side of the room when I heard a crash. I thought maybe it was Dane and I immediately thought the worse. I ran down the same hallway Dane turned into when we first got here. I followed the noise of clanging metal until I found a light on in an old office. I was seconds from opening the door when I heard Dane's voice. He was talking to someone. It wasn't just the two of us in here.

I pressed my hand onto the door, opening it enough to hear what Dane was saying.

"Didn't think he'd leave you alive." Dane said.

Another voice in the office whimpered, letting out a scream of pain.

"I kind of wish he killed you. That'd be less work for me. Let me guess, he wants me to keep you healthy, keep you breathing." Dane asked.

The other man in the room let out a grunt.

"Stop moving, you're fucking up the stitches." Dane complained.

I could hear Dane moving around the room. The same metal noises I heard before happened again. It was like he was dropping something over and over again.

As soon as I heard what Dane was talking about I should have walked away. I should have closed the door and gone back to the main floor, but I couldn't. I wanted to see him, I needed to see what he was doing. This was his life. It was just another day of work for him and it might be my only chance to see the real Dane. I opened the door a little bit more to let in more light.

A man was tied to a chair with blood running down his legs. Behind him was Dane, cleaning a table full of tools. The metal noise from before was him dropping them under the table into a bucket. From where I was standing I could see a bloody axe and a few smaller power tools.

I held onto the door frame to keep myself from fainting. Was this the package Apollo needed Dane to pick up? Who the fuck was this man? The man in the chair started to stir. Before his eyes opened I hid behind the door. Dane noticed he was conscious again, so he moved to check his pulse.

"I'm taking you to the docks." Dane said.

The man tried to speak.

"You should really be saving your energy. If you think Apollo's going to show mercy and put you out of your misery you're fucking crazy." Dane said.

This time he spoke loud enough to be heard, "Fuck you."

"You know, it's not Apollo you need to worry about. It was my night you interrupted. I was having a good night, a great night even, and you ruined it. I'd keep your mouth shut if I were you. I'd hate to have to explain to Apollo you showed up to the docks with a few more injuries than when he left you."

The man tried fighting out of his restraints, but it was useless.

"You made a mistake going after Eliana like you did. Eliana's family now. There isn't a man alive that works for Apollo that doesn't want you dead, me included. Eliana's one of the good ones, she deserves better than to be used by you to try and take Apollo's place as head of the family."

I'm guessing this was Gio. The one Apollo and Dane went chasing after. I'm surprised he's still alive. I get the feeling if it was up to Dane he wouldn't be alive. I should have been afraid, but I wasn't. If anything this was only making him hotter. I couldn't wait another minute. I wanted this version of Dane to fuck me.

I opened up the door the rest of the way and stepped out of the shadow. Dane looked over in shock, surprised to see me standing there. He dropped a medical bag he was holding and rushed over to the door. Before Gio found enough strength to look over at the door, Dane had carried me into the hallway.

"What the fuck are you doing? I told you to stay in the main room."

"I heard a noise. I thought maybe you'd gotten hurt and came to make sure you were okay."

Dane grabbed my shoulders and tried to turn me away from the room.

"You need to go. I don't want you anywhere near him."

"No." I said.

"I'm not playing around Kate. This isn't something you should be watching."

"I'm not going anywhere! I'm tired of you trying to protect me from everything bad in your world. I would have left a long time ago if I didn't think I could handle it. I know who that man is. I know what he did."

"You say you're fine now, but you might just be in shock."

"I'm not in shock!"

"Don't lie. I saw you at the wedding tonight. You didn't say a word all night and you kept your distance from everyone you met. I've been doing this job long enough. I know when someone is having a hard time adjusting."

"You're terrible at reading people, you know that? I can't keep spelling this shit out for you Dane." I said.

"I like to think I'm pretty good at reading people."

Dane was so frustrating, so oblivious. So blind to the attraction I felt for him. He would never be able to understand how I felt for him, even in moments like this.

I grabbed his suit and kissed him. I wrapped my arms around his neck and stepped closer to him until our chests were touching. He grabbed my waist and leaned into the kiss.

"I'm not in shock." I said, putting some distance between us. "I was trying to restrain myself until we got home, but then you brought me here. I'm running out of patience."

Dane smiled and lifted me up into another kiss. I forgot where I was, where we were standing. Dane deepened the kiss, pressing his tongue to my lips. I was trying to fight against Dane's dominance, but he squeezed my ass. It surprised me enough to give him the access he needed. He held me tighter with every moan I let escape.

"Kate, stop. We can't do this here."

"Why not?" I asked.

"Because, because Gio's in the room behind us."

"That doesn't bother me." I answered, kissing his jaw.

"Romeo and Alex will be here any minute with the van. I don't want them walking in on us."

"Then you better fuck me before they get here. But, for the record, I don't mind them watching." I teased.

That was enough to set Dane off. Dane made it very clear our first night together, he didn't like sharing. He grabbed my thighs and motioned for me to jump. I wrapped my legs around his waist and continued to kiss along Dane's jaw. He kept one hand on my thigh but used the other to lift my dress up. He pushed it up against my stomach, leaving me exposed. He wasted no time ripping the thong I was wearing and tucked it into one of his pockets. He turned around and leaned me up against the wall. I arched back at the coldness of the wall. He paid no attention to that, and instead started teasing me. He grabbed in between my legs and gently pushed a finger into me.

I gasped at the sudden contact. He was taking what he wanted from me, and it was driving me crazy. I stopped kissing him to steady my balance. I grabbed his shoulders and whispered into his ear.

"You said we don't have a lot of time. Don't waste it teasing me, just fuck me already."

Dane kept me pinned against the wall as he messed with his zipper. He threw me up, forcing me to loosen my grip on him. He gave me a warning look when I tried to set my foot down.

"Don't move. I'm fucking you like this, in my arms."

He pushed into me which forced me to almost sit down on his dick. He didn't wait for me to adjust to his size. He simply grabbed my hips and started lifting me off his waist. With each lift I slid even further onto him. He held my dress tight to keep it from falling. He shifted my weight onto the wall and grabbed my legs. I leaned against the wall to give Dane a different angle to hold me at. With every thrust my core started to ache more and more. My arms had no place to go so I held Dane's neck with one and used the other to put pressure on my clit.

Dane watched me play with myself as he pumped into me. I watched him drop his head onto his shoulders, trying not to let go before I'd finished at least once. I closed my eyes and rested my head back against the wall. I had to take deep breaths to keep myself from finishing too soon. I knew we were running out of time, but I didn't want this moment to end.

Dane picked up the pace and grabbed my chin, "Look at me."

I opened my eyes.

"I'm the only one that gets to see you like this. I'm the only one that gets to make you moan like this." He said.

I bit my lip to keep my screams from echoing down the hallway. We both heard a garage door open from the same entrance we came in earlier. Dane looked over at the main floor and then back at me. He held onto my hips tight and quickened his pace. He thrusted to the same rhythm I circled my clit with until I finished with a gasp. Dane was close after me. He let go of my legs and helped me find my balance right as Romeo and Alex walked towards Gio's door.

Dane fixed his shirt before leaving me to follow after Romeo. I held my hand out against the wall and tried to steady my breathing. I slowly walked over to the room Dane was in and watched Alex clean up the rest of the room. When Alex started to cut Gio's ties and get him ready to go to the van Dane came back out.

With a smug smile on his face he looked me up and down. How he looked normal, like nothing had happened was just unfair. You'd never guess what he'd just done, but I was still struggling to walk straight. I could still feel my legs shaking.

"You ready to go home?" He asked.

"I'm ready."

Dane told Alex where he wanted him to take Gio and then grabbed my hand and walked back to the front with me.

"You've got until we get home to recover because as soon as we get home I'm fucking you again." Dane warned, before opening my car door.

The drive back to Dane's was suspenseful. Every minute we drove built up more and more anticipation. I wasn't sure about Dane, but one quick fuck in a warehouse wasn't going to be enough for me. I needed more.

If I didn't diffuse the sexual tension between us we weren't ever going to make it back to the house.

"I have a few questions."

"I have a few answers." Dane said, squeezing my thigh.

"Why were there so many car parts in that warehouse? I thought Apollo was a weapons dealer. Do you hide the guns in engines or something?" I asked.

Dane laughed, "No we don't stuff Glocks into engines. Although that's not a terrible idea. A lot of Apollo's businesses are legit. He runs legitimate import and export services. It makes it easier laundering and sneaking supply past borders. There was a time he even owned a small chain of diners. Whatever Apollo's interested in at the moment he buys. Right now it happens to be cars. We sell to a few mechanics across the East Coast and ship foreign parts over from Europe into the States."

"So then what's the point? Why sell illegal shit if you can make money legally?" I asked.

"I don't know. That's just always how it's been. For generations his family has run guns. I don't think the Costa's would make it out alive if they tried to go legit."

Dane thought my silence meant he'd told me too much, "I'm sorry, there's probably a better way to word it. I just thought you wanted me to be honest."

"No, it's fine. I guess I'm still trying to figure out where you fit in. I only know the Dane that sits and solves crosswords in my shop all morning. It's hard to picture you working with Apollo."

"I promise, one day I'll tell you all about my time working for Apollo."

"But not now?" I asked.

"No, not right now."

"Why not?"

"Because it would seriously kill the mood and right now I want to take you home and take you straight to bed."

"Distracting me with sex is low, even for you Dane. Absolutely deplorable." I laughed.

"It's only deplorable if it doesn't work." He said, reaching underneath my dress and sliding his fingers into me.

"You're just as wet for me as you were in the warehouse. I guess I'm not the only one in a rush to get back to the house."

It was infuriating how naturally talented Dane was. He was good at everything he tried. Becca asked him to pipe some cupcakes as a joke last week and he came out to the front with gorgeous cupcakes decorated to look like sunflowers. We had to watch the security camera in the kitchen to prove it was him that decorated them.

There was nothing he couldn't do. He was the perfect employee. If he ever decided to retire early he'd be employee of the month in no time. He was currently helping a customer pick a dessert to take home. He had his obvious favorites from the menu, but he was always unbiased when helping another customer pick out a new favorite.

On the nights I didn't have to close we spent our nights at his house. I didn't love spending all of our time there because of how cold and bland it was, but I was making small improvements to make living there less sufferable. The trick was to bring stuff over on nights Dane would come back too tired to notice. I was still waiting for him to notice the purple loveseat Junior helped me bring into his study.

The nights Dane had to leave for a late work meeting were the worst. I always tried to stay awake until he came home, but I usually failed. Most nights I fell asleep alone, waiting for him to come back. Tonight was one of those nights.

"How important is this meeting? There's no chance you can call in sick and spend the day with me?" I asked.

"I'm afraid there's no getting out of it. Apollo is meeting a new client tonight and he asked me to cover for him." Dane said.

"That's a shame. I had a really fun night planned."

"Oh yeah?" Dane asked, walking up from behind and wrapping his arms around me. He kissed my neck until he found the back of my ear. He thought if he laid on the charm I would forget I was upset.

"I guess if you're going to be gone I'll have to find someone else to invite over for dinner."

"Not funny Kate." He kissed.

"I'm being serious. You can't expect me to sit around bored all-night waiting for you to get back. I have needs Dane."

Dane spun me around. Ever since he came back from Italy I've been seeing how far I could push him. I learned the night of Apollo and Eliana's wedding that jealous Dane fucked better.

"You're killing me, you know that?" He said.

"You should probably leave. I'd hate for you to be late to your meeting."

"Let's see if you keep this same attitude when I get back." He warned.

"Be safe." I smiled, kissing him on the cheek.

Dane rolled his eyes and walked to the front door.

"Don't forget to lock this." He said before leaving.

With Dane gone I focused on finishing up closing. Before working on the dining area I had to close the register. I went to the office to grab an envelope for the receipts. When I walked back through the kitchen I heard the doorbell chime.

"What did you forget this time?" I asked, expecting to see Dane near the register.

When I walked out from the kitchen I didn't find Dane. A man dressed in all black was waiting for me near the door.

"Sir, we're closed. You need to leave-"

"I'm not here to buy a coffee. I'm here for you." He said.

I looked over at the counter and saw my phone a few yards away. I tried to grab it, but I was stopped. The man pulled out a gun and held it right at my chest.

"Don't move."

"You don't want to do this."

"Get on your knees." He ordered.

"Take anything you want. There's money in the register, and more in the office."

"I don't want money. I want to know everything you know about Apollo Costa."

"Who?" I lied.

"I know you're sleeping with his number two. I've seen you with his wife. Don't act like you don't know who I'm fucking talking about. I know he's planning something, and I know it has something to do with the Russians."

"I don't know anything I swear." I cried.

I could see the man's mouth moving, but the blood rushing to my ears was the only thing I could hear. It didn't matter how hard I tried to focus; it was impossible to hear what he was shouting at me.

The next thing I saw was a gun being swung in front of me. The man had stepped closer to me. He leaned down and ran the gun down my arm. My knees were going numb. I couldn't feel the ground anymore.

"If you aren't going to talk then maybe I'll just go find Dane myself. I wonder if Dane will believe me if I tell him you talked."

When he mentioned Dane's name I snapped. I brought my eyes up and stared directly down the barrel. He was trying to scare me but it wasn't going to work. I couldn't show this man any fear.

"Oh trying to be brave, are we?" He asked.

The man laughed and then stood up. He walked around me in a circle, dragging his gun through my hair. I ignored him and stared straight ahead.

"We'll see how brave you are in a few minutes." He said.

While the man turned towards the windows and lowered the curtains I knew I wasn't making it out of here alive. It didn't matter if I gave him information or not. I was dead before he even walked in here.

If I was going to die then I wasn't going out like a coward. I owed it to Dane and his family. This was about more than just Dane and Apollo. I couldn't betray Eliana and the kindness she had shown me.

My only regret was that Dane would be the one to find me. He'd come back and think I'd forgotten to lock my door. He would walk in all mad, ready to give me another lecture but instead he'd see me lying here in my own cold blood.

"I don't know anything. You're wasting your time. Do you really think they trust me enough to tell me anything important?"

"It doesn't matter if you're not someone they trust. Dane trusts you enough to spend his nights with you. Even Dane must have let something slip, something you aren't supposed to know about." He said.

"If you think Dane would tell me anything then you're dumber than you look."

That pissed him off. He didn't appreciate the attitude. I could have been more careful, but there's something about a gun being held against your head that really gets your blood flowing.

"If you're going to kill me, just fucking kill me." I spoke, hiding the fear in my voice.

"Trust me, the Costa's aren't worth dying for. Tell me what you know and you'll never see my face again."

"If I tell you everything I know will you let me live?" I asked.

"If your information is good I'll walk out of here and you'll never see me again."

I looked at the gun sitting in his lap, I watched his fingers tap the cold metal again and again. The longer I stayed quiet the more impatient he became. Before I knew it his face was right in front of mine.

I sat a foot away from the man that was going to kill me.

Taking a deep breath I looked right at him and spit in his face.

"Fucking bitch!" He yelled, wiping his face.

He stood up, kicking his chair away. He pointed his gun at me and pulled the trigger. I took in a deep breath and closed my eyes. A quiet click went off and then the room fell silent.

I thought maybe I'd died, but if I was dead then why could I still hear the noise of traffic outside, or the kitchen door swing? I tried to force myself to open my eyes, but I was afraid to see the man who had pulled the trigger. Maybe he'd see I was still alive and try again.

The only thing I knew for sure was that we weren't alone in the bakery anymore. I could hear another set of footsteps.

"I told you not to pull the trigger." A familiar voice spoke out.

"Chamber's empty." The man in black said.

I opened my eyes and found Apollo standing in my bakery. He took off his gloves and winter coat and set them down on one of my tables.

"Leave." He ordered.

The man walked out of the bakery, leaving me alone with Apollo.

Apollo held out a hand and offered to help me stand. Still in shock I fell back, catching myself with my hands. Apollo took a step back and waited for me to stand on my own.

"Did you- did you send him? Did you know he was here?" I asked.

Apollo pulled over a chair for me. I hated accepting his kind offer, but it felt like I was going to pass out. I dropped my head between my knees and tried to take deep breaths.

"I'm sorry Kate. Angel wasn't supposed to use the gun."

"What the fuck was he supposed to do then?" I asked, trying not to cry.

"You and Dane are becoming more serious, I needed to know I could trust you."

"So you sent one of your men to *pretend* to kill me."

"It's nothing personal. I think it's great you and Dane met each other."

I stood up, still staring at Apollo.

"You fucking psychopath. What the fuck is wrong with you? You needed to be sure you could trust me, so you sent one of your men to threaten me?"

Apollo's jaw clenched. In any other situation I would have been more careful about how I talked to him, but I think I earned a few minutes of immunity.

"You're a part of the family now Kate. Dane sees a future with you, and Eliana seems to really like you. There's nothing more important to me than Eliana's safety. I needed to be sure she would be safe with you."

I wanted to hurt Apollo the same way he'd just hurt me, but I couldn't move. My body wasn't reacting the way I needed it to. I was betrayed by adrenaline. I thought maybe this was all a nightmare. That I would wake up and Apollo wouldn't be standing in my bakery but this wasn't a dream.

"Does Dane know?" I asked. "Does he know you're here right now, and not at dinner with a new client?"

Apollo looked surprised to see I knew about his dinner plans.

"No, he doesn't."

"And how do you think he's going to react when he finds out where you really were tonight?"

"I don't plan on him finding out." He said.

"Are you suggesting I don't tell him about you and Angel coming to see me?"

"Well now that we know you're good at keeping secrets. I doubt keeping one more would hurt." He tried to joke.

"What's to stop me from calling him as soon as you leave?" I asked.

"Because you know better than anybody what that would do to him. It would have been easier for you to tell Angel everything you knew about me even if it was all a lie, but you didn't. You put protecting Dane before your own life. Him finding out about tonight would ruin him. If you called him you'd be tearing him from his family."

"He has a family, a family that's not you." I said.

"There's more to family than blood Kate. You proved that tonight. If Dane found out I was here he'd never forgive me. He's fallen too hard for you. His judgment is clouded, it would be impossible for him to see the bigger picture. He wouldn't care I did this to protect him."

"What would you have done if I did talk? What was Angel supposed to do if I told him all about you and Dane?"

"Angel was only supposed to scare you. I was waiting in the kitchen ready to take care of you if I needed to."

"You were going to kill me." I said.

"I never planned on killing you Kate. Traitor or not you're important to Dane. We would have discussed your options on how to leave Dane's life, but I wouldn't have hurt you."

"I need you to leave now."

Apollo walked to the door, "Don't do something you'll regret tonight just because you're mad at me Kate. Dane would be proud to hear you held your own. You've earned my trust tonight, which believe me, is not an easy thing to earn."

"Fuck your trust, Apollo. Get out!" I yelled.

The adrenaline was wearing off. My hands had begun to shake again, and I was struggling to slow my heart down.

"I can't promise this is the last time you'll be put in danger because of my family Kate. I'll do my best to protect you, but no one is safe from the life I live. Dane may act invincible, but one day all of the sins we've committed will catch up to us."

Apollo grabbed his coat and left the bakery. I locked the front door and then ran to the bathroom to throw up. Exhausted, I leaned against the wall of the bathroom.

When I thought that I would be able to walk again without throwing up I went back to the front. I found my phone and debated calling Dane. I wanted him to leave whatever job he was on and come back to me. Apollo had no right asking me not to tell Dane.

I took a few deep breaths and called Dane. I dropped my phone on the counter and held onto the glass of the display case. The cold of the counter calmed my shaking hands. I let out the breath I was holding in when he answered.

"Hey baby." He answered.

As soon as I heard his voice I began to cry. I tried to cover my mouth with my hands so he couldn't hear me.

"Kate, are you there?"

"I'm here." I whispered into the phone.

I had to bite down on my lip to keep him from hearing my cries.

"Is everything okay?"

"Everything's fine, just needed to hear your voice." I lied.

I can't do it. I can't tell him.

"Miss me already?" He laughed.

"How'd you know?"

"I can hear it in your voice." He said.

He'd never forgive Apollo.

"It's been a long day and I didn't realize how tired I was until you left."

"Don't worry. I'll be home soon."

"Promise me you'll be safe tonight Dane."

I could hear someone calling for Dane in the distance, "I promise, now go get some sleep. I'll be home soon."

Dane hung up and I dropped my phone onto the counter. Apollo was right. Dane would never forgive him. It would ruin him to know what happened tonight, he could never find out.

CHAPTER SEVEN

Dane

The lights were off in Ivy's again. Kate had closed early almost every night this week. When I walked in I found Becca and Amanda putting on their coats and scarves.

"Why are you closing early tonight?"

"She had another panic attack again. I accidentally hit the lights in the kitchen and she freaked out on me. She yelled about being more careful in the kitchen and then told us to leave. Her screaming scared away the customers, so now we're leaving." Becca explained.

"What about your hours?"

"She says she'll still pay us what we would have made tonight and asked us to leave before cleaning or doing the register." Amanda said.

"I don't know what's going on with her, but she needs to get her shit together. We're losing money every time she sends us home because she's having a bad day." Becca complained.

"I'll talk to her." I said.

"Good luck." Becca said, walking out with Amanda.

I followed the music to the back of the kitchen. Kate was mixing batter. She'd been baking more than ever, so it didn't make sense why she was closing her shop early.

I wasn't thinking when I walked up behind her and grabbed her shoulder. At the surprise contact Kate threw the bowl that was in her hands into the air.

"Fuck!" She shouted, turning around, surprised to see me behind her.

In what felt like slow motion, batter fell onto Kate. Onto her hair, her clothes, the counter. It even dripped off of her nose.

"You can't sneak up on me like that Dane." She cursed, trying to catch her breath.

"I'm sorry. I thought you heard me. I was out there talking with Becca. I just assumed you heard me come in."

Kate dropped to her knees and started cleaning up the batter that was spilling down the counter. Her hands shook as she tried to keep the batter off the floor.

"Kate, let me." I tried to offer.

She ignored me and continued cleaning. I had to grab the rag from her hand before she paid any attention to me.

"Stop." I said.

Kate paused and stood up.

"Go upstairs, get out of these clothes, and wash up. I'll clean up down here and meet you upstairs."

"But-"

"No buts, go and get cleaned up." I said, reaching for the bowl on the floor.

Evergreen Ivy

I watched Kate walk up the stairs to her apartment, and then I got to work. I cleaned the counters and floors first and then washed the bowls that were left sitting out. There was more to be done down here, but my main concern was Kate.

She wasn't her normal self. Kate never had a problem with me sneaking in like that before. She usually found it exciting. This wasn't the first time I scared her. On nights when I come over late she usually slept through me coming to bed, but now when I came over she's been awake. I find her in bed with the lights on, ready to jump if it's not me.

I walked into the apartment and heard the shower running. I grabbed her clothes she tossed on the floor and threw them in her laundry hamper. I wasn't sure how long she'd spend in the shower so I went looking for something for dinner.

I found a few leftovers and started making a chicken bake. Every minute or so I listened to hear if the shower was still running. It eventually stopped, but Kate never came out. She was stalling. The table was set and the food was getting cold. I was grabbing two wine glasses when she finally came into the kitchen.

"You cook now?" I heard her ask.

"I've always cooked. I just rarely have the time to. My nights are too unpredictable to cook. Dinners on the table. Let me know if I need to reheat it." I told her.

I expected her to sit down at the table, but when I walked over to my seat I found her staring down at her plate. Was there something wrong with it? She told me she didn't have any allergies, but maybe what I made wasn't something she wanted. My doubts disappeared when she walked over and wrapped her arms around me. She leaned her head into my chest and let out a deep sigh.

"Thank you." She whispered.

She eventually let go and sat down. She took a bite of her salad and let herself relax. I'd been busy this week. Most nights I came over late. The way she ate had me doubting she'd been eating. The empty fridge was my first clue. Tomorrow I'd make sure Junior stopped by regularly with meals on nights I couldn't be here.

Kate ate quickly and then stood to clear her plate. I followed her to the sink.

"Do you want to talk about what happened today with Becca?" I asked.

"No."

"I think we should Kate. You've been closing early, sending people home, it's not like you."

"There's nothing going on. I'm a little overwhelmed and tired, but I'm working on it."

"This is more than you being a little stressed Kate. Let me in, all I want to do is help."

Something flashed across her eyes, but then it was gone. For a minute I thought she might tell me what was wrong, but then her expression became cold.

"I'm tired. I'm going to bed."

Kate left her dishes in the sink and walked to her room. I turned off the lights in the apartment and followed after her. I couldn't tell if she was actually asleep or just pretending, but I didn't bother her. I took off my pants and unbuttoned my shirt then laid next to her. I reached over for her but she stiffened and curled her legs up. I moved my hand back and folded it under my pillow. After all the patience she showed me I have to trust that she will tell me what's wrong when she's ready.

I waited for Kate's morning alarms, but they never came. Kate slept until almost noon. I had a few meetings in the morning that were easy to cancel and I already had the evening free. I would be here when Kate woke up.

She must have thought I had already left because she ran through the living room in a rush.

"Kate." I spoke.

Again I scared her. She tripped over her own feet when she saw me.

"Fuck, Dane. You have to stop doing that!" She snapped.

"I didn't mean-"

"Just forget it. I'm late. I have to go."

She left me alone in her apartment. I was left standing there like a fucking idiot, holding her lunch for her and she didn't even notice. It's like she was on autopilot.

I walked downstairs and sat down at my usual table. I waited for Kate to come by, but she never came. I walked over to the counter and ordered with Becca.

"Did you talk to her last night?" She asked.

"Didn't get the chance. She shut me out, just like you. I can't even get her to look at me."

"Did you do something? Did you two fight?"

"No, we were doing fine. I thought we'd finally worked out our issues."

"And what issues did you two have?" Becca asked.

I stared at her. She was already pushing her luck.

"It was worth a shot. I thought maybe you'd open up because you're desperate."

"Maybe I should go." I said.

"That's your solution?" Becca asked, grabbing me my drink. "She needs help Dane, serious help, and your best idea is maybe you should give her space?"

"I don't know. Do you have any better ideas? She clearly doesn't want me to be here right now."

"She needs a break from this place. Maybe it really is just work stress that has her acting like this."

"We did have plans to go on a trip, but it didn't work out." I explained.

"Why not?"

"Work."

"Is there a chance work has anything to do with why Kate is acting like this?" She asked.

Maybe.

"That look on your face tells me it is." Becca said.

"Would you be willing to close tonight?" I asked her.

"Why?"

"Because there's somewhere I need to take Kate."

"Right now?" Becca asked.

"Yes, right now."

Becca looked around for Kate and saw her struggling with bringing out a few coffee orders. Her regular warm daisy smile gone.

"Okay."

"I owe you one." I said patting her shoulder and running over to Kate.

"We have to go." I told her.

"What?"

"Take my hand. We're going out. Becca is going to close."

"Are you on something?" She asked.

"Kate, do you trust me?"

"Of course."

"Then take my hand. We're leaving."

Kate laughed and threw her apron off. It was the first genuine smile I'd seen from her in weeks. It confirmed I was making the right choice getting her out of here.

Kate waved at Becca on our way out and held onto my hand tighter.

In the car her excitement settled.

"Where are we going?"

"Jersey."

"Jersey?" She asked, now regretting leaving with me.

"There's something I want to show you."

Kate doubted me the entire drive. I had to nearly drag her out of the car when we made it to the bar. She hesitated on the sidewalk, probably asking herself why she agreed to leave work to come to a run-down bar with me. I didn't blame her; it was a little out of character for me.

"Let's go." I said, taking her hand.

I walked into the bar and led Kate to a quiet corner of the bar.

"Dane I'm not really in the mood for drinks."

"We aren't here for drinks. I've been meaning to bring you here for a long time."

"Why?"

"Because this is the bar where I first met Apollo."

Kate looked around and took a closer look at the bar where it all began.

"You pulled me away from work to take me to the bar where you first met Apollo? Are you feeling nostalgic?" She asked.

"It's the only way I know how to show you how much you mean to me. You've never pushed me or forced me to talk about my relationship with Apollo. When I ask you to trust me you always do, without doubt or question. I know there's something you're keeping from me, something that's hurting you. Becca and I have been trying to think of ways to help you, but nothing seems to be working. I'm wondering if maybe you haven't come to me because you don't really trust me to handle it."

"Dane, that's not it-"

"Just listen, please."

Kate agreed and nodded for me to continue.

"You've been dying to know more about my life with the Costa's since Apollo and Eliana's wedding. I was afraid to tell you everything about my life because a small part of me knows you'll want to leave but it's unfair of me to keep secrets and then get upset when you keep secrets from me."

"So you're going to tell me everything about you and in return I have to tell you my secrets too?" She asked.

"I'm not asking you to tell me anything. It's about building trust. If I show you my hand maybe it'll bring us closer and you'll stop feeling like you're all alone. Maybe one day you'll decide to let me help you." I explained.

"Anything I ask you'll tell me about?" Kate asked, a smile growing on her face.

"Anything, don't hold back."

"This bar is where you met him, how and why?"

"I was nineteen and at Duke on scholarship."

"Duke?" Kate asked, surprised to hear my answer.

"My grades were good and the essay I wrote about the sacrifices my family made was even better. Admissions ate it right up. They offered me a full ride. Until Duke I wasn't even sure I wanted to go to college, but I wasn't going to turn down free money."

"You mean to tell me you graduated from Duke?" Kate asked.

"I never said I graduated."

"Then what happened?"

"I was undecided and taking a bunch of classes my first year to figure out what I wanted to major in. I took a criminology course my first semester and got close with the professor. Our last class of the semester he brought in a RICO agent to talk to us about a few cases we'd studied. He brought up a few cases he'd worked on, one of them being the Costas. Later a few of us were invited out to drinks with the professor and this agent. A few beers turned into a couple more and before the end of the night this agent was telling us everything he had on the Costas. He was a textbook narcissist. He was dying to tell us about his top secret cases. He spent the whole night bragging about how close they were to arresting the entire family, Apollo's dad included."

"What did you do?" She asked.

"My first night home for winter break I came here. I knew a little about the Costas because of their involvement at the docks. I knew they were in town for a few months. I got Apollo's attention by beating the shit out of one of his men at the front door. Less than five minutes later I was brought back to his office to meet him."

I pointed over to the back wall of the bar. Kate looked around until she saw a closed off door, barely noticeable in the dim lighting. While Kate looked around the bar I waved down the bartender and asked for two beers. Kate said she wasn't in the mood to drink but she would be after I answered her questions.

"I told him I'd tell him anything he wanted to know about the RICO case against him for a hundred thousand. Apollo laughed and had me thrown out. A week later on Christmas a car pulled up in front of my house while I was taking out the trash. A man I didn't know threw a suitcase out of the car. In it was a hundred thousand in cash and a burner phone."

"So what, you just took the money and started working for Apollo?"

"No, a few months later back at school Apollo came to visit. Coincidentally he was taking care of a job and needed my help. He offered me more money than I'd ever seen in my entire life to work for him. So I dropped out of college and never looked back."

Kate finished her beer and grabbed mine.

"I thought you weren't in the mood to drink."

"I had a change of heart." She said.

I gave Kate a few minutes to process everything I'd just told her.

"How many people have you killed?" She asked.

"I don't know. I lost count years ago." I told her honestly.

"And these jobs you take for Apollo. Do you have any say in whether you take them or not? What would happen if you told him no?"

"I don't know. I've never not taken a job." I admitted.

"Ever?"

"Every job he's given me made sense. Big or small it was to protect the family."

Kate picked at the coaster on the table. That answer upset her.

"Would you ever leave?"

"I don't know. I've never thought about wanting to leave."

"Would Apollo even let you leave?" She asked.

"Probably not. I like to think he would, but now that he's taking over for his father I'm sure he'd struggle letting me walk away from everything we've been through together. Apollo's family, and you don't walk away from family."

Kate waved for another drink.

"He's family?" She asked, so quiet I barely heard her.

I nodded my head yes. That seemed to hurt her more than anything else I'd told her today.

"What happens if one day I want to leave? Would Apollo kill me?"

"Kate, how could you even say that? Of course not!"

"I'm serious. Would you ever let Apollo hurt me?"

How could she possibly think I'd ever let anything happen to her? I reached over the table and held her hands.

"I would never let anything like that happen to you Kate. I promise."

"I'm not saying you'd intentionally let anything happen to me, but it comes with the territory Dane. You'll do your best, but you aren't invincible."

These words coming out of Kate's mouth weren't her own.

"Never said I was invincible Kate, but I am promising to protect you."

Kate smiled and looked down at her beer. She smiled like she knew my words were empty. We sat in silence for a little while longer. She nursed a beer and watched the night crowd shuffle in. Soon we were surrounded by people all here for drinks after work. The noise of an old jukebox and the laughs of strangers filled the room.

Kate asked to leave when the crowd grew beyond comfort. We were surrounded by people and it was starting to overwhelm her. We were back in the car, driving to my house. I didn't want to take her back to Ivy's tonight.

Almost to my house Kate looked at me, "I want to learn how to use a gun."

"Excuse me?"

"I want to learn how to shoot."

"No." I told her.

"If you won't teach me I'll get someone else to do it. I want to be able to protect myself in case anything happens to me."

"You hate guns. You barely put up with me bringing mine with me to Ivy's." I reminded her.

Evergreen Ivy

"Doesn't mean I'll never need to know how to use one." She mumbled.

We sat in silence for the rest of the drive. I wasn't going to argue her learning how to shoot a gun when she was drunk. Tomorrow we'd have a serious conversation about it, but now wasn't the time.

Kate barely made it up to my front door on two feet. If I wasn't behind her holding her up she'd have fallen in the rocks on the way up the stairs.

"I think it's time for bed, babe." She laughed.

Kate only called me babe when she had too much to drink, "I think so too."

"Tomorrow if I have more questions will you answer them? Should I be trying to ask as much as I can before the clock strikes twelve?" She teased.

I looked at my watch and then back at Kate, "How many more questions do you have?"

"Not a lot, but now that I know what I know I'm going to have a hard time not asking you about work. It's going to get harder to ignore."

I kissed the top of Kate's head as she slid out of her work clothes and slipped on one of my shirts.

"Anytime you have questions or doubts you come and ask me about them, okay?" I told her.

"Okay." She smiled.

"Come on, let's get you to bed."

Kate grabbed my hand and walked over to her side of the bed. She fixed her pillow and then fell into the silk covers.

"I do have one more question."

I sat and waited for her to open her eyes.

"Are you happy?" She asked.

"Am I happy?"

"Working for Apollo. Living like this, are you happy?"

How did she expect me to answer that? How could someone be happy living the life I do? Did I deserve to be happy after all the pain I've caused? Did I tell her she made me happy? Would she believe me?

"Yeah, I'm happy Kate."

Kate closed her eyes and moved further into her covers.

"He was right." She whispered.

"Who was right Kate?"

"You'd never forgive him."

I laid next to Kate while she slept. I tried to fall asleep but I couldn't get Kate's words out of my head. I was up until the morning wondering what Kate meant. Who would I never forgive?

I thought being honest with Kate about my life working for Apollo would make her feel better, but it only seemed to hurt her. I guess I was wrong in thinking she'd open up to me now that I had. Kate was less reactive at work, but when we were alone together she still kept her distance. Most mornings when I woke up I saw she'd moved to the couch in the middle of the night.

I was doing my best to be patient, but watching Kate suffer like this was killing me. There was nothing I could do to get her to open up to me, so for now I kept a close eye on her.

I was there at closing, I was up in the morning to prep dough, I ran to the market for her. She was still taking quite a bit of time off, so on the days it was hard for her to get out of bed we did anything that made her happy. I quickly learned Kate's version of self-care was going to bookstores and taking drives out of the city. Some days we drove until we were the only two left on the road.

Spending all my time with Kate came at a cost. I got a call from Junior early this morning that we were short a few crates at the warehouse. That meant one of two things. Either someone was stealing from us before our guns made it to inventory, or we had idiots working the docks and not checking our imports at the gate. I'd spent all day in the office tracking payments and the schedule for the past month.

Angel and Fabian were in the office with me trying to follow our paper trail. They're the only ones that haven't worked at the warehouse for a few months. Apollo sent a few of his security guys to help me at the warehouse until I could figure out why our inventory was short.

"All our numbers from last month to the first match. Every shipment that arrived, day or night, adds up. It doesn't look like anything went missing until a few weeks ago." Fabian said, dropping a stack of papers on my desk.

Being able to keep receipts of our weapons would make this all easier, but it wasn't something we could afford to risk. We were left filtering through the little documentation we had and our security cameras. Angel was on hour six of surveillance videos of the gate. He knew he wasn't allowed to stop until all trucks going in and out had been put into a timeline.

"Start with our night crew this time. If someone's stealing they aren't doing it during the day when I'm here." I told Fabian, pointing to another box on the floor.

I looked over at Angel. His head was starting to drop again, so I threw a pen at him. He shot back in his seat, cracking his neck.

"I'm awake." He lied.

"Bullshit." Fabian laughed, walking back to the table.

Ignoring both of them I started working on a way to stretch our current inventory to keep our customers happy. We'd lose clients if they knew we were missing their regular pieces.

Someone singing out in the hallway caused all three of us to look up towards the door.

"What is that?" Fabian asked.

"That's how Junior lets me know he's back. He thinks if I have time to prepare for his arrival I'll be less likely to kick him out when he gets here." I answered.

"Is it working?" Angel asked.

"No."

Junior also thought if he announced himself by singing he didn't have to knock. He walked right into my office and sat down with Angel. His only job today was to drop food off at Kate's, so it was confusing why it took over two hours to get back to the warehouse.

"What took you so long?" I asked.

"Kate needed help rearranging the bookshelf. She had the books all scattered around on the tables; it was a mess. Plus she offered a piece of cake as a thank you. It would have been rude to not accept."

"Did you at least pay for the desserts you ate?"

"Why do you assume it was more than one?" He asked.

"Answer the question."

Junior's eyes dropped, "They were on the house."

"They were what?" I asked.

"They were on the house." He spoke up barely loud enough to hear.

I rolled my eyes and went back to my desk. While I worked I tried to think of anyone I trusted enough to run dinner to Ivy's. Until I found someone else I'd have to talk to Kate about Junior spending all his time there.

I looked over at the table and saw Fabian and Angel giving Junior shit for being late. Junior, who had yet to do any work today, was throwing a fit.

"Would it kill you to lie?" Fabian laughed.

Junior tried to ignore them, but they weren't even close to being done.

"There's only like twenty books at Ivy's. How did it take you two hours to organize? They all fit on one fucking shelf." Angel said.

I thought about Kate's shop. I'd never paid much attention to the layout of the place. I was usually too distracted by Kate to notice. I only ever spent time by the books if I was working on the crossword. Gun to my head I'd not be able to say how many books there were at Ivy's, but Angel knew.

"How do you know?" I asked.

"How do I know what?" Angel asked, confused by my question.

"How do you know how many books there are at Ivy's?"

Angel sat back further in his chair. He gripped the edge of the table until his knuckles were white.

"I just guessed." He tried to lie.

"No you didn't. You knew exactly how many books there were."

"Junior must have mentioned it after one of his trips over there." He lied again.

"Junior, leave." I ordered.

"Why?" He asked.

"Because Eliana said I have to stop shooting people in front of you. She says I have to stop making you an accomplice."

Junior looked over at Angel and Fabian and hesitated. He waited to see if I was being serious. He got his answer when I reached behind my back for my gun. He dropped the papers he was holding on the table and ran out of the room.

"I was never a big fan of yours but because Apollo likes you I'll go easy on you. Tell me the truth and if I think you're being honest I won't shoot anything vital." I warned.

Angel's eyes grew wide when he realized I was being serious.

"Dane, this is crazy. You aren't going to shoot me."

To make sure he knew I wasn't kidding I shot at the chair behind him. The leg of it shattered and left splintered wood at his feet.

"Okay, okay. I'll tell you. But you can't shoot me for orders Apollo gave."

"What orders?" I asked.

"He asked me to go to the bakery and scare Kate. He told me to threaten to hurt her unless she gave me information on you two. But Dane I swear, I didn't actually hurt her. As soon as Apollo realized she wasn't going to talk he came and stopped it."

My brain was failing to process the words I was hearing. The more Angel talked the farther away I drifted. What was Angel even saying? If he had actually gone to Ivy's and scared Kate she would have told me.

"You're lying. There's no way Kate wouldn't tell me something like that." I said, keeping the gun aimed at Angel.

"Apollo convinced her not to tell you. When we left her that night I asked him how he knew she wouldn't talk. He just said something about loyalty. After a few days of silence from you we knew she decided not to tell anyone."

It was getting harder and harder to keep calm. I steadied the gun in my hand, noticing the smallest of tremors.

"What did you do to her?" I asked, unsure I was ready to hear his answer.

Angel said nothing.

"What did you do?" I asked.

Angel made the mistake of taking too long to answer. I shot his left knee and watched him fall to the ground.

"You promised not to fucking shoot!" He screamed.

"I didn't promise shit. You're lucky I'm only shooting once." I said.

If Angel wasn't going to give me the answers I needed I would get them from Kate. I found Junior waiting in the hallway. I grabbed him by his coat and dragged him down the hallway with me.

"You're going to drive to Kate's and wait outside her shop. You'll wait there however long it takes Kate to pack a few bags. When she's ready you'll take her to my house. No stops, no visitors. Do you understand?"

Junior shook his head yes.

"Wait for my call. If you walk into Ivy's before I give you permission to and you interrupt us I'll kill you."

I left Junior in the parking lot of the warehouse and drove to Kate's.

I thought about knocking or ringing the doorbell, but when I got there and saw Kate up in her apartment I let myself in. I pulled her front door open, breaking the lock even more than before.

When I walked into her apartment I found her cleaning up dinner. I watched her for a minute. She looked at ease, comfortable in her own space. I dreaded what I was about to do. Soon she'd be reliving what Angel did to her.

She heard me walk into the living room and drop my keys on her coffee table.

"I thought you were working late tonight. You should have called. I would have left dinner out."

There were a million questions I wanted to ask her, but I didn't even know where to begin.

"Is everything okay?" She asked.

I watched her walk over from the kitchen to the living room. Even standing in front of me now I couldn't believe what Angel had told me.

"Dane, what's going on? You look like you're about to pass out."

She tried to reach her arms out and comfort me, but I stepped back. It was taking everything in me to stay calm. If Kate came too close to me I wouldn't have the nerve to ask her what I needed to know.

"He knew how many books you had." I said.

"Is this because I asked Junior to stay and help? I didn't mean for him to be here so long, but we lost track of time and-"

"No. Angel. Angel knew how many books you had."

Kate froze. The warm smile on her face fell and was replaced with a blank stare.

"Who's Angel?" She asked.

"You know who Angel is Kate."

"I don't know anyone named Angel." She tried to lie again.

"Damn it Kate! I know. I know everything. He told me what he did to you!" I yelled.

Kate shook her head no and walked out of the living room. She went back to the kitchen and started cleaning again. She put away tupperware, threw dishes in the sink, did anything to distract herself from what I was about to say next.

"Kate, look at me." I said, walking over to her.

She ignored me. Pretended I wasn't in the room.

"Kate!" I shouted.

She finally looked at me only this time she was angry.

"No! Just stop it, please. We aren't supposed to be talking about this. You weren't supposed to find out!"

She stopped and leaned against the counter.

"You weren't supposed to find out." She cried.

I grabbed her shoulders and wrapped my arms around her. She tried to push away but I held her tight. Her erratic breathing finally slowed down and I could hear her take a few deep breaths. I whispered in her ear a few times to keep her from spiraling out of control again. She held onto me and matched the ups and downs of my own chest. When I thought she had calmed down enough I let go and gave her some space.

"I need you to tell me what happened."

"I can't." She cried, wiping her tears with her shirt collar.

"Why not?"

"I promised Apollo I wouldn't."

Those words sent a rush of rage through my heart. Everything stilled, time moved slower. I wanted to scream, but I was paralyzed. In a cold, level tone I spoke again.

"I don't give a damn what you promised Apollo. I need you to tell me everything Angel did to you."

"Promise me you won't hurt him."

I laughed; she had to be fucking kidding right now.

"It's too late for that, Kate."

"It wasn't his fault. He was doing a job. Just like Apollo makes you do."

"What happened?"

Kate sighed. Defeated, she walked over to the couch.

"Do you remember that night you went to a meeting for Apollo because he was meeting a new client?"

I grabbed her hands to try and ground me.

"There was no client. Angel came in as soon as you left. He tried to scare me, get me to talk."

"What else?"

"He forced me down on my knees and then tried convincing me to give up info on Apollo."

"He touched you? I swear to God if he laid a hand on you Kate..." I snapped.

"No, God no. He didn't have to. The gun he tossed around was enough to do whatever he said to do."

I brought Kate's hands up to my face and kissed her knuckles. I knew what she was doing. She was trying to turn this into a joke to make what she'd been through easier to stomach. Only Kate would try to use humor to ease my discomfort.

"What happened when you told him about us?"

"Nothing happened. I didn't tell him anything." She said.

"Why not?"

"Because I thought I was dead either way. I didn't want something I told him to hurt you or the Costas."

My hands were shaking. I looked down and saw Kate's were too. I'd never felt fear and anger like this.

"You thought you were going to die and still you protected us?"

"It was a test. Apollo needed to know he could trust me."

I'm going to kill him.

I stood up from the couch and walked back over to my keys. Kate was at the front door ready to stop me.

"I'm not letting you leave."

"Move, Kate."

"No. If you leave here you'll do something stupid. Something you won't be able to take back."

"Move."

"Dane, look at me. I'm fine. I'm not hurt, I'm not in pain. It was all fake. There weren't even bullets in the gun. As soon as Angel took it too far Apollo stepped in."

Everything Kate was saying only made things worse. I had to get out of here.

"Pack a bag, Junior is waiting downstairs to take you to my place."

I grabbed the front door and swung it open. Kate moved out of my way but continued to run after me. I heard her screaming my name until I was in my car and driving off.

I don't remember how I got to Apollo's or how I got to his front porch. All I could think about was finding him. I ran up his stairs and found his office empty. The rest of the second floor was empty, so I went back down and went searching through the living room and into the dining room. When I heard voices in the kitchen I froze.

Nearly breaking off the door that connected the dining room to the kitchen I found Apollo talking with Eliana who was sitting at the counter.

"Dane, what are you doing here?" Eliana asked.

"He knows why I'm here." I said, walking up to Apollo and punching him.

Apollo fell back, surprised by the attack.

"Jesus." Apollo spat, wiping blood from his lip.

"Dane what the fuck are you doing?" Eliana asked, jumping out of her seat.

I ignored her and rounded the corner of the counter. I grabbed Apollo by the shoulder and lifted him up enough to hit him again.

"Dane!" Eliana shouted, "Stop!"

"It's fine. Dane here has some things he needs to process." Apollo said.

Another hit seemed too forgiving so while Apollo was grabbing for the counter I swung my knee into his chest.

"I'm surprised it took you this long." He wheezed. "I didn't think she'd last this long keeping it a secret."

"It wasn't Kate that told me. I had to find out about what you did from Angel."

"You can be upset I didn't tell you, but you can't be mad I asked Angel to test her. The family always comes first." He said.

"You crossed a line."

"What did you do Apollo?" Eliana asked, terrified to even hear his answer.

Apollo kept quiet, couldn't even bother to stand up off the floor.

I looked at Eliana and answered for him.

"He sent Angel to threaten Kate. Wanted to test her loyalty to me and the family. He sat in her kitchen and watched as Angel held a fucking gun to her head."

Eliana looked over at Apollo, "Please tell me you did not do that."

"I needed to know you'd be safe spending time with her." Apollo told Eliana.

"I should kill you."

"You should be thanking me. Now we know she can be trusted. And can I just add how impressed I am with her. She really stood her own that night. If it weren't for me stepping in when she spit in Angel's face, who knows what would have happened."

Apollo was enjoying this.

I grabbed him one more time and punched until he was half dead on the ground.

"I came to you a month ago and told you about my concern for Kate. I asked you why she was on edge, losing her temper at small things, why she was shutting me out. The whole time you knew what was wrong with her and you said nothing."

"I was waiting to see if she'd tell you."

Eliana tried to step in between Apollo and me.

"Dane, I get you're upset, but hurting Apollo won't make you feel any better. Let's be smart about this."

Apollo finally made it to his feet.

"I needed to know Kate was someone that Eliana would be safe hanging out with. This was about more than just the company. You would have done the same if you were in my position. It's my job to keep this family safe. I wasn't going to risk the safety of our entire organization because you're fucking the barista you met when you were supposed to be working."

I thought I had calmed down, but Apollo just didn't know when to quit. Even Eliana knew he'd gone too far. She sucked in a breath and waited for the next hit. I hit Apollo again and watched as he tried to shake off the pain.

I watched the blood drip from Apollo's face. I hoped it hurt, but I knew it wasn't anywhere close to what I felt right now.

I walked over to the door I'd ruined and turned to face Apollo.

"I'm done."

Apollo shouted after me, but I ignored him. I'd given up my life to protect a man undeserving of being saved. If I stayed any longer Kate was right, I'd do something I would regret. I had to put my anger aside and leave before I didn't get the chance.

Apollo ran after me to my car.

"Think this through, Dane. Leaving isn't something you get to do."

"I couldn't figure out what was causing Kate to be in so much pain, this entire time it was a mystery. Now I know why and it makes me sick. I told her you were family Apollo. You should have seen the look on her face when I told her that. I'll never forget the fear in her eyes when I told her you were the person I trusted more than anyone else in the world."

"Dane." He said again, trying to block my way to the car.

"Go back inside Apollo. If Kate leaves me because of what you've done I'll come back here and actually kill you. Go and pray I don't come back."

I opened my car door, pushing Apollo out of the way. He winced as the car door slammed into his probably broken ribs.

"You don't want to do this Dane."

"Yeah, I do."

CHAPTER EIGHT

Kate

I sat on the couch in the living room and waited for Dane to get back. A terrified Junior kept watch outside. A few hours later Dane walked in. He slammed the front door shut and walked to the bathroom that connected to his bedroom.

He didn't even bother looking at me. He walked right past me like I didn't exist. I followed him to the bathroom but kept my distance.

Dane turned on the hot water and watched it run, his bloody hands rested on the marble sink. He went to grab the first aid bag from below the sink but ended up dripping blood onto the rug.

"Fuck." He spat, gripping onto the sink even harder than before.

I couldn't just stand there and watch any longer. I walked over and picked up the dropped bag. Dane watched my hands but refused to look up at me.

I grabbed the hand that was bleeding the worst and held it under the water. Dane's entire body flinched when I touched him. His shoulders tensed and dropped.

Neither of us said anything while I cleaned up the cuts between his knuckles. None of them were split enough for stitches, but it would take a while to heal. When I reached across Dane for an extra wash cloth he finally spoke.

"You should have told me."

I had nothing to say to make the situation better. He acts like I haven't been dying to tell him since it happened.

"I almost did. The night it happened; I was so close to telling you everything." I confessed.

Dane's jaw clenched. I continued to clean his cuts with saline.

"Why didn't you?"

"When you picked up the phone and I heard your voice I just broke. I couldn't stomach telling you what Apollo had done to me. A man you trusted more than anything. I knew it would ruin your relationship with him."

Dane finally looked up at me. He looked into my eyes, trying to calm himself down.

I could only imagine the anger Dane was feeling, but for the first time in a long time I felt calm. The weights that had been dropped on my chest were finally gone. I could breathe again.

I let out a quiet laugh that grew into a manic fit. Dane looked at me like I'd gone crazy. He let go of the extra gauze he'd begun wrapping. He was debating reaching out to me to calm me down.

"Kate…" He tried to soothe.

"Sorry, I just-" I laughed, losing my breath.

"Kate, breathe."

"I'm just so relieved you finally know. I know I shouldn't be, but God this feels so good."

My tears of laughter quickly turned into real tears. I continued to struggle to breathe, my lungs felt tight. I could only get quick breaths out as the tears continued. Dane threw his arms around me and rubbed my back.

"Breathe with me."

I wrapped my shaking arms around him and leaned into his chest. I listened to his deep breaths and did as he said. My breaths slowed down and my heart began to beat a little more normal.

"I'm really struggling, Dane. I don't even know who I am anymore. My heart is full of anger and fear. It makes me sick." I whispered.

"I know, baby. I'm so sorry." He said, kissing the top of my head.

"I'm just so mad. I'm mad at Apollo for what he did. I'm mad at myself for not being more careful. I'm mad that he asked me not to tell you. I'm mad that even though I should have told you I didn't because I was afraid of what he'd do to me." I cried.

He let go of me and grabbed a few tissues. Throwing the bloody washcloths behind the bathroom door along with his bloody shirt he grabbed my hand.

"Let's go." He said.

"Where are we going?"

"It's a surprise. Go change into pants and long sleeves." He said, walking into his closet.

I grabbed my painting overalls and put on an old long sleeve underneath it.

"And wear shoes you don't mind getting ruined." Dane shouted from the closet.

Walking into the garage he tossed me the keys and motioned for me to get in. He disappeared into the back of the garage where all of his work tools were set up and came back with a large duffle bag.

He drove out of town to the same neighborhood we drove through the night of Apollo and Eliana's wedding. He didn't say anything, but his hand brushed over mine every few minutes. The scratch of the bandages had me picturing what he'd done to Apollo.

Dane pulled into the parking lot of a warehouse just like the one we'd been in before only this one wasn't blown up to bits.

"Dane, where are we?"

"This is where Apollo moved product after the incident with Gio. We've been working out here until the other warehouse gets cleared by the city to work in again."

"Why are we here?"

Dane smiled and tossed the duffle bag onto the concrete in front of me.

"We're here to break some shit."

"Excuse me?"

"Open the bag."

I did as he asked and opened it to find a baseball bat, a torch, a few axes, and a few knives.

"Dane what the fuck is this?"

"Apollo broke into Ivy's; he violated your space. You're angry, acting out, you feel like you're not in control anymore. So, eye for an eye. We're going to hurt Apollo where it hurts."

"You want me to vandalize a mob bosses' warehouse. Great idea, I'm sure that won't piss him off at all. Are you fucking crazy?" I asked.

"Come on, don't pretend like it doesn't sound fun."

"I'm not breaking into one of Apollo's warehouses, Dane."

"You don't have to break in. I know the code."

I hesitated. Was he for real? Did he actually expect me to go through with this? Dane grabbed the bat from the bag and walked over to a window near the front door. He took one swing and shattered the first layer of the window. Glass went flying.

Holy shit.

"Your turn." He smiled.

You know what, fuck it.

Dane opened the door and let it swing open. He held out the bat to me. I took it from him and went to the front desk. I walked around the counter and got ready to swing, but Dane stopped me.

"Wait."

I gave him an annoyed look for trying to stop me. He only laughed and pulled out a pair of safety goggles.

"Put these on first."

I slid them on and took aim at the desktop sitting on the desk. Chipped plastic went flying. Dane had to duck to miss getting hit by a corner of the screen.

I looked over at Dane. I couldn't believe what I'd done, but I was in even more shock at how good it felt. Dane gave me a reassuring nod to continue. I looked over at the broken computer and picked it up and threw it across the room. It slid until it hit a wall leaving a small dent.

I walked into the main floor and walked around with Dane. He knocked over a few crates from the first shelf we found. Wood shattered all around us. I picked up a piece of the broken crate and threw it in the air. I swung my bat to hit it midair. It went flying.

"That was so hot." Dane said, running his hands over his lips.

"I want the axe."

Dane handed over the axe and watched me as I hacked at every crate I could reach. Foam peanuts went pouring out of every crate I broke. I grabbed for anything I could reach and sent it hurling down the aisles. Dane sat back and kept a close eye on me.

I dropped the axe and went back to the bat. I'm not sure what came over me, but I just didn't stop. I hit and I hit and I hit until my shoulders physically ached. I screamed until I lost my voice. I cried until the tears ran out.

"You tapping out, or you need more?" Dane asked.

"More."

Dane stepped away from the wall he was leaning on and went over to a locked door.

"Do your worst." He said, unlocking the door.

Dane turned on the lights and waited for my reaction.

"Dane, I can't."

"Eye for an eye babe."

"This is his office. He'd never forgive me." I told him.

"Then we'd be even because I don't think I'll ever be able to forgive him for what he did to you."

"Toss me a knife." I told him.

Dane threw me a hunting knife. I clipped off its guard and spun Apollo's chair around. I sliced at the expensive material and watched the seams rip.

"Are you just going to watch?" I asked.

"Apollo and I already worked our problems out. Seems a little over-kill to smash inventory after breaking his nose."

"What are those?" I asked, pointing to Apollo's bar cart.

"Liquor?"

"No, like are they sentimental? Family heirlooms?"

"No the interior designer bought them. Said it fit the room aesthetic."

"So, he wouldn't be upset if I accidentally dropped them?"

"Not any more upset than seeing the shit you broke out there." Dane laughed.

I walked over to the glass bottles and dropped the lids next to the glasses. I offered a drink to Dane, but he declined. Oh well, more for me. I took a big gulp of the smoothest whiskey I'd ever drank.

Damn. What a waste.

I took another sip and then threw the bottle against the wall.

"Fuck you!" I screamed.

The vodka was next.

"You fucking asshole!" I screamed again as I watched the liquor drip down the walls. Dane walked closer to me, the glass crunching under his shoes.

"Feel better?" He asked.

"A little."

Dane walked over and brought the tequila to me. I grabbed it by the neck of the bottle and handed Dane the knife I was holding.

"I want to go home now."

Dane nodded his head and grabbed the duffle bag. He threw it over his shoulders and reached for my hand. The tequila was empty by the time we made it to the car. I let the last few drops fall in the parking lot while Dane packed up the car. I carefully set the bottle in the back seat of the car. Dane got in the car and immediately grabbed my hand. Dane's thumb running across my hand lulled me to sleep.

I slept the whole way back to the house. I don't even remember Dane carrying me in from the car. All I remember is waking up and feeling better than I had in a long time. I slept through the night for the first time since Apollo came to the bakery.

I walked into the kitchen and found Dane on the phone. His sweatpants were hung low on his hips, I also appreciated that he'd gone without a shirt this morning. I watched his tattoos move every time he moved around the room. His muscles tensed with every step. When he heard me behind him he hung up. I knew it was Junior on the phone because of how he talked. He was more patient with Junior than any of his other men. He wouldn't ever admit it, but he was always taking care of Junior like his little brother. His pauses in his directions told me he was giving Junior a chance to ask questions. A privilege few got when on the phone with Dane.

"How'd you sleep?" He asked.

"Good. Great." I hummed.

"Breaking shit and tequila have that effect on people."

Last night came rushing back. Holy shit. That was real. Dane sensed my panic and came over to me.

"If you're worried about last night you shouldn't be. I promise there's nothing Apollo can do to you. I don't plan on letting him hurt you again."

"I'm not even scared, just in shock maybe. I've never done anything like that. I didn't even know I was capable of that type of destruction."

"You're also probably really sore."

"Oh my God! I didn't want to say anything, but I'm dying. I need like an ice bath or something." I laughed.

Dane smiled and spun my shoulders around. He ran his hands underneath my shirt and threw it off. He gave my back muscles a much needed massage. I relaxed at his touch. Dane and I had spent a lot of time together these last few weeks, but there was a distance between us. Neither of us had mentioned it to the other but standing here with him instantly calmed me. Having his hands on me again woke me up, it ignited the fire I'd been missing.

"That feel good, baby?" He whispered in my ear, leaving soft kisses down my neck.

I leaned back into his chest letting him wrap his arms around my own chest. Dane brushed his fingers along my chest causing me to shiver.

"I missed you." He whispered.

"You missed me?" I asked.

"Mhmm." He kissed my shoulder.

"How much did you miss me?" I asked, teasing him, hoping for a reaction.

"Like you wouldn't believe." He said, letting go of me and softly pushing on my back to lower me onto the counter. One of Dane's hands slid down my back and past my ass, sliding in between my legs.

I let out a whimper at the sudden contact. It had been forever since Dane touched me like that. I'd been distracted, distant since the break in.

"I missed this." He said, playing with my pussy.

I pressed my arms against the cold countertop and opened my legs a little wider.

"I missed being able to kiss you." He said, leaning in to lick me.

"I missed hearing you scream." He spoke, muffled between my legs.

"I missed how you shake when you're close and you tighten on my cock."

"Dane." I begged.

He'd barely touched me and already I was close. My brain was screaming, my stomach was in knots. I wanted him, I wanted him to fuck me.

"Did you miss me?" He asked.

"Yes."

"What did you miss Kate?"

Dane stopped touching me. He leaned back on the floor and softly blew against my wet folds. It caused me to shake.

"I miss you touching me like this. I miss feeling your cock slide into me while I play with myself." I confessed.

"You like touching yourself when I'm in you?" He asked.

I nodded yes.

"Is that what you want Kate?"

"Yes." I whispered.

I heard Dane stand up and move around to the other side of the counter. I started to stand up straight, but he stopped me.

"Don't move."

I laid my head back down on the counter. Dane moved into my line of sight.

He began to stroke himself. He ran his precum down his cock. I had to squeeze my legs together to keep me from moving and going over to him.

"You like that?" He asked, now teasing me for his own pleasure.

"Yes."

"I want you to touch yourself." He ordered.

I leaned farther down on the counter so I could slide my hand in between my legs.

"I'm going to fuck you, but I want to see you touch yourself first. I want to watch your cheeks get red and I want to hear your little whimpers."

Dane continued to touch himself while I rubbed a finger between my cunt. I finally gave in and started circling my clit.

Dane knew instantly what I was doing. I reacted to my touches by biting my lip.

"You aren't going to last long if you're already pushing against your clit like that Kate."

"Dane, please."

Dane moved back behind me and spread my legs as wide as he could. He ran his dick up and down my folds pushing into me in one thrust. No warning, no going slow, he was already as deep as he could get.

"Fuck." I sighed.

Dane sucked in a deep breath. This was killing him just as much as it was killing me. Neither of us were going to last very long and we both knew it. There would be other times to enjoy each other, to soak up every touch and moment. But right now I wanted him to fuck my brains out. I wanted him to help me forget.

"Faster." I told him.

Dane gripped my hips and fucked me just like I needed him to.

"Are you touching yourself?" He asked.

"Yes. Don't stop, please."

Dane let out a few curses and slightly lifted up my hips. I was on my tip toes trying to keep up with him. I barely touched myself. Even the slightest movement had me going crazy.

"Shit Kate." He cursed leaning into me.

His thrusts were quick, sloppy. He wasn't going to last much longer. I sped up and started to press harder into my clit. I wanted to come before him. I wanted to come with his cock still inside me. I wanted to send him over the edge.

I rocked with Dane's thrusts and let go. I let out a moan that caused Dane to squeeze me harder. I closed my eyes and relaxed which sent the orgasm to take over my entire body. My fingers froze on my own clit. I couldn't move if I tried. I pulsed against Dane's cock.

It sent him over the edge. He laid one hand on my lower back and came in me. I felt him spasm still inside me.

"Fuck." He groaned. He leaned against me on the counter as the two of us climbed down from our highs.

When he finally slipped out of me I felt his cum slide down my thigh. Dane might have been ready to walk but I wasn't. I needed another minute. Dane came around and brushed hair out of my face.

"Can you grab me my shirt?" I asked.

Dane lowered down and picked it up off the floor. When I was sure my legs weren't going to give out I stood up and wiped his cum off my thighs. Dane looked at me with so much lust I was afraid he'd push me back down and fuck me again.

"No." I laughed.

"What?"

"I need like at least an hour before you fuck me again."

"I'll set a timer." He said, grabbing my arm and walking me to the bathroom.

Dane was making dinner while I sat and looked through a cookbook that had to be a hundred years old. The pages nearly dissolved each time I turned the page. It was full of recipes from Dane's family passed down from generations. How he ended up with a book this special is a mystery.

I looked up and saw Dane lost in thought staring at the mug cabinet.

"What's wrong?" I asked.

"I'm trying to figure out where all these cups came from. I don't remember buying them."

Oh no.

"Well I doubt they appeared out of thin air. Even you couldn't possibly remember every purchase you've ever made." I said.

If I didn't play this cool he'd figure out how much stuff I'd snuck over here.

"Dane grabbed two mugs from the top shelf. One of the mugs he was holding was my heart shaped cappuccino mug. The other was my clementine mug. The one I only used when I wanted orange juice.

"I have literally never seen these in my entire life." He said.

Crap, I was about to get caught. In an attempt to distract I hopped out of my chair and walked over to Dane. I walked into his arms still holding the mugs and gave him a kiss.

"You look so sexy right now." I said.

"Kate…"

"Maybe after dinner you can be dessert." I smiled.

"Nice try." He said, giving me another kiss.

Dane set down the two mugs he was holding and moved me to the side of him. I had to watch as he pulled out another cup with a picture of me drunk at a party on it. The photo was faded, but it wasn't hard to tell I was flashing whoever was taking the picture while holding a bottle of cheap tequila. I was instantly nauseous looking at the photo and remembering how that night ended.

"Classy." Dane laughed.

"That was a birthday gift from Becca."

"And it's in my cabinet because?"

"It's my lucky mug. I've used it literally every day for coffee since I've started spending the night here. It's your own fault this is your first time noticing it."

Dane put all the mugs back and looked around his house like it was his first time being here. Every time he noticed something new he shook his head.

"Unbelievable." He said to himself.

"I think your onions are burning." I shouted over to him when he started to walk into the living room.

"No they aren't."

Damn.

A few minutes later Dane came back still trying to calculate all of the changes I'd made to the place. He talked to himself while finishing up his sauce.

While he finished getting dinner ready I tried to think of anything else that was hiding here he didn't know about. I needed to hide it for a few days until he adjusted to what he'd already seen.

Dane sat next to me at the table in the kitchen and handed me a fork. A fork that I brought from home. The only one I liked to eat pasta with.

I laughed and thanked him for the food. A few bites in I reached over and grabbed the wine. Plan B was getting Dane drunk and hoping he forgot about all of his new discoveries. Maybe by morning he'd forget I had practically moved my entire apartment over here.

"It's going to take a lot more wine than what we have here to get me drunk, Kate."

"Damn."

"You know I don't mind all the changes you've made, but maybe the next time you bring something new here you give me a heads up."

"Does that also apply to things you haven't noticed yet? Because if it does it's going to take a while to write up a list."

"What else could there possibly be?" He asked.

It was time to change the subject before he found out I'd turned one of his spare bedrooms into my own personal closet.

"What were you talking to Junior about earlier?" I asked.

Dane gave me a cheeky smile but accepted my attempt at avoiding having to explain what I'd done.

"I had him call someone to come fix your door. I'm installing a new security system."

"Dane, I don't think-"

"It's nonnegotiable Kate. End of story."

I looked up at him and saw the same anger on his face from last night. I could argue with him. Stand my ground, but I didn't want to. He was right. I didn't feel safe at Ivy's anymore. This was a small change that might help me feel comfortable at home again.

"Fine."

"Thank you."

"I don't know when the new system will be set up, but I'd like to go home tomorrow. As much as I love it here I can't stay here forever."

"I'll take you back tomorrow whenever you're ready." Dane offered.

Remembering Ivy's brought me back to that night again. I should be over it already. Nothing even happened, but I can't get the image of Angel threatening me with his gun out of my head. I remember what it smelled like that night, how cold I was. The way his voice echoed throughout the empty bakery. I'd been through a lot worse in my life, but that night was stuck in my brain on repeat.

Dane dropped his fork and ran his hand down my back. His warm touch brought me back to the table.

"If you aren't ready to go back I understand. You know I like having you here with me. There's no rush." He soothed.

"I can't spend forever here. I need to go home and get back to work."

"You don't need to do anything you aren't ready for Kate. It's understandable you wouldn't want to spend your time there."

"But every day I avoid going back to Ivy's or close early because I can't stand to be alone there at night it's another day Apollo wins."

"How could you possibly think that? Apollo only wins if you give him that kind of power over you. There are no words to describe how proud I am of you for standing up to Apollo. There are few men alive who have the nerve to put him in his place. I can understand feeling disconnected to Ivy's, but don't give up on your home and dream of running Ivy's because you're afraid."

Leave it to Dane to say exactly what I needed to hear. Ivy's was mine. I wasn't going to let anyone take that from me. Not Apollo, not anybody."

"Is the security system Junior's setting up good?" I asked.

"It's the best. There's no chance of anyone coming into Ivy's without you knowing about it. I've asked him to set up sensors on all entrances. And you'll be the sole admin. You're the only one who can change settings and set alarms."

"Not even you?" I asked.

"Not even me."

"I like that." I smiled.

"I thought you might."

"Is it that same system that lets you play any song you want for the doorbell?"

"No."

"You're lying."

"No I'm not."

"Fine, lie. But jokes on you because I know Junior will set it up for me if I bribe him."

Dane knew he was beat. There was little chance Junior turned down free food.

"Have I told you how gorgeous you're looking today?"

I rolled my eyes. How dare he use my own tricks against me. I wasn't falling for it.

"Nice try." I laughed.

"Damn." He sighed.

Weeks had gone by since Dane found out about Angel. I thought after the dust settled he'd go back to work, but he never mentioned Apollo or the warehouse. I only saw Junior when he snuck in the back for yesterday's leftovers. Junior did his best not to talk about the Costas. I got the feeling Apollo had something to do with his hesitation to talk about work.

Dane had been nothing but supportive these last few weeks. He never questioned my irrational fears of going back to Ivy's. He even suggested I spend a few nights alone at Ivy's to help me feel better about being alone. He swore he went to his place on those nights, but I had my suspicions he waited down the block in his car in case I called. He was so supportive, which is why it hurt so much to see him send Apollo's calls to voicemails.

Eventually Apollo stopped calling which Dane pretended to be glad about, but I knew it upset him. One night after dinner I tried talking to him about going back but he shut it down. He didn't want to hear anything about going back to work for Apollo. I haven't brought it up since that night. I had months to process what Apollo had done to me but Dane was just now finding out about it. I couldn't ask him to make peace with Apollo until he was ready.

It was a quiet Tuesday morning and Becca and I were finalizing the menu for spring while we had some down time. The two of us were sat near the bookshelf so we could see anyone come in. Becca was trying to convince me to add cake pops at our front counter when the doorbell rang.

Fuck.

"Good morning." Apollo said, walking over to the counter and looking over our desserts.

"Becca take your things and go work on this in my office please."

Becca looked over at our customer and then back at me. She was looking at me to see if I needed her to stay. I nodded for her to leave. She grabbed her notebook and hurried into the kitchen. When I heard the office door close and lock I stood up.

"You look terrible."

"You can thank Dane for that. Eliana isn't a fan, but the bruises are really starting to grow on me. It makes me look tough."

"Interested in ordering something?" I asked.

"I hear the scones are good."

"They're Junior's favorite. Dane's go to is an Americano with a croissant."

"That surprises me."

"Why?" I asked.

"Dane hates coffee." Apollo said, standing up straight and looking right into my eyes.

"What?"

"For as long as I've known him he's refused to drink it. Even when he was dead tired. Said it made him too jittery."

It took everything I had not to react. He was trying to rile me up, remind me just how new my relationship with Dane really is.

"Why are you really here Apollo?"

Apollo sighed, "I'm here to apologize."

I laughed. Apollo Costa doesn't apologize.

"Nice try, come on be serious."

"I'm serious. We need to talk about Dane."

I pointed to the table I was working at and offered him a seat. Apollo sat across from me and leaned back in his chair. He tapped against the hardwood table and waited for me to sit.

"Dane needs to come back." He said.

"I agree, but that's not my choice to make. Dane has to decide for himself when he's ready to go back."

"Dane won't ever come back, not until you forgive me."

"Dane must have fucked you up real good if you think there's any chance in hell I forgive you Apollo."

Apollo's jaw clenched, "Kate."

"No. I don't care who you are Apollo. You have no right coming here for a second time to try and intimidate me again. I'm not afraid of you. Nothing you could say would make me forgive you."

"I'm not asking you to forgive me. I expect you to hate me for the rest of your life. I'd be disappointed if you were actually considering forgiving me. I'm asking you to pretend to forgive me."

"I don't understand."

"Apollo is like a brother to me, Kate. I don't want to see him hurt. Do you know what will happen if he doesn't come back to work?"

I shook my head no.

"If he leaves I won't be able to protect him anymore. There's a long list of people that want him dead and there would be nothing I could do to protect him if he wasn't my number two anymore. I could give a shit if you ever accept my apology, but I need Dane back. I know what you think of me. You can barely even sit here with me now without showing disgust for me and my family. You think I'm a monster that doesn't deserve the life I have, and that's fine. I'm not asking you to support the decisions I've made, but you knew who Dane was when you met him. You knew shit like this was part of the arrangement when you agreed to be with him."

"It's not that simple."

"Yes it is Kate. You knew exactly who Dane was, but you didn't care until the person that got hurt was you. You were fine pretending not to know what Dane did when he left in the morning or when he came back late. You ignored all the signs that told you what me and my family did. You agreed to be a part of my family when you fell in love with Dane."

"I'm not- we aren't."

"He's falling in love with you Kate. It's why he's out shopping for that special brand of vanilla extract you like right now instead of running my shipments. It's why he's been sending me to voicemail and ignoring my texts."

"You've been following him."

"I just told you there's an actual list of people who want him dead. Of course I'm following him. I'd never forgive myself if something happened to him. It's the same reason I had Angel test you. I can't risk losing him, not after everything we've been through."

I sat and looked out the window behind Apollo. It was crazy to admit, but Apollo was right. I knew the risks of dating a man like Dane. There was no Dane without the Costas. I didn't get to choose to love one and not the other.

"What do you want me to do?" I asked.

Apollo pulled out a burner phone.

"Call me when you think Dane's ready to hear what I have to say. Until I get your call I'll give you two as much space as you need."

Apollo stood up and walked towards the back entrance.

"That's a beautiful vase." Apollo said, pointing over at my cash register.

I looked at the glass tequila bottle that I stole from his office. It now held a bouquet of dahlias from Dane. I had to bite my lip to hide my smile.

"I bought it at a flea market a few days ago." I lied.

"Is that so?"

"Mhmm, I think it really ties the whole room together."

Apollo shook his head and laughed quietly to himself as he walked out through the back. I waited until the back screen door closed and then ran to the office.

"Who the hell was that?" Becca asked.

"It's a secret. A secret you can't tell Dane about."

"Kate, if you're cheating I'll actually kill you. It doesn't matter how hot that man was, it's no excuse."

"Oh shut up." I laughed and hit her arm.

"I'm planning a surprise for Dane. I needed one of his friend's help to pick some stuff up for me."

"Okay, but I dibs the next hot mystery man that walks in here. It's not fair you get to have all the fun." She sighed.

Becca and I walked back out to the front just as Dane walked in. In he walked carrying my tote bag over his shoulder and looking so dreamy. He reached into the bag and pulled out a chicken Caesar wrap and a shit ton of vanilla extract.

"They didn't have the extract in bulk, but I convinced the guy at customer service to sell me four of their smaller bottles for the price I'd get the larger one. I think they're really starting to like me over there. I didn't even have to threaten this one. Oh and I brought you lunch because I know you lied when you said you had a big breakfast." He smiled.

Becca looked over at me and rolled her eyes, "You are the luckiest bitch in the whole world."

"He's my karma for something good I did."

Dane laughed at Becca's sighs while he walked to the kitchen.

"You'll find someone Becca."

"Who? The guy that said he didn't have time to buy flowers so he brought actual weeds he pulled out of the ground on his way to dinner? Or the guy that had a lizard on his shoulder when I showed up to our first date?"

"There's no way that actually happened." I laughed.

"The lizard's name was Leo, and we were asked to leave when my date tried to order lettuce for the table so Leo would have something to munch on."

"Where are you finding these men Becca?" Dane asked, genuinely concerned.

"I swear there's something wrong with me, they attract to me like a fucking magnet. They appear out of thin air."

"Neither of those dates sound as bad as the guy who took you down the river with a boat he'd stolen earlier that day." I reminded her.

"How do you steal a boat?" Dane asked.

"I don't know, which is exactly what I told the cops when they tried to question me about it."

Dane and I looked over at each other and broke out into laughter. I totally forgot about that night until just now. I remember her calling me from the police station and having to pick her up.

"I hate both of you." Becca said, walking back to the kitchen.

Dane walked over to me and gave me a quick kiss.

"Have you ever stolen a boat?" I asked.

"No, but now I kind of want to see how hard it'd be."

"How about instead of stealing a boat you help me crumb coat some cakes."

"Fine." He compromised.

Dane walked over to the display case and took a scone back to the kitchen with him. Apollo's words played back in my head. I wonder how long it would take Dane to admit he didn't like coffee. How much longer would he be able to pretend he was happy working here at the bakery and not working with Apollo?

Dane had been the biggest help at the shop which made it so hard to admit he was driving me crazy. I loved having him at Ivy's to help, but I could tell he was missing working with Apollo. He was going crazy not having work as an outlet. He was up before me most days ready to prep the kitchen. He never took a break; he never took lunch. He was a few days away from breaking the most cookies iced in a day record that I didn't even know existed until he started working here.

It was time to call Apollo. It was almost painful watching Dane work. He didn't belong here.

I called Apollo and asked him to meet at the bakery after closing. I was a nervous wreck all day. I was afraid if I got too close to Dane he'd be able to tell something was wrong with me. He'd know I called Apollo. It was impossible lying to him. I had to keep busy all day until the final customer left.

When the front door was locked I finally found the courage to go find Dane. He was in my office organizing my old file cabinet. He heard me before I was even in the room.

"What are we going to do for dinner?" He asked.

"Actually I was thinking I'd cook tonight."

"Why?"

I didn't know how to tell him. If I told him before Apollo showed up he'd try to leave. But if I didn't tell him there was the possibility he would lose it again.

I heard the alarm sing from the back of the store. It meant someone had come in. Dane sat up straight and looked out into the hallway.

"Someone's here."

"I know." I told him.

"Who is it?"

"Just promise you won't be mad."

"Why are you acting so weird?" He asked.

"I called Apollo, I asked him to come over."

Dane stood up from the chair he was sitting in and walked over to me.

"You called Apollo?"

"I thought it was time you two had a talk."

"I don't have anything to say to him. Tell him to leave."

"Dane, look at me."

Dane calmed down and gave me a chance to talk.

"You miss it, you miss the thrill and excitement of working with him. I felt the exact same anger you felt when I thought about what he did, but every day I wake up I feel less angry than I did the day before. After talking about it with you I started to understand why he did what he did."

"It doesn't make it right." He argued.

"No, it doesn't. But at the end of the day he did what he did to protect you. It was fucked up, but he was only trying to protect his family."

At the word family Dane's brows softened.

"This wasn't your problem to fix, you've already been through so much because of me."

"Then go fix it. Go out there and give Apollo a chance to explain himself. I will forever appreciate the love and patience you've shown me these past two weeks, but it's time to move on."

"This is really what you want?" He asked.

"If I'm ever going to move on I need you to forgive him."

Dane kissed my cheek then pressed his forehead to mine.

"Thank you." He whispered.

Dane let go of me and walked out to the front of the store. It was time; time to move on.

CHAPTER NINE

Dane

"You're a fucking pussy going to Kate instead of me." I said, as I walked out from the kitchen.

"It worked." Apollo grinned.

"I should be asking you to leave right now."

"But you won't." He said.

"What you did Apollo…"

"I know it was fucked up but I panicked. I saw how quickly your relationship with Kate was moving and I needed to make sure she would be able to handle all of this." He said, pointing between the two of us.

"You knew it was wrong, that's why you kept it from me." I told him.

"If it's any consolation Eliana's been giving me the silent treatment since you left that night. Plus the broken ribs serve as a constant reminder."

"Now what? How do we come back from this?" I asked.

"I don't know. I was hoping tomorrow you'd come back to work. I spent one day with Junior at the docks and wanted to blow my brains out. There's no off button on that kid."

"God I miss that little shit."

"The never ending talking I can handle, but it's the singing that drives me crazy." Apollo joked.

"You figure out why inventory was short yet?"

"Not yet. I'm too busy keeping customers happy with the inventory we still have. The warehouse is dying without you."

"I won't work with Angel. One look at him and I'll wish I hit somewhere other than his leg."

"Done. I'll keep him away when he comes back."

"And you won't ever pull shit like that again. Not with Kate, not with me." I continued.

"As long as you promise not to set Kate loose in one of my warehouses again."

"I'm not paying you back for any damages. We're even now." I told him.

Apollo laughed and ran his hands over his jaw.

"What's so funny?" I asked.

"Remember all the shit you gave me when Eliana and I became more serious?"

Of course I remembered.

"It's just funny to see you defend Kate the same way I tried to defend El."

"Look Apollo, I'm sorry…"

"No, please don't. I get it. Before El I would have given anyone in my position the same talk about priorities. It's terrifying isn't it? Doing what we do knowing everyday they're at risk of getting hurt because of us."

"It keeps me up most nights." I admitted.

"Yeah, I know the feeling." Apollo walked over to me, "No more tests, no more destroying warehouses. We're even."

I took a step forward and shook his hand, "Deal."

He pulled me towards him and patted my back. Apollo walked around to the front and looked over at the kitchen.

"Whatever you do, don't fuck this up."

"I won't."

"I'm serious Dane, you're all she's got now. Don't hurt her now that she's beginning to trust you."

"What do you mean I'm all she has?" I asked.

"Shit." Apollo mumbled, stepping closer to the door. "I really need to learn to keep my mouth shut."

"Apollo, what do you mean I'm all she has?"

"Just, ask her if you want to know. I promised not to use anything I learned about Kate to hurt her. El would be pissed if she found out I told you before Kate did."

"Apollo…"

"No, I can't." He apologized, raising his hands in surrender.

Apollo messed with the new door handle and grabbed his keys out of his pocket.

"I'll call you when I need you."

I didn't waste a minute after Apollo was gone to go find Kate. I found her back in the apartment. She nearly jumped off of the couch when I came in. She was worried, afraid she'd done the wrong thing.

I grabbed her jaw and pulled her into a kiss. We nearly fell back at how fast I'd ran up to her. She had to hold onto my shirt to keep herself from falling.

"Thank you." I said, kissing her a final time.

Kate held onto my arms as I kissed her. Her smile turned into quiet giggles with each kiss.

"You two work things out?" She asked.

"I think so."

Kate let out a sigh of relief.

"Now, what's for dinner? I'm starving."

Kate gave me a guilty grin and put her hands on my shoulders.

"I was going to make dinner, but then I was craving burgers and I knew I couldn't make a burger better than that place that will put onion rings on them. And I was nervous about what you two were doing downstairs and I wasn't really sure how to handle the stress, so I ordered some burgers and then ordered some more and I might have gotten a little carried away."

"What did you order Kate?"

"A few burgers, a few fries and a couple milkshakes."

"How many is a few?" I asked.

"Enough to last us for a few days." She laughed.

"I'll go set the table." I sighed.

"You're the best." Kate shouted after me.

Nearly a dozen burgers later Kate and I sat down for dinner. The two of us sat together at her small kitchen table. It barely fit the both of us, but it was my favorite place in her whole apartment. I was sat barely an inch from Kate, our knees touching every time she leaned over the table to dip her fries in her ketchup. It felt so intimate to eat here like this with her. The reason she invited Apollo over tonight was because she thought he was family. I wish she knew when I sat here with her like this she felt like family too. Kate felt like that calm feeling you get when you come home after being gone for a long time.

What did Apollo mean I was all she had? Surely there was someone else in her life she called family.

"Kate."

"Hmm?" She mumbled after a bite of her burger.

"Are you close with your family?"

"What made you think to ask that?" She asked.

"I don't know. Nothing really. I was just thinking about how you've never mentioned them before. Is there a reason you haven't?"

"I have a brother." She answered quickly.

"And your parents?"

Kate sighed and set down her burger. She licked off some ketchup from her knuckle before looking up at me.

"You really want to know?"

"Yes, I want to know."

"They're both dead. Mom got sick when I was in middle school. By the time we found out she had cancer she only had a few months to live. Chemo wouldn't have done anything."

"And your dad?"

"He killed himself my freshman year of high school. Said he didn't want to live in a world without Mom."

"Kate, I'm so sorry. I didn't know- I shouldn't have asked."

"It's fine. You were going to find out sooner or later."

"What about your brother? Are you two close?"

"He's seven years older than me. I moved in with him and his girlfriend when Dad died. My senior year him and his girlfriend got married. At my graduation party she told me they were excited to start a family but couldn't because they were stuck taking care of me. She told me Nick would never say anything to me but I was starting to become a burden. In August I moved into the dorms and never went back home."

Oh Kate.

I pulled Kate's hands into mine. I shouldn't have asked. It wasn't fair of me to ask her to bring up those memories.

"I know what you're thinking, Dane. I know you feel terrible for asking about them and wishing you hadn't. But please, do not feel bad. I made my peace with it years ago. I had no idea the pain my dad was in when Mom died. After Mom died he put his career on hold to try and give me a normal childhood. I try to focus on all the times I thought he was the best dad in the world, and not why or how he left."

"Kate…"

"Some people only get to spend a few years here on Earth. I think deep down Dad always knew he was one of those people."

"You don't have to be okay with how he left Kate. You're allowed to be angry, upset even." I told her.

"I know and believe me I was. I spent most of my teen years angry at the world. But then one day I was tired of being angry. I was tired of being mad at the world, mad at the universe. I hardly remember my high school years. One night I went to bed after my mom's funeral and when I woke up I was a freshman in college."

"When was the last time you went back to visit your brother?"

"I never did. We call on birthdays and on Mom and Dad's birthdays, but other than that I don't even remember the last time we called for something other than a family obligation."

"Does he have any kids?"

"Two boys."

"And his wife?"

Evergreen Ivy

"Hannah doesn't call, but I get the family Christmas newsletter every December."

"I'm sorry Kate."

"Hey." She smiled, "At least now you don't have to worry about an awkward meet the parent's dinner. There's no one for you to impress, which is great considering what you do for work."

I let out a surprised laugh, "Yeah I guess there's that."

"The scariest person in my life is Becca and so far she likes you."

"It gets me out of a meet the parent's dinner, but you have to meet my family, which believe me will be an absolute nightmare."

"I'm sure it won't be that bad!" Kate said.

"My sisters have been waiting for this moment their entire lives. The stories they've been waiting to share, it will ruin me Kate."

"I can't wait." She smiled.

"Can I ask one more question?"

"Sure."

"Why did you name your shop Ivy's?"

"Before my mom died we lived across the street from a house that was covered in Ivy. I used to sit outside on the porch swing with my mom in the morning before she left for work. She would sit and drink her coffee and I'd lay in her lap and watch the wind rustle through the ivy. She used to complain and say the neighbors didn't take care of their yard and if they weren't careful it'd ruin the side of their house but I loved it."

Kate picked at the plastic lid on her milkshake as she talked.

"Even in the winter the ivy would still be there, it's green so beautiful against the snow. After Mom died I spent every morning on the porch. It was where I felt closest to her. A few months later we moved to be closer to my grandma. After Dad's funeral I made my brother drive back to our old house. When we pulled up in front of my neighbor's house I saw that the ivy was gone. Someone had cut it down. Before college I thought I'd move somewhere far away from New York and I'd buy a house covered in Ivy. I guess naming the store Ivy was a way to hold onto my memories with my mom."

"Is that still your dream, to buy a house covered in Ivy? Somewhere far away from New York?" I asked.

"Maybe one day. But dreams change." She smiled.

As Kate went back to her burger I wondered if she knew she was my dream. Maybe soon I'd be brave enough to tell her growing old with her was all I would ever want.

I'd barely gotten a few hours when my phone woke me up. I could hear it ringing from Kate's kitchen. I must have left it there last night. I fixed the covers over Kate and went out to see who was calling.

"Dane." I answered.

"Still asleep?" Apollo teased.

"It's not even five."

"That's late for you." He answered.

"I'm going to guess you called because you need me and not because you wanted to piss me off?"

"We have a meeting with the Irish. They figured out we're missing guns."

"When's the meeting?"

"In a few hours."

"Brunch with the Irish, can't wait." I lied.

"Call Junior for me. He's coming with us." Apollo said.

"Why?"

"Dunne likes him. They find Junior's constant annoyance charming."

"I'll meet you at the house in an hour." I told him, hanging up the phone.

I went back to the bedroom and found Kate awake. She was throwing a shirt over her head when I came in.

"Was that Apollo?"

"He needs me to go to a meeting with him."

"Okay." She answered, grabbing her square brown glasses from her nightstand.

"Are you heading down to the shop?" I asked.

"Yeah. Come find me and say bye before you leave."

Kate walked around the bed and gave me a quick kiss on the cheek before leaving to go downstairs. I showered and got dressed in Kate's closet and then went down to find Kate. She was in the kitchen cleaning the counters.

"Good morning." She smiled.

"Morning." I said, kissing the top of her head.

"When do you think you'll get back tonight?" She asked.

"I have no idea. I imagine after our meeting with the Irish Apollo will want me working to figure out who's been stealing our product."

"That's still happening?"

"They stopped working on it when I left. If I'm lucky Junior and I can figure out who's behind all of the missing guns, but it could take a few days."

"Oh, that reminds me!" Kate nearly shouted right in my ear before she walked towards the fridge.

"We had a few extra red velvet cupcakes from yesterday. Take them to work with you."

"I don't like red velvet." I told her.

"They aren't for you." She laughed.

I looked at the perfectly packaged cupcakes. Bright red frosting and pink sprinkles.

"Then who-"

"Red velvet is Junior's favorite. I used the beet powder he suggested for the color."

"Beet powder?"

"He thought it'd be a healthier alternative to the dyes Becca and I use. Wait to tell him about the beet powder until after he's eaten it in case it sways his opinion. Let me know what he thinks."

"I'm not bringing Junior cupcakes." I argued.

"Why not? Is he not going to be at the meeting?"

"No, he'll be there."

"Then I don't see what the problem is." Kate questioned.

I took a deep breath and grabbed the box from Kate.

"Don't throw them in the back of your car either. I spent a lot of time decorating them!"

I ignored Kate and kept walking.

"Have a great day at work sweetie!" Kate called after me.

I gave a wave behind my head and walked out to the car.

Forty minutes later I was driving up to Apollo's house. I threw the cupcakes in the back seat and walked into the quiet house.

I met Apollo in his office, unable to find Junior. I'd sent him a text to be ready to go at eight, but odds are he was still sleeping. Apollo was working on inventory to bring to the Irish. I'm sure they were pissed we'd lost some of our supply. He threw a folder on his coffee table for me and then went back to his desk.

I grabbed the folder and scanned over Apollo's tracking information. It took us too long to figure out someone was stealing from us, and now if Apollo couldn't keep the Irish happy we'd lose millions. It would slow production down all over the East Coast and it would hurt us in Italy.

"This is bad." I said.

"No shit." Apollo snapped.

"What are you going to do to keep the Irish from going to other sellers?"

"I have no idea. I can't offer them anything without losing a shit ton of money. I can't decide if I want to lose profits for the next quarter or lose the Irish."

"Have you considered dropping smaller jobs and backfilling until we figure this out?"

"Run the numbers, but I don't think it's worth the risk."

"We could just tell them what happened. Be honest about our thief. They've stuck with us through worse." I suggested.

"I don't want-"

Apollo was interrupted by a knock on a door.

"Come in."

"You promised me today off." Junior complained.

I looked over at Apollo and then snapped my head back at Junior.

"What the fuck was that?" I shouted.

Junior and Apollo looked at each other confused.

"When the fuck did you learn how to knock? Where's the singing? The shrieks from the hallway?" I asked.

"Mr. Costa doesn't like the singing." Junior answered.

"And I do?!" I asked.

"Oh please, you love my singing. It's the best part of your day." Junior joked.

I looked over at Apollo, "I'm going to kill him."

"Wait until after the meeting."

I hit Junior on the head with the folder I was holding and then went back to work. Junior sat on Apollo's cigar couch and struggled to stay awake. His head fell every few seconds.

"Why do I have to go?" He yawned.

"Dunne likes you. Your only job at this meeting is to keep him laughing. If he's happy he might not notice how much of his order we're missing." Apollo explained.

The garage door slammed shut and someone came in screaming. Alex's shouting echoed off the wall.

"Shit!" Junior yelled before jumping out of his chair.

"What did you do this time?" I asked.

"I broke one of the guesthouse windows." He admitted.

"How?" Apollo asked.

"Juliette and I were playing golf ball hockey out by the pool."

Apollo pinched his nose and dropped his shoulders. He let out a deep sigh and then looked up at Junior.

"How bad is it?"

"We hit one of his bedroom windows." He admitted.

Alex stormed into the office looking for Junior. I took a step in front of Junior, giving him a chance to hide behind me.

"Stay out of this Dane." Alex yelled.

"I can't do that Alex. We need him."

Junior poked his head out above my shoulder. It only pissed Alex off more.

"It's colder than a fucking freezer in my room right now. My fish tank has frost on it."

"I know you're mad, but we need him at the meeting with Dunne today. Torture him when we get back, but I need him alive for the next three hours." Apollo told him.

Alex pointed a finger at Junior, "I'm going to drown you in my frozen fish tank you dipshit."

Junior being the idiot that he was, stepped out in front of me.

"Would an apology help this situation at all?" He asked.

Alex looked at Apollo, almost waiting for permission to drag him out by his collar.

"Three hours." Apollo ordered.

Alex left Apollo's office as angry as he came in. I looked over at Junior and gave him a disappointed look.

"Golf ball hockey?"

"We couldn't find any pucks." He explained.

"You know he's going to destroy everything you love right? He's probably ripping your posters off the walls and snapping your records in half right now. I'd be surprised if you're still living in the guest house when you come back." Apollo told him.

"Are you and Eliana interested in having a guest for a few days? At least until he cools down?" Junior asked.

I laughed at the idea of Junior staying in the main house. Apollo didn't find it as funny as I did.

"If I come back to the house tonight and find you in any of my guest rooms I will throw you out of the window." Apollo said.

I had to bite my tongue to stop from laughing. It was day one and I didn't want to piss Apollo off more than he already was.

"We should go." I told the both of them.

Apollo gave Junior a death glare then left for the garage. I followed behind him still struggling to hide my smile. Junior scanned the hallway before running to catch up with us.

I waited for Apollo to get in the front seat before walking over to the driver's side. Junior quietly stepped into the back of the SUV. We were driving out of the neighborhood when Junior grabbed both of our seats.

"Wait!"

Apollo and I looked back at him, confused again by his weird behavior.

"I smell cupcakes." He said.

Apollo hit his head on his head rest, "I can't. I just can't Dane."

"Red velvet, behind my seat." I told him.

"They're upside down! The icing is all over the place." Junior complained.

"I'm sure that won't stop you from eating them." I told him.

"I'm telling Kate you dropped them."

"And I'm going to let Alex actually kill you." I threatened.

Junior took the hint and ate in silence. Apollo and I worked through ways to work with the Irish as we drove.

"I really do think you should just tell them what's happening."

"I can't risk them telling me they don't trust our ability to come through for them. I would rather lose money from other clients than have them doubting us or spreading word about what's happened." Apollo said.

"These are really good." Junior interrupted.

I looked through the rear view window, "She used beet powder this time."

"No shit." He smiled, "I told her that would work."

"It's like I'm fucking invisible." Apollo complained.

"Oh sorry, beet powder is an alternative to aggravating red dyes used in food. I told her about different ways to keep her color in her desserts. She promised me so long ago she'd make them. I almost forgot all about it." Junior rambled.

"Junior." Apollo said.

"Yes?"

"Eat your cupcakes." He said turning around to look at him dead in his eyes.

"Yes sir."

Apollo sat back in his seat and then looked at me.

"How many more minutes?"

"Fifteen." I answered.

"Make it five."

I stood behind Apollo with Junior next to me. We sat with Dunne in the bar his nephew ran. He wouldn't meet with us at one of our locations. Apollo walked into this meeting unsure what he was going to do about the inventory problem. I'm still not sure he has any idea what to do.

The guns hadn't even been brought up in conversation. Dunne was too busy talking to Apollo about their busy winter season. It was a busy year for his family. Apollo sat and pretended to care. For a minute or two they talked about distribution out in Chicago. Junior kept hitting my shoulder to tell me something, but I kept ignoring him. He became frustrated and hit me harder than he probably should have which caused Dunne to look up at us.

"And how are you doing Junior?"

"No complaints." He smiled.

"Apollo working you too hard?"

"Never."

"You look nervous boy." Dunne told him.

"If I'm being honest sir, there's a friend of mine waiting to throw me in a fish tank. I'm kind of hoping this meeting lasts for a while."

Dunne let out a deep laugh. Apollo just shook his head.

"A fish tank?"

"Pay back for a broken window, sir." He admitted.

"You wouldn't be the one threatening our Junior now would you Dane?" He asked.

"Of course not." I answered.

"It's been a while since I've seen you Dane. Everything okay?"

"Everything's fine. I've been a little busy with work." I lied.

"That's code for he met a girl." Junior joked.

Dunne let out another energetic laugh. It echoed across the empty bar. I gave Junior a side eye I hoped would kill him and then looked back at Dunne.

"You're just as bad as Apollo." He said. "Ever since that wedding you've caused a few problems for the family."

"I can promise I haven't." Apollo answered, a little too short.

"Oh don't worry Apollo. I'm not upset, I remember those first few months after my wedding with Claire. Enjoy it now while you can. Soon you'll be in your fifties and you'll wonder where all the time went."

Apollo nodded his head in agreement.

"Are you the reason my deliveries have been short this past month Dane?" Dunne asked.

"No, sir."

"Dunne, I promise you we're doing everything we can to fix your deliveries. We just need a little more time."

"How much time?"

"A week, two weeks tops."

"And what am I supposed to do in the meantime? You hurt us all when you fuck up and lose your supply. I'm hurting here Apollo."

"I know you are. So tell me what I can do to make this better and I'll do it."

"I'll give you two weeks. If I don't have my full order by the end of the month I'll find another distributor. And you won't like how I leave. I'll make sure any future clients of yours wonder if they're going to the right family."

"Two weeks, and the next three months of deliveries are on us. Consider it our apology for causing problems for you."

"You're too kind Apollo." Dunne smiled. "Deal, I'll call you in two weeks with a location I want my guns sent to."

"Thank you."

Dunne's men stood back from the table and waved to the door. It was time for us to leave. Apollo walked over to the exit with Junior and I close behind him.

"Give Eliana my best Apollo."

"Of course." He smiled.

The three of us walked back to the car and then sped off back to the house.

"Two weeks." Apollo scoffed, "Two fucking weeks."

"That's not that bad." I lied.

"We have no leads and months of missing inventory. It is bad."

"I just don't get it." Junior said.

"What don't you get?" Apollo asked.

"How did no one see anything? I mean it's not like they stole something small, they stole guns. You don't just walk out with a crate of guns in broad daylight."

I tapped on the steering wheel at a red light. Junior's right. No one walked out with the guns. That would be too obvious.

"He's right." I mumbled.

"What?" Apollo asked.

"Junior's right. No one walked out with our guns. We let them leave."

"I don't understand."

"What would we have done if someone working at the docks or warehouse tried leaving with a truck of our guns?"

"We'd ask them where they were going, who they were meeting with."

"Exactly. We already know that none of our trucks that left the warehouse left without approval. They all had approved, paid for, deliveries. But what if each time a truck left it drove off with one or two extra crates. Not enough to sell all at once, but enough to get past the gates without raising suspicion." Apollo said.

"Someone's been packing up our trucks with more than they should and dropping them off somewhere before getting to their planned drop off location. We wouldn't have noticed anyone loading up the truck with one too many crates and no one at the gate is going to question an approved delivery. Especially if I've already signed off on it." I said.

"Who knows how long it took someone to steal as much as they did. A few deliveries a week with one or two crates would mean they've been stealing for months. A lot longer than we thought they were. We only noticed the missing inventory from a few weeks ago because they got cocky and started to take more." I continued to explain.

"So what changed a few months ago that we wouldn't have been paying attention to? We've been running guns out of that warehouse for over a year. What changed between then and now?" Apollo asked.

"I don't know." I told him.

Junior leaned closer into the middle console and joined the conversation.

"Let's figure this out. One: You get engaged to Eliana. Two: You two go to Italy. Three: Raff takes over Chicago. Four: You go rogue and hunt down Giovanni. "Five: You magically make it back in time for the wedding. Six: You and Eliana get married, it's magical. Seven: Guns go missing.-"

"Wait." Apollo said, interrupting Junior.

"Did I solve it?" Junior asked.

Apollo ignored him, "Chicago."

"What about it?" I asked.

"A few months ago Raff hired his own men to run guns from our warehouse to Chicago. Those are the only deliveries we don't track because all the payments and orders go through Raff. They've been coming to us for our supply and taking it to Chicago. It took so long to notice because until a month ago Raff only had three drivers. He hired more when we started delivering to the West Coast."

"Someone from Chicago is stealing our guns. What do you want to do?" I asked.

"We're going to Chicago." Apollo said.

"When do you want to leave?" I asked.

"Right now."

"Can I come?" Junior asked.

Apollo rolled his eyes, "Call Alex. He's coming with us."

"Never mind, I think I'll stay here."

Apollo looked behind him, "You're coming with."

"Great." Junior groaned.

I pulled up to the house and waited until Junior and Apollo left before calling Kate. I walked into the house and waited for her to answer.

"Hey."

"Hi." I replied.

"How'd your meeting go?" She asked.

"Better than I thought it would."

"What's wrong?" She asked.

"How do you know something's wrong?"

"I have this terrible feeling you're about to tell me something bad."

"Apollo and I have to go to Chicago." I told her.

"When are you leaving?"

"Right now."

"Why?"

"We think we figured out our thief problem."

"When will you be back?" She asked.

"I don't know. That's why I'm calling. It could be a few days."

"Well I'll miss you, but this is a good thing."

"How is this good?" I asked.

"Because you're back where you belong, which is helping Apollo." She said.

"Yeah, I guess you're right."

I was leaned up against the stairs talking with Kate when Junior came running down.

"Is that Kate?" He shouted.

"Go away." I told him.

Evergreen Ivy

He ignored me and grabbed the phone, "Kate!"

I tried but failed to get the phone back from him. He was too fast. He ran right past me down the stairs.

"They were incredible. I wouldn't have known about the powder if Dane hadn't said anything. You have to use it to make those pink mini cupcakes."

I reached for Junior's shoulder and pulled him back to me.

"Kate, I have to go. Dane caught me. But please try those mini-"

I grabbed the phone out of Junior's hand and held it back up to my ear. On the other line I could hear Kate having a laughing fit. I listened to her try and catch her breath.

"Is he going to Chicago?" She asked.

"Unfortunately." I scowled at him.

Junior gave me a satisfied smile and stuck around to hear the rest of our conversation.

"I'm sure you have lots to do before you leave, so I'll let you go." She said.

"Text me when you close." I told her.

"I will, promise."

A loud crash echoed through the phone, "Dane I have to go. A bird just flew into the window!"

"Of course it did." I laughed.

"Be safe, call me later. Love you, bye!" She shouted through the phone before hanging up.

Love you, bye.

I looked over at Junior to see if he heard what she'd said before she hung up. He quickly turned around and looked right up at the ceiling like it was the most interesting thing he'd ever seen. That meant she definitely said what I thought she said. Apollo walked in and looked at the two of us.

"What happened?" He asked.

Junior opened his mouth to tell him what he'd heard, but I pulled him closer to me and covered his mouth.

"Nothing." I lied.

"Then let's go. Alex is outside waiting."

Apollo walked out ahead of us. Junior walked right beside me with a grin that stretched from ear to ear.

"She *loves* you." He teased.

"Shut the fuck up."

"And you didn't say it back." He sighed.

"I didn't get the chance. She hung up on me too fast."

"So you're saying if she hadn't hung up you would have said it back?"

"Shut. The. Fuck. Up." I warned.

Junior ran to the car laughing. His laughing died down when he saw how angry Alex still was. I pretended I needed to catch up on some sleep so that I could hide in one of the back rooms for the flight. When we landed Junior was still smiling, forcing me to relive my phone call with Kate.

Junior was right. I should have said something back before she hung up, but I panicked. I never panic. I had to talk to Kate. I needed a chance to explain myself. I tried calling her again, but it went to voicemail. I tried one more time, but Apollo came over to the car ready to leave. I hung up and threw my phone in my pocket.

"We're going to visit Raff first."

"Does he know we're coming?" I asked Apollo.

"No."

Alex and I were waiting outside Raff's office together. Junior was standing beside me doing his best to get Alex to forgive him. Apollo was in Raff's office alone talking to a pissed Raff. Eliana's brother, Raffael, was not happy we paid him a surprise visit. He threw a fit and demanded we leave immediately. It only took a little convincing to let us onto the property of his warehouse. We could hear parts of Apollo's conversation with Raff and it wasn't going well.

"So, you back for good?" Alex asked me.

"Yeah."

"I'm sorry for what happened to Kate."

I didn't answer him. Remembering what Apollo did to Kate was still a little raw.

Alex ignored my annoyance and kept talking, "From what I've heard from Eliana she seems really great."

Again I ignored him.

"Kate's great." Junior answered for me.

"I wasn't talking to you." Alex snapped.

"You know what would really make this moment special? If you forgave me." Junior said.

Alex leaned off the wall and looked past me at Junior.

"I thought we agreed on a no talking rule for you on the plane."

"And I thought we were best friends, but sometimes life disappoints us." Junior said.

Why did I come back? I was happy at Ivy's. I got to spend all of my time with Kate. Junior and Alex never went anywhere near the bakery. It was a good life.

I tuned back into the conversation when I heard my name.

"Just ask Dane. I am full of remorse. I reflected on the hurt I caused you the whole drive back from Dunne's." Junior argued.

"Are you comfortable in small spaces?" Alex asked him.

"Yes actually. Perfectly fine." Junior lied.

Thank God the office door opened and Apollo waved for me to come in. Before I walked inside I looked at Alex.

"He's lying. He's terrified of the dark."

I could hear Alex's laugh and Junior's cries even after the door closed. This might be my first time ever happy to be stuck in a room with Raff.

"Raff here swears he has no idea who's stealing our guns." Apollo said.

"Why would I steal from you?"

"If it's not you then who is it?" I asked Raff.

"That's what you get to find out. Raff agreed for you to meet all of his drivers."

"Apollo says you shouldn't need more than a few days to figure it out, but I can't lose two days of work. Figure out who your thief is and let the rest get back to work." Raff said.

"How do we know it's not all of them?" I asked.

"You really think all of my men have been stealing from you?" Raff asked.

"I guess we'll find out. Anything off limits?"

Apollo shook his head no, "Do your worst."

"I want all of your men in the warehouse in five minutes." I told Raff.

Raff looked back at Apollo to see if I was serious. Apollo's face stood cold, unbothered.

"Sure thing." He sighed when he saw just how serious Apollo was.

Raff left the two of us alone in his office.

"The sooner you take care of this the sooner we get to go home." Apollo said, standing up.

"It won't take long." I promised.

"If Raff gives you any trouble I want to know about it. He understood who was in charge when we agreed to work together. This may be his company, but I don't have any problems taking it away from him. Do you need Alex to help with this one?" Apollo asked.

"No."

I left the office and waited out front of Raff's warehouse. I watched the drivers come in one by one. This was my first job since being back. I wanted to really enjoy it, take my time, but I couldn't. Kate was waiting for me back home.

Raff walked over to me and handed me a paper with a few names on it.

"This is everybody. I wrote down their names and their schedules for you." He said.

"I won't need that."

Raff folded the paper up and put it into his pocket, "Make it an easy clean up please."

He closed the door and left me alone with his men. A few of them were annoyed that I'd interrupted their work. A few looked nervous. The rest were too young to be working here.

"Do you know why you're here?" I asked.

None of them answered.

"I'm here because someone here has been stealing from me. Well, not me exactly, but let's just assume from here on out that when you steal from Apollo Costa you're also stealing from me."

The men who were leaned against the wall or sitting down stood up. I had their undivided attention the minute I mentioned Apollo.

"Who's idea was it?" I asked.

Silence. No one answered me.

"I have to admit it was a solid plan. It would have been months before either of us noticed our missing guns." I walked over and locked the door.

"Problem is you got greedy. You wanted more."

"If Mr. Costa really is upset about his missing guns then why did he send you? Shouldn't he be here right now?" A man in the back of the room asked.

"You all are my welcome back gift." I explained.

"We didn't steal anything from you." The same man shouted out.

"I wish I believed you Will. That is your name right? William Campbell?"

The man took a step back.

"How's Carly adjusting at her new school? The move to Chicago must have been hard on her. Middle school can be so tough."

At the mention of his daughter's name Will stepped forward.

"Kristen must be pretty close to her due date right? Is this baby number three or four?"

"This has nothing to do with them." He seethed.

"It has everything to do with them. Before you were hired I did background checks on every single one of you. There isn't anything you can hide from me. You may make runs for Raff but it's me you work for. I know all about your dirty little secrets. Isn't that right Jacob."

Jacob, our newest driver, looked up at me.

"Having a hard time after the divorce? It must be hard watching your ex-wife move on with that new husband of hers. Is he Navy or Marines? I keep forgetting." I asked.

"Fuck off." He spat.

"You've been spending a lot of your time and money at that dancer's club right off the exit on your way to Dolton. Money I'm betting you got from selling guns."

"I don't know shit about your stolen guns." He lied.

I pulled out my gun and set it down on a desk near the front of the room.

"You all have ten minutes. I either leave here with the men who stole from me, or I leave with no one. You decide."

Panic grew in the room. Almost instantly I knew who was innocent. They looked around at their friends confused and pissed off to be put in a situation like this.

Jacob tried to run to a narrow hallway off behind me. He barely made it a few steps before I grabbed him. I threw him to the ground in front of the other men and dislocated his shoulder. Jacob dropped to the floor screaming.

"Who else helped?" I asked Jacob, towering over him.

"No one else knew about the guns."

I knew he was lying so I grabbed his hurt arm and pulled him up by it. The other men watched as I dragged Jacob around the room. I forced the men he worked with to watch him pay for what he'd stolen. Eventually Jacob got used to the pain and was able to shift his weight. I forced Jacob onto his feet and pistol whipped him. Not hard enough to knock him out, but enough to drop him back to the floor.

Like I knew he would, he tried to stand up again. He held his bleeding temple with his good hand. I raised my arm to hit him again but was stopped by Leon.

"For Christ's sake, let him go. It wasn't his idea."

The man who stepped forward wasn't new to the life. Raff hired Leon as one of his drivers after Leon retired. He was barely a part timer, but he had the connections to run guns. Leon worked his entire life for Raffael's dad. It was a surprise to find out he was behind the missing guns.

I turned from Jacob to Leon. With my eyes off him Jacob sulked back into the group.

"When did it start?" I asked him.

"A few months after Raff hired me to be a driver. I needed the money and I knew the market."

"Why Jacob?" I asked.

"It was easy. You've met him. He's not the brightest. I told him how much we could make and after the first job he wanted more." Leon said.

"Who were you selling to?"

"Some small-time guys trying to make a name for themselves. A few people who thought Raff was charging too much."

"How much of it do you still have? What hasn't sold?"

"Not a lot. We were able to sell a lot of pieces individually. No one in this area bought in large quantities. They didn't want that kind of attention."

"You know what happens next right?" I asked.

"Just make it quick." Leon said.

I held up my gun and shot him twice in the chest. I walked over to him and watched until I was sure he was gone. I grabbed Jacob and looked around to the others.

"Get back to work."

I took Jacob back with me to Raff's office.

"Shit." Raff cursed when he saw me carry in Jacob.

"Raff, I can explain." Jacob tried to convince.

"Shut the fuck up." Raff warned.

I looked over to Apollo, "It was Leon's idea. It'd be a waste of time to hunt down what they sold. It's scattered all over the place. No one bought in large orders to keep the heat off them."

"Where's Leon?" Raff asked.

"Warehouse. You'll want someone to come in and clean that up."

"I'll send over our inventory losses. You have two months to recover whatever they still have hidden away somewhere plus interest on what they've already sold." Apollo told him.

"That's bullshit!" Raff argued.

"Is it?" Apollo asked.

"I think it's more than fair." I told Raff.

"I don't owe you shit. It wasn't me who stole from you."

"When I agreed to give you my Chicago operations you promised me there wouldn't be any problems. And while you might not think so, two of your drivers stealing my guns is a big problem. Is this you telling me you can't handle your responsibilities here? Should I be looking for a replacement?" Apollo asked.

Raff said nothing.

"Two months." Apollo told him again before leaving his office.

I tried to walk out behind Apollo but was stopped by Raff.

"Forgetting something?" He asked.

"I don't think so."

Raff pointed over at Jacob, "So you just plan on leaving him here in my office?"

"You'll need all the help you can get if you plan on getting any of those guns back to us."

"It's nice to see you back at work. I thought maybe when I heard you'd agreed to come back to work it meant you negotiated a better job, but I see you're still Apollo's bitch."

Raff has always been all talk. He's angry and he can't take it out on Apollo. I had my hand on the door handle already halfway out the door when he made the mistake of bringing Kate into this.

"Are you sure that girl of yours is fine with you coming back to work? Seems a little too soon don't you think? I mean, I'd bet money Kate's still having nightmares. This must be torture for her."

As soon as I turned around Raff knew he'd made a big mistake. He took a step back, fear in his eyes.

"You know, I never liked you Raffael."

He took another step back.

"If it weren't for Apollo I'd have killed you by now. Apollo says you're off limits because of how devastating it would be for Eliana to lose a brother, but I've never felt that way. I think to lose you she would only benefit. How pathetic to even call you a brother. To call Eliana family."

Raff was running out of steps to take.

"I'd hate to have to tell Eliana I killed you but I would enjoy every minute of watching you beg for your life."

I grabbed Raff's collar and punched him until his body dropped to the floor. I let go when his head fell back onto the hardwood floor. He lifted his head up to look at me.

"If I ever hear Kate's name leave your mouth again I will stitch your lips together and slowly and carefully watch you bleed out. I will watch you squirm and listen to your muffled cries as you die alone with no one to truly mourn you."

I left Raff's office before I got carried away and hit him again. Apollo was waiting for me in the hallway.

"Is he still alive?"

"Unfortunately." I told him.

Apollo grabbed my shoulder as he walked past me down the hallway, "Let's go home."

As soon as we took off back to New York I snuck up to the front of the plane to hide from Alex and Junior. They'd been bickering since leaving Raff's. The only minute of peace we got on the drive to the plane was when Apollo threatened to leave them both in Chicago if they said another word. I had almost fallen asleep when Apollo came over with drinks. He sat my drink down in front of me and sat on the chair across from me.

"That might have been the fastest you've ever taken care of a job. I thought for sure you'd take your time with this one." He said.

"I didn't want to be stuck in Chicago any longer than we needed to be."

"Sure." He smiled, taking a sip of his drink.

"You have something to say?" I asked.

"Junior told me about your phone call with Kate."

"Alright, good talk." I said standing up.

"Sit down." Apollo laughed.

I sat back down and watched the ice in my drink swirl.

"It's terrifying isn't it?" Apollo asked.

"What?"

"The feelings you have for Kate. It makes you feel so human, so vulnerable." He said.

"Is this how you felt with Eliana?"

"Worse." He admitted.

"Am I doing the wrong thing? Is it selfish of me to want her in my life?" I asked.

"I think Kate being a part of her life is her choice to make."

"Still, I'll never be able to explain to her the danger she's putting herself in by just being with me. I'm afraid one day she'll feel pressured to stay and won't know how to tell me she's miserable. She'll feel stuck."

"Does Kate ever do anything she doesn't want to do?" He asked.

"No."

"No, she doesn't. Kate chose you; she's changed her life to better fit you in it. Only a fool would doubt that kind of commitment Dane."

Apollo's wise advice was interrupted by a crash towards the back of the plane. I looked over my shoulder and found Junior in a headlock. I looked over at Apollo and saw him watching Junior with worry.

"He's a good kid Apollo." I told him.

"I know."

"You can't keep blaming yourself for what happened to his dad. It wasn't your fault."

"I know." He said again, "It's just sometimes I'm afraid we're doing the wrong thing by letting him work with us. I promised his dad I'd keep him safe. Some days I'm afraid Alessio is going to come back from the grave just to yell at me for dragging Junior back into this life."

"Who was it that just told me we aren't responsible for the choices others make?" I asked.

"This is different. This isn't about you or Kate. This is about doing what's best for that kid over there." Apollo said.

"And the safest thing for him is being a part of your family. I promise Alessio wouldn't want it any other way."

Apollo looked over at Junior, still not convinced.

I pointed over at Alex and Junior, "There is nothing that boy wants more than to be here working for us, Apollo. He's better off here where we can take care of him.

"Yeah, you're right." Apollo sighed.

"I'm always right."

Apollo and I watched Alex torture Junior all the way back to New York. As soon as we landed I rushed off the plane. There were two cars waiting for us on the tarmac. Apollo walked down the stairs and stood with me.

"I had an extra car sent over. Thought you wouldn't want to drive back with us to the house."

"Thank you."

"It's the middle of the night but I figured you didn't want to wait until morning to see her." He said.

I grabbed the keys from one of Apollo's men and threw my bags in the back seat. As I drove off I could hear Alex and Junior shouting after me but I didn't care. Whatever they had to tease me about wasn't worth my time. All I cared about was getting back to Kate.

The lights were off in Ivy's when I pulled up. I quietly let myself in the front and walked up to her apartment. There was a good chance I scared her with my surprise arrival, but I didn't care. I needed to see her.

I found her asleep, covers tangled all about. I turned on one of her lamps and sat near her. She must have been exhausted because nothing could wake her. She didn't even notice when the mattress dipped as I sat down.

I ran my hands through her hair trying to softly wake her up. A sleeping Kate swatted my hand away and let out an annoyed grunt. I tried again to wake her up, but she was out cold.

I leaned down and left kisses on her cheek all the way down to her neck. Finally I got a reaction out of her.

"Dane?"

"I need you to wake up for me, baby." I whispered in her ear.

"Why?" She whispered, already falling back asleep.

"Because I have something important to tell you."

"Can it wait until morning?" She asked, eyes still closed.

"No." I said, kissing her temple.

"Okay, fine. I'm awake." She lied; eyes still closed.

"Kate."

"Ugh, okay you win. I'm up." She said, crawling out of the covers and sitting across from me, "What did you need to tell me? It better be important. You know what happens when I don't get my six hours. It's bad enough I had to open Ivy's every day this week. Last night Amanda canceled on me and I had to close. Everyday I get a little closer to selling the shop and running away to the desert. I wouldn't match the aesthetic and I hate the heat, but at least no one would be able to find me. I might finally actually get a good night's sleep-"

When Kate began to ramble like this there was no stopping her. I grabbed her by the jaw and kissed her to get her to shut up.

"Kate, I love you."

"What?" She asked.

"I love you and I had to wait all day to tell you. I know how important your sleep is to you, but it felt like I might actually explode if I had to wait another minute. And as much as I hate the desert, if you ever do decide to move there just promise to bring me with you."

"Is this a dream? Am I dreaming?" She asked.

"You're not dreaming Kate."

"You love me?" She asked, reaching out to touch my face.

"I love you."

I grabbed her hand and kissed her palm.

"You love me."

"Mhmm."

"Well I love you." She said.

"Good." I smiled.

"Good." She whispered.

I watched Kate's eyes bounce around the room. She looked around like she still wasn't convinced this wasn't a dream. I ran my thumb over her hands to remind her this was real. She looked down at our hands tangled together.

"Come on. Let's go back to bed." I told her.

I leaned off the bed and walked over to Kate's closet. I threw my clothes near her door and walked back to the bed. When I looked over at her she was already staring, a big grin on her face.

"You open tomorrow?" I asked.

"Unfortunately." She groaned.

"Then we really need to get to bed. I can't have you angry at me tomorrow because you didn't get a full night's sleep."

"It's too late for that. I can feel it in my bones. I'll be mildly annoyed all day thanks to you." She said.

"I'm the worst."

"Yeah, the worst." She smiled.

I pulled her into my arms and played with her hair. We laid together, foreheads nearly touching. I waited for her eyes to close, but her eyes followed mine.

"Kate…"

"Yeah?"

"We won't be going to bed if you keep looking at me like that." I told her.

"Just say it one more time."

I pulled her head into my chest and wrapped my arms around her.

"I love you."

Kate squeezed my arm in excitement.

"Go to bed, baby." I whispered.

Kate finally relaxed in my arms and let herself fall back asleep. I ignored the voices in my head that told me Kate deserved better. For tonight all I could worry about was getting to hold the woman I love more than anything in the world as she slept.

CHAPTER TEN

Kate

"We could try pies?" Becca suggested.

"Ugh."

"No, listen! It could be really cute. We could make mini ones and we could display them in cute little baskets!" Becca said, trying to convince me.

"I'm just not a pie person." I told her.

"Oh well then that settles it. Forget how much money we'd make selling cute little adorable still warm from the oven pies. If you don't like it then what's the point?" She said.

"You know what I mean. I've just never been able to master the perfect pie."

"Kate, it's just pie. It doesn't need to be perfect."

"I do like the idea of getting to buy mini pie tins." I told her.

"And we could make the crusts look like cute little flowers or we could do that cute cross stitch pattern. It would be perfect for summer."

"Okay."

"Okay we can do pies?" She asked.

"Okay, I'll think about it."

I grabbed my phone and saw that it was already past six. I promised Dane I'd be at his place for dinner by now.

"Shit."

"What's wrong?"

"I was supposed to be at Dane's ten minutes ago."

"Do you think Dane likes pie?"

"I doubt it." I said, grabbing my purse and jacket, "I just don't get the pie vibe from him."

"You're only saying that because you don't like pie."

"Not true."

"You just don't want to admit you could potentially be dating a pie guy."

I can't believe this is an actual real conversation I'm having right now.

"How about this, I'll ask Dane if he likes pie and if he does you can add it to the menu."

"Deal." Becca smiled.

I walked over to the back alley door with Becca right behind me.

"Text me if anything happens before closing. And make sure you lock up, don't leave until you hear that beeping from the security system."

"Oh my God, I left one time without checking to make sure the sensors were on. Just leave already, please."

By the time I made it to Dane's place it was almost seven. I let myself in and found take out on the table. I had found the food but not Dane. I walked around the entire house but couldn't find him.

"Dane!" I shouted into the empty house.

Nothing. I made one more trip around the house. I heard the water turn on from one of the guest rooms, so I went snooping. Well, it technically wasn't snooping, but I did do my best to sneak into the room without Dane hearing me.

I tried to slowly creak open the bathroom door but was caught immediately.

"Kate?" Dane asked, turning around in the shower.

"Crap."

"What's wrong?"

"How did you hear me?" I asked.

"That was you trying to be quiet? You ran around the house three times. It took you nearly a minute to get across the bedroom and into here."

"I was trying to go slow. I thought that was what people did if they didn't want to be heard."

Dane laughed and shook his head. I watched through the blurred clear glass as he rinsed down his arms. I considered joining him but stopped when I saw his bloody clothes in the hamper.

"How was work?" I asked.

"Not great."

"You want to talk about it?"

"No." He answered.

I couldn't join Dane in the shower but I didn't want to leave, so I sat up on the sink counter and waited for him to get out. Dane turned around surprised to see me still here in the bathroom with him.

"How was Ivy's?" He asked.

"The warm weather means we have more customers coming in. It will be time to open up the patio again soon."

"Is Becca okay closing alone tonight?"

"She practically kicked me out the door. Speaking of Becca, do you like pies?" I asked.

"Yeah, I guess so. Why?"

"Damn, he's a pie man." I whispered to myself.

"What'd you say?" He asked, his head thrown back under the running water.

"I asked what type of pies you liked."

"Oh um, cherry, chocolate, pecan's always good." He said.

"I don't think this is going to work out."

Dane shut off the water and slid the glass door back.

"Say that again?"

"I had fun, but I don't think this is going to work. I just don't see myself settling down with someone who likes pecan pie."

Dane stepped out and grabbed a towel.

"Well we had a good run."

"We sure did." I smiled.

Dane came over to the sink and towered over me. His hands dropped to either side of me. His hair dripped onto my shirt.

Dane tried to give me a kiss but I pushed him away. I jumped off the sink and walked back into his bedroom.

"Where are you going?" He asked.

"I have to go call Becca."

"Why?"

Evergreen Ivy

"I have to tell her she gets to sell pies at Ivy's." I sighed.

Dane got dressed and met me in the kitchen for dinner. I was doing my best to ignore him but it wasn't easy. After a failed attempt at getting my attention Dane finally cracked.

"It's not my fault! My grandma made the best pies. Every time we went to visit her there was always a pie on the counter."

"I understand cherry, blueberry even, but pecan? I feel like I don't even know you anymore." I told him.

"Would it help our situation if I lied?" He asked.

"It might."

"I hate pecan pie. It's terrible. There are no good childhood memories associated with it."

Dane waited for a reaction, "Feel any better?"

"No."

"You were right. Becca was wrong, pies are a terrible idea." He lied again.

"I can't even look at you right now." I told him.

Dane got up from the table and kissed the top of my head, "I'll be in the kitchen doing the dishes. Let me know when you aren't angry at me so we can hang out."

As Dane walked away I continued to shout at him.

"It could be a few days. I might not even be able to stay here tonight!"

"Tragic." Dane yelled back.

When I heard the bell ring the last person I expected to walk through the door was Dane. It was too early for him to be off work.

Dane laid on his biggest, charming smile as he walked over to me. *Oh no.*

"Hey." He said.

Of all the terrifying things about Dane this smile was the scariest thing about him.

"What happened this time? Apollo sending you away again? Did another warehouse blow up?" I asked.

"You always assume the worst."

"Okay so it's good news?" I asked.

"You look radiant today. So gorgeous." Dane said, trying to distract.

"Dane..."

"Okay fine. We've been invited to dinner."

"That doesn't sound like a bad thing." I said.

"We've been invited to dinner with Eliana and Apollo."

"Ah, there it is."

"I told them I wasn't sure if you'd want to go. I even asked El not to spam call you and pressure you into going. They said they'd totally understand if you aren't ready for something like that." Dane said.

"Why wouldn't I want to go?" I asked.

"Eliana and I weren't sure you'd want to spend your Friday night stuck at a dinner with Apollo. As excited and anxious as Eliana is to spend time with you she knows you and Apollo don't have the best relationship."

While I wasn't thrilled about having to spend time with Apollo I had been missing Eliana. It'd been a while since she'd visited me here. No doubt because she was trying to respect my space.

"Yeah, let's do it."

"Really?" Dane asked.

"Why not? Could be fun."

"Okay, I'll go call Eliana."

Dane looked over his shoulder one more time when he got to the kitchen door.

"Are you sure?" He asked.

"Yes. I'm sure." I told him.

Dane disappeared into the kitchen and I continued on cleaning the front of the shop. When he came out he grabbed the broom that was leaning against the wall and helped me clean.

Every few minutes he would look over at me, worry on his face.

"Dane, you're killing me." I finally snapped.

"Sorry." He said, going back to cleaning.

I watched and waited for him to look at me again. When he looked up I was already staring.

"It's just. We've never really talked about how we'd handle situations where you and Apollo would be forced to hang out."

"I promise you I can handle dinner with Apollo. I appreciate your concern but I knew there would be times we'd want to hang out with our friends. Should I bring anything?"

"Anything you have left over from tonight? Oh and Apollo has Junior working security tonight so bring him something for later. He said he'll need the sugar to stay awake."

I looked over at Dane with a smile.

"What?" He asked.

"It's real sweet you remembered to bring Junior something."

"I didn't remember. He heard our dinner plans from the hallway and hasn't stopped texting me about dessert since I drove over here."

"Right, that's the only reason." I smiled.

"It is. I just want the texts to stop."

"Mhmm."

"I hate when you do that." He said.

"Do what?" I asked.

"That." Dane pointed at my knowing smile.

"Not sure what you're talking about." I lied reaching for a chair.

Dane came over and grabbed the chair I was reaching for, "Go upstairs and get ready."

"But-"

"I'll take care of things down here. Go."

I kissed Dane on the cheek and ran up the stairs into the apartment. Now that I was alone I had time to figure out how I felt about dinner. I hadn't spoken to or seen Apollo since that night he came back to Ivy's. It was no secret I didn't like him. At best he was tolerable. I thought it'd be easier to avoid spending time with him but I failed to consider Eliana wanting to spend time with me.

After grabbing a coat and turning off the lights I walked downstairs with Dane. He went to the kitchen and grabbed a few boxes of treats and then met me at the door. He handed me a falling box and used his now free hand to rest his arm over my shoulders. It wasn't until we were driving through Apollo's neighborhood did I start to feel the nerves.

"What happens if I say the wrong thing? Is there anything I shouldn't bring up? What if we run out of things to talk about? You should have made a list of approved conversation topics." I rambled.

"Kate, breathe." Dane laughed.

"I'm serious Dane! I don't know anything about Apollo. The only thing I sort of know about him is what he does for work and our last two visits with each other weren't that great."

"I don't think you'll have anything to worry about but if you find yourself struggling to talk about something just signal for me."

"We should have a planned topic ready just in case things get awkward." I said.

"I'm sure we don't need that."

"When's Apollo's birthday?"

"Why do you need to know that?"

"I need to know what his sign is. I can't go into dinner not knowing what he is. I bet he's a Gemini, no Virgo-"

Dane interrupted my panic rambling with a laugh. He grabbed my hand from the middle console.

"You're overthinking this. Once we get inside and you catch up with Eliana you'll feel better."

Dane pulled into Apollo's driveway while I counted to ten to keep myself calm. Dane was right. There was nothing to be nervous about. This was just a dinner with my friend Eliana and her mafia don husband. It'll be a piece of cake.

Eliana must have heard us driving up because she was waiting for us on the porch. With a big wave she greeted us at the front door. I helped Dane grab the boxes from the back seat before walking over to her.

"You made it! How was the drive?" She asked.

"Traffic from the city wasn't terrible. But oh lordy the drive through your neighborhood is something else."

"It's gorgeous isn't it?" She asked, helping me with my boxes and walking up the stairs into the house.

"How hard do you think it would be to convince Dane to get a place near here?" I asked.

Eliana looked back at Dane who was walking a few paces behind us.

"I already asked him why he lives so far away from us. He said something about needing space away from Apollo. He doesn't want to be reachable when he's not working."

"That's a stupid reason. He spends all of his time here with Apollo and when is he ever not reachable?"

"I think he's just terrified of being my neighbor. I'm sure the mere idea of living near me gives him nightmares. I've traumatized the poor boy."

I let out a laugh and walked with Eliana to the kitchen.

"You talking about me?" Dane asked.

"Of course not!" I lied.

Somewhere between the porch and the kitchen Eliana and I lost Dane. I'm sure he went to find Apollo.

"What's with all the boxes?" Eliana asked.

"I brought over a few desserts for dinner and any leftovers I had to give to Junior."

"Well now I'm wondering if three boxes are enough for us plus Junior."

"Don't worry, a few of these are packed pretty tight."

"I'll hide a box just in case." Eliana said.

Coming back from the pantry Eliana handed me a glass of wine.

"So." She sighed.

"So."

"How are you doing?" She asked.

"Great, Ivy's is busier than ever. Becca is finalizing our summer menu, things are great."

"No, I mean how are *you*?"

"Oh um, fine." I answered.

Eliana had more questions. I could see the curiosity in her eyes but she was too afraid to upset me. I didn't want to talk to Eliana about what happened because I was afraid she'd side with Apollo. I'm sure hearing what he'd done to me was upsetting but nothing was more important to Eliana and Apollo than family. Dane was an important person in both of their lives and I got the feeling they'd do anything they needed to do to keep him safe, protected.

"Is there anything I can do to help with dinner?" I asked.

"The table's set, the dessert is hidden, I think all that's left to do is go find Apollo and Dane." Eliana smiled.

Eliana walked back to the front staircase and shouted up to the second floor. Apollo and Dane came out of a room that looked like Apollo's office. When Apollo saw me standing next to Eliana he froze.

Dane caught the tension between the two of us and came over to stand by my side. Apollo brushed off his minor hesitation and walked to Eliana. The four of us made our way to the dining room.

I sat to Dane's right across from Eliana at the table. We all helped each other pass along plates of food and then sat in silence and enjoyed our meal for a few minutes. Apollo was the first one to break the silence.

"Kate, how's it going at Ivy's?"

While the question was awkward I appreciated the effort.

"I was just telling Eliana how busy we have been lately. Numbers are looking good heading into summer."

"Is there anything exciting Becca is making for the new menu?" Eliana asked.

I looked over at Dane and let out a sigh. Dane avoided my eyes and focused on cutting his steak.

"Should I not have asked? Is it a secret?" Eliana asked.

Dane looked over at me and then to Eliana, "They're thinking about selling pies."

"Is that a bad thing?" Eliana asked.

"It's Dane's fault. I didn't want them."

"What's wrong with pies?" Dane asked.

"What isn't wrong with pies?" Apollo mumbled.

"Yes! Thank you!" I shouted pointing my fork over in Apollo's direction.

"You just don't like them because there's too much out of your control. Pies aren't a science, they're an experience." Dane said.

I looked over at Dane, half ready to kill him with the knife I was holding.

"Go ahead, tell them what your favorite pie is."

Dane's smile disappeared, "You promised you wouldn't say anything."

"What is it?" Eliana asked.

"Pecan. It's pecan." I told them.

Apollo looked over at Dane full of disappointment.

Eliana laughed while she refilled her wine.

"Remind me not to ask about the menu next time we invite them over for dinner." Eliana said, looking over at Apollo.

"Or pies." Apollo agreed.

Dane was desperate to change the conversation, "How's the firm El?"

"Terrible. Horrible." She sighed.

"No it's not." Apollo said.

Dane and I waited for one of them to explain what the problem was.

"I'm having a hard time convincing my clients to take their cases to court."

"Why?"

"Most of the women who reach out to me for help end up going back to their partner's. After meeting with me about their options they struggle to take the next steps."

"What's holding them back from taking their case to court?" I asked.

"They worry about being able to financially support themselves or their families if they leave. They won't take the risk of losing their income whether it be shared or dependent on another person." Eliana explained.

Apollo reached over and held Eliana's hand.

"What if income wasn't a problem because you could offer them a job." I spoke up.

Eliana looked over at me, "What do you mean?"

"Maybe more of the women you work with would press charges if they found a job with flexible hours and a really cool boss. A boss who'd let them leave for family emergencies or for court. They wouldn't have to worry about paying next month's bills without their partner's help because they'd be able to work."

"Well yeah, that's the ideal situation but a job like that just doesn't exist." Eliana said.

"But what if it did? What if they came to work for me at Ivy's?"

Everyone at the table stared at me like I was crazy.

"Are you serious?"

"Why wouldn't I be? I need the help and they need the money and flexible hours. Ask Dane I've been short staffed for months. I could offer them part time or full time hours and I'd work with them to help them build up their resume. It wouldn't have to be permanent, just a chance to help them get back on their feet." I offered.

"I can't ask you to do that!" Eliana said.

"Why not?"

"Because…" Eliana thought about it and paused.

"See? It's not a bad idea." I smiled.

Eliana looked over at Apollo.

"It's a good idea my love." He told her.

Apollo looked over at me and gave me a nod of appreciation.

"What do you think?" I asked Dane.

"Kate has been looking to hire more staff. She's been working thirteen hour days just to keep the place open. Any help would mean that Kate could get back to being the boss."

"Do you think Becca would be fine with it?"

"Becca and I are going crazy working together as much as we have been. She would love getting to work with someone that isn't me." I told her.

"You'd really do that for me?"

"Of course!" I told her.

"Are you sure? I can't promise there won't be risk." Eliana said.

"Like what?" Dane asked.

"All of my clients live in fear their abusers will find them. I'd hate for something like that to happen while they're working at Ivy's."

"You're kidding right?" I laughed.

Eliana looked at me and then back at Dane to try and understand what I found so funny.

"You're afraid I'll get an unwanted guest? Someone who might try and break into Ivy's to try and intimidate me? Someone who would try to scare or hurt me?" I asked, looking at Apollo.

"This is different." Apollo said.

"Is it?" I asked.

Eliana squeezed Apollo's hand, "What if I offered security? Having someone at Ivy's would make me feel better during trials or hearings."

"No." I said.

"It's not a bad idea. Having someone there like Junior could help Eliana's clients feel safer." Dane suggested.

I looked at Apollo hoping he could save me from having another one of his men in my shop. He knew I would never agree to it.

"I think one of my guys at Ivy's would only escalate the situation. We don't want anyone working there to feel like they're in danger every time they're at work. They won't be able to move on if we're convincing them they aren't safe at work. They'll struggle to find their own independence." Apollo said.

"Fine but promise me you'll tell Dane if you notice anything suspicious or out of the ordinary. I want you to tell me if something feels wrong or you think someone is intimidating my clients." Eliana compromised.

"I promise. I'll give you daily updates and call Dane as soon as something doesn't feel right. Just tell me when you want to start working out the details."

"I want to start right now, like literally right now. I want to know everything. Hours, availability, training, tell me everything." Eliana said.

Apollo stood up from the table and kissed Eliana on the cheek. He nodded to Dane who stood up from the table. The two of them walked back up to Apollo's office. If Eliana saw them leave she didn't seem to care. She practically jumped out of her seat and grabbed my hand. She dragged me up the stairs and past the office Apollo and Dane had disappeared to.

Eliana's office was just as magnificent as the rest of the house. Every decoration, every piece of furniture was intentional. Not a single thing was out of place. I accidentally laughed out loud.

"What's so funny?" Eliana asked.

"I'm just thinking about my office back at Ivy's. It takes me ten minutes to dig through piles of papers to find a pen. Just prepare yourself if you plan on spending any time there working with me."

"I'm surprised Dane hasn't snuck down in the middle of the night to organize and clean it for you while you're sleeping."

"He cleans it a few times a week but it doesn't take very long for me to get it back to normal. All it takes is one busy morning and the chaos is back. It's usually the first place he checks when he comes over. Sometimes he just stands at the door and sighs." I laughed.

"I get those sighs too." Eliana said, sitting down at her desk.

"I've just started ignoring them." I told her.

"When Apollo and I first got engaged there was a good month where Dane didn't say a single word to me. He communicated entirely in sighs."

"It took me a week before I finally broke him and got him to say more than a few words to me." I told her.

"How you two found each other will forever amaze me." She said.

"Believe me, I know. Dane and I being together will always be a mystery to me." I said.

"He's one lucky son of a bitch." Eliana said, opening up her laptop.

"Mhmm." I laughed.

Eliana and I were interrupted by a knock on her door. I walked over to open the door and found Dane standing in the hallway.

"Hey, sorry to interrupt but we need to talk." He said.

I looked over my shoulder at Eliana. She shrugged her shoulders, unsure what he wanted to talk to me about. I stepped into the hallway and closed the door behind me.

"Apollo just got a call. There's a problem at the docks. We have to go take care of it."

"Oh okay, do you have time to take me home or is someone driving me back?" I asked.

"Actually we thought maybe you'd want to stay here. You don't have to if you don't want to but I know you and Eliana are excited about working together. I can take you home, but this shouldn't take long. We'll be back before you know it."

"Yeah, that'd be great!" I said.

"Really?" He asked.

"Eliana and I want to get started on a schedule. I'd hate to leave now."

"Okay then. I'll give you a call in an hour or so to check in?" He said.

"Sure." I smiled.

Dane grabbed my hips and dipped into a kiss.

"Have fun. Be safe."

"Always." He said, walking back to Apollo's office.

I waited until the door to Apollo's office door closed and then walked back into Eliana's office.

"What was that about?" Eliana asked.

"Apollo and Dane have to go to the docks. I asked to stay here instead of going home. I thought maybe we could work on getting a training schedule set up." I told her.

"Perfect. I can't give you specifics about my clients until I get their permission, but I thought you'd want to see what my hours look like at the firm. I want to spend as much time as I can at Ivy's this week figuring out the best way to pitch our idea to my staff."

"Let's get started then." I said, pulling a chair next to her and grabbing one of her notepads.

Eliana and I spent the next few hours working on schedules for her clients. We changed my current schedule to fit the needs of her clients. We had an early morning shift, a shift for any parents that could only work when their kids were at school and an evening shift for anyone that wanted the closing shift. Eliana gave me all of her contacts for her staff and the shelters and group homes she worked with. My next step was working with my accountant to figure out the best way to set up pay. Anyone that came to me from Eliana's firm would be part time until we worked out a more permanent schedule. The goal was to let them work at Ivy's while they worked on getting a more permanent job.

The two of us needed a break so we were having drinks in the living room. We were waiting for the boys to call when the front door slammed shut. Eliana finished her drink in one gulp and then set down an empty cup. She stood up from the couch and walked over to the front door.

"Let's go see what that was all about." She said.

I followed in Eliana's footsteps by finishing my drink and rushing over to the front door. Standing on the staircase in a giant coat was Apollo's younger sister Juliette. The two of us met at the wedding. After spending only a few minutes with her I quickly learned she was the complete opposite of Apollo.

"I'm going to kill him!" She shouted.

"I can't help you if you don't explain, Juliette."

"Junior, I'm going to actually kill him!" She screamed again.

When Juliette saw me standing behind Eliana she paused her anger for a few seconds to wave and smile at me.

"What are you doing here?" She asked.

"Dane and I came over for dinner." I said.

"Is Dane here?" She asked.

"No, they went to the docks." Eliana told her.

"Good, that means there won't be anybody to stop me from killing Junior."

Junior, with the worst timing in the world, walked in through the front door.

Eliana and I looked at each other as soon as he walked in. I ran over to the staircase just in case Juliette actually did attempt to hurt him while Eliana stood in front of Junior.

"Hey Kate!" Junior waved, completely oblivious to the danger he was in.

Seeing Juliette upset and angry like this had me finally seeing the resemblance between her and Apollo.

"Can someone please tell me what happened?" Eliana said to the two of them.

"Do you want to tell them or should I?" Junior asked Juliette.

Juliette lunged for Junior from the stairs. I caught her before she made it to him.

"Junior, Kate brought you some desserts, why don't you go with her to the kitchen." Eliana said.

I let go of Juliette and walked with Junior to the kitchen.

"I hope you choke on a fucking cupcake asshole!" Juliette yelled at the two of us as we walked.

In the kitchen I grabbed Junior the desserts and sat with him at the counter.

"What happened?" I asked.

"She snuck out and went to a party. I got a call from one of my friends that she was there so I went to pick her up."

"Why?" I asked

"Apollo asked me to keep an eye out for her. When I heard she was out at that party I knew she wasn't safe."

"What did you do to make her so mad?"

"How do you know I did something?" He asked.

I gave Junior my best *bitch please* look.

Junior shrunk into his seat, "When I found her at the party I freaked out a little. I threatened to call Apollo on her in front of all her friends and then I threw my jacket around her and carried her out of the house all the way to the car."

"Oh Junior." I sighed.

"She isn't actually going to kill me is she?"

"If I were you I would go hide. Take your cupcakes and don't come out of the guest house until Eliana tells you it's safe." I told him.

"If tonight's my last night on Earth at least I go out with a couple of your cupcakes by my side."

"Just go." I told him.

When I heard the garage door close I went to go find Eliana and Juliette. Eliana was sitting on the floor of the hallway with her head against a closed door.

"She locked you out?" I asked.

"She didn't even tell me what happened before slamming the door in my face."

"I know what happened." I told her, sitting down next to her.

"What'd he do?"

"He crashed a party she was at and lectured her in front of all of her friends."

"No." She gasped.

"And then he threw her in his coat and dragged her out of there."

"Is he hiding?" Eliana asked.

"I told him he isn't allowed to leave the guest house until you tell him it's safe to come out."

Eliana knocked on the door, "Junior told us what happened Juliette. Why don't you let us in so we can talk about it?"

I leaned against the door and heard slow footsteps walking over. When the door opened Eliana and I fell back into Juliette's room.

"I'm getting too old for this shit." I whispered, standing up.

"Tell me about it." Eliana said, reaching out a hand to help me.

Juliette sat down on the bed; Junior's coat still wrapped around her.

"What happened?" I asked.

"He stormed into Harrison's house like an ass. He shouted my name in every room until he found me. It was so embarrassing. He threatened to call Apollo and have him pick me up if I didn't leave with him!"

"I just don't get why he felt like he had to come and rescue you from the party. You two used to be super close. He went to that prom after party with you a few months ago." Eliana said.

"I didn't even tell him I was going! Emily texted him even though I told her not to invite him. I'm literally going to have to drop out of St. Katherines. I'll never be able to show my face there again."

"I doubt anyone will even remember what happened by tomorrow." I tried to comfort.

"Emily said everyone was watching including Cameron-" Juliette froze.

"Including who?" Eliana asked.

"No one." Juliette lied.

"It doesn't sound like no one." I said.

"Did you being at this party with Cameron have anything to do with Junior crashing?" Eliana smiled.

Eliana and I gave each other the look. Now we know why Junior stormed into the party.

"Are you going to tell Apollo?" Juliette asked.

"No, of course not." Eliana said, "But I do need more information about this Cameron kid. Does he go to St. Katherines?"

Juliette shook her head no.

"Oh a rival romance." I swooned.

"You two are so pathetic." Juliette said, rolling her eyes.

"And did Junior know about Cameron asking you to the party?" Eliana asked.

"Maybe."

"How long have you been seeing Cameron?" I asked.

"I'm not having this conversation with you two. Don't you have more exciting things to be doing?"

I looked over at Eliana, "I don't have anything else to be doing, do you?"

"Nope, I'm totally free and super bored." Eliana laughed.

"So, what's Cameron like? How did you two meet? Does he play any sports? Have you gone on any dates?" Eliana asked.

"Get out!" Juliette shouted, jumping off of the bed.

Eliana and I both raced to the door. Juliette held up a pillow and was ready to use it.

"We'll be downstairs if you need anything." Eliana told her before closing the door.

Eliana and I kept a straight face until the door was closed. After we were in the hallway all bets were off. Eliana nearly lost her balance trying to calm herself down. I laughed so hard I gave myself hiccups.

The two of us had to hold onto each other to keep from falling down the stairs. We carefully walked to the backyard and sat down on the patio swing.

"Does Apollo have any idea those two are totally in love with each other?" I asked.

"He has no idea."

"Oh this is so painful." I cried.

"I'm pretty sure they don't even realize it. I'm so glad you see it too. I've been going crazy having no one to talk to about it. Ever since Junior moved into the guest house Juliette's been spending more time here. And of course Junior would never be able to admit his feelings for her because she's Apollo's sister. It's killing me to sit and wait for the inevitable."

"Juliette's right. We are pathetic." I laughed.

"Our lives are boring now. Sue us for using Juliette and Junior's drama to help us feel alive."

"What's Junior's story? Isn't he a bit young to be working for Apollo?" I asked.

"Junior's father, Alessio, died a few years ago. Alessio and Apollo's father Cristian were close. Like Apollo and Dane. No one talks about it but I think Alessio died because of a debt the family had. After Alessio's funeral, Junior's mom went off the deep end. She stopped being a mother and looked for comfort in others. She lost everything Alessio had worked to build."

"That's terrible."

"Out of guilt Apollo took Junior under his wing. Kept him in school, helped him graduate. Then last year when Apollo started to help him look at universities, Junior told him he wanted to stay and work for the family instead." Eliana said.

"And Apollo was okay with that?" I asked.

"I guess so, I mean he's still here. Apollo brings up college as a threat when Junior fucks up but that's it. I don't think he's ever serious about it. Apollo would miss him too much if he actually left."

"I'm too drunk for this." I told her.

"I'll make you a flowchart or something. It took me forever to figure all this shit out when I first moved in here. Come on, let's go inside. I'm cold and I need another drink."

Eliana and I found our way back to the couch.

"What are you going to tell Apollo when he asks why Juliette's here?" I asked.

"I haven't decided yet. I'm not sure I should get involved. Juliette and Junior need to figure out a way to coexist together. I can lie tonight and keep Juliette from getting in trouble for going out but I don't know how to protect the peace between Junior and Juliette for much longer."

"Do you think they'll ever figure out their feelings for each other?" I asked.

"Maybe, maybe not. They've known each other their whole lives. Anywhere Juliette went Junior was close behind. If they haven't figured it out by now they probably won't. If you'd have told eighteen year old me I would marry Apollo I would have laughed in your face. Who knows where life will take them."

"Do you ever miss being that young?" I asked.

"God no. I was a miserable bitch when I was their age. I don't miss it for a minute."

"Here. Take this." I said, handing Eliana one of the almost empty wine bottles.

Laid almost flat on the couch, unable to sit up, she still managed to hold the wine bottle high above her.

"To being old." I toasted.

"Cheers." Eliana laughed.

"What are we celebrating?" A voice behind the couch asked.

Eliana reached for anything to hold onto to lift herself up but failed. I ended up having to grab her arm and drag her up.

"To being a couple of old boring bitches." I cheered.

"Amen." Eliana shouted, falling back down onto the couch.

"You two need to crash here tonight?" Apollo asked Dane.

"I think I'd better get her back home."

"Did we see Junior's car in the driveway?" Apollo asked Eliana.

Eliana finally found her strength and sat up. She leaned over the couch and looked at Apollo.

"He brought Juliette home from a party." Eliana said.

"Why is he still here?" Dane asked.

"We had to send him to the guest house. He isn't allowed to leave until Juliette calms down." I told them.

"What happened?"

Eliana and I looked at each other.

"It's a secret." I whispered.

Eliana laughed and handed her empty bottle to Apollo. She tried to stand up but fell right into Apollo. He dropped the bottle to catch her before she fell.

"I think it's time for bed."

"Ready to go home?" Dane asked.

I nodded my head yes and reached over to him. He walked me to the front door and helped me find my shoes. On his way out he shouted to Apollo he'd see him tomorrow then helped me get to the car.

I must have fallen asleep in the car because I woke up to Dane helping me get out of my dress and into one of his shirts. I let my eyes close again and waited for Dane to join me back in bed. When he crawled in he reached over for me.

"Kate." Dane whispered.

"Mhmm."

"I want to know the secret." He said.

"I can't tell you."

"Why not?"

"Because it wouldn't be fair for you to know the secret before Juliette knows the secret."

"Kate, you're not making any sense." He complained.

"Believe me when I say you definitely don't want to know what the secret is. Now, let me go to bed in peace. It's real low of you to try and ask me questions when I'm too drunk to defend myself. I could sue you for unlawful interrogation."

"I knew introducing you to Eliana was a mistake." He whispered in my ear.

Dane gave up and kissed me on the cheek. He rolled over to give me a bit more space while I fell into a much needed deep sleep.

CHAPTER ELEVEN

Kate

As the days grew longer my life at Ivy's turned into absolute chaos. The idea was that I would hire more staff and it would mean I was spending less time working but so far that hadn't happened.

If I wasn't working in the kitchen I was managing all of our new employees. My to-do list was never ending and we were busier than ever but it was worth it to give Eliana's clients a chance at starting over. As soon as I told Becca she'd get to work with someone other than me she fell in love with the idea. We all took over different roles. Eliana was in charge of helping build resumes and working on more permanent jobs, Becca was in charge of training and I was in charge of everything else.

It took a month but we finally got into the rhythm of things. We worked through the hiccups of last minute court dates, custody battles, balancing new work trainings. We'd come a long way in just a few weeks. The dust was finally starting to settle.

"Are you sure you don't need me next Thursday?" Becca asked.

"I say we give the new girls a chance to run the place on their own. We need to stop hovering." I told her.

Becca was currently sitting on the desk in my office scrolling through the schedule. I was next to her filling the gaps in the schedule we couldn't find coverage for.

"I'll give Avery a chance to open by herself and come in before the lunch rush to make sure everything's running like it's supposed to." I told her.

"Who did you put down for closing?" She asked.

"I have Natalia closing with Amanda. She asked for the late shifts so I'll have Amanda work with her until she's ready to do it alone."

The front door alarm rang on the computer. Becca pulled up the security cameras to see who came in even though we already knew who it was. Every night just after closing Junior came in to grab leftovers. In any other circumstance I might believe Junior really was here for leftovers but I knew why he'd been stopping by more and more. I knew Dane had him stopping by at night to make sure things were fine here at Ivy's.

"We should give him a punch card. Tenth visit free." Becca said.

"He'd bankrupt me if I did that."

Becca and I watched as Junior stuffed the tip jar full of hundreds. He looked around his shoulder to make sure no one saw him do it.

"He knows we can see him right? You have to tell him we know he's the mystery tipper." She asked.

"I just don't have it in me to ruin his fun. Look how proud of himself he is. He thinks he's being sneaky."

I know Dane's been sending him with tip money every night. It was Dane and Apollo's way of supporting Eliana's clients. Until Dane brought it up I'd pretend not to see Junior sneak in to leave a tip.

"Run through next week for me one more time and then you can head out." I told Becca.

Walking out to the front Junior was already eyeing his picks for tonight. He was counting how much of everything was left and how much he'd be able to take home with him.

"Junior, what a surprise to see you here again."

"Hey Kate." He smiled.

"What can I get for you tonight?"

"Do you have any of those cinnamon twists left?" He asked.

"Those went pretty fast this morning but I saved a few for you in the back. Go sit down and I'll fix you up a box."

I went to the kitchen and grabbed a box I set aside for Junior. When I came out he was sitting near the register.

"So, how's it going?" He asked.

"You can tell Dane nothing exciting happened here. It was a slow day full of regulars stopping by for their morning coffee and breakfast. Nothing out of the ordinary."

"Oh I wasn't asking for Dane. I was just curious to see how it was going." He lied.

"It's been perfectly peaceful here. Just like it was yesterday and the day before." I said, handing him his box.

Junior tried to hand me cash but I pushed it right back to him.

"These are on the house tonight."

"I can't not pay you. Dane said if I ever left without paying I'd never come back." Junior said.

"Well it will be our little secret. I won't say anything if you don't."

Junior pocketed the fifty and opened up his box to see what I'd packed tonight.

"How's Dane?" I asked.

Junior looked up at me with a frown on his face.

"That bad?" I asked.

"There was a small problem with the Russians. He asked me to tell you he might not make it back home tonight. Told me to tell you he'd call you tomorrow."

"Anybody hurt?" I asked.

"Not yet."

"Well then you should probably get back before it gets too late."

"Yeah, probably." He said, walking over to the door.

"I'll see you tomorrow Junior." I shouted after him.

"See you tomorrow."

With Junior gone I locked up and went back to the office. Becca was putting away her apron and grabbing her purse.

"I left today's receipts in the top drawer. Schedule looks good but I left it pulled up in case you wanted to take another look. You headed over to Dane's?" She asked, digging through her purse for her keys.

"Yeah, maybe. I haven't decided yet. You got any plans?"

"Another long night of getting drunk and having to talk myself out of adopting a cat." She said.

I laughed and watched her walk down the back hallway and out into the patio.

"Be safe, I'll see you tomorrow." She waved, closing the door behind her.

I finished cleaning up the kitchen and then went to the office to clean up a bit. While I cleaned up I debated going over to Dane's. He probably wouldn't be home tonight but I still wanted to be there in case he did. He shouldn't be going home to an empty house after a day like today.

I closed down Ivy's and headed over to Dane's. On my way I grabbed dinner. After eating and leaving some leftovers in the fridge I took a quick shower. I was determined to stay awake until Dane got back but that didn't last very long. I was asleep on his couch with the tv on low when his front door opened.

I sat up and waited to hear his footsteps walking into the hallway but they never came. Instead all of the lights in the house shut off. Scared and confused I grabbed the closest thing I could reach and ran to the hallway. I snuck around the corner of the living room and waited to see who was here.

I held my breath when I watched someone holding a gun step into the hallway.

"Kate?" Dane whispered.

"Dane?" I whispered back.

"Jesus, Kate! I thought someone had broken in."

Dane lowered his gun and turned the hallway lights back on.

"What are you doing here?" He sighed.

"I came over after work. I wanted to be here when you got off work." I explained.

"What are you holding?" He asked.

I looked down at the tv remote in my hand.

"I grabbed it in a panic. I thought someone was breaking in here to hurt me."

Dane walked into the kitchen and slid his gun onto the island counter. He leaned against the counter with his head dropped.

"You should have texted me and given me a heads up you were planning on coming over. I almost shot you."

"I'm sorry."

Dane turned around and reached out for my hand. He pulled me closer to him and wrapped his arms around me. He took a deep breath in and rested his head on mine.

"Junior told me about your problem with the Russians. I didn't want you to have to come home alone. I needed to see you weren't hurt." I explained.

Dane let go of me and held out his arms turning around slowly.

"I'm okay, not even a scratch."

"What happened tonight?" I asked.

"Not tonight Kate. I can't give you the answers you need tonight."

Dane looked drained. With how busy work has been for the both of us we haven't been able to spend a lot of time together. It had been a few days since we spent a night together, just the two of us. Just for tonight I'd help keep Dane's mind off work. For the next few hours I'd help him forget.

"Come on." I said, holding out my hand.

Dane grabbed my hand and followed me to his bedroom. I put my hands on his shoulders and asked him to sit down on the edge of the bed. Dane sat down and waited to see what I'd do next. While I grabbed his wrist to take off his watch his other hand ran down my thigh.

I walked his watch over to the dresser and took off my shirt and jeans. I walked back over to Dane and helped him unbutton his shirt. He shook it off his arms and threw it to the other side of the room.

I leaned into him leaving kisses on his neck, "Go lay down."

Dane did as I asked and sat against the bed frame. I crawled over to him on my hands and knees. Left only in my bra and sheer panties, Dane's eyes roamed my body. He no longer looked tired and drained. He looked hungry, ready to devour me.

I stopped at Dane's hips and started to slowly unbutton his pants. I stuck my thumbs underneath his boxers and slid them down with his pants. Dane kicked them off which left him completely naked. He tried to lean forward and touch me but I pushed his chest back.

"Wait your turn." I smiled.

Dane dropped his arms back at his sides and watched as I ran my nails up and down his stomach. I teased Dane for a minute or two until he relaxed. He was too wound up. Finally I grabbed his already erect dick and started to slowly stroke him. He reacted immediately.

I leaned over his cock and ran my fingers over my tongue. I licked some spit onto my hand and then went back to massaging his hard cock.

"Baby." He groaned.

"You like that?" I asked.

Dane grabbed a lock of my hair and forced my head back up.

Locking his eyes to mine he spoke, "I like anything you do Kate."

"Even this?" I asked, lowering down onto his cock, and taking all of him in my mouth.

Dane let go of my hair and let out another groan. I slowly pulled away letting my spit roll down Dane's hard shaft. I ran my fingers down him and twisted a few strokes as I watched him react. It was addicting watching Dane respond to my touch. I'd never get tired of seeing him so vulnerable like this.

I licked over his head and then took a deep breath taking him in my mouth again. I continued to twist and stroke what I couldn't fit in my mouth. I swirled my tongue around as I sucked up and down on his dick. I could taste his precum at the back of my throat. He was hard, losing his cool with every stroke. Dane finally lost his patience and pulled me off him. He sat up and threw me onto my back.

He crawled up to me and left a sloppy kiss on my lips. He kissed down my chest, sucking on my nipples as he traveled down. When he got to my core he paused and looked up at me. He ran his fingers over my folds and slid a few fingers into me.

"I want to taste you but I need to fuck you now or I'm going to lose my God damn mind." He said.

"Then fuck me."

Dane didn't wait a second longer. He pulled me by my hips closer to him. He ran his dick over my folds. He gave no warning before thrusting deep into me. I had no time to adjust to his size. He was fucking me at a pace I couldn't keep up with. I bit my lip to try and keep myself from screaming. I couldn't let Dane know I was already close to coming.

"This is your dirty little fantasy isn't it, Kate? You told me you thought about getting to fuck me after I come home from work. You said it turned you on."

He was right. Before our first date I would picture Dane coming home from work and fucking me like this.

"You said you pictured me fucking you with my bruised fingers. Dane ran his fingers over my clit and rubbed it in circles.

Dane fucked me harder than he ever had. He had to hold my hips tight to keep him from sliding out. He didn't want to lose the connection we had. He wanted to thrust his entire cock in me so deep I'd feel it in my stomach.

"Is this what you want Kate? You want to know I beat a man half to death with my bare hands tonight? Does that turn you on?" He asked.

It was so fucked up and had me considering finding a therapist but I still nodded my head yes.

"Fuck baby I'm going to fuck you so hard you won't be walking tomorrow. Turn around." He ordered.

Dane slid out of me and waited for me to turn around. He pushed me down into the pillows and grabbed my ass. He held my hips high in the air and spread my legs wide. He ran a finger from my folds to my ass before sliding his cock back into my pussy.

After a few thrusts he reached for my neck. His hand reached around my throat and forced me to lean back into his chest. He kissed my shoulders and then ran his tongue over my neck up to my lips. He took advantage of my moaning and slid his tongue into my mouth. He turned my head back and kissed me until I nearly forgot how to breathe. While pressing me into his chest he didn't slow down his thrusts. He kept me close enough to fuck me without needing to hold my hips.

I leaned my head against his chest and let him do whatever he wanted to me. I closed my eyes as his hands let go of my throat to grab my tits. He pinched my nipples and squeezed my left breast in his hands. Tomorrow I was sure there'd be bruises of his hand prints on my soft skin but I didn't want him to stop.

Dane had complete control, I wanted to come but I wasn't ready for this to end.

"Dane." I moaned.

"What's wrong baby?"

"I'm going to come."

"Then come."

With Dane's permission I let go. I relaxed into his arms and let my muscles spasm. Afraid he'd stop now that'd I'd come I grabbed his hands and held them to my chest.

"Tell me what you need Kate." He whispered in my ear.

"Whatever you do, don't stop."

Dane let go of my chest and let me fall back onto the bed. With my face pressed against the pillow Dane rested a hand on my lower back. With his dick still inside me he spread my legs even more.

I let out a surprised cry at his new angle.

"That feel good, baby?"

He knew it did, he just wanted to hear me moan. I relaxed my arms above my head and let Dane fuck me how he wanted. Grabbing and slapping my ass he refused to slow down. He kept a fast pace the entire time. When he knew I was close again he dipped his hand in between my legs and rubbed against my clit.

I pushed back against his thrusts to make him hit deeper. I continued to bounce on his dick as he fucked me. Dane's breathing got short and his sighs turned into grunts. He was close. I replaced Dane's fingers with my own so that he could grab my hips. In a few final thrusts Dane unloaded in me and slowed down his movements. I finished to the sound of Dane's groans as he pumped into me.

Collapsing onto the bed I reached out for Dane. He wrapped an arm under my shoulders and tried to get me to sit up.

"What are you doing?" I protested.

"I need to clean you up before we go to bed."

I didn't want to have to leave Dane's bed but he was right. I let him help me to the bathroom and then back to bed as soon as we'd cleaned off.

I crawled under the covers and waited for Dane to join me. I opened my arms for him to come lay on my chest. He laid down next to me and wrapped an arm around my stomach. I ran my fingers through his hair and waited for him to fall asleep before falling asleep myself.

Too short after falling asleep Dane and I were woken up by an alarm on my phone. Eyes closed I ran my hand over the bed stand table in search of my phone but Dane found it first. I was close to falling back asleep when Dane shook me awake.

"Kate wake up."

Dane ran to his closet and grabbed a pair of sweats. He came back to bed and pulled on a sweatshirt.

"What's going on?" I asked.

"One of your alarms at Ivy's just went off."

"What?" I asked, now completely awake.

"I have a few guys going over there now to check it out. I'll call you when I get there."

"No, I'm going with you." I argued.

"Kate…"

"I'm going with Dane. End of discussion. If something happened at Ivy's I need to be there."

Dane stood with his hands on his hips and considered his options. In the end he knew it was best for me to go.

"Go get dressed. Meet me at the car." He said, leaving to go make another phone call.

By the time Dane and I made it to Ivy's a few of Apollo's men were already there.

"What happened?" Dane asked, moving me behind him as we walked up to the door.

"Back door window is broken. Someone threw a rock at it." A man I didn't recognize told Apollo.

"Who was it?"

"We don't know. They were wearing a hoodie. When the alarm went off they ran. Alex is looking at street cameras now to try and figure out which way he went."

I walked past Dane and tried to walk upstairs.

"Where do you think you're going?" He asked.

"Upstairs?" I said.

"No."

"We already did a sweep. The place is empty. Whoever tried to break in was working alone."

I pointed to the man talking, "See? It's safe to go up."

Dane looked out at his guys and then back at me.

"I want two people at every entrance. No one goes in or out without me knowing about it."

"Yes, sir."

Dane followed behind me up to my apartment.

"You have ten minutes to pack up things you'll need for the week."

"I'm sorry?" I asked.

"Until we know who tried to break in tonight you're staying at my place. You can call Becca tomorrow and tell her Ivy's will be closed for a few days."

"Yeah no, that's not happening."

"Kate, it's not up for debate."

"I'm not closing Ivy's. Not now, not ever. I just put three of Eliana's clients on as full time staff. I can't take away their hours. That's not fair to anyone."

"Someone just tried to break in here. God only knows why. What if they were here to hurt you?" He said.

Dane leaned against the counter and folded his arms against his chest. He was upset, there was no convincing him to be logical about this. His emotions were shot.

"I know you're worried Dane but I'm fine, nothing happened. And even if I had been here your men made it here in record time. Do I look worried?" I asked.

Dane looked me up and down.

"I understand your concern but I'm not closing Ivy's. I can't do that to my employees. They won't understand why we had to close. If I tell them the truth about what happened here tonight they'll quit. Everything Eliana and I have been working for would be over, ruined."

"I don't want you here alone."

"Okay then let's figure out a way to make it work." I said.

"I'm putting Junior here full time. No more surprise drop ins. I want him here from open to close."

"Dane, that's going to freak out my workers."

"He can hide in the back, but I need him here."

"Okay." I compromised.

"And you're staying at my place. I don't want you here alone when I'm working late and can't be here with you."

That I had no problem agreeing to, "Deal."

"Go pack up anything you want at my place. I have to go call Apollo."

I tried to reach out to him as he walked by me but he ignored my touch. He was scared and in an attempt to not lose it he was shutting me out. I tried to ignore his cold attitude towards me as I packed up some clothes to bring over to his house.

After packing I went back down to the shop. I stopped at the bottom of the stairs and listened to Dane yelling at his men. He was ordering them around Ivy's like he owned the place. When he saw me hiding over on the stairs he sent all of his men away.

He tried to avoid me again by walking over to the windows to check the alarms.

"Dane." I spoke.

"Hmm." He mumbled back.

"Dane." I spoke again only louder.

He finally turned around.

"I need you to see that I'm okay. That I'm not upset, not hurt."

Dane looked me up and down and let his shoulders relax, "I hate this."

"I know."

Dane closed the space between us and pulled me into a hug. He held my head and rocked me back and forth. I held onto his sweatshirt and ran my hands down his back.

"I've never worried like this. I don't know how to handle the fear that someone was here tonight to try and hurt you." He confessed.

I didn't say anything. I was just as terrified as he was. Someone had broken into my home and I had no idea why. I could lie and say it was a failed robbery but the odds of that were slim. My gut told me it was probably someone who wanted to hurt Dane by hurting me.

The excitement of tonight finally caught up with me. I let out a quiet cry and felt the tears fall down my cheeks. Dane lifted my chin up and saw the tears. He looked broken as he wiped my tears away with his thumb.

"I love you Kate." He spoke softly.

I was afraid if I said anything the tears would fall harder so all I could give him was a nod.

"I love you." He repeated.

Unable to look Dane in his eyes I dropped my head into his chest.

"You ready to go home?" He asked.

I gently nodded my head against his chest.

"Then let's go home." He said, grabbing my hand and walking out to the car with me.

On the drive back to the house I thought about my life with Dane. I thought about our future. I wondered if this is what it would always feel like. Would we always be driven by fear, forced to react out of anger to situations out of our control? Dane's hand on my thigh felt heavy as I imagined what the future looked like for the two of us.

CHAPTER TWELVE

Dane

"Okay, run through it one more time."

Kate took a deep breath and fixed her posture, "Tera, the oldest, is married to Mateo. Owen and PJ are their oldest and twins, then comes Mattie and Evelyn. Evelyn, her youngest, tolerates everybody but loves your mom, Grandma. Josie's sister number two, married to Robbie who we hate. Their kids are Keenan and Samantha"

"You forgot about Joey." I told her.

"Right, baby Joey, little over a year old only knows how to say bad words." Kate repeated to herself.

"Who's next?"

"Kimberly, labor and delivery nurse super into yoga and healing energies. She works nights and her husband Andrew has the kids tonight."

"Good one more to go." I told her.

"Mayra, manager at Rosie's Diner. Oh my God I can't remember what her kid's names are."

"Remember we talked about this. They both start with C's." I said, trying to help her remember.

"Clara! Cade!" She shouted.

"And how old are they?"

"Clara is about to start preschool; Cade is only a few months older than Joey."

"I think you're ready." I told her.

"I should have made flashcards." She said, getting out of the car.

"Trust me as soon as we get in there and you meet everybody you'll feel better."

I grabbed the boxes of dessert from behind my seat and walked to the front door of my parents' house with Kate right beside me.

"I don't think we brought enough dessert. I told you we should have packed up a fourth box."

I ignored her worrying and rang the doorbell.

"Should you not have rang the doorbell? Will it be weird that we're standing out here and not just going in? Isn't this technically your house?"

"I don't know I just panicked but we can't go in now after I rang it that would be weird. Are you telling me you never rang the doorbell at your parents' house?" I asked.

"My parents are dead! I've never had to worry about ringing a doorbell." Kate whisper yelled.

"Right." I laughed.

Kate looked up at me and let out a laugh just as the door opened.

"Dane? What are you doing standing out here?" Tera asked.

"Told you we should have just gone in." Kate laughed.

Tera looked over at Kate and put on a big smile, "Oh my God! She's real!" She shouted behind her into the house.

Everyone raced to the front porch and piled behind Tera.

From over Tera's shoulder I saw Josie take a look at the two of us outside.

"Why didn't you two just come in?" She asked.

That only made Kate laugh harder as she leaned further into my side.

"Fuck off." I sighed as I helped Kate get into the house.

"Language!" Mom shouted from the kitchen.

"How did she even hear that?" I whispered to myself.

As soon as Kate's coat was off she was guided into the kitchen by Tera and Josie. I was left behind in the living room holding Kate's jacket and all of the dessert boxes. The only person who stayed behind was Owen.

"Help me take these boxes to the kitchen."

Owen held out his hand, "Twenty bucks."

"Ten."

"Twenty-five." He argued.

The boxes started to slide. I didn't have a choice so I gave Owen a few boxes and walked with him to the kitchen. When we got in there Kate was talking with Mom.

"I can't believe it took Dane this long to invite you over for dinner!" Mom smiled.

"You should have seen him on the car ride over. I've never seen him more nervous." Kate told her.

"I can hear you." I shouted at them.

Kate laughed with Tera and Josie at the counter as they talked with Mom. Into the kitchen ran Samantha, stopping right in front of Kate.

"You must be Samantha." She smiled.

"What's in the boxes?" Samantha asked, ignoring Kate's hello, and getting right to business.

"I brought desserts. A little of everything. Do you like cupcakes?" She asked.

Samantha nodded her head yes.

"The only problem is I only brought cupcakes for people that help with dinner." Kate said.

"You better go get your cousins to help you set the table before Kate gives your cupcake to someone else." Mom said.

In a near full sprint Samantha left the kitchen and ran upstairs shouting Evelyn's name. The two of them came back down stairs with Mattie right behind them. They ran right to me.

"Will you help us set the table?" They asked.

"Why me?"

"Because we can't reach the plates. Grandma keeps them way too high up." Mattie said.

"What's in it for me?"

"Did you not just hear her? If you don't help you don't get a cupcake!" Samantha nearly cried.

"Alright, alright, Samantha go get silverware, Mattie and Evelyn you're in charge of napkins."

The three scattered off. I walked towards the dining room but stopped when I noticed Kate wasn't behind me. I turned around and waited for her to follow.

"What are you doing?" She asked.

"We're setting the table. I wanted to show you around the house on our way to the table."

"No, you're setting the table. I want to stay in here and catch up with your sisters." She said.

"Yeah that's not happening." I told her.

"Uncle Dane!" Mattie shouted from the dining room, "We're waiting!"

"They're calling for you." Josie said, pointing to the hallway.

I didn't love the idea of leaving Kate alone with Tera and Josie but I didn't have a choice. I had about a minute to get to the table before all three girls came in looking for me.

When I walked into the dining room Mattie was sitting at the table trying to fold the napkins into what I guess was a flower.

"What cupcakes did Kate bring?" Evelyn asked.

"She brought like a hundred different flavors. I think I even saw a few with sprinkles." I told them.

"What kind of sprinkles?" Samantha asked.

"Does it matter?"

"Yes!" They all shouted.

"Well I don't know. I guess it will be a surprise."

I tried to help Mattie with the napkins but she was struggling.

"Mattie I'll fold the napkins for you if you do me a little favor."

"What do you want?" She asked.

"Go into the kitchen and pretend we need more spoons or something."

"Why would I do that?"

"Because then when you come back you can tell me what your mom and Auntie Josie are talking about."

"They're probably talking about you." Samantha chimed in.

"Yeah, I know. That's why I'm sending Mattie in."

"I'll do it if I get your cupcake after dinner." Mattie told me.

"Deal." I said, shaking her hand.

Mattie ran into the kitchen and I finished folding up her napkins.

"You should have sent Evelyn in. She probably could have snuck in and listened forever." Samantha said.

She was probably right but it was too late now. I finished setting the table with Evelyn and Samantha. Evelyn was helping me place the forks down when Mattie came back in.

"Well?" I asked.

"They're telling Kate everything." She said.

"That's it? That's all you got?"

"Oh, one more thing! Mom told me to tell you to send someone better the next time you want one of us to spy for you. She said she's going to make sure she shows Kate your swim team photos from middle school." Mattie said with a smile.

"Told you." Samantha said on her way out of the room.

All three girls went running to the front door when they saw Maya walk in with Cade and Clara.

Halfway to the door Mattie ran back into the living room, "I still get your cupcake right?"

"Yeah." I said.

"Awesome."

Clara ran into the living room with the girls. Cade was asleep in Mayra's arms. Mayra saw me in the dining room folding napkins and walked over to the table.

"She here?"

"In the kitchen right now." I sighed.

"This is what you get for waiting so long to introduce us to her. We have months of catching up to do." Mayra said.

Mayra was the sister I was closest to growing up. She was the only one who knew what I really did for work and she was the first sister to know about Kate. This whole dinner was her fault.

"Will you go in there and make sure they aren't telling any of the really embarrassing stories?" I asked.

"Sure. I'll make sure we wait until after dinner before we tell her anything that might ruin that scary reputation of yours."

I stood up from the table and gave Mayra a quick kiss on the cheek, "Thank you."

Mayra tossed off her jacket and threw it at me. She left me alone in the dining room as she left to go save Kate. I knew if I went back to the kitchen I'd get kicked out so I went looking for Dad.

I found him watching the news in his office. Joey was asleep in Dad's lap. Joey's favorite person was his grandpa which is why his favorite words were all curse words. Wherever Dad went Joey was right by his side.

When Dad saw me come in he turned down the volume.

"You already get kicked out of the kitchen?"

"They're all in there talking about me. It's karma for all the shit I caused when they brought home boyfriends."

"Not just when they brought home boyfriends. Josie and Robbie have been married for years and you still make his life a living hell."

"That's because Robbie sucks. I'll stop picking on him when he grows up." I defended.

Joey was now wide awake and getting anxious. He wanted to roam. I stood up and walked around the room with him; his fingers wrapped around mine as he stumbled around.

"You bringing Kate to meet the family means you two must be pretty serious." Dad said.

"It is pretty serious. Kate's the one."

"Don't let your mom hear you talking like that. She'll start planning the wedding."

"Yeah, she might." I laughed.

From the hallway Mattie ran into Dad's office, "What are you guys talking about?" She asked.

"Nothing." Dad and I both shouted.

"Grandma wanted me to tell you dinner's ready and you have to come to the kitchen."

I grabbed Joey and walked out to the kitchen with Dad. Josie took Joey to lay down in her old room and then came back to join us in the kitchen.

"Alright kids get your plates!" Mom said.

Like a herd of lions all the kids came rushing into the kitchen. They quickly filled their plates then disappeared into the basement. They were in and out in less than a minute. After the rush of the kids settled the rest of us sat down in the dining room.

After a quick prayer we spent the next few minutes stacking our plates with Mom's roast and her homemade bread rolls.

Kate sat in between Josie and me at the table. Mom and Dad took the ends with Mateo, Robbie, and Tera across from us. Mayra was next to Mom's left. After filling plates and digging in, mom broke the silence.

"Dane, Kate told us all about Ivy's and how busy you've been this past month." Mom said.

"Kate's been working nonstop to keep up with their sales." I told her.

"That is just amazing. Not many people have what it takes to open and run their own business like that." Mom beamed.

"Isn't it hard running that place all by yourself? All those long hours?" Mayra asked.

"It's definitely not been easy but I wouldn't want to be doing anything else. I can't imagine being stuck in an office from nine to five every day. I make my own hours, that's enough for me." She said.

"Girl after my own heart." Dad smiled.

"Dad was head of maintenance for the city for twenty years. Never spent a minute in the office. If he wasn't out on sites he was making home visits to anyone who sent in a complaint to the city." I told Kate.

"Running Ivy's sounds like a walk in the park compared to that!" Kate said.

"Didn't matter how many people told me to retire or take my job back to the office, couldn't imagine myself doing anything else." He spoke proudly.

"And what does everybody else do? Dane told me Kimberly works at the hospital and Mayra runs Rosie's, but that's all I know. It's hard keeping track of everything."

"Tera is an assistant principal at Hodgkin's and Josie works at the medical examiner's office." I told her.

"Medical examiner's office? That's exciting!" Kate replied.

"I love it, but it's nothing like the movies." Josie laughed.

"And Mateo?" She asked, setting her fork down to hear Mateo's answer.

"I run a construction company." He answered, surprised Kate had asked.

Mateo was a quiet person. He was a good father and husband, but in all the years I'd known him I hadn't heard him talk much. His calm personality balanced out Tera's energetic personality.

Interrupting the conversation Robbie pointed over at Kate.

"How long you two been dating?" Robbie asked.

I laid my hand on Kate's thigh, letting her know I'd answer this one.

"Few months."

"You couldn't find anyone better so you settled for Dane?" He asked, looking right at Kate, trying to intimidate her.

"Well I actually think Dane's pretty great." Kate smiled.

Robbie was pushing his luck with me tonight. Him and Josie got married way too young. He's tired of me reminding him he's a nobody, and I'm tired of having to send him money. I thought he'd be on his best behavior tonight, but I guess I was wrong.

Tera spoke up, trying to change the subject. She knew I wasn't a Robbie fan and would say something to upset Josie if he stepped out of line.

"Kate says you two met at Ivy's." Tera laughed.

"And why's that funny?" I asked.

"Kate said you showed up one day and never left. Said you were just a little lost puppy who refused to leave."

"Okay I didn't say it in exactly those words." Kate laughed.

"I was hardly a lost puppy. I just had a hard time leaving after meeting Kate. And with how many hours she worked the odds of me running into her were pretty good."

"Sure." Kate smiled.

"Kate says you're even pretending to still like coffee." Josie laughed.

I looked over at Kate, "You know I don't like coffee?"

"Maybe."

"For how long?" I asked.

"Like a long time."

"So this whole time you've been letting me drink all that coffee?"

"I was waiting for you to finally admit it. And to be fair the first day we met you drank at least twelve lattes so I figured anything less than twelve wouldn't kill you." She said.

"I can't believe you've known this whole time." I laughed.

"If it makes you feel any better I've been giving you decaf since I found out."

"I wondered why the shakiness stopped a few weeks back. I thought I was just getting used to all that caffeine."

"You're welcome." Kate joked.

"I love her." Mayra said.

"Same, I like her so much I forgive you for hiding her from us for so long." Tera agreed.

"Kim's going to love her." Josie smiled.

"I can't wait to meet Kimberly!" Kate said.

"You're going to love her. She's the one Dane's most afraid of. She's been waiting years to meet Dane's girlfriend. She's looking for payback." Josie told her.

I looked over at Dad hoping he'd save me but he had checked out of the conversation a long time ago. I was on my own here. Mateo was trying to avoid anyone asking him to join the conversation and Robbie was the last person I'd ask for help.

"Who's ready for dessert? Kate brought some amazing treats." I said, hoping to distract my sisters.

"Why don't you and Dad clean up and get dessert ready. I want to show Kate all of Mom's photo albums." Tera said.

Shit, I should have paid one of the twins to hide those before we got here. Maybe it wasn't too late.

All the girls left to the living room while the rest of us cleaned up. Robbie went to check in with the kids while Mateo and I cleared the table. Dad was busy packing up the leftovers.

When the two of us made it to the living room Kate was laughing at an old photo of mine.

"I understand the swimsuit, it was middle school, but the blonde streaks? I mean it's just painful to look at." She laughed.

"Hey, that hair was popular back then. Everyone was dying their hair like that."

Kate pulled her phone out of her pocket but I stopped her.

"Oh come on! El and Becca are going to die when they see this!"

"No."

Kate looked over to Mayra who gave her a wink. I'm sure later they'd send her a picture of it. After flipping through all of Mom's old photo albums the kids came back upstairs. They were ready for dessert.

Mattie, Evelyn, and Samantha all helped Kate plate the desserts in the kitchen. I grabbed PJ and Owen and snuck them into the hallway to help me.

"I need that photo album to disappear." I told them.

"Define disappear." PJ said.

"Hide it somewhere in the basement where none of your aunties will be able to find it. No permanent damage but I need it gone long enough they'll forget about it. In a few months you can tell Grandma where you hid it." I said.

"Fifty bucks." They shouted together.

"Thirty."

"Two hundred." They said.

"Fine, fifty each." I agreed.

PJ and Owen snatched their fifties right out of my hand and then snuck back into the living room. I saw them leave back down to the basement with the photo album hidden between them. If I'd known those two were going to raise their prices I would have brought more cash with me.

Kate was right. We should have brought another box. We cleaned out three boxes of cupcakes and desserts in minutes. We sat and talked in the living room and ate our dessert for the next hour. I wish she knew how little my mom complimented other's food. Even though Kate refused to accept everyone's appreciation for her desserts I knew she was happy to hear they loved them.

When I snuck down in the basement with Tera we found most of the kids asleep on the couches and floor. Only PJ and Owen were still awake. They had their video game on mute and they played quietly to not disturb the girls.

Tera dimmed the lights on and woke up her four. Mayra came down with Cade to come wake Clara up and bring her upstairs. All of Josie's followed behind us back up into the living room. Keenan was struggling to keep his eyes open as Robbie took him to the car.

I found Kate in the living room with Mom. The two of them were saving their numbers into each other's phone. When Kate saw all of us come back into the living room she stood up and walked over to me.

"You ready to go home?" I asked.

Kate nodded her head yes and leaned up against my shoulder.

"I'll go grab your coat."

"Thank you for dinner Margo." Kate smiled, giving Mom a hug.

"Oh my pleasure Kate. You call me anytime, and I mean it."

Just in case it came up I told everyone about Kate's parents. I didn't want them to make her uncomfortable with questions about her family. It meant the world to me that Mom had been so warm and kind to Kate tonight.

"I'll call and give you updates about those turnovers Becca is making for the fall. Maybe you and Joe can stop by and visit Ivy's soon." She said.

"I'd come tomorrow if I could." Mom smiled.

"I'll text you when I know when we're having Mateo's birthday dinner. I'll make sure to pick a day that works for Kimberly." Tera said, taking her turn for hugs.

"I'll be there, just let me know when." Kate said.

We said goodbye to the rest of the group and then headed back to the house. On the drive back to my place Kate was quiet. As soon as we were pulling away from Mom's house her energy dropped. She sat and watched traffic through her window all the way back to the house.

She walked into the house faster than I could park and turn off my car. I found her in my room taking off her jewelry.

"Is something wrong?" I asked.

"I'm fine."

"Kate…"

"I just don't think there's any way to tell you how I'm feeling without sounding like a jealous asshole."

"Give it your best shot."

"Before tonight all I knew about you was that you worked with Apollo. And then tonight I got to meet your real family and it's just not fair. You have these two incredible families that want you and love you and I don't have anybody."

"Kate." I sighed.

"My mom died; my dad killed himself because the thought of living was too much for him. My own brother didn't even want me! It's just not fair."

"Come here." I told her, pulling her into a hug.

Kate tried to hold back her tears but I could tell she was frustrated.

"You aren't alone Kate. You have me. We're family."

"You're just saying that to make me feel better."

I moved Kate over to the bed and sat down with her. I ran my thumb over her cheeks wiping away her tears. It didn't matter what I said to Kate right now. She'd lived a life full of loss and heartbreak. I don't care how long it takes to convince Kate how important she is to me. I'd spend forever proving to her she was family.

"I hate to break it to you Kate but you're already family. You're stuck with me. I'm not sure it's the family you thought you'd have but you're a Russo now. My sisters already love you and my mom couldn't stop raving about how amazing you were. Even on a good day we're dysfunctional and there will be days my sisters will annoy the hell out of you but that's what family is for. I know it's hard not having your parents here with you but mine will always be a phone call away."

"You know sometimes I just can't stand you." Kate laughed.

"Why's that?"

"You always say the right thing. It's a little irritating." She said.

"I just can't help it. It's a gift."

Kate hit my shoulder and climbed off the bed. She walked over to the bathroom and came out with a few tissues.

"You ready for bed?" I asked.

"Yeah I have an early morning tomorrow. I need to get ahead of the wine hangover I'll have tomorrow. If we don't go to bed now I'll be miserable all day."

As Kate and I got ready for bed I kept a close eye on her to make sure she was okay. I really did mean it when I told her she was family but I'm not sure she believed me. It doesn't matter how long it takes me, one day I will prove to Kate just how much she means to the people around her.

CHAPTER THIRTEEN

Kate

"I need Saturday off." Avery shouted from the kitchen.

"Why?" I asked from the office.

"Sophie has an away game. Can't find anyone to drive her there."

"I thought the season ended last week?" I asked.

"They made it to the championships." Avery said, disappointment on her face.

"You complain now but one of these days Sophie will be playing for the national soccer team and winning gold." I told her.

"God I hope not. I'm so tired of driving to these games. I can't imagine having to do that for fifteen more years."

"I'll cover Saturday morning. Pick up a shift sometime in the week if you need the hours and tips." I said.

"You're the best."

"I know!" I shouted back at her.

Most of Eliana's clients left Ivy's after a few months until they found a better place to work but Avery was slowly turning into a manager. She ran this place better than Becca and me. Last week she took over scheduling which meant my life got a whole lot easier. Her two daughters, Sophie and Tessa, were both in middle school. Eliana and I helped Avery move out of the halfway house and into an apartment of their own near the middle school.

My plan for today was to get some work done in the office and spend some time out on the floor but there was nothing left for me to do. I was standing in my own office and none of it was familiar to me. Avery and my new staff had made Ivy's their home. They treated it with more love than I did some days. Having nothing to do I went out to the floor. I may not have any office work to do but I could help out until closing.

My favorite customer was sitting at the back of the room which meant it was nearly closing. Junior spent most of his time in my office but just before closing he always came out to the front. It took a few days to get used to having him here all day long but after about a week I hardly paid any attention to him. He kept to himself and was always there for me when I felt uneasy about a customer. He was the perfect guard dog. He took my leftover desserts as payments and he rarely complained when I made him help me clean up at night.

When the last customer left I tossed Junior the broom, "Chairs and floors."

"Can't I do the kitchen? It's spooky in here when it's just me."

"We've been over this Junior. I promise you Ivy's is not haunted." I assured him.

"That's easy for you to say. The ghosts here like you. They wouldn't cause problems for you."

"Just go." I laughed.

Junior cleaned up the front while I crumb coated a few cakes for tomorrow. I was cleaning up the counters when I heard a loud crash come from the front. The sound of shattering glass echoed through the shop just before all of my alarms went off.

I ran back to the front and found a man standing in my store pointing a gun at Junior. I immediately stepped in between the gun and Junior.

How the fuck was this happening again?

"Move." The tall man said.

"I can't do that. Not until you tell me why you're here."

"You know why I'm here." He said, pointing his gun at me and off of Junior.

Junior didn't like that one bit. He tried to step in front of me but I wasn't going to let him do that. He wasn't going to get hurt because of me.

"Who are you?" I asked calmly.

"I'm Wesley, Avery's husband." He spat.

"Avery's ex?" I asked.

That pissed him off. He shook his gun.

"She's not my ex, she's my wife and you're going to help me find her."

"I can't help you do that." I told him.

Wesley saw Junior reaching in his pockets, "Don't fucking move!" He yelled.

"Okay, okay, no need to get upset. Junior, show him your hands." I said, still holding mine up.

Junior took his hands out of his pockets and held them palm up. Junior took one big step to his right, standing by my side.

"I know Avery works here. I know you and that lawyer bitch convinced her to leave me. She took the kids and ran. I know she's here somewhere. She's coming home with me."

"Avery's not here Wesley. I sent everyone home early." I tried to explain.

"No, no fuck!" He shouted.

"Why don't you put the gun down and we can talk." I said.

The alarms to the bakery were still ringing which meant Dane and his men had to be close. If I could keep Wesley calm until he got here we'd be okay."

Wesley paced around the floor and talked to himself. Finally, he looked back at me.

"Let's go." He said, pointing the gun to the back door.

"I can't go anywhere." I told him.

"Yes, you can. You are going to take me to wherever Avery's staying right now. I know you know."

"I don't know where she lives." I lied.

"Yes you do!" He screamed.

"I don't."

"Tell me or I shoot."

"Wesley I promise I don't-"

Wesley didn't wait for me to finish. He shot Junior in the shoulder and sent him dropping to the floor. My knees gave out. With shaky hands I reached out to Junior and tried to put pressure on his shoulder.

"It's okay Junior, you're going to be okay. Dane will be here soon; he'll know what to do. He always knows what to do." I whispered to him.

Junior's blood quickly covered my hands as I held pressure on his wound.

"Get up!" Wesley shouted.

Afraid he'd shoot again I stood up. Wesley grabbed my arm and led me out back. The last thing I heard was the cries of

Junior as he begged Wesley to let me go. I heard his screams until the doors to Wesley's truck were closed.

I was no longer worried about me. All I could focus on was if Junior would be okay until Dane could get to him. He couldn't die because of me.

"Drive." Wesley said, resting his gun onto my thigh.

I put the car in drive and pulled out of the driveway. I held on to the steering wheel as tight as I could to keep my hands from shaking. If I braked too hard or accelerated too fast Wesley's gun pressed harder down into my thigh.

Turning left onto my block I pulled into oncoming traffic and drove towards Avery's apartment. Part of me wanted to drive him there to keep him from getting angry but the other half of me knew I couldn't bring this man back into Avery's life.

"If you want Avery back I can talk to her for you. Help her realize she shouldn't have left you." I cried.

"I don't need you to do that. I can tell her myself."

"Can you put the gun away? I don't need it pointed at me while I'm driving."

"Just shut the fuck up and drive." He said.

While driving around town I tried to figure out where I could drive to before Wesley caught on I wasn't taking him to Avery. I could drive to Dane's but chances are no one would be there. If I went back to Ivy's he'd know. My best bet was to drive to Apollo's. It was farther than Dane's but I knew someone would be there. Even if Wesley figured out we were going the wrong way there was a chance one of Apollo's men would find me.

I took the backroads to Apollo's. It was a few minutes after six which meant the roads would be full of people leaving work. I couldn't let anyone else get hurt because of Wesley. I had barely made it ten minutes before Wesley started to get suspicious.

Realizing I was taking him the wrong way he raised the gun so that it was sitting just below my ribcage.

"I know Avery can't afford this shit." He spat, pointing at the condos we were driving by.

"She moved out of the city to be closer to the kid's new school. We still have quite a long drive." I lied.

"Bullshit!"

"I'm telling the truth!"

There was no convincing Wesley I was going the right way. If I had to guess I'd say he was drunk out of his mind. There was no way to reason with him. I took a left on a side road I knew would get me to Apollo's where there wouldn't be any houses for Wesley to look at. I was going ten above the speed limit. I was running out of time to make it to Apollo's alive.

Something I did must have tipped Wesley off because he blew up.

"You fucking bitch!" He yelled.

He pulled his gun off my waist and aimed it right at my temple.

"I warned you not to test me."

"Wesley, you don't want to do this." I cried.

"I told you I needed to talk to Avery and you're keeping her from me. Give me one reason I shouldn't shoot you right now."

"If you kill me you'll never find Avery."

"I found you, I found where she works. I don't need you to help me find her."

I looked at the gun through the rear view mirror. Wesley was starting to lose control. His fingers were starting to slip against the trigger. There was a good chance he killed me by accident if I didn't do something.

"You know what. Fuck you Wesley. Now I know exactly why Avery left you. You're a fucking coward."

If I wasn't going to make it to Apollo's the least I could do was make sure this piece of shit died with me.

"You're nothing but a coward and a drunk."

Wesley shook his gun in his hand and shifted his weight in his seat. It was then I saw he wasn't wearing his seatbelt. I couldn't wait for Wesley to pull the trigger. I'd made my decision. Wesley and I were going out together. It wasn't enough for me to only delay his reunion with Avery. He had hurt his family for the last time.

I drove until Wesley and I were nearly out of the city. I knew he was losing his patience and soon he'd doubt I was going the right way. I drove until we were the only ones on the road. Making sure no one was around and could get hurt I hit the gas as hard as I could. I took Wesley's truck from twenty to ninety in under a minute. The momentum of our speed caused him to lose his tight grip on his gun. It was sliding across the middle console. I took one more look at the road and made sure my seatbelt was buckled in.

I cranked the steering wheel as hard as I could to the left. It sent the truck skidding into a ditch. The front two tires hit mud and sent the truck spinning. Wesley wasn't wearing a seatbelt which meant he hit the dashboard hard. I let go of the steering wheel completely and let the truck take over. The last thing I remember before being knocked out cold was feeling the car flip into the field I'd crashed into. I could hear the screams and cries of Wesley as we flipped but all I could see was darkness.

I wonder if this is how Mom felt. We were with her when she died but did she even know? Could she feel us beside her? I couldn't feel anything. I knew I had to still be in the car but I was numb to everything around me. Everything was still, quiet, and cold. Could Mom feel me holding her hand or did she feel as alone as I did right now?

Maybe it was different for Dad. Maybe this feeling of being alone was what brought him relief. Did he regret it? Did the numbness make him wish he'd never left us? Would I get to see them again?

As I laid against broken glass I thought about Dane. I thought maybe if I held on a little longer I'd get to say goodbye to him. It wasn't fair. To die and not get to say goodbye to those you love. To not be able to see their faces one more time. It just wasn't fair.

CHAPTER FOURTEEN

Dane

"I need you in Chicago next week." Apollo said, walking into the living room.

"No thanks."

"It wasn't an offer. I have meetings here I can't leave but Raff requested a meeting."

"Send somebody else. If you put me alone in a room with Raff again I might kill him." I said.

"I'll text you details tomorrow." He said, ignoring my complaints.

"Did you not hear me? I said no."

"And I don't care." Apollo said, sitting down next to me.

I tried to punch his shoulder but he leaned to his left too fast.

"Hey!" Alex shouted through the hallways.

"We're in here." Apollo called back.

"Dane, your phone's blowing up. There's like twenty alarms all going off at once."

I immediately sat up, "Where is it?"

"Kitchen. How didn't you hear it from in here?" He asked.

I ignored him and ran into the kitchen where I left my phone charging. When I unlocked it I saw the alarms to Kate's security system all going off. I also had missed calls from Junior. I tried to call him back but he didn't pick up.

I ran from the kitchen to the living room, "We have to go!"

"Where?" Apollo asked, jumping to his feet.

"Ivy's! The alarms are going off."

Alex was right behind us. The three of us ran to the car. While I ran I tried to call Kate but her phone was sending me to voicemail.

"Shit. Shit. Shit." I cursed, throwing my phone onto the dashboard.

"I'm sure everything's fine." Apollo said.

I kept calling Kate's phone the rest of the drive over. Every time I got sent to her voicemail I imagined the worst. I was looking down at my phone as Apollo pulled up to Ivy's.

"Dane..." Alex said, tapping my shoulder.

When I looked up I saw the shattered window. I ran from Apollo's car and sprinted into Ivy's. I found Junior passed out on the floor covered in blood.

"Fuck." Apollo sighed, running in behind me.

Alex ran in between the two of us and fell to the floor beside Junior. He removed Junior's hand from his shoulder and tried to stop the bleeding. When Alex applied pressure to Junior's shoulder he woke up. He gasped in pain and shock when he saw us standing over him. He let out a whimper as Alex stuffed his ripped shirt into his wound.

"You're okay, you're okay." Alex said.

Apollo and I both knew he wasn't but we needed Junior to stay calm.

"What happened?" I asked Junior.

"Wesley." He choked.

"What?" I asked, leaning down closer to him.

"Wesley... took Kate. She's gone."

"What do you mean she's gone?" I asked, trying to grab Junior.

Junior tried to talk but nothing came out. I tried to reach out to him and slap his cheek to keep him awake but Apollo pulled me off of him. I rushed Apollo, trying to get back to Junior.

"Where is Kate?!" I screamed.

"Dane." Apollo shouted.

"Where is she!"

"Dane!" Apollo yelled again.

He held me until I calmed down. When he was sure I wouldn't run to Junior he let go of me.

"She's gone." I whispered.

"We'll find her."

"Alex. Alex you have to find her." I said.

"Can't really do that right now." He said, nodding his head to an unconscious Junior.

"Go, I'll take care of Junior. Go figure out a way to find Kate." Apollo said, taking Alex's place.

Alex started to run back to the car but stopped when he realized I wasn't behind him. I tried to move but I just couldn't. I looked around the empty bakery praying, hoping Kate would walk in from the kitchen. I waited to confirm that this was all a joke, that she was right outside waiting to run in with a smile on her face.

"Dane..." Apollo said, "Go."

Alex grabbed my shoulder and ran with me to the car. He wiped his bloodied hand against his suit and opened his phone. I wandered around outside and looked for Kate in the crowd of strangers on the sidewalk. Any minute now she'd turn the corner.

Alex put his phone on speaker and walked over to me. The look on his face told me he was about to give me bad news.

"Just tell me."

"Kate left with someone in an old pick up. They left the parking lot together. Romeo's using traffic cameras to find out where they went."

"I want to see." I told him.

"I don't think that's a good idea-"

"Show me the fucking video." I yelled.

Alex tossed me his phone and showed me the video of Kate leaving with an older man. He looked sleep deprived, probably high. When Kate climbed into the driver's seat the man made the mistake of showing the camera the gun he was holding.

Fuck.

"No one's faster than Romeo when it comes to tracking. We'll find her." Alex said.

Alex's words meant nothing. We both knew he was only saying that to make me feel better. He left me alone on the sidewalk to flag down a few more of Apollo's men that were just arriving. They ran in to help Junior. I tried to walk through them to find Alex but I couldn't see straight. Everything in front of me was blurry. Thinking I found Alex I ran into someone else.

"I got you." Apollo said, holding me up by my shoulders.

"He took her." I told him.

"I know. Alex told me everything."

"I don't know what to do."

"You and I are going to find her." He said.

"What if she's already-"

"No. We aren't going to think like that. Kate's a fighter. She's going to be just fine."

"I can't feel my legs." I said.

"Come on, let's go inside."

Apollo brought me inside and walked with me to Kate's office. He pulled out her chair and had me sit. Without Apollo I probably would have passed out. All of my fears were coming true. Kate was gone and probably dead.

"Dane, breathe."

Apollo sat with me and waited until I calmed down.

"You good?" He asked.

"Yeah."

"Alright, then let's go figure out what's going on."

I nodded my head and followed Apollo back out to the main floor and saw that Junior was gone. All that was left was the spreading pool of his blood.

"What do we know?" Apollo asked.

"Avery Shaw, one of Eliana's clients filed for divorce a few months ago from her abusive husband. The divorce went through this week which also included a restraining order. Wesley, Avery's ex-husband, came in here looking for her. Instead he found Kate and Junior." Alex said.

"Why did he take Kate?" I asked.

Romeo spoke up through Alex's phone, "We don't know. It looks like Wesley lost it when Kate told him Avery wasn't here. He tried taking Kate out the back and shot Junior when he tried to stop him. We have no idea where they're going or why he took her."

"Does Kate know where Avery lives?" Apollo asked.

"Probably. Eliana's been working with Kate to set up new places to live that are close to the bakery and schools in the neighborhood."

"Romeo start looking for Kate and that truck on the traffic cameras. Alex call Eliana. Tell her we're sending a few guys over to watch Avery's house in case Kate shows up. Tell her to let us know if Avery doesn't pick up. Worst case scenario Kate's already there." Apollo said.

"What can I do?" I asked.

"Nothing. You're staying here with me until we figure out more." Apollo said.

"No."

"You're not thinking straight, I can't have you going out and making the situation worse."

"I'm not going to sit around and do nothing while we wait to find out if Kate is even still alive!"

"I'm not asking Dane. You don't go anywhere until we get in touch with Avery."

I looked over at the door. Everyone watched and waited to see what I would do. They were all expecting me to freak out and storm out on Apollo, maybe beat the shit out of him on my way out. They were waiting for me to explode.

"Okay." I agreed.

Apollo gave me a quick nod. I leaned against the counter and watched as everyone sprang into action. Alex called Eliana, a few guys left for Avery's house, and Apollo worked with Romeo over the phone.

With every second I stood there doing nothing it got harder to breathe. My chest tightened as I watched Apollo order his men around Ivy's. I tried to focus on the positive instead of the negative. Apollo was right. Kate's a fighter; she's smart. I waited until I was sure no one was looking for me and then I snuck into Kate's office. Alex showed me Kate leaving with

Wesley but I know they were intentionally avoiding showing me what happened in Ivy's before that. I logged in and started watching from the minute Wesley showed up. I had to turn off the computer when I saw Wesley point his gun right at Kate's chest.

    Even with a gun pointed right at her she still stood tall. She didn't show him any fear. She stayed calm even though I'm sure she was freaking out. I turned off her computer but I stuck around in her office for a few more minutes. I looked around at her cluttered desk. I looked to my left and saw one of her drawers open. It was the one drawer I wasn't ever allowed to go in.

    Every time I tried to open it Kate got all flustered and kicked me out of her office. I opened the drawer a bit more and found nothing but scraps of paper and used napkins. When I pulled out the drawer a few more inches I saw that it was more than used napkins and old receipts. Kate's secret drawer was full of every note I'd ever left her. Every single note. She kept them all. In the bottom of the drawer was an envelope. When I pulled it out I found a note from Eliana. It was the note from our first dinner together when I came over with the gift basket. She'd even kept the little sticky notes I would leave in her apartment on mornings I had to leave early.

    One piece of paper stood out from the rest. It was the first note I ever left. The one promising I'd be back the next day to see her. I was so afraid that day to say goodbye to her in person. I hid the note under my tip and waited outside for her to find it. I hid just past the window and waited to make sure she got my note.

    I carefully put all of her notes back exactly how I found them and closed the drawer. I stood up and walked back to the front. This wasn't how our story was going to end. I deserved a life with Kate. I wanted to grow old with her. She deserved a better ending.

    I ran out and found Apollo, "I can't just sit and do nothing. I'm going to find her. You can come if you want but no one here is going to be able to stop me."

"Dane..." Apollo said, stepping closer to me.

"No, you aren't talking me out of this. She's out there somewhere, alone, and scared. Probably hoping that we are looking for her and coming to save her. I'm not waiting-"

"Dane." Alex said.

I looked around the room. Everyone was still, frozen in place. The rush of finding Kate was gone. Everyone stood with worried eyes and they were all staring at me.

No.

"They found her."

No.

"Eliana just called. They're taking her to the hospital now."

"Is she- is she alive?" I whispered.

"They found her unconscious on the toll road. It looks like the truck flipped a few times before rolling into a ditch." Apollo said.

"Is she alive?!" I asked louder.

"Eliana says when they got her into the ambulance she still had a pulse. It wasn't strong but it was there." Alex said.

I looked around the room at Apollo's men. All of them were carefully placed around the room. They were blocking the door. When I looked over at Apollo he was already shaking his head.

"Give me the keys." I said.

"I can't do that Dane."

"Keys."

"Eliana says they're taking Kate into surgery. It won't do you any good to get to the hospital right now. We need you calm before you get there."

"Apollo." I threatened, stepping closer to him.

"I can't let you leave here alone Dane."

"What would you do if it was Eliana? " I asked.

Apollo looked around the room. We both knew his answer. He pulled out his car keys and tossed them to me.

I have no memory of driving to the hospital. One minute I was standing in Ivy's and next thing I knew I was running into the emergency room. I found Eliana in the waiting room. She was pacing around and talking to someone on the phone. When she turned around and saw me she hung up.

She ran over and pulled me into a hug, "I'm so sorry."

"How is she?" I asked.

"They just took her back. They're taking her into surgery now in case she has any internal bleeding."

"How bad is it?"

Eliana paused; afraid I was going to freak out. I relaxed my shoulders and gave her a small nod letting her know I'd be okay.

"They're worried about her head. She was unresponsive when they got to the scene. The surgeon said she wouldn't know how bad it was until they ran a few tests."

"I need to see her." I told Eliana.

"You can't. Not right now at least. They're taking her back for an MRI then straight into surgery. They wouldn't even let me see her when she got here."

I walked over to the staff only doors of the hospital. I thought maybe I'd be able to see her from the window but there was no one on the other side of the doors.

Eliana walked over and waited with me at the doors. I took a deep breath and looked down at Eliana.

"What if she..." I stuttered.

Eliana held my hand.

"What if she doesn't make it?"

"Kate's strong. She's not going down without a fight." Eliana said.

I really needed Eliana to be right. I needed Kate to fight until the very end.

Eliana stayed by my side all night. We sat together and waited for Kate's doctor to come and find us. I don't remember much but I do remember Apollo showing up to keep me company. He sat with me while Eliana left to make more phone calls.

Hours later a doctor came through the doors, "Kate Kelley?"

"How is she?" I asked.

"She's being taken to the ICU. For now she's stable but she suffered a lot of injuries. We will have to monitor her closely these next few days to make sure there's no long term brain damage and her lungs heal properly."

"She's alive?" I asked.

"Yes, she's alive. If you'd like I can take you back to see her. She's not awake but I'm sure you'd rather be waiting with her than out here. I just need to confirm with the front desk you're family."

"I'm her husband. Don't waste your time checking with the front desk."

Apollo gave me a knowing look but played along with my lie.

"Alright then, let's go."

I walked with the doctor down a long hallway. We stopped at the end of the hall in front of a room full of nurses. There were so many people working around Kate I couldn't see her through the crowd. I stopped at the door and leaned against the glass.

"You can go in and see her if you'd like. They're just setting up her monitor." The doctor smiled.

I stepped into the room and nearly fell to the floor. I thought getting to see Kate would make me feel better but it only made me feel worse. She was hardly recognizable. I sat down in a chair next to her and carefully ran my thumb over her hand. With shaky hands I reached out to her.

"Oh Kate." I whispered.

Her shoulder was bandaged and set in place. I looked over her face and counted every scratch, every cut, every bruise. The doctor came to the other side of her bed and started listing off her injuries, one after another.

Broken and fractured ribs. Punctured lung. Broken collar bone. Thigh wounds, head wounds, damage to the brain from impact, concussion. The list went on and on.

"I'd like to keep her sedated for a few days to give her a few days to heal. We won't know the extent of any potential brain damage until the swelling goes down. Her MRI isn't showing any bleeding or damage but it's too soon to say when she'll wake up. Would you like a moment alone?" She asked.

"Yes, please."

The doctor grabbed her binder and asked for the nurses still working on Kate to leave. Finally alone I pulled my chair closer to Kate and carefully pulled her hand into mine. I kissed the palm of her hand and ran my fingers up and down her arm. I sat beside her, in disbelief of what I was seeing. I tucked her hair behind her ear and leaned in to kiss her temple. I was afraid to hold her too tightly. I was afraid even under sedation I would cause her pain.

"You did so good Kate." I cried.

I carefully ran my fingers between hers. Her hand fell limp in mine.

"I need you to keep fighting, baby. I'll never forgive you if you leave me."

I knew she couldn't hear me but it was comforting to talk to her.

Evergreen Ivy

Every thirty minutes a nurse would come in to check her IV and her vitals but then they'd leave us. I stayed right by Kate's side all night. I assumed it was morning when a different nurse came in to check on her. The next time the nurse came in he brought Eliana with him.

I didn't bother to look up when she came in. I couldn't take my eyes off of Kate. I was afraid if I did she'd disappear.

"How's she doing?" She asked.

"How do you think?" I snapped back.

Eliana ignored my rude comment and stepped closer to Kate.

"The nurse who brought me up said they have a great cafeteria. Let's go grab some breakfast." She said.

"No."

"Dane, you have to eat."

"I'm not leaving her."

Eliana sighed but didn't try to argue. She knew I wasn't leaving Kate's room.

"If I bring you food will you eat it?" She asked.

When I didn't answer her she took my silence as a yes and left me alone. She came back a few minutes later with a smoothie and pancakes. She pulled out the table from the corner and slid it over to me. I tried ignoring the food next to me but Eliana wasn't giving up.

"When Kate wakes up and finds out you stopped eating she's going to kick your ass."

"I'll worry about that when she wakes up." I told her.

"Worry about it now because as soon as she's up I'm telling her that you stopped taking care of yourself because of her."

I let go of Kate's hand and sat back in my chair. I grabbed the smoothie and took a sip.

"Happy?" I asked.

"Finish it."

I rolled my eyes but finished off the whole smoothie in a few gulps. I showed Eliana the empty cup.

"Thank you."

Eliana moved the table back into the corner and then came to stand by me.

"Do you want me to stay with her for a while so you can take a break or get some air?"

"No."

"Dane-"

"I'm not leaving her." I said.

"Okay."

"I just can't."

"I'll come back in a few hours for lunch." She told me, leaving the room.

Apollo was the next one to visit. He came in carrying food. I'm going to guess Eliana thought if anyone could get me to eat it'd be Apollo.

"How is she doing?" He asked, sitting down next to me.

"Fine."

"Eliana said you have to eat the sandwich I brought."

I ignored Apollo like I had tried to ignore Eliana when she came in with food. Apollo set down the sandwich on the table and pulled out his phone. He pulled up a text and cleared his throat.

"El says if you don't eat your sandwich she will show up for dinner and spoon feed you soup. She said you can eat some protein now or she'll be back with a big bowl of chicken noodle."

"She's not going to do that." I said, looking over at Apollo.

He showed me her text to him and it did in fact promise she'd be back if I didn't eat.

I let go of Kate's hand and pulled out Eliana's sandwich. I was about to take a bite when Apollo held out his phone for a picture.

"What the fuck are you doing?"

"She needs proof it was you who ate the sandwich. She said she'd know if I ate it."

"She's fucking crazy."

"Hey, that's my wife you're talking about." Apollo laughed, trying his best to sound angry.

"Why is she acting like this? She doesn't even like me that much." I asked.

"She doesn't give a shit about you. She's worried about Kate. I think she feels responsible for Wesley attacking Ivy's. She's channeling all of her anxiety towards you." Apollo said.

"Is there any chance you can get her to back off a little?"

"Sorry no can do. For once she's not worried about me. I'll enjoy you being her distraction for as long as I can. Plus, we both know El's never listened to me a day in her life. There's nothing I can say to get her to back off."

A small mumble from Kate caused both of us to look over at Kate.

"Is that her waking up?" Apollo asked

"No, the doctor said it was too soon to take her off sedation. She says Kate needs a few more days to heal."

Apollo came over and rested his hand on my shoulder.

"She's going to be okay Dane."

I shook my head in agreement unable to say anything. I had a hard time believing anyone that told me she was going to be okay. It felt like they were lying to me.

Apollo sat with me for the rest of the night. After sending Eliana proof I ate he left me alone and kept his distance. I barely noticed him in the room with me.

On the third day Kate's doctor came in and took her off sedation. Eliana convinced me to take a quick walk around the hospital in the morning. I didn't want to leave Kate alone but Apollo promised he'd keep a close eye on her until I got back. I hated to admit it but I desperately needed some fresh air. It helped me clear up my mind. When we got back to Kate's room Apollo was sitting with Kate.

"Anything?" I asked.

"Nothing yet. Doctor came by looking for you." Apollo told me.

"What did she want?"

"She said the cops are anxious for Kate to wake up. They want to get their report started. I heard the nurses talking about Wesley. He's in custody but they can't charge him until Kate wakes up."

"How that fucker survived will never make sense to me." I said.

"I can keep the police away from Kate for a few days but eventually they're going to need her statement." Apollo said.

"I don't want her talking with them. Wesley's mine. He's not leaving with the cops." I said.

"I'll make a few calls, see what I can do." Apollo agreed.

I sat down next to Kate and tried to calm down.

"You guys don't have to stay. Doctor said it could be a while before she's up."

"We aren't going anywhere." Eliana said, taking the chair next to me.

Eliana and Apollo stayed with me through the night. I was asleep in the chair when Eliana hit my shoulder.

"Dane!"

I looked around the room and saw Eliana pointing at Kate. Kate had begun to shift in her sleep. It looked like she was in pain and starting to wake up.

"Go get a nurse."

Apollo left the room while Eliana and I waited for Kate to wake up. She threw her hand to her face and tried clawing at her ventilator. She scratched and pulled at her throat and mouth. Apollo came back with the nurse just in time. They held her hand down and gave her a few minutes to wake up.

"Why can't you take it out?" Eliana asked.

"She needs to be able to breathe on her own without it for a few minutes. I can't take it out until she's completely conscious."

We were forced to sit and watch Kate struggle to breathe on her own. Eventually she calmed down enough and stopped resisting against the nurse.

After removing the ventilator the nurse gave Kate some space. Time slowed, everything blurred. All I could focus on was getting to see Kate's eyes again. Getting to see her smile.

Slowly, her eyes fluttered open. When she realized where she was, panic set in. I leaned over the bed so that I was in her eye line. I grabbed her hand and held it in mine.

"Kate, you're okay. You're safe."

Kate heard my voice and began to calm down. Her eyes searched for mine. I had to clench my jaw to keep myself from crying again. She was in so much pain and there was nothing I could do to help her. She was calmer than before but she was still moving too much. If she kept trying to climb out of her bed she was going to hurt herself.

"I need you to stop moving Kate. Slow down, take a deep breath." I said.

I tapped Kate's hand and helped her slow down her breathing. I gave her a small smile when her breathing became more normal.

Kate let go of my hand and tried to reach for my face. She had no strength to be pulling me anywhere but when she placed her hand around my neck I let her move me where she wanted me. She leaned me down closer to her. I could hear her trying to whisper something.

Her voice was too scratchy to understand. All that came out was short painful breaths. I leaned away from her to try and read her lips. She became frustrated when I didn't understand her.

"Say it one more time, slowly."

I read Kate's lips and tried to match the shapes she was making. She continued to repeat herself in a panic.

"Junior!" Eliana shouted out, finally understanding Kate.

"Junior?" I asked.

Kate shook her head yes.

"He's okay. He's at Apollo's right now recovering."

"You shouldn't be worried about Junior. You should be worrying about Alex. I gave him orders to take care of Junior until he gets better. He's worse off than Junior is at the moment." Apollo said.

Kate smiled at Apollo's joke. That smile was the only memory I had of Kate to hold onto these past few days. It was a relief to see that smile again. The way her eyes light up, God I'd never forget that smile.

"Are you in any pain?" I asked Kate.

She nodded her head yes.

"Where?"

Kate pointed to her ribs. The nurse came over to fix a few pillows on Kate's bed and to give her some more pain medication. Kate didn't know it yet but these next few days were going to suck. Recovering would be nothing compared to the pain she felt during the accident. Her body needed time to heal and to do that it would be painful for her.

The medicine the nurse gave Kate made her sleepy. She struggled to keep her eyes open.

"Don't fight sleep baby. I'll still be here when you wake up." I promised her.

Kate reached for my hand and then fell back asleep. Apollo and Eliana gave me a quick hug then left the room. They were glad to see Kate awake but they needed to get back to the house. They were still trying to decide who could help us with our Wesley problem. I could worry about Wesley later. All that mattered right now was being with Kate.

Sometime in the middle of the night Kate woke up. Her meds must have worn off. I woke up when I heard her whimpers. I sat up in my seat and watched her struggle to find a comfortable position to sleep in.

"What hurts?"

"Everything." She whispered.

I stepped into the hallway and flagged down the night nurse. She came back to increase Kate's morphine. Immediately Kate felt relief. I leaned over Kate and gave her a quick kiss on the forehead.

From the corner of the room Kate's nurse let out a sigh.

"Is something wrong?" I asked.

"Oh no everything's fine." She said.

"Are you sure?" Kate asked.

"Forgive me for saying so, but you are a very lucky lady." She said.

"I don't feel too lucky right now."

"Girl, with a husband like him, you won the lottery. I've been a nurse for over fifteen years and I've never met anyone more attentive and caring than that man right there. Believe me when I say you are very lucky."

Kate squeezed my hand and let out a laugh, "He sure is one of a kind."

"I'll let you two get some rest."

When the door was closed Kate repositioned herself in her bed to stare down at me.

"Husband?" She asked.

"They weren't going to let me be in here with you if I wasn't family. I panicked. I'm sorry."

"Oh don't apologize. I should be thanking you. I'm married to all this." Kate said, grabbing my arm and trying to give my muscles a squeeze.

"Kate!" I laughed.

"What?"

"Those pain meds you're taking are causing you to forget where you are right now."

"I know exactly where I am. I'm lying next to my caring, attentive, deliciously hot husband."

"Oh my God." I sighed, covering my face with my hands.

"Hey, you can't be embarrassed right now. You chose to marry me." She continued to tease.

"You know the best part about those pain meds the nurse just gave you?" I asked.

"What?"

"You aren't going to remember any of this." I said.

"I will too."

"Tomorrow you'll forget all about our little conversation and I'll get to save this story until our real wedding. You'll have to explain to our friends and family what you meant when you called me *deliciously hot*." I smiled.

Kate's smile dropped when I mentioned our real wedding. Maybe it was too soon for her to be talking about that.

"Is getting married something you've thought about?" She asked.

"All the time." I told her honestly.

Kate's eyes got big.

"What you don't?" I asked.

"No, no I do. I just didn't think you were also thinking about, you know, marrying me."

"I think about a hell of a lot more than just marrying you."

"Really?" Kate asked.

"Really."

"I don't believe you."

"It's true. All I've been able to think about these past few days is what the future looks like for the two of us."

"And what does it look like?" She asked.

As excited as Kate was I could see her eyes start to droop. Soon the medicine would kick in and she'd fall asleep.

"I'm not sure now is the best time to have this conversation Kate. Maybe another time."

"No, I want you to tell me now. It will help me fall asleep. I need something nice to dream about."

"Alright." I agreed.

I fixed her pillows and helped her shift her weight off of her shoulder before sitting down beside her.

"Marrying you has never been an if but a when. I knew the night of our first date we were going to be together for a long time."

Kate smiled at my confession. She squeezed my hand in excitement.

"Our engagement will be a short one. We'll have a small wedding, inviting only our closest friends."

"You've really thought this through haven't you?" She asked.

"You haven't?"

"No I have. I wonder what it would be like to see you become a dad. To get to have a family with you." She whispered.

"I dream about that too. I'm a little terrified but I'm sure with you by my side we'll be okay."

"You're already an incredible husband. How much harder could fatherhood be?" She teased.

As much as Kate was enjoying our conversation I could see her medicine catching up to her. She closed her eyes and held onto my hand a little tighter.

"Tell me more. I want the full timeline." She yawned.

"Well, we both struggle to balance work and the kids but we make it work. Junior will pretend to hate babysitting but he'll be the best uncle to our kids. He'll be there for all their birthdays and graduations. Eliana and Apollo will be the fun aunt and uncle that spoils them with toys and cars." I said.

"What else?"

"One day, our kids will be all grown up, Apollo and I will be ready to retire and even though it will be hard you'll find someone you trust to take care of Ivy's for you. We'll be ready for the next chapter in our life. Our journey will end how it began, just the two of us."

"Where does it end?" She asked.

"I don't know, somewhere warm. I'll buy you a house somewhere on the West Coast where the ivy grows all year long. We'll get a cute little house on the water. You can have that garden you've always dreamed of and I'll pick up fishing. During summers our grandkids will visit and we'll take them to all the coolest spots in town. On rainy days you'll keep busy with baking and I'll be right by your side happy to help. Just like now." I whispered to her.

I stopped because I thought Kate had fallen asleep but she tapped my hand a few times.

"That sounds nice." She whispered.

I watched as her muscles relaxed as she found a little bit of relief.

"I love you, Dane."

"I love you. Kate." I whispered to her as she fell asleep for good.

I was hoping Kate wouldn't remember our conversation in the morning. It would ruin a few secrets I'd been keeping from her. It was too soon to tell her about the proposal I had been planning with Eliana and the summer house in Washington I'd bought for us.

CHAPTER FIFTEEN

Kate

I woke up the next morning to arguing. I opened my eyes and saw Dane and Apollo out in the hall. I sat up and tried to eavesdrop. Apollo was trying to convince Dane of something.

"I told them not to wake you but they don't know the meaning of quiet." Eliana said from a corner in my room.

"You scared the shit out of me!" I gasped.

"Sorry."

"Could you have picked a creepier corner to hide in?" I asked.

"How you feeling?"

"Sore. Like I got hit by a bus."

"Well, getting hit by a bus might have hurt less." She said.

"You think you're funny, don't you."

"A little." She smiled.

"I missed you." I told her.

"Yeah, me too."

"So, what are they arguing about?"

"They're fighting about Wesley."

At the mention of Wesley my body froze.

"Cops are waiting to book him but they're waiting to talk to you first."

"Why does that make Dane angry?" I asked.

"If you tell them what Wesley did to you then they'll have to arrest him."

"Isn't that a good thing?" I asked.

"Not to Dane. Once he's in custody we lose control of the situation. Dane and Apollo won't be able to get to him. Apollo could call in a favor and get them to drop charges but he doesn't want anyone to find out how we're connected to Wesley. Right now no one knows I'm helping Avery build a case against him. If Apollo asks for Wesley they'll want to know why. The cops are only here because of the report the hospital made. If Apollo gets involved it makes things messy."

"I don't get how any of this is my problem."

"Dane told Apollo your first night here that Wesley was his to take care of. He wants payback for what he did to you and Junior."

"So if I tell the cops what Wesley did then Dane doesn't get his revenge?"

Eliana nodded her head yes.

"But Wesley hurt me. If anyone deserves revenge for the pain he caused it's me."

"And that's exactly what I told Dane. You're the only person that gets to make this decision Kate. You decide what happens to Wesley."

I sat with Eliana and considered my options. I wanted Wesley to suffer for what he did to Junior and me but would I be able to live with myself if I gave Wesley over to Dane instead of the cops?

"Can you tell the detectives I'm ready to speak with them?"

"Kate, I highly advise against that. There's no rush. Let's take a few minutes to process the past couple of days. I don't want you rushing into this." Eliana said.

"I'm not rushing into anything. Just go get them please."

Eliana walked over to the door, nervous at my decision to talk to the cops.

"El?" I called out to her.

"Yeah?"

"Could you take Dane and Apollo with you. I think I need to be alone right now."

"Sure."

Eliana dragged Apollo and Dane down the hallway and back into the waiting room. A few minutes later Eliana came back with the detectives. Dane was the first one to enter the room. He cautiously let in the two detectives.

"Ms. Kelley we're glad to see you awake and recovering." The shorter detective smiled.

I looked over at Dane and Apollo, "I'd like to talk with the detectives alone please."

I ignored Dane's complaints and looked over at Eliana. I gave her a nod letting her know I needed them to leave. She understood them being in the room would probably escalate the situation, so she kicked out an angry Dane and then came back to stand by my side.

The two detectives sat down next to my bed and pulled out a small recorder.

"We have a few questions about the night of your accident." One of them told me.

"You're here because the hospital made a report." I said.

"Yes."

"Well I appreciate you coming down here to see me but what happened that night was an accident. I lost control of the truck when a fox ran out across the street."

The two detectives looked at each other.

"Are you sure? There's evidence that suggests it wasn't an accident."

"What evidence?" Eliana asked.

One of the detectives coughed and shifted in his seat.

"Well, our crime scene investigators found a gun in the truck that had recently been fired and gun residue on Mr. Shaw's fingers. Not to mention the paramedics found handprint bruises on your arm in the ambulance."

"Is Wesley's gun not registered? Does he not have a permit to carry?" I asked.

"No, he does but there is doubt it was concealed appropriately."

"So at best you have a misdemeanor?" Eliana asked.

"Well, not exactly. Not if Ms. Kelley has something she'd like to tell us."

"You want me to tell you why a gun was in the truck that I flipped? Would it have helped if I kept a close eye on the gun falling out of the glove compartment? Next time I'm rolling into a ditch and I think I'm going to die I'll do a quick check of everything around me. Would that be better?"

"No of course not but our investigators found gun powder residue on Mr. Shaw's fingers. We need your statement to help us fill in some missing pieces of the story."

"I'm not sure what you're asking me to say to help you with your case against Wesley but I did not see him using his gun. I didn't even know it was there in the truck with us."

The taller detective gave me a look of disbelief, "While that may be true we're still concerned about the bruises on your arm."

"After I lost control of the truck Wesley freaked out. He wasn't wearing a seatbelt. Out of panic he grabbed onto me for stability. Have you ever been in a car while it flipped?" I asked them.

"No, Ma'am."

"Well then I don't expect you to understand the panic Wesley was experiencing as he knocked around inside the truck."

The two detectives weren't buying my story. They gave each other a knowing look as they clicked off their recorder.

"Was there anything else?" I asked.

"No."

"Great. If you don't mind I'm still not feeling well so I'd appreciate it if you'd leave now."

Before leaving the room one of them took a step forward.

"Please let us know if you think of anything else. We're just a phone call away if you change your mind and want to share any more information with us." He said, looking over at Dane and Apollo.

"Thank you." I smiled, taking his business card.

The two detectives stalled outside my room. They stopped to talk to Apollo. I couldn't read their lips but their conversation wasn't a pleasant one. Eliana and I watched Apollo send the two detectives off before Dane said something he'd regret.

Eliana was tired of Dane and Apollo's arguing. It seemed to be all they were good at these days. She closed the curtain around my bed that blocked my view of the hallway. I finally had some peace and quiet to myself. I closed my eyes to enjoy this moment alone.

I thought Eliana might leave the room but when I didn't hear her leave I opened my eyes. I saw her standing over near the curtains with tears in her eyes.

"I'm so sorry." She cried.

"What for?" I asked.

"This is all my fault. You would have never gotten hurt if I hadn't asked you to let my clients work at Ivy's. You're in here because of me."

"You didn't ask Eliana, I offered. I knew there was a chance something like this could happen but I didn't care. Helping your clients find their freedom and independence was more important than the fear of something like this happening."

"I should have never agreed to let you help."

"Hey, come here." I said, patting the bed next to me.

Eliana wiped the tears on her cheek away quickly, hoping to hide them from me.

"None of this is your fault. I should be thanking you for bringing those incredible women into my life and for making my life easier. I was feeling burnt out and struggling to run Ivy's on my own and now they take care of it like it's their own shop. You have nothing to apologize for."

"You almost died!"

"But I didn't. I'm still here and you can bet your ass as soon as I'm walking and out of this annoying brace I'll be back at Ivy's helping your clients get back on their feet." I smiled.

"I can't ask you to do that."

"I'm not going to let someone like Wesley ruin all the hard work we put into Ivy's. If you ask me to quit and stop working with you he wins. So I'm a little banged up but I'll live. And trust me, Dane is going to take care of Wesley. The only bad thing to come out of this accident is how much money I'm going to lose when Junior recovers."

Eliana let out a laugh in between her crying.

"I'm serious. How can I ever ask him to pay for his desserts when he risked his own life to save me? He's now entitled to a lifetime of free cupcakes."

"You really think Dane is going to let you keep working with me?" She asked.

"I'm not worried about it. I can be quite convincing when I need to be." I said, giving Eliana my best attempt at a slow wink.

"Stop no, I don't want to hear about the weird things you two do in bed." She laughed jumping out of my bed.

"You good?" I asked.

"I'm good."

"Great because I have one more favor to ask."

"Nope. I'm not doing that."

"You don't even know what I was going to ask!"

"I'm not telling Dane he can't come back in here. He's already upset with me. I can't be the one to tell him he can't come see you."

"You're one of Dane's favorite people. He'll listen to you." I told her.

Eliana raised her eyebrow and looked right at me.

I laughed and rolled onto my side, "Okay fine! So you're not his favorite person but if you told him not to come in here he would listen to you. You're my attorney, he has to do everything you say."

"That's not how it works." She laughed.

"Damn."

"Best I can do is stall him for a few minutes." She said.

"Fine." I sighed.

Eliana did her best to leave the room without moving the curtain too much. When I heard the door slide open and then close again I did my best to move my pillows and blankets around. Maybe if I pretended to be asleep he wouldn't bother me.

The door opened one more time and through the curtain I could see Dane's outline. He slipped through the opening in the curtain and sat down next to me in his chair.

"I know you're awake." He said.

Damn, I was acting my heart out. How did he figure it out?

"Your toes are wiggling." He answered.

I opened my good eye and looked over at him.

"Hi." I whispered.

He looked mad.

"You shouldn't have done that." He said.

"Done what?" I asked.

"Lied to the cops. You should have done what was best for you, not what was best for me."

"I did do what was best for me. I considered telling them the truth and sending Wesley to prison. But I knew him going to prison is what he would have wanted. He deserves to pay for what he did to Avery all those years. He doesn't get to take the easy way out. Just promise me one thing."

"Anything." He said.

"You'll tell me when it's finished. When he's finally dead. I don't want to know what you do but I do need to know when he's gone."

To hide the tears that were falling Dane ducked his head down. I ran my hand through his hair and down his neck. His emotions from the last few days were finally catching up with him.

"I can't believe I almost lost you."

"Dane, look at me."

Dane refused to look up. He sat with his head in between his arms.

"Baby, look at me."

Finally he lifted his head and grabbed my hand.

"I need you to really look Dane. I need you to see that I'm going to be okay. I'm going to heal and this is all going to be a thing in the past. This will all be just a bad memory, a short chapter of our lives."

I took one of Dane's hands and brought it up to my heart. He was careful not to get too close to my brace and bandages as I laid his hand down on my chest.

"I'm alive because of you Dane. You're the reason I kept fighting. The doctor says all of my injuries were relatively minor and I'll live a long and healthy life. That means you're stuck with me for a really long time."

Dane wiped his tears and stood up to kiss my forehead.

"I can't imagine wanting to be stuck with anyone else. I love you Kate."

"If you really love me, you'll do me one more favor." I told him.

"Anything you need, it's yours."

"I need you to break me out of here. I'm ready to go home."

"I'll go find the doctor." He smiled.

Dane worked his magic and had me discharged before dinner. I probably could have gone another day recovering in the hospital but I had to get out or I was going to go crazy.

It took longer to leave the parking lot than it did getting discharged. I fought with Dane about pillow support for twenty minutes. After threatening to walk home he finally gave up and agreed two pillows was enough support for my brace.

I thought I'd sleep on the drive home but my pain meds were wearing off and I wasn't allowed to take any more for a few hours. When Dane finally did make it to his house I was exhausted. All I wanted right now was to get to sleep in a bed that wasn't the shitty hospital bed I'd been in for over a week.

Dane took my things and pillows into the house before coming back to help me get in. He was right by my side in case I needed any help getting up the porch stairs.

"God it feels so good to get out of that hospital."

"Doctor says you need to eat something before you take your medicine. Can I fix you something?" Dane asked.

"I don't want food. I just want to go to bed."

"I really think we should eat something first." Dane said.

"No Dane, please I just want to sleep."

"Did I hear someone offer to make food?" A familiar voice called out from the living room.

I looked at Dane and saw him hiding a smile with his hand.

"Is that who I think it is?" I asked.

"I don't know. Maybe you should go see for yourself."

When I walked into the living room I found Junior sitting on the couch with his legs kicked up.

"Oh my God." I cried.

"Hey Kate." He smiled.

"It's really you."

Junior slowly stood up from the couch and walked over to me. He carefully wrapped an arm around my good shoulder and gave me a light squeeze.

"How are you feeling?" He asked.

"Like shit." I told him.

"Well you look amazing."

In between the tears I let out an embarrassing laugh. I wiped the tears and snot away while I looked Junior up and down. He looked perfectly normal. A stranger looking at him would never be able to tell he'd just been shot.

Junior tried to pull away from the hug but I held onto him tighter. Realizing Junior was still healing I let go to give him some space. He helped me sit down on the couch, moving around a few pillows for me.

"Dane told me what you did, how you lied to the cops." He said.

"I had to. I want Wesley to pay for what he did to us."

Junior held my hand and gave me a knowing nod, "You did the right thing."

I still couldn't believe he was here sitting in front of me. I looked over Junior's chest one more time just to make sure he was really okay. He looked down at his left shoulder and held up his shirt.

"Bullet went right through. Doctor stitched me up in no time." He assured.

I looked at the bandages on Junior's chest. They were similar to mine. The tears began to flow again as I thought about Junior lying on the floor as Wesley pulled me to the truck.

"I thought he'd killed you. There was so much blood" I cried.

"Don't worry I'm not going anywhere. It's going to take a lot more than one little bullet to kill me." He joked.

"Not funny Junior." I said, wiping away my tears.

"I'd do it all over again if I had to Kate. All that mattered in that moment was protecting you. Plus recovery hasn't been all that bad. Apollo has Alex running around like a little bitch."

"Poor Alex."

"I heard you got a few plates in there." Junior said, pointing to my collarbone.

"They had to piece my clavicle back together, the x-rays are brutal."

"That's badass." Junior said.

"Yeah I guess it's pretty cool."

"It still kind of feels like a dream. Like that night never even happened." Junior said.

"Yeah, I get that. I keep waking up forgetting where I am but it doesn't take long for the pain to remind me of what happened."

Junior pointed to my brace and then at his shoulder.

"You know what this means don't you?"

What?" I asked.

"We're going to have matching scars." He smiled.

I shouldn't have found any comfort in that or found it funny but I did. Maybe it was the way he said it that made it sound less awful.

Junior and I sat together for a few more minutes before Dane came in to check on me. As excited as I was to see Junior I was exhausted and I needed sleep. Alex came back in to help get Junior to the car even though he was totally capable of walking on his own. I walked outside with Dane to see them off. As Junior was getting into the car I grabbed Dane's hand.

"Can you help me get down to the car?" I asked.

Dane held my hand and helped me walk over to the car. I stopped Junior's door from closing and looked around at Alex and Dane.

"Could you two give us a minute?" I asked.

Alex and Dane walked over to the garage leaving me alone with Junior.

"Miss me already?" He joked.

"I just wanted to tell you how proud your father must be of you. I know he's somewhere in the stars thinking about what an incredible young man you've become. And for what it's worth I think you've more than earned the name Alessio. If he were here now I'm sure he'd agree."

Junior grabbed my hand and clenched his jaw. In the year I'd known Junior I'd never seen him get emotional. He was always making deflecting jokes to mask the pain of losing his father.

"Thank you." He whispered, a few tears falling down his cheek.

"And even though they'd never admit it I know Apollo and Dane are proud of you too."

Junior looked over at Dane near the garage. Both Alex and Dane were keeping a close eye on the two of us. I leaned off the car door and gave Junior a minute to himself. He needed a minute to calm down before Alex got in the car. Dane stood with me in the driveway as we watched the two of them drive off.

"Thank you, for inviting him over. I needed that." I said, resting my head on Dane's chest.

"Come on, let's go inside. I made dinner, you'll have a few bites before we go to bed."

"And then maybe I could take a shower?" I asked.

"The doctor said we can't get your stitches wet for a few more days." Dane said.

"Then I guess that means we just have to get creative." I smiled.

"If I'd known you weren't going to follow any of your doctor's orders I wouldn't have helped you leave a day early."

"I should switch with Junior. I bet Alex is easier and complains less."

I knew that was going to piss Dane off, so I turned around as fast as I could and tried to walk up the stairs on my own before Dane caught up to me. I didn't even make it to the first step before he stepped in front of me.

"What did you say?" He asked.

"I love you?" I lied.

Dane rolled his eyes but still held out his hand to help me get up the steps.

"You're lucky I like you." He said as he helped me to the kitchen.

CHAPTER SIXTEEN

Kate

"Kate, you're really bumming out the customers." Becca said.

"Sorry."

Becca came over to the cash register and stood next to me.

"Why do you look so upset?"

"Because Ivy's all grown up. It doesn't need me anymore."

"What?" Becca laughed.

"There's nothing here for me to do. Avery took care of everything in the office, someone already went to the market, nothing out here needs to be done, the kitchen is all caught up on afternoon desserts. It's like you guys don't even need me anymore."

"That's why we agreed to work with Eliana's clients in the first place. You were working overtime and drowning. This is what you needed, what you wanted."

"I know, it's just hard coming here and seeing the place run without me."

"Ivy's still needs you Kate just in different ways. You should be proud of how far we've come in just a few months. You should be enjoying every minute of this. You should be out there taking orders, getting to reconnect with your customers." Becca said.

"Do you ever wonder what would have happened if we never started selling cookies? If we never found each other?" I asked.

"All the time. I'd still be working at my parents' accounting firm. And you, you'd be traveling the world. Eventually I'm sure you'd have found your way back to New York but it wouldn't be the same as it is now."

"Yeah, I think you're right."

"I'm always right. Now, get back to work. Breaks over."

Becca slapped my ass with a rag and ran back to the kitchen. I grabbed a tray and cleared a few tables and refilled a few coffees. Becca was right. This was exactly where I belonged. It was time to take a step back from Ivy's.

I spent the rest of the day running tables up front. By six I was exhausted but it felt good to be back at work. My entire body was sore but I didn't mind. I was so tired I had to drive home with my windows down and the radio blasting. I had been taking it slow after my accident but today was so busy I'd gotten carried away. Tomorrow I needed to be more careful to not overwork myself.

The lights were on in the living room when I came in from the garage. I usually beat Dane home from work so it was weird seeing him waiting for me in the living room. The living room was empty so I went searching for him. I found him bringing up some wine from the cellar.

"What are you doing?" I asked.

"It's complicated." He said.

"How so?"

"Well I have something to tell you but I wasn't sure if after I told you we'd be celebrating or not so I prepared for any scenario."

"Any scenario?" I asked.

Dane nodded his head to the dining room and motioned for me to walk with him. When we walked into the dining room I found the table full of food and desserts. Dane set down the wine which completed the spread.

"What is all this?" I asked.

"It's all of your favorite foods."

"No I can see that but why did you buy all of this?"

"Maybe you should sit down first." He said.

"Dane just spit it out."

"Wesley's dead."

Okay so maybe Dane was right, I should have been sitting. I reached for the chair behind me and sat down at the table. My bag dropped on the floor at my feet.

"He's dead?"

Dane stood by my side waiting to see how I'd react. He was waiting for me to lose it, to freak out, but that didn't happen. Instead I felt calm. I felt free.

It's over.

"Were you the one, the one that-"

"It was me. I killed him."

I reached out to grab Dane's hand. He sat with me for a few minutes while I processed Wesley's death.

"Have you told Junior yet? Does he know?" I asked.

"Apollo talked to him earlier. He's doing okay."

"Well, that's good."

"Do you want to know more?" Dane asked.

I shook my head no. I didn't want to know what he did. All that mattered was that he was gone.

"Was all this food really necessary? How did you even know to buy all this?" I asked.

"I have a list of all your favorite things. When I asked Eliana what to get you that would make you feel better she didn't know so I bought everything I could find on such short notice."

"What didn't you buy?"

"The deli was out of those mini caramel cheesecakes you like. Oh and we're running low on wine so we'll have to make these two work."

"I don't think we can eat all this before it goes bad." I laughed.

"I got that covered. Junior wants any leftovers."

"I guess I'll go grab the plates." I said.

Dane followed me into the kitchen. He stood near the fridge and watched as I grabbed some plates for dinner. He stood watching, waiting to see how I was going to react to his news. I thought maybe he was upset and anxious to see how I would react but then I saw his stone cold expression break for just a second. I'd never considered the guilt that Dane must be experiencing right now. How had killing Wesley affected him?

I left the plates on the counter and went over to pull Dane down for a kiss.

"The world is a better place now that he's gone, Dane. You did the right thing."

Dane nodded his head in agreement and wrapped his arms around my shoulders. Knowing Dane had done the right thing didn't make it any easier to stomach. Killing Wesley didn't erase the horrible things he'd done but maybe now Junior and I would be able to move on.

"I thought we agreed nothing over ten pounds." Dane shouted from upstairs.

"This box is labeled kitchen towels and napkins. I think I can handle it."

Dane came into the kitchen after me and took the box from me.

"You've been out of your brace for a week. Doctor says no heavy objects. I thought we agreed you'd take it easy."

"We also agreed you wouldn't be an ass."

"I don't remember agreeing to that."

"Well then maybe I dreamed that part." I said.

"You dreamed it?" He asked.

"Dream Dane is so understanding. He doesn't try to tell me what to do and he believes me when I say I can handle carrying in a box of towels from the truck."

"Dream Dane sounds awful."

I grabbed the box back from Dane and sat it down on the counter. I ripped off the tape and pulled out my dish towels.

"My physical therapist says I need to start challenging myself. She says I'll never get back to my normal level of mobility if you keep doing things for me."

"I just don't want you to hurt yourself after all the progress you've made. It's not even been two months Kate. There is no need to rush recovery. You'll never be cleared for physical activity if you push yourself too hard before your body is ready." He said.

"Speaking of physical activity." I winked, grabbing Dane's shirt, and pulling him closer.

I almost had him but before I could pull him down into a kiss he pulled me away.

"Not until you're ready."

"I've been ready." I argued.

"I don't want to hurt you."

"You won't. You're the last person on Earth who would ever hurt me."

"It's too soon." He said.

"No it's not."

Dane looked over his shoulder at the front door, "We'll talk about this later. After we're done moving you in."

"Fine." I said, rolling my eyes.

Dane saw my disappointment when I walked past him to the front yard. He grabbed my waist and pulled me back to him. I crashed right into his chest. He wrapped his hands behind my neck and leaned down to kiss me. I wrapped my arms around his shoulder and deepened the kiss. Ever since my accident Dane's been afraid. Afraid to kiss me, afraid to hold me, to fuck me. He was afraid he'd hurt me.

He pulled away and ran his fingers down my lips, "Soon." He whispered.

Dane walked away and left me frozen in the hallway. God I was aching for Dane's touch and little moments like this weren't nearly enough. I needed more. How was I going to survive the day?

I grabbed a box from the stairs and walked it up to the guest room I had taken over as my office. I was unboxing some of my desk things when the door opened.

When Apollo saw he wasn't alone in the room he took a step back.

"Sorry, I didn't know you were up here. Dane just asked me to bring your computer up."

"It's fine. Could you set it over there on that shelf? I haven't decided where I want to move my desk to."

"Sure."

After setting down my computer Apollo looked over at me, "Is something wrong?"

I fixed my face and answered him, "I'm just a little surprised to see you here helping me move in. I thought you had guys to do that type of work for you."

"I told Dane I wanted to help. Needed a break from the office." He answered.

"Sure." I said.

"You don't believe me?"

"It sounds like maybe you're here because Eliana said you had to come and help."

"I'm not here because of Eliana. I'm here-" He started to explain, but he stopped himself.

"Because why?"

"Because I'm trying to prove I'm more than just an irredeemable bastard. I'm trying to make amends."

I let out a small laugh. I don't remember exactly when I would have called him a bastard but it sounds like something I would say. I'd never been a big fan of Apollo but his efforts to be a better person hadn't gone unnoticed. He was there for Dane during my accident and he gave me his full support when I had to tell Dane I was ready to go back to work at Ivy's.

Apollo wasn't sure if he should stay or leave so he went back out to the hallway. Guilt ate at me as I watched him leave. It would have been so much easier to let him walk away. To continue to ignore Apollo's kind gestures but I just couldn't do it. I ran to the hallway unsure what I would say to Apollo when I found him. When I caught up to him all I could do was shout his name. He turned around confused to see me standing there.

"Should you be running?" He asked.

"I forgive you." I shouted at him, struggling to catch my breath.

"What?"

"You sent your own men to find me when I was missing. You were there for Dane when I was in the hospital. You've helped Eliana and I reopen Ivy's. I should be thanking you for all you've done for me."

"I didn't do any of that for a thank you Kate."

"I know and that's why you get my forgiveness. I'm offering a chance for the two of us to start over."

"I think I'd really like that." He said.

"I would too." I smiled

Apollo held out his hand for me to shake, "No more treating my warehouses like your own personal rage room."

"That happened one time."

"Kate…"

"Fine but I hope one day I'll get to call Dane family which means you and I will be family. I need you to trust me and come to me when there are problems between us."

"Deal, but you should know you're already family Kate. If you ever need anything at all you give me a call."

I couldn't believe it. Apollo and I were totally having a moment. This scary irredeemable bastard wasn't so terrible after all.

"You should probably head back down now. The pain meds I take for my shoulder make me super emotional. If you stick around any longer I'll start crying and neither of us want that."

Apollo went down the stairs and out to the truck to pick up a few more boxes. I followed behind him and found Dane in the living room.

"There was a suitcase in the truck that broke open. I brought you another box if you want to throw some stuff in there so we can bring it into the house and figure out where it all goes." Dane said.

I stepped into the truck and walked to the busted suitcase. While picking up my clothes I felt the truck shift as Dane stepped in.

"You okay?"

"Yeah, I'm good." I smiled.

"You look like you were crying." He said, running his hand over my cheek.

"They're happy tears."

"You sure?"

"Yeah, promise. You should probably get back to work. You and Apollo have the furniture to bring in still. You'll want to bring that in before it gets dark."

"Well with your help it shouldn't take too long. We can make it work." Dane said.

"Oh no, I am going inside and starting dinner. You two can figure out how to bring in my reading couch on your own." I said.

I gave Dane a kiss on the cheek and carried my boxes of clothes out of the truck.

"What happened to being a team, moving in together?" Dane shouted after me.

"I'd love to help but I can't, doctor's orders. Sorry!" I waved back at him.

Dane and Apollo took care of the rest of my things while I worked on unpacking photos in the living room. After bringing in the last box Apollo came to say a quick goodbye then left.

Dane was somewhere in the house I just wasn't sure where. I had finished unpacking all of my photos in the living room but now the room just didn't feel right. The energy felt forced. I moved the coffee table out of the way and laid down on the rug.

"Kate?" Dane asked.

"I'm in here."

"What are you doing?" He asked as he walked into the living room.

"I'm waiting for the room to speak to me."

Dane sat down on the floor next to me, "Has it said anything yet?"

"She says we need to paint. She said she's sick of the bland gray walls."

"Any idea what color the room wants?" He asked.

"Something warm. Maybe yellow." I told him.

Dane laid down next to me and grabbed my hand.

"Do you have a ladder?" I asked.

"I have a few."

"I don't know how we're going to be able to reach the ceiling. We might need to hire someone to come in and do it for us."

"I don't think you're supposed to paint the ceiling." Dane said.

"Why not?"

"Well, I don't know. I thought it was a painting rule."

I leaned over onto Dane's chest, "I don't think that's a rule. Besides, it would bring in so much light."

I ran my hand down Dane's chest and pressed further into his chest.

"I know what you're doing." Dane smiled.

"And what am I doing?"

"You're trying to seduce me so I'll let you paint the living room yellow. That's not fair."

Dane sat up and sent me rolling back to the floor. I grabbed his arm and pulled myself up so that I was sitting next to him.

"I am not seducing you!" I lied.

"You're using every trick in the book!"

"Is it working?" I smiled.

"A little." He said, grabbing my neck and pulling me into a kiss.

Dane grabbed my hips and pulled me into his lap. I pulled away from the kiss to leave sloppy kisses down Dane's neck. Dane immediately reacted. He pulled my hair back and brought my lips up to his. I thought maybe Dane was finally ready to go further but when I started to grind my hips into his he pulled back. Our hot make out session was over before it even began.

"Nice try." He smiled.

"Damn, so close."

"Let's go. Dinner's getting cold." He said.

Dane sat up and walked to the kitchen but I stayed in the living room for just another minute. I finally got up and walked to the kitchen. I found Dane grabbing our plates and dancing to the music I had left on earlier. I walked over to the counter and leaned against his shoulder.

"Is this you still trying to seduce me?" He asked.

"No, not this time." I laughed.

Dane put down the spoon in his hand and turned so that he could give me a hug. I fell into his arms and nearly melted. Being here with Dane just felt right. I was finally home.

"I love you Dane."

"Not as much as I love you Kate."

CHAPTER SEVENTEEN

A Few Months Later

Dane

"Dane!" Junior shouted from the hallway outside Apollo's office.

"I thought we told him to leave. Why is he back?" Apollo complained.

Junior stormed into the office with Alex right behind him smiling.

"Who wins in a fight, me or Alex?" He asked the two of us.

"Alex." We both answered in unison.

"Okay but in this scenario I'm completely healed from my injury."

"Alex." We repeated.

"Bullshit." Junior argued.

"I told you." Alex smiled, crossing his arms over his chest.

"I can't believe this." Junior said.

"If you want Dane can train you, help you get into shape." Apollo offered.

"No I can't." I said, slapping Apollo's shoulder.

"Great, when can we start?" Junior asked.

"How about never."

"Oh come on! Why not?" Junior asked.

"Because I already spend too much time with you."

"I'll train with you." Alex offered.

While watching Junior and Alex argue Apollo's phone rang.

"Costa." He answered.

I couldn't decide who to watch. On one side of the room Apollo was yelling at whoever called him. On the other side Alex had somehow gotten Junior into a headlock. There was too much going on.

"Where?" He asked.

Apollo ran his hand over his forehead.

"Yeah, we'll be right there." He said, hanging up.

"What happened?" I asked.

"Kate and Eliana got into a bar fight."

Immediately Junior and Alex stopped their fighting.

"I thought they said they were going out for one drink?" Junior asked.

"What bar?" I asked, standing up.

"My bar. They got in a fight at my own fucking bar." He said, dropping his phone on his desk.

"How?" Alex asked, trying not to laugh.

"I have no idea. Romeo said he needs us to come pick them up."

"I'll drive. They took Eliana's car. You can take that home." I said.

Apollo and I ran to my car and rushed to the bar. Apollo sent a few texts to Romeo asking him to keep the girls in his office until we could get there.

"I can't for the life of me picture Kate and Eliana in a bar fight. I hope Romeo saves the security footage. Who do you think started it?"

"I have no idea. Eliana has a short temper when she's drunk. It was probably her."

"I'm never going to let Kate live this down." I laughed.

"Speaking of Kate. Have you proposed yet?" He asked.

I gripped the steering wheel, "Not yet."

"Why not? You bought the ring months ago."

"I'm waiting." I said.

"Waiting for what?"

"I'm just waiting for the perfect time to ask her. I thought I'd propose to her when we went on our trip to Rome."

"The trip you've had to cancel three times now because of work?" Apollo asked.

"I just want it to be memorable for her. I don't want her to have any regrets about the engagement."

"Dane, your only regret will be waiting this long to ask her. Trust me, waiting is only hurting you. Wait any longer and she's going to give up hope you'll ever ask her."

"I don't think you're the best person to ask for proposal advice."

"Fine don't believe me but I'm telling you man, you'll regret waiting this long. It's not about the perfect proposal, it's about getting to spend the rest of your life with her. Every second you don't propose is a second wasted."

I'd spent too much of my time worrying about the proposal rather than getting to spend the rest of my life with Kate. Even though I wouldn't admit it to him, he was right. By the time we made it to the bar I was so anxious to see Kate I was nauseous.

Apollo and I walked past the line for West End and went straight to Romeo's office. We found a very drunk Kate and Eliana on his couch.

"Shit." Eliana cursed as soon as she saw us.

Kate hid her face, her hair covering her red cheeks.

"What happened?" Apollo asked.

"A guy at the bar got a little handsy with one of the waiters. These two thought they'd handle the situation rather than let the bouncers deal with it. They got a few punches in before we were able to pull them off of the guy." Romeo explained.

"And what happened to the guy?"

"Scotty threw him out when the girls explained what happened. They kicked out him and his friends"

Apollo rolled his eyes and leaned against Romeo's desk.

"Really El? You thought the best way to deal with a perv at the bar was to fight him?"

"You weren't there okay! He'd been saying shitty things to the bartenders all night. When we saw him actually try to put his hands on Georgia we just sort of lost it!"

"You do any damage?" I asked.

"Dane." Apollo said.

"What? It's a valid question."

"Kate broke his nose." Eliana smiled.

That's hot.

"You have anything to say for yourself Kate?" I asked.

"I hope it hurt?" She said, finally looking up at me.

Apollo, who was still trying to look upset, let a quiet laugh slip.

"Alright, let's go home." He said, holding out his hand for Eliana.

Kate stood up with Eliana and walked out of Romeo's office behind Apollo and Eliana.

"Put that guy on our no fly list and let me know if he ever comes back." I told Romeo.

After saying goodbye to Romeo I caught up with Kate near the front.

"We have to get you home so we can ice that hand." I teased.

"Shut up." She laughed, getting into the car.

The whole drive home Kate was quiet. It might have been my fault. She thought I was upset about the bar fight but really I was thinking about my conversation with Apollo.

Kate tried to sneak up into the bedroom before I made it inside but I stopped her in the living room.

"Kate…"

"Look I know you're mad but-"

"Marry me."

"Excuse me?" She asked.

"Marry me."

"I think I might have hit my head. It sounds like you're asking me to marry you."

"I am." I said, digging around in my pockets for the ring.

"Dane, stop it this isn't funny." Kate said.

"I'm not joking. Look, I even have a ring." I said.

Kate took a step back so I grabbed her hand as I kneeled down on one knee.

"I've actually had the ring for months. I was waiting for the perfect time to propose to you but I just can't wait any longer."

"Oh my God." Kate cried.

"Kate I love you and if you'll let me I want to spend the rest of my life with you. While I can't promise what our life will look like in the future I can promise to do everything in my power to keep you smiling. If when I die all I did with my life was make you happy then I will have lived a good life. It's you and me for forever Kate. Will you marry me?"

Kate nearly fell from shock. I had to stand up to hold onto her.

"Yes." She answered.

"Yes?"

"Yes I'll marry you Dane!" She continued to cry.

With shaky hands I grabbed Kate's hand. Between the two of us and our nerves it took forever to actually put the ring on her finger. When I'd finally slipped it on all the way she held it up in the air.

"I love you." She said, pulling me into a kiss.

I wrapped my arms around her and held her tight. Kate held onto my shirt, pulling me closer to her. She tried to bite my lip to deepen the kiss but I stopped her.

"Kate, we can't."

"Dane, please."

Fuck, it was impossible saying no to her. I grabbed her ass and lifted her off the floor. She instantly wrapped her legs around my waist. She wrapped her arms around my shoulders and kissed up and down my neck.

"Are you sure?" I asked.

"I need you Dane."

I carried Kate upstairs while she left sloppy kisses on my jaw. I barely made it to the bedroom before she began unbuttoning my shirt. I threw her onto the bed and tossed my shirt off to the side.

"Promise you'll tell me if you need me to stop. I don't want to hurt you."

"You could never hurt me Dane."

"You know the rules Kate. Use your safe word if you need it." I said, unzipping my pants.

"Fine." She said, rolling her eyes.

"Did you just roll your eyes at me?" I asked.

"Maybe." She smiled.

Stepping out of my pants I grabbed her ankles and pulled her to the edge of the bed. Kate let out a shriek as she slid down the comforter. I didn't notice it until now but the dress Kate was wearing was way too short. I could see her entire pussy hiding underneath her lace panties.

When I reached beneath Kate's dress and ran my fingers over her folds she let out a gasp. It had been too long since I'd heard that sound. Just the thought of getting to touch Kate again had me harder than I'd ever been before.

"What do you want Kate?" I asked.

Kate replaced my hand with hers. She shuffled against the bed causing her dress to ride up to her hips. I was left watching her play with herself and fuck it was so hot.

"I want you to taste me, touch me, lick me."

I wasn't going to last long if she kept talking like that. I kneeled down at the edge of the bed and pulled her closer to me. Her hips were nearly hanging off the bed. I hooked my thumb under her panties and ripped them off of her. Throwing them next to her on the bed I wrapped her legs around my shoulders.

Kate wanted me to eat her out but I wanted to tease her a little first. I wanted to see how wet she was. I ran a finger over her folds and watched her squirm underneath me. His legs tightened against my shoulders the deeper I slid my fingers in. While twisting my fingers in and out I kissed up her thigh until I was just above her clit.

Kate was anxious for me to stop teasing her, so I finally gave in. I pulled my fingers out and replaced them with my tongue. I sucked and licked and felt her legs tightened around me. It'd been too long since getting to pleasure her like this. I was always afraid of hurting her ribs or slowing down her recovery but now that she was healed all bets were off.

I circled my tongue in and out of her folds all while using my fingers to shake pressure against her clit. Kate's thighs shaking told me she was close. Her fingers held onto my hair while I fucked her.

I spit on Kate's pussy and ran my fingers down her folds, giving her a break from my tongue. While I fingered Kate again I grabbed my dick and gave it a few strokes. It was too soon to come for the both of us. Not wanting to give her the release she was looking for just yet I pulled away and watched her legs drop off of my shoulders.

"Why'd you stop?" She asked.

"Because I want to fuck this sweet pussy of yours before I make you come."

I pushed her back onto the bed and spread her legs down. Kate watched as I rubbed my dick a few times before entering her. Kate sucked a deep breath in as soon as I entered her, so I gave her a few minutes to adjust.

"Does that feel okay?" I asked.

"More, I need more." She gasped.

Normally I'd grab Kate's waist to help me hit a deeper angle but I was afraid to grab her too tight. What if I hurt her?

Kate must have understood my hesitation because she grabbed my hands and brought them up to her waist. She dragged her nails against my forearms and then brought her hands back up behind her pillow.

"I'm not in any pain Dane. I need you to make me feel good."

I let go of my fears and began to slowly thrust. Kate reacted immediately. She shifted her hips up as she adjusted to my size. I picked up the pace and found a pattern with Kate. She grinded her hips against mine as I fucked her. I let go of her waist and pressed my chest against hers. I held most of my weight off of her by leaning onto my elbows while I picked up the pace and fucked her harder. Kate ran her fingers through my hair.

I dipped down to kiss her shoulder, the one she'd hurt. When I kissed her sensitive scar Kate shuddered. I leaned off of her to look her in the eyes. She looked like she needed more, so I dipped down and kissed her breasts. I softly bit her nipple and pulled. She liked that; she clawed my neck begging for more.

I softly let go of her tit and blew on the sensitive skin. I repeated my kissing and sucking with her other nipple. Picking up the pace I thrusted harder into Kate, I could feel her start to lose control so I quickly pulled out. I wanted to watch her come on my tongue.

I leaned down below her hips and ran my tongue slowly down her mound. She shook when I got to her clit. With two fingers I fucked her; my tongue never leaving her pussy.

"Dane." She cried.

"Relax baby, let go." I mumbled against her, my words vibrating her core.

Kate relaxed and came all over my tongue. I licked and ran my fingers all over her folds as she came down from her orgasm. When she stopped shaking I flipped her over.

I wanted to watch her come one more time. Kate liked it when I held her tight against my chest from behind. I held her ass in the air and teased her with my cock.

"Dane..." She begged.

I finally slid back in and began to slowly thrust. I held her by her elbows and watched as her hair fell over her face. Bringing her elbows to my chest I fixed her against me and then held her with one hand against her back. My other free hand ran my fingers through her hair, fixing it behind her back. I wanted her to be able to see me.

"I love you so much, Kate." I whispered in her ear.

Unable to speak Kate let out a whimper.

"So fucking beautiful like this baby." I said, kissing her neck.

Kate grabbed my hand and pulled it across her chest. She dug her nails into me as I twisted her nipple in between my fingers.

"You ready to come again?" I asked.

Kate nodded her head yes against my chest. My thrusts grew sloppier as I grew closer to coming. Kate could tell I was just as close as she was. She dipped her head back for a kiss. I grabbed her cheek and pressed my lips against hers.

"Fuck!" She cursed, letting her second orgasm take over.

Watching Kate lose control sent me over the edge. I followed after Kate and let go, my orgasm exploding.

Kate dropped to the bed. I laid next to her and brushed her hair out of her face. A few strands stuck on her lips.

"I love you Dane." She said, while catching her breath.

I'd gotten so caught up in the moment I didn't think that my grip on Kate was too tight. I forgot to go easy on her shoulder and her ribs.

"Did I hurt you? Are you okay?" I asked.

"I'm fine." She said, running her hand over my chest.

"You're not hurt?" I asked.

I ran my hand down Kate's ribs, afraid she wouldn't tell me the truth even if I asked.

"I've never felt better. In fact, for round two I don't want you to hold back. I want you to fuck me rough, like you've always done."

"God I love you so much." I smiled, pulling her into my chest.

"I know." She laughed, wrapping her arm over me.

While Kate and I laid with each other I ran my fingers down her shoulder. As Kate ran her hand over my chest we both watched her ring glisten in the moonlight. Kate didn't know it yet but I was marrying her as soon as I could. I couldn't go another day not being able to call Kate my wife; to call her family.

"I thought this was supposed to be relaxing?" I asked.

"It is. You're just doing it wrong." Kate said.

"How am I doing it wrong?"

"I don't know. Maybe you're too stressed. You can't get into the right mindset if you're too stressed."

I tossed my paintbrush back down onto the tray. We'd been painting the living room for hours and we weren't anywhere close to being done.

"I told you we should have just hired a professional to come in and do this." I said.

"We're making memories. Quit complaining and go grab me a few rags from the closet."

"Yes ma'am." I saluted, walking to the hallway.

When I came back to the living room Kate was up on the ladder trying to reach the corners. I watched her ass sway back and forth with every stroke. I walked up behind the ladder and cupped her ass.

"Dane, get your hand off my ass." She warned.

"Or what?" I asked.

"Or I'll kill you with my bare hands and my paintbrush."

"I love when you talk dirty to me baby." I smiled.

"Hands off Dane." She threatened.

I moved over to the other side of the room and finished off the wall closest to the front windows. After another hour Kate set down her paintbrush and tossed me a rag. She walked out of the living room without saying anything to me.

"Where are you going?" I asked.

"It's time for dinner."

"We still have half a room to paint!" I shouted after her.

"I'm hungry. I need food if we're ever going to finish the rest of the living room."

I could have been petty and made an argument about following through with a task but I also didn't want to paint anymore so I said nothing. I followed Kate to the kitchen and grabbed a few things for dinner.

Kate and I talked about work while I cooked.

"Eliana told me you two are looking for a bigger place to move into." I said.

"Eliana's looking; I'm not. She wants to move Ivy's to a bigger shop but I don't want to leave the building we're in now. I'm too attached."

"She made it seem like you two had already found a place."

"She probably has. She's been begging me to go look at a few places but I've been avoiding it."

"Well there's no harm in looking right? Just because you go and look at a few new places doesn't mean you have to move. Who knows you might fall in love with a new shop." I said.

"Yeah, maybe. I'll talk to Becca about it. See how she feels."

Kate set the table in the kitchen while I finished up the chicken.

"How's Junior doing? He make it back from Chicago?" Kate asked.

"He's supposed to be back at work but no one's seen him in weeks." I said, bringing the food to the table.

"Where is he?" She asked.

"Who knows. He texted Apollo and said he wasn't taking the plane back from Chicago and hasn't checked in since. My guess is he's on a beach somewhere down south or hiding out in Italy."

"God I'm so jealous."

"You're jealous of Junior?" I laughed.

"He's off the grid somewhere, enjoying a vacation away from you and Apollo. He's living the dream right now. We used to be young and fun like that too but now all we do is go to work and come home to paint a living room." She complained.

"We could be like Junior if we wanted to be." I said.

"Yeah, right. Like either of us could take a week off work without the world ending." She said.

"I'm serious. We should just get in the car and drive until we hit a coast."

"Okay." She laughed.

"I'm not joking Kate. Let's go."

"We can't just leave right now!" She argued.

"Why not?" I asked.

"Because we both have work and because our living room is half yellow."

"You know Avery would be able to cover Ivy's until we got back and as for Apollo he can't ask me to come into work if I don't pick up his calls. And the yellow walls will still be here when we get back. It will just give them some extra time to dry."

I stood up from the table and walked over to the sink with my plate, "Go pack a bag. I'll meet you at the car in fifteen."

Kate ran from the kitchen to the bedroom to pack a bag. I followed behind her and grabbed some clothes. I wasn't sure where we were going or for how long so I packed more than I probably needed.

"Are we really doing this?" Kate asked from the bathroom.

"Yes we're really doing this and now you only have ten minutes to pack."

I could hear Kate's laughter all throughout the house as she ran around turning off lights and locking doors. I hadn't seen her this excited in a while. It only confirmed how badly she needed a break.

"You ready?" I yelled out from the garage.

Kate came from the kitchen with two bags. One full of clothes and the other full of snacks.

"I thought we better bring food just in case." She said.

"Good idea."

I had no idea where we should go so I just drove. We drove out of the neighborhood and onto the highway. When we'd driven a few hours south I pulled out a map from the glove compartment.

"You did not just pull a map out." Kate sighed.

"What's wrong with my map?"

"Look how many folds it takes to get this thing open! We're trying to be cool and young and this is anti that. Just use your phone."

"The map is perfectly practical. If you dig around in the glove box you might find a magnifying glass."

"You're making it worse. Please stop talking." Kate laughed.

"Just pick a place to drive to and tell me how to get there."

"There's too many choices." She said.

"Just pick somewhere."

"But there's too many factors. If we want beaches we have to go south. If we want some fun roadside attractions to stop at we need to go west. Plus there's no telling what the weather will be like once we start driving. And what if my road trip playlist isn't long enough for where we want to go then we either have to add more songs to it or listen to repeats."

"Is this how your brain works all the time?" I asked.

"Yes, it's exhausting."

"Okay how long is your playlist?"

"A little over ten hours." She said.

"And how many skips are there?"

"None, it's the perfect playlist. I'm hurt you'd expect any of the songs on it to be skips."

"It's nothing personal Kate but I've never seen you go longer than three songs before hitting skip." I said.

"Okay fine, at best we have seven hours after the skips."

"Alright I know where we're going." I said.

"Where?" She asked.

"I'm not telling you."

Kate shuffled around in her seat to get comfortable, "Can I have a hint?"

"No."

"If I can guess where we're going will you tell me?"

"No."

"Would you be open to bribery?" She asked.

"No."

"You are turning out to be the worst road trip partner ever."

"Insulting me isn't going to work either. You better hurry up and get your phone connected to the stereo. We only have a few hours of driving to listen to this perfect playlist of yours."

Eight hours later Kate and I finally made it to our destination. It was almost the morning. We'd driven through the night to get here before the sunrise. I shook Kate's shoulder to wake her up.

"Kate baby, we're here."

Kate sat up in her seat and looked out the window.

"Where are we?"

"Georgia."

"Georgia?" She asked.

"Mhmm, now come on. We only have a few more minutes to get to the cliffs before the sunrise. Bring the blanket."

As we walked closer to the water the morning air woke Kate up. I had forgotten how cold it could get in the morning before the sun was up. I grabbed the blanket from Kate and sat down on the sand. Kate laid down on the blanket with her head resting on my thigh. I ran my fingers through her hair while we waited for sunrise.

"What made you decide on Georgia?" She asked, her eyes closed.

"My grandma moved her after my grandpa died. It was their dream to retire and move to Georgia together but they never got the chance. He spent his entire life working at an electrical plant and it cost him his life. His lungs gave up on him, they couldn't take the damage they'd suffered working at the plant. We used to visit her every summer but then we stopped coming. I haven't been back since high school."

"Your grandma, does she still live here?" Kate asked.

"No, she moved back to Jersey a few years ago. She moved closer to Mom so that she'd have someone to take care of her."

"Why did you stop coming here?"

"I don't really know. It wasn't on purpose but we were all busy with our own lives. Mayra and I were the only ones still at home. Tera, Josie, and Kim were all at school or busy with their own family. It just got harder to make it down here and then Grandma got sick and it was time for her to move back home."

Finally, the sun began to rise over the water. Kate sat up and rested her head against my shoulder. The water reflected the warm oranges and yellows of the sky.

"It's beautiful."

"I used to hike this with Dad in the mornings. We'd get up early and then bring breakfast back for everyone. There's a diner down the road with the best French toast you'll ever have."

Kate and I sat together and enjoyed the quiet Georgia morning. I was having a hard time believing I was really here with Kate and not in New York right now. I wasn't sure how long we'd be able to stay here but I'd stay for as long as Kate wanted.

"It only took a year but we finally got our vacation." Kate laughed.

"We might need to call Eliana and Apollo to let them know we aren't dead."

"And maybe Becca. She's probably started putting up missing posters of me."

Kate curled closer into me to protect herself from the wind. While the sun rose we watched the beach get its first few visitors. A few runners jogged past on their morning run; others brought their dogs to play in the water. I could have sat here with Kate forever.

"What do we do now?" Kate asked.

"I don't know. We could get back in the car and keep driving or we could find a hotel and stay for a while. I'll go wherever you want to go."

"I want to stay here for a few days. We could drive into town and find a cute hotel or inn to stay at. And maybe in the morning we could come back here and watch the sunrise again."

"Sounds good to me." I smiled.

"We should come back here every year and we can invite the whole family. I'm sure your sisters would want to bring the kids out here now that they're getting older."

"I'd love that." I said, kissing Kate's temple.

Kate and I sat together on the cliffs long after the sunrise. We could come back to this same spot tomorrow but there was something special about this moment here together that made us not want to leave. Being here with Kate felt like the beginning of a new chapter for us. While sitting here on the cliffs I was positive there was no one else I'd rather be on the run with than her.

Evergreen Ivy

EPILOGUE

Four Years Later

Kate

"What do you think?" Eliana asked.

"It's perfect."

"I know right! The realtor wouldn't tell me why the Mastin's decided to move but I have a feeling it's because they were tired of living next to Apollo and me. They were always out in the front doing yard work giving us these disapproving looks."

Eliana carried a sleeping Theo in her arms as we walked around her neighbor's house. I tried telling her to bring the stroller because Theo never misses his afternoon nap but she chose to ignore me. So now she was stuck carrying him around.

"I love it…"

"But?"

"I have no idea how I'm going to convince Dane to move. We just redid our kitchen."

"Just tell him a new kitchen adds to the resale value! He won't be able to say no when he finds out there are more rooms here than at your other place." Eliana said.

"Oh my God look at the backyard!"

"And there's a movie room. It's better than ours." Eliana said.

"Wait, how did we get in here without the realtor? I didn't just accidentally break into this house did I?"

"Let's just say I know the code. Plus I figured no cop is going to arrest you right now." She shrugged.

"And why not?"

"Bitch please, you're about to pop! If we did get caught all you'd have to do is pretend you were going into labor and you'd probably get a free ride to the hospital."

"I can't believe you made me and my unborn child an accomplice to a break in." I laughed.

"It's not like I sent you in here alone. I came with, that should count for something." She argued

"Yes, you're right. Thank you for also bringing my two year old with us as we break into your neighbor's house. That makes me feel so much better about this whole situation."

"Alright, fine, we can leave, but you're going to regret not taking a look upstairs."

I looked out the front window to make sure no one was outside ready to arrest us and then I looked over at the stairs.

"Five minutes." I said.

After giving me a quick tour of the second floor Eliana and I snuck back over to her house. Eliana ran without picking up her feet to not wake up Theo and I was doing my best to run but it was more of a slow walk. All bets were off this close to my due date. I was afraid a big sneeze would be enough to break my water. If there were security cameras watching us then they were getting quite the show.

Before Theo was even born Eliana and Apollo turned one of their guest rooms into his own room. Eliana took Theo to finish his nap while I looked for something to drink in the kitchen. I was struggling to climb into one of the barstools when Eliana came into the kitchen.

"You good?" She laughed.

"Fuck off."

I found my balance and got comfortable at the counter.

"Dane's going to kill you when he finds out you kidnapped me."

"I didn't kidnap you! You were literally begging me to pick you up and help you break out of the house."

"That's not what I'll be telling him. I'll tell him you showed up unannounced and refused to leave."

"Fine, I'll take the blame for this one. I can't have him angry at you. You're the one that's going to have to convince him to move." She said.

"He's never going to agree to it. We're busy enough as it is. The last thing I want to be doing right now is moving. Two babies and Dane and me both working full time is already more than I can handle. The last thing I need is coming home from work to take care of a newborn and then still having to pack for a move."

"Oh please, Theo's practically three. Give him some tape and a box and he'll do half the packing. Plus you have me and Apollo to help and as soon as Alessio finds out you want to move closer to us he'll do whatever it takes to make it happen. He loves babysitting Theo."

I rolled my eyes; Eliana was making a lot of sense.

"You know I'm right."

"I would love being closer to you and Apollo."

"Ever since Alessio moved out of the guest house it's been too boring here. Even Apollo misses the excitement."

"What's the deal with Alessio?" I asked.

"What do you mean?"

"I'm just surprised he didn't tell me he wanted to move to Italy. I mean he tells me everything. He's always come to me when he has a problem. I supported him when he was ready to tell everyone he was tired of being called Junior. I convinced Dane to let him move out of the guest house and into his new place. But I was the last to find out he wanted to take over shipments for Apollo in Italy. I don't like it. It's like he's in a rush to grow up or something."

"Kate, he is grown up. He's not a kid anymore. Apollo thought it was time for him to take on a little bit more responsibility."

"But it's like he's running away from something. I've never heard him mention wanting to live in Italy and now he's in a rush to move? It doesn't make sense."

Eliana took a sip of her drink, "Is Theo awake? I think I hear him?"

She was definitely hiding something from me. Something about Alessio.

"El, you know something!"

"No." She lied.

"What is it? Did something happen?"

Eliana sighed, "I wasn't supposed to say anything."

"Like that's ever stopped you before!"

"I think I might know why he's trying to run away to Italy."

I leaned closer to Eliana, dying to know what happened.

"Juliette met someone."

"No." I gasped.

"She asked to bring him to a family dinner. I told her I'd talk to Apollo about it."

"Have you told Apollo yet?" I asked.

"No, but if she's willing to bring him to meet the family that means she's serious about the relationship."

"Does Alessio know?"

"He overheard us talking about dinner and stormed out of the house." She said.

"I thought they worked things out. They were getting along at Christmas."

"I don't know. I can't keep up." Eliana said.

"So Alessio is running away to Italy because Juliette met someone and is ready to introduce him to the family? That seems a little dramatic."

"There's more." Eliana said, stretching her arms out to reach me.

She looked like she was ready to explode. She'd been hiding all these secrets from me for who knows how long.

"That night Juliette and I were talking about dinner I think he might have heard her say she could see herself marrying this new boyfriend. She said she was really happy and saw a future with him."

"Oh my God!" I shouted.

"I know."

"If he's that bothered by Juliette's new boyfriend then why is he choosing to run away rather than tell her how he feels?" I asked.

"I think he's trying to move on and to do that he needs to create some distance between them. More than anything he just wants her to be happy."

"What does Apollo think of him moving?" I asked.

"Apollo wants him to go. He knows he can't run the family forever. Alessio wouldn't be the worst person to replace him. Apollo's treating Alessio moving to Italy as a trial run. He wants to see how he does on his own." She said.

"And he still has no idea those two are crazy in love with each other?"

"No, whatever fling they had at Christmas is over. He had absolutely no idea what was going on."

"This is giving me a headache." I sighed.

"Tell me about it."

"I'm almost terrified to find out what happens when Apollo and Dane do figure it out."

"Apollo wouldn't kill Alessio would he?" I asked.

While we were talking Eliana's phone rang, "Speak of the devil."

Eliana picked up her phone and stood up.

"How much longer?" She asked.

I watched Eliana's mood drop. She was getting bad news.

"No, don't worry about it. She's here with me now, I'll tell her." She said, looking over at me.

Eliana hung up the phone and came back to the counter, "They aren't going to make it back tonight."

"What happened?"

"I don't know. All he said was that Dane was busy and was worried about you being home alone tonight. He didn't know you were already over here."

"Did he say if Dane was okay?" I asked.

"He didn't say much. Only that he would be busy tonight."

I left the kitchen and walked to Theo's room. I stood at the door and watched him sleep.

"Why don't we go back to your place? I'll stay with you tonight until Dane gets back." She offered.

"No, you don't have to do that. We'll be okay."

"Dane would kill me if he found out I left you alone right now. Let me be there for you, just in case." She said.

I held Eliana's hand and gave it a squeeze, "Thank you."

Eliana went back to the living room to pack up Theo's bag while I woke Theo up.

"Hey, bubs." I whispered.

Theo rolled over, confused to be at Eliana's house.

"We have to wake up Theo, we're going home."

"With Daddy?" He asked.

"No, not with Daddy. He's working."

Finding out Dane wouldn't be home when we went home upset Theo. He turned his back to me and curled up into a ball.

"Auntie El's coming with us though. Maybe after dinner you can show her all your books."

"Auntie El?"

"Mhmm, she's going to stay with us until Daddy gets home."

"Okay." Theo smiled.

Theo sat up and reached out to me. I grabbed his hand and walked with him to the living room.

"Ready to go?" Eliana asked.

Theo nodded his head yes and held out his arms for Eliana to pick him up.

"Theo you can walk to the car." I said, grabbing his backpack.

"Um no he can't." Eliana said.

"Yeah." Theo agreed.

"You are creating a monster El. We can't keep holding him every time he wants to be picked up."

"If Theo wants to be carried to the car I'm carrying him to the car. Plus in like a year he's not going to want me to hold him. He'll be all grown up and he won't love me anymore. Just let me have this." She argued.

"Yeah." Theo agreed again.

That was their thing. Theo agreed with everything Eliana said. It drove me crazy.

"Fine, let's go."

On the drive home Theo found his energy. He was fully awake and ready to play. From the rear view mirror I could see his tiger being thrown back and forth.

"Should we pick something up for dinner while we're out?" Eliana asked.

"No I have some leftovers at the house we can heat up."

"I want trees!" Theo shouted.

"Trees?" Eliana asked.

"He means broccoli." I whispered so he couldn't hear me.

"Why are you whispering?"

"Because you have to call them trees or he won't eat them."

"Why not?" Eliana asked.

"I have no idea. It's probably something Alessio taught him."

"Where do you want me to park?" Eliana asked, pulling into the driveway.

"Out by the side of the garage. I'm not walking in all the way from the front." I told her.

Eliana helped me get Theo out of the car and then grabbed the rest of his things. I walked into the kitchen with Theo.

"Can we do books?" He asked.

"Why don't you go out and play for a few minutes while I warm up the food. Go enjoy the sun before it gets dark."

"Didn't Uncle Alessio get you a new bike?" El asked.

"It's big!" Theo shouted, running out to the back yard.

"Will you be okay?" Eliana asked.

"Yeah, go play. I'll come get you guys when dinner's ready." I smiled.

After getting the food started in the oven I sat down at the table. I couldn't stop worrying about Dane. I didn't want to think about the trouble he'd gotten himself into this time. It never got any easier watching him leave for work.

The timer went off on the stove so I grabbed a few plates and cut up some broccoli for Theo. I was grabbing Theo something to drink when I got a text. I found my phone in my bag in the living room.

The text was from Dane.

** Miss you baby, be home soon **

I read over the text a few times before putting my phone back in my bag. Hearing from him made me feel better but I wouldn't relax until he was actually home.

Eliana and Theo raced through their dinner so that they could get ready for bed. Theo's favorite time of day was getting to read his bedtime stories. He especially loved it when Dane was home to put him to bed but on days Dane couldn't be here he'd take anyone he could get.

I kept telling Eliana she could go home whenever she wanted but she insisted on staying until Dane came back, so I let her help with Theo and took a break in the living room. I was all stretched out on the couch when she came back to sit with me.

"You should go lay down." She said.

"No, I want to be awake when Dane gets back."

"If you're tired you should try and get some sleep."

"Fine. Why don't you tell me about your cases? That usually puts me to sleep." I said.

"Rude but I actually do have some cases I need someone to help me brainstorm so you're in luck."

I got comfortable on the couch so that Eliana could tell me all about the boring case paperwork and trials she was working on. I'm not sure when I fell asleep but listening to Eliana about her firm worked. I was knocked out.

A few hours later there was someone rubbing my shoulder, shaking me awake.

"Kate, baby." Dane whispered.

I opened my eyes and saw Dane sitting on the couch next to me. With Dane's help I sat up.

"Hey." I smiled.

"Hey."

Dane pulled me into a kiss before pulling away and leaning down to kiss my belly.

"How are you feeling?" He asked.

"Tired."

"And how's my baby girl doing?" He asked.

"We don't know it's a girl Dane."

"It's a girl, trust me."

"Well then she's driving me crazy with all her kicking."

Dane ran his hand over my belly, waiting to feel a kick from the baby.

"What happened tonight?"

Dane sighed, "We lost a big shipment, someone was waiting for our trucks up north."

"Who?"

"We don't know. The two men we caught aren't talking."

I grabbed Dane's hand off my belly and brought it up to my lips. I left soft kisses against his bruised knuckles.

"Come on, let's get you to bed." He said.

Dane helped me get from the couch to the bedroom. I walked into the bathroom to get ready for bed but he didn't follow into the room.

"What's wrong?" I asked.

"I'll be back in a minute."

Dane left the bedroom and walked towards Theo's room. After changing into pajamas and brushing my teeth I went looking for Dane. He was leaned against Theo's bed holding his hand. When he heard me walk into the room he turned around. I walked over and stood behind him and rested a hand on his shoulder.

"I hate not being here for bedtime." He whispered.

"I know."

"How was he today?" He asked.

"He got to spend the day with Eliana so it was the best day ever for the both of us."

Dane kissed Theo's forehead then stood up.

"How did you end up at Eliana's house today?"

"One day when you're in a better mood I'll tell you why I was there." I said, leaving Theo's room.

Dane followed me back to our room.

"She brought you over to see her neighbor's house didn't she?"

"You know that house is for sale?" I asked.

"Apollo told me about it as soon as it went on the market."

"Why didn't you tell me?" I asked, sitting down on the bed.

"I thought you were busy enough as it is. We don't need to be adding house hunting to the list."

"Wait, hold on. What are you saying? Would you consider moving closer to Apollo and El?" I asked.

"I mean I've thought about it. It would be nice being closer to them after the baby is born. We're going to need all the help we can get."

"I was thinking of ways I could trick you into moving and here you are telling me you want to move." I said.

"And how were you planning on tricking me?" Dane asked.

"I thought for sure I'd have to seduce you. Lay on my charm." I winked.

"Yeah?" He asked, walking over to my side of the bed.

"Mhmm, but I guess now that you want to move I don't have to."

"I think I'm having second thoughts. I might need to be convinced."

Dane wrapped a hand behind my neck and pulled me into a kiss. I licked his bottom lip, teasing him with my tongue. He smiled against my lips as I deepened the kiss. My hands pressed against his chest to keep myself from getting lost in the kiss.

"Is it working?" I whispered, pulling away from him.

"A little."

Dane stood up and dragged his hand up my leg. He curled his fingers and squeezed my inner thigh. I reached my arm up and dropped it onto his shoulder. While he traced his fingers over my thigh I ran my hand down his neck. Dane pulled his hand away to rest it on my bump. I watched his smile grow while rubbing my belly. He relaxed and dropped his shoulders. He took a deep breath before looking over at me.

"I love you." He said.

"You love me?" I asked.

"More than anything in the world."

Dane's words hit me harder than I thought they would. It took everything in me not to cry. I wish I could go back in time and tell my younger self that one day she'd finally get the family she'd been dreaming of.